# LOVE, LOVE ME DO

MARK
HAYSOM

piatkus

PIATKUS

First published in Great Britain in 2014 by Piatkus

A CIP catalogue record for this book
is available from the British Library.

ISBN 978-0-349-40389-2

Typeset in Sabon by M Rules
Printed and bound in Great Britain by
Clays Ltd, St Ives plc

Papers used by Piatkus are from well-managed forests
and other responsible sources.

MIX
Paper from
responsible sources
FSC® C104740

Piatkus
An imprint of
Little, Brown Book Group
100 Victoria Embankment
London EC4Y 0DY

An Hachette UK Company
www.hachette.co.uk

www.piatkus.co.uk

After graduating from Leicester University, Mark Haysom had a thirty-year career in newspapers, during which he rose from trainee journalist on a local weekly to managing director of Mirror Group. In 2003 he moved into education as head of a large government agency. In recent years he has served on the boards of a number of charities dedicated to overcoming poverty, disadvantage and addiction. He was awarded an honorary doctorate from Leicester University in 2005 and the CBE in 2008. Mark lives in Brighton with his wife, Ann. This is his first novel.

For Annie

# FRIDAY, 2 AUGUST 1963

# THE ASHDOWN FOREST, SUSSEX

# 1

# Baxter: 5.24 a.m.

*Baxter had stood there, angrily
swishing a favourite stick*

It was like a clock going slowly tick ... tick ... tick ...
tick ... tick ... Baxter could hear it now and he could feel
it ticking not just in his head but somehow too inside his
stomach as he lay in the grey light of dawn, hot and sleepless
in the narrow tousled bench bed at the back of the cramped
caravan.

No, that wasn't it.

It was more like when you turned a key slowly in a clockwork toy and you could feel it getting tighter and tighter and
you knew that if you kept turning it around it would break
but you still did it anyway and it made you feel as if at any
moment something really bad was going to happen. It was
like that and the clock thing both together and it was a nervous sick thing in your stomach as if you were empty and
sick both at the same time.

The ticking had started inside him and the empty sick feeling had begun as soon she said it.

'It will be good, you'll see, Baxter,' she'd said, sitting in the sunshine on the low step of the caravan one afternoon.

She was peeling potatoes, sending them plopping one by one into a saucepan of water. From the caravan had come the muffled sound of the radio; Buddy Holly gave way to Ray Charles.

'Oh, this is one of my favourites,' she said with a small distant smile.

♫ *Take these chains from my heart and set me free* ...

He had wanted her to look up at him, not think about music. But when finally she did look he had twisted away.

'Just you and your dad together for the day,' she said to reassure him. 'You've never done that before, have you? It'll be fun, you'll see.'

And the ticking had started and the sickness and the clockwork key thing had turned tighter. Like that time, Baxter thought, that time with the stupid tin soldier with the stupid drum and the key turned so tight it wouldn't work any more and *he*, he had yelled at him and Megan had cried even though she was nine and then he had gone slamming out through the door and it wasn't Baxter's fault. Not really.

He always yelled.

'Just boys together, you and your dad,' she said, gouging an ugly black bruise from a potato, sending it tumbling into the pan.

'But, Mummy ...' Baxter started to say.

But it was no good; she wouldn't listen.

'It'll be good,' she said quickly. 'Go down to Brighton for

4

the day, go to the house, pick up things we need. Clothes, more books, games. He'll buy you an ice cream, probably.'

Again she had smiled, but it was a funny smile as if she didn't believe it. Not really.

Baxter had stood there, angrily swishing a favourite stick backwards and forwards through the long grass. As he scythed at the grass, he could see their small white terrace house in Brighton on the road that ran so steeply, so narrowly, down to the sea and he was back in his room with his train set spread out on the floor and downstairs his mother was singing along to Helen Shapiro or Brenda Lee on the radio and Megan was laughing. But even though they seemed all happy and everything, he knew that really they were just waiting for the sound of the front gate. Waiting for that click of the gate.

It was always the same. Whatever else was happening in the house, whatever game they were playing or song they were singing, he knew that it was all just a kind of pretend. What was really happening was that they were waiting and listening.

And sometimes it was all right. Sometimes when his father came through the door he had presents for them and everything *was* happy. For a while.

But most times it wasn't like that. Most times.

Baxter stopped swishing, took the stick in both hands and bent it until it snapped.

It was days ago that she had said about boys together and the clock and the stomach-ache sick thing had been going ever since and the key had turned inside him almost until it was breaking. And it wasn't fair and now in only a few hours his father would be there.

5

Just him and his father.

As he lay listening to the faraway call of a wood pigeon, Baxter writhed with the injustice of it all. Irritably, hotly, he kicked the crumpled sheet from his legs. He didn't want to go, he wasn't going. His father could take Megan instead, she was nine, she was the oldest by a whole year. He should take her: she was the favourite anyway.

He wasn't going. They couldn't make him. And when his mother and Megan and the baby were up and dressed, he would tell her that he had been thinking about it for a long time and he had decided something.

'Mummy . . .' he would say with a serious face, although he would be a bit happy and laughing inside. 'I've been thinking that I won't go to Brighton today after all.'

'Why's that, my best boy?' his mother would say softly, with her eyes big.

'I just don't think it's fair on Megan,' he would say, and he would probably say this bit really slowly to make it sound even more serious, as if he really had been thinking about it very hard for a very long time.

'She's the oldest,' he would say. 'It's only fair that she should go instead of me.'

'Why, Baxter,' his mother would say with a big smile. 'That's very thoughtful of you.'

'Dad could buy her an ice cream,' he would say. 'Probably.'

And if that didn't work he would say he was sick and couldn't go. And, if they still tried to make him, he would just run away into the woods and hide there all day with Soldier and they would build a camp together.

# 2

# Christie: 5.37 a.m.

## *That was what she had wanted for Baxter*

With a mother's unbreakable habit, Christie listened to the children's breathing: Megan in her deep untroubled sleep, the baby mercifully quiet in the carry-cot on the floor next to her, Baxter awake and sighing, restlessly kicking the sheets from his legs.

Baxter, poor Baxter.

Lying on her cramped makeshift bed, Christie propped herself up on her elbows and whispered to him.

'Is everything OK, Baxter?'

He sighed again; but said nothing.

Taking care not to knock the baby's cot, Christie swung her legs from her bed and negotiated on tiptoes the few feet of the confined space of the caravan. She bent over, put her head close to his. 'It's all right,' she said, straightening his blanket, smoothing his sheet.

'There's nothing to worry about ... I've decided that you

7

don't have to go with your dad after all. Go back to sleep now ...'

She bent again and felt the warmth of his forehead on her lips as she kissed him.

Making her way back to her bed, she listened once more. The sighing had stopped. All the children were sleeping now.

It had been a stupid idea anyway; another fantasy.

Somehow Christie had managed to convince herself that what Baxter and his father needed was to spend time together, just the two of them; to really get to know each other.

For too long they had been locked in this unbearable cycle of anger and tears. Truman had no patience with the boy, he was a storm always waiting to erupt; and Baxter was so clumsy and tongue-tied whenever he was with him. The more anxious he became, the more that seemed to fuel Truman's rage. And that, of course, made Baxter more desperate still.

It had never been quite the same with Megan. With her, Truman's anger would soon subside and he would scoop her into his arms and make her laugh even as she cried. Sometimes Christie could see in Baxter's eyes that all he wanted was for his father to pick him up and hold *him* close. What *he* wanted to hear was his father's voice making *him* laugh. What he needed to feel was his father's arms about *him*. Instead what he so often heard were more harsh words and what he felt was the weight of his father's hand: a bruising wallop across the legs or the backside or a stinging cuff around the ear.

Christie drew some small comfort that at least it had never been more than that. She was certain that Truman would never, *could* never really hurt his own son. He wasn't capable of it. And she, more than anyone, should know just what he was and wasn't capable of. But it was too much to bear to see Baxter so unhappy.

Since they had been at the caravan, Baxter had taken to disappearing into the woods or hiding in the long grass as soon as he heard his father's car approaching. It couldn't go on like this and the more Christie had thought about it, the more she had convinced herself that all they needed, father and son, was some time together. She was sure they would then grow close.

She had this picture in her mind of herself as a child of about Baxter's age, standing next to her own father. She was looking on as he worked in the musty warmth of the potting shed, with the rich honeyed smell of his pipe tobacco wrapping itself around them. There was not a word spoken between them, it was enough just to be there.

That was what she had wanted for Baxter. A child needed a father, she had told herself, a son especially so. But it had all been another of her fantasies, another fairy story where everything would somehow come right in the end. Instead of a happy ending, all she had succeeded in doing was to give Baxter days of torment. She had seen it in his face, in the anger and the hurt in his eyes.

# 3

# Soldier: 5.42 a.m.

## *Blackness before; blackness after*

Hunched over a battered, blackened kettle as it steamed on the glowing embers of his early-morning fire, Soldier let the tears run down his cheeks and gather in the clumped grey tangle of his beard. He could taste their bitter saltiness.

Tiredness, like an ache, washed over him; it had been another night of little sleep. Once more he had been too full of them: her and the children. All night they had run and played inside his head, the careful, serious boy, the teasing ponytailed girl, the mother in her blue-and-white print dress, with her coal-black hair. Sleep had come only fitfully. They had been in his dreams and in his waking thoughts.

Shivering now in the thin pale light of the summer dawn, Soldier pulled his long dark coat more tightly about him. Worn shiny and thin, muddied, stained and torn, it hung from his shoulders like a tattered cape. He warmed his hands over the fire, straightened a little to ease the stiffness in his back.

Still the tears continued to run. It seemed as if an inexhaustible well had been opened up in him.


The first time had been on a February morning.

Half-starved, he had reeled and stumbled through the numbing, knee-high, glistening white drifts. The cold had drilled into him as never before. It had reduced him, worn him away, and made him desperate to seek out the warmth that it had been impossible for him to create for himself in his shelter in the woods.

On the doorstep of her cottage there had been no words spoken; just a contemptuous glare and the door left open. After he had followed her shuffling footsteps through to the kitchen, she had stabbed at the headline in the *Daily Express* in accusation. As if he was to blame. It was the 'Big Freeze', she said; the worst winter for nearly three hundred years. He had no cause to be out in it. Soldier had turned away, shame-faced, guilty.

All the way to the cottage the black dog had run beside him, its tongue lolling from its mouth, its breath misty in the biting cold. Soldier had looked to the door.

'That dog of yours again?' Mrs Chadney said, reading his mind, scorn rising in her voice.

Soldier had nodded and pointed urgently to the door. The dog was left outside in the snow.

'It's all in your bloody head,' she spat at him. 'Bloody fool.'

She had struck a match to light the gas ring.

'Never has been no bloody dog ...'

Soldier heard the whimper at the door.

11

She came over to him, jabbed at his head with a bent finger.

'It's all in here ... All in your bloody head,' she said. 'There is no bloody dog. Understand? There never was no bloody dog in all these years. I've told you a hundred times. Bloody stinking fool ...'

As the pan simmered on the hob, her anger had rumbled on.

'Coming here, stinking up my house ... A-jabbering and a-gibbering, muttering away to God-knows-who about God-knows-what ... Like some raving bloody lunatic ... Like you're soft in the bloody head ... Bloody stinking fool ...'

But she had fed him.

'Eat it,' she said, rattling the plate down on the table in front of him, the harshness of her words at odds with her soft Sussex burr.

'And I hope it bloody chokes you.'

The rabbit stew and dumplings had steamed in front of him. And Soldier had wept. Exhausted tears. Tears of mute gratitude.


Soldier warmed his hands again, rubbed them vigorously together over the fire, and then shifted his position to free the ache in his knee. Finally, he wiped at his tears with the frayed cuff of his coat. Still they came.

After that first time, it had seemed as if there was no stemming them. Later that same day, making his way back to his shelter, he had thrown his head back and cried with elation at the crisp brilliance of a clear blue winter sky. Then, as the March thaw had finally set in, he had wept as the birds had tentatively started to find their voices once more. He had cried too one morning at the sudden return of the yielding softness of the forest floor. And much later, he had cried at the first sight of her, alone on the caravan step as the evening had settled about her and as the night had gathered her in.

The kettle had finally boiled and Soldier reached for his mug. Army-issued, somehow it had survived all the years in the forest with him. Cupping it carefully in his hands, he closed his eyes and tried to summon up the memory that it held.

*He was half lying, half crouching in a shallow hole ripped from a rolling meadow. Above him the air thundered and sang. Thundered. Sang. His uniform weighed him down, thick and heavy. His hands were blackened and bruised. He touched his face. There was blood now on his fingers. The mug had been left behind by someone else and it was standing half full when he found it; the water was gritty and warm. He gulped it down, it spilled over his chin and he wiped it quickly away with his arm. He was still thirsty, his mouth still dry. The sleeve of his jacket had a jagged tear, threads stood out in coarse tufts. He decided to claim the mug for himself and stuffed it into his kit bag. He was tired, too tired to move. There was a muffled shout in the far distance. He braced himself, breathed deeply, looked up: there were white clouds scudding across a blue sky above.*

And then nothing. It was no good, he could get no further. Every time he held the mug and closed his eyes, it was the same. There was only blackness before; blackness after.

Chipped and veined as it was, he treasured the mug; it was his only possession that held even this much of a fragment of memory. He owned little else. An ancient pair of Taylor Hobson field-glasses, the kettle, a pair of dented saucepans with their Bakelite handles long gone, an army knife, rusted and pitted now, and the few blankets and clothes that Mrs Chadney had thrown his way over the years.

Soldier reached into his coat pocket and pulled out a handful of the leaves that he had collected the previous evening. He worked them carefully to the bottom of the mug and poured the water from the kettle. Waiting for his nettle tea to brew and to cool, he squatted beside the fire, pushed his long thin grey hair from his face and scratched at his matted beard. Picking the mug up, he blew at the slicked surface of the muddy green water and took a gurgling sip.

Close by he heard a wood pigeon's echoing call. A first weak shaft of sunlight broke through the canopy of the trees above. The day was beginning, the day the boy had spoken of.

Suddenly Soldier's heart raced. He swallowed the tea noisily and threw the dregs on to the fire.

## 4

# Christie: 6.01 a.m.

## *She had felt for a moment like a girl again*

Christie couldn't settle. The bed was too hard, too ridiculously narrow; it was yet another day to be spent in this hot ugly caravan in the middle of a wood in the middle of nowhere; she was worried about Baxter, about Megan, about the baby. And all night her head had ached with the same questions that she had now spent weeks asking herself.

How *had* she ended up here? With a husband she so rarely saw and little more than the clothes that she and the children stood up in.

How had she, that young girl of not that many years ago, with her head so full of dreams and possibilities, come to be living in such a place? How had *any* of it happened? How had she *allowed* it to happen?

\*

Truman had told them that it was a surprise holiday.

Turning up unexpectedly one June afternoon, he had come bursting through the door with his lopsided foolish smile, clutching a big battered leather suitcase to his chest. And he'd never come home early before, not even for the children's birthdays.

'Come on, kids, get packed quick!' he shouted.

'But Truman . . . ' she said.

And now, in the half-light of the breaking day, alone in her bed in the caravan, she couldn't believe that she could have been so naïve, so gullible.

'But Truman . . . ' she said, finding herself, despite herself, caught up in the electric storm of excitement he'd generated. 'We can't just drop everything and go, can we?'

'Of course we can, princess,' he said, and he'd thrown the suitcase on to the kitchen table and had swept her up and twirled her around and the children had laughed. And even though she could smell the drink on him, she had felt for a moment like a girl again in his arms.

'There's nothing we can't do if we set our minds to it,' he said, plonking her unsteadily down. 'Fifteen minutes, everyone! Let's get packed and let's get going!'

'But *where* are we going?' she said.

'You'll see . . . ' he said mysteriously, tapping his nose with a nicotined forefinger, winking like a pantomime conspirator.

'But what about the children's school?' she said.

'Won't do them any harm, will it? To miss a few weeks,' he said to squeals of approval from Megan and Baxter.

'But you've never even mentioned a holiday before?' she said, unsure and breathless as she ran upstairs after him, the children excitedly jostling behind. And he never had, not in their ten years together, not even a honeymoon.

'Met a man in a pub,' he said, as if that was all the explanation needed.

'And . . . ?' she said.

'You'll see!' he said, as if to an impatient child. 'Fourteen minutes! We're wasting time!'

Foolishly, madly, she had thrown as many clothes into the suitcase as she could for herself and for the children. She'd then emptied the contents of the larder into a cardboard box and hurriedly packed another bag with the baby's things.

He, meanwhile, had gone to the top of the wardrobe and taken down his own smaller suitcase, the one he'd been carrying when she went to meet him at the station when he came back from National Service, and he had deftly folded his spare suit and his freshly ironed shirts and fitted them neatly inside.

Just a few minutes after the allotted fifteen, all the windows had been closed, the back door had been checked, the gate had clicked shut behind them and they were gone.

In the car, as they made their way up through Seven Dials and past the grand houses of Dyke Road Avenue towards the rolling South Downs, they'd sung 'We're All Going on a Summer Holiday'. And they'd never sung in the car before. It was magical; it was how a family was meant to be.

But then suddenly and without warning he had stopped singing.

And then he shouted at the children to be quiet.

When, still bubbling over with laughter and excitement, they didn't stop at once he swung round in his seat while he was still driving and with his left hand he swiped at them, missing Megan but clipping Baxter hard on the head. The boy had cried and he'd shouted at him again. And then Baxter had felt ill and Truman had bellowed at him not to be sick on his leather car seats and they had to pull over.

After that they had driven north and inland in a silence broken only by the baby's occasional fretful sobs. Under gathering clouds they had crossed the great green swell of the Downs and then gone on through tree-lined twisting country lanes, canopied with branches so heavy with leaves that they met from either side and formed a darkly dappled tunnel, the day's weak sunlight struggling to find a way through.

Christie had shivered, suddenly cold, and held the baby tightly to her.

The tide of exhilaration that had swept her up and along and into the car had long since passed and she had a sense now that something had happened that she didn't understand, that something was terribly wrong.

'Is everything all right, Truman?' she asked, her voice lowered to prevent the children from hearing.

He either hadn't heard or he had chosen not to answer and she hadn't wanted to risk provoking him by asking again. She had to take care. She always had to take care.

They had driven on in silence and Christie had found her mind turning to more immediate concerns. How long would they be travelling? Where and when would they stop to feed the children? How long would they be away? Had she packed everything they would need? Where were they going?

Where *were* they going?

She could stay silent no longer.

'Truman . . . ?' she started to say.

But at that moment they turned abruptly from the road

and followed a narrow potholed track through densely over-hanging trees and nettled verges until finally they emerged into a large clearing in the woods.

In the middle of the clearing, squatting in the tall grass, was a small grey-white caravan.

'Where are we?' Christie asked in a whisper.

'We're in the forest, of course,' he said as if she was stupid, as if she should have known. 'It's the Ashdown Forest and they call this place Tabell Ghyll,' he said proudly, showing it to them like an enthusiastic tour guide with his outstretched hand.

'And *that* . . . ' he said, pointing excitedly, emphatically, towards the caravan as Christie and the children looked on, open-mouthed and disbelieving, '*that* is your holiday home.'

# Soldier: 6.10 a.m.

## *It had run through his fingers like dust*

Soldier pushed on through the glossy, waist-high bracken, he pushed on to where the track neared its end, to where it widened and the bracken thinned, to where the splintered branches of a fallen oak lay like bleached bones.

There he stopped, he swayed; he almost buckled, almost fell. The pain raged in his knee. He could feel the accumulating shortness of his breath, the quickening beat of his heart. He leaned forwards, bent double and tried to steady himself, to collect himself.

He allowed his eyes to close, to rest. A minute passed. More. Finally he straightened and pressed on once more to where the dark edge of the wood met the clearing. There, beneath the spreading shadows of the beech trees, he crouched low in the warm earthy tangle of the brambles, the ferns and the scrubby gorse.

Easing his legs from under him, he sat back against the

trunk of a tree and looked out across the grassy clearing to where the hunched caravan stood like a small white ship adrift on a swaying sea of green.

And there he began to wait and to watch.

For so many years Soldier had thought of these woods as his alone. Now, though, he shared them willingly with her and the children. When he had first come across the caravan, there in the woods, *his* woods, he had immediately wanted it gone. It had no place there, no right to be there. Studying it suspiciously, apprehensively, from the shadowed edge of the clearing, he had been confused. Outraged. Afraid. Diminished. Hurt.

But then *she* had stepped hesitantly through the caravan's door and had sat quickly down on the low step. In the evening's fading light, her eyes had nervously scanned the clearing. Settling back against the door, her shoulders had slumped and she had hung her head.

Soldier had shrunk back into the brambled margins of the wood, had squatted low and watched. Barely breathing. His lips working on the words that ran through his mind. Over and again.

She didn't belong there.

She didn't want to be there.

She was afraid.

And that had been enough. In that moment he had known it. That it was his duty. There had been no choice, no decision to be made; it was his duty to keep them safe. Lest violence and harm should come to them. He had known that it was for him to be their guardian angel. A grizzled angel in a stained and tattered long dark coat.

She didn't belong there. She didn't want to be there. She was afraid.

As the last light drained from the day and a cool evening breeze whispered through the long grass, he had stooped lower in the musky ferns that fringed the clearing and he had begun to watch. To watch over her, her and the children. And he had watched faithfully. For hour after hour. From dawn to dusk and beyond. Day after day.

And then later the boy had come to him and they had sat together on the rough flint wall.

He had built the wall far into the woods some years before, when a thought had settled on him that he should have a cottage of stone to replace his lean-to wooden shelter. And, although the thought had soon faded, had quickly been taken from him, the short length of flint wall had stubbornly remained.

Soldier had hoisted himself up next to him, next to the boy.

They had sat there swinging their legs, the two of them, knocking their heels against the coarse stonework. And, just for a moment, it had felt to Soldier as if he was a child again, sitting on a wall, somewhere else, with someone else, a very long time before.

*He was a child again, sitting on a wall, and the sun's heavy warmth was on his back and there was a blue carefree sky above his head and a lingering low stirring of a breeze on his face. Green fields rolled away from him like the sea and somewhere in the distance a dog was barking and a lark was serenading high above a scented billowing hedgerow ...*

For as long as he could, Soldier had held fast to this splinter of a memory. But as he had reached towards it, to try to understand it more fully, to know it for what it truly was, it had broken down, disintegrated.

He had knocked his heels harder against the wall, trying to reassemble it in his mind, trying to summon up the warmth of the sun on his back, the breeze on his face and the distant barking of the dog.

But it was no good; it was gone. It had run through his fingers like dust.

And, as the boy had looked on with a silent question in his eyes, Soldier had quickly wiped away a solitary tear.

# 6

# Christie: 6.14 a.m.

## *The king's stone rolled down the mountain once more*

It had been a shrieking animal cry in the shadowy darkness two weeks after they had arrived in the forest that had first set Christie's mind racing. It had been harmless, of course; she had quickly realised that there had been nothing to fear. But the sound had cut through her sleep and made its way murderously into her dreams. Her eyes had snapped open and in the long moments that followed, Christie had found herself lying rigid, with her hand clasped to her mouth in disbelief. Her heart pounding, her senses stretched, she had waited for the cry to come again.

Megan's sudden whisper had made her heart jolt once more.

'What *was* that, Mummy?' she said. The fear evident in the smallness of her voice.

Christie had gone to her and tucked her more securely in.

'It was nothing,' she said, as matter-of-factly as she could. 'Just a silly noise in the night.'

Until Megan was asleep again, Christie had perched on the side of her bed. Finally she had been convinced that silence had settled back on the forest; although she had learned in those first weeks that it was never a true silence, there was always something scratching, something snuffling, rustling, whirring somewhere in the night. When she had been sure that she and the children were safe and that Megan was sleeping, she had given a small bewildered shake of her head.

What on earth was she doing in such a place? How had she come to this?

It was not the first time she had asked herself such questions. Before, though, it had been easy enough to shake them quickly off: Megan, Baxter and the baby had filled every moment of her days and tiredness had sent her tumbling into sleep at night. But this time it had been different. In the weeks that had followed, the questions she had begun to ask herself in the dead of that night had taken an exhausting hold on her.

How had she *allowed* it to happen? To the children? To her?

Whether she was sitting on the caravan step as the sun dipped or whether she was trying to settle back on the absurdly narrow bench bed, resting her head on the cushion that doubled as a pillow, pulling the worn, fusty eiderdown up tightly to her chin, wherever she was, Christie would close her eyes and would find herself instantly plunged back into trying to make sense of it all.

The more she had tried to wrestle with it over the weeks, the more a piecemeal jumble of memories had come to her.

Oddly, each of them had begun in the same way. Whenever she closed her eyes, the first thing she would see would be a tiny smudged black-and-white snapshot, like one of those she used to take with the old Box Brownie camera her father had given her for her twelfth birthday.

Some of these snapshots were fading, some dog-eared and yellowing, some crisp and new. Gradually the image on the photograph would come into focus. There would be a face smiling or her bicycle propped against the cobbled school wall or a child running or the stretched sun setting on a spangled sea.

At first, as the picture began to emerge, Christie had gone diving recklessly into the memory. In time, though, she had learned to become more circumspect. Too often she had been shocked and disappointed, too often she had been misled; the memory had not been what she had thought it was. The image would shift and the face would suddenly not be smiling. The child would be both running and crying. The sea would be dark and churning on a stormy windswept day.

And this morning, halfway between waking and sleeping, in the misty light of the breaking dawn, the bicycle had been propped against a different wall.

It was to be the day that she would remember for the rest of her life, everyone said so; and nothing was to be allowed to spoil it.

Having tiptoed across the landing to the bathroom and washed and dressed as quickly and quietly as she could, Christie carefully slid back her bedroom curtains. The sun was shining, the sky was a faultless blue, the seagulls were up and circling high, their cries carried away by the gentlest of breezes coming from the sea. And her bicycle was waiting for her, gleaming against the garden wall.

It was perfect.

As she went down the stairs, and as each tread creaked loudly enough to wake the whole house, Christie had to fight back an attack of the giggles. It was too ridiculous. Here she was, the day after her twenty-first birthday, and she was creeping around at dawn as if she was thirteen years old again and sneaking out of the house to meet Jenny and go swimming in the sea before breakfast.

Still trying to stifle her laughter, Christie pushed open the kitchen door.

'Oh!' she said, the laughter vanishing.

Her mother was sitting at the kitchen table in her dressing gown, nursing a cup of tea.

'I don't know what you've got to laugh at,' she snapped at Christie.

Christie flinched.

'Because I'm happy, Mum,' she said apologetically. 'Because it's my big day.'

Her mother reached across the table for her packet of Consulate. They were so much more refined, she always told people; she wouldn't be seen dead smoking anything else.

'Your big day,' she parroted, her voice heavy with sing-song sarcasm.

'It is, Mum,' Christie said quietly, determinedly.

Nothing was going to spoil it. Nothing.

'You're up early,' Christie said, trying to move on.

'What do you expect?' her mother hissed. 'How could I

sleep? *You* may be happy but this is the *un*-happiest day of my life.'

'No, Mum . . .' Christie said.

It wasn't fair, she wasn't having it. Not today.

'Yes, Mum,' her mother said mockingly, refusing to let go.

'Because I'm marrying Truman?' Christie said.

They'd had the argument a hundred times; despite herself, she was being sucked into it again.

'Because of *who* you are marrying and because of *where* you are marrying him,' her mother said, clicking her lighter and sending a billow of smoke in Christie's direction.

'I wish you'd change your mind, Mum. You could still come, it's not too late,' Christie said.

Why was she being so conciliatory, even now? She didn't want her there. Not if she was going to be like this.

'Come?' her mother said.

'To the wedding,' Christie said.

Her mother sat back in her chair and gave Christie a look that said she must have completely taken leave of her senses. She shook her head.

'As far as I'm concerned there *is* no wedding,' she said. 'If it's not a church wedding then it's not a wedding at all. And I for one will have no part of it.'

Again she put the cigarette to her mouth; this time she let the cloud of smoke rise up from her as she spoke.

'I didn't bring you up so that you could shame me,' she said. 'Getting married like this . . .'

Apart from christenings and funerals, Christie couldn't remember the last time her mother had set foot inside a church. It was just an excuse. She didn't want Christie to be happy; she had never wanted her to be happy. She had waged such a long, bitter war with her husband, and Christie had always been on the side of the enemy.

For a moment there was silence between them. Silence was better, Christie thought. It didn't last long.

'Anyway, what are you doing up at this time?' her mother demanded.

'Well,' Christie said. 'If you must know, I'm going to see Dad.'

Her mother took the cigarette from her mouth, rocked back in her chair and laughed throatily.

'I might have guessed,' she said. 'Daddy's special girl ...'

'Leave it, Mum,' Christie said, feeling tears suddenly come to her eyes.

Still her mother laughed.

'Useless dreamers, both of you,' she said. 'Always with your noses in some book or other and your heads in the clouds.'

'No, Mum,' Christie said.

She turned from the kitchen and ran to the front door.

'But do say hello ...' her mother shouted after her, still laughing. 'Do give him my regards!'


Some of the memories that had come back to Christie as the weeks passed had seemed to have no part to play in answering the questions that nagged at her. Here she felt her mother's hard hand for the broken buckle on her new school shoes; there she was being carried shoulder-high by her father along the seafront with an ice-cream cone dripping in her hand; here she was hugging her friends on her last tearful day at school; there she was shivering with nerves in Mr

Bonfield's office on her first day at work. These she had tried not to linger on for too long, however diverting and tempting at least some of them might have been.

Others had been almost too difficult to dwell on at all and she had promised herself she would try to return to them again.

But as she had worked conscientiously through all these memories, Christie had come to realise that her main preoccupation was to try to understand how each one was connected to the next, how each might have a consequence that would *lead* it to the next. This, she had told herself, was what she meant by making sense of it. She needed to be able to say to herself, 'Because this happened, that then happened.' Because of this, that.

But it had been exhausting. And frustrating. And defeating.

Her father had once told her a story. Her father had told her so many stories; stories for her alone. Most of his stories, told when she was very small and snuggling in to him only half awake, were of knights and dragons, hope and laughter, where the moral was always that courage and honesty brought their own reward, where dreams could come true. But this much later story, recounted as they walked together along the seafront on a wet November day, was a strangely dispiriting one about a king who had been condemned to spend eternity rolling a stone up a mountainside. She hadn't thought much of it at the time, although she hadn't told her father so; she wouldn't have wanted to disappoint him. But now she felt she understood it because it seemed as if she had been similarly condemned to spend her own eternity of nighttime hours picking through all these pictures from her life and trying to join them together.

And, just like the king and the stone, she had done this in the knowledge that however hard she might try they could never finally be pieced together.

There had been no story of her own where *she* had done this and so that, then, had followed; where because *she* had decided that, then this had come about. Instead, there had been all these decisions made about her life that she seemed to have had no part of. There had been so many things that, unknown to her, must have been decided elsewhere, must have happened elsewhere and had then come spilling, crashing into her life. In the end there had been simply too many things that she should have known about her life, her life with Truman, but didn't.

The king's stone rolled down the mountain once more; everything was broken again into separate pieces. Nothing joined. It made no sense.

31

# 7

# Christie: 6.27 a.m.

## *Six weeks*

Lying on the thin mattress of the cramped uncomfortable bed as the early-morning light filtered through the skimpy net curtains, lying there listening to a wood pigeon greeting another day, calling over and over in the distance, Christie, of course, knew exactly how long it had been since she had first set her eyes on the caravan. None the less, as she found herself doing each morning now, she counted through the weeks that had passed.

Six weeks, she confirmed to herself as she tried to remember at what point she had truly begun to confront the thought that this was something much more than a holiday.

Six weeks. And in all that time she hadn't found a way to talk to Truman about it, to ask him why they were still there, when they were going home.

*Six weeks.*

Six weeks of boiling kettles to wash nappies in a bucket.

Of stamping on the wheezing foot pump for cold strip-washes in front of a trickling tap over a sink the size of a saucepan. Of trying to scrub mud and grass stains from clothes that would be stained and muddy again within hours, within minutes. Of juggling pans on a single guttering Calor Gas ring to cook for them all each day. Of skinning her knuckles as she struggled on her knees to put the beds together each night and again as she packed them away every morning.

Six weeks of fighting to keep her fraying temper, to keep hold of her sanity, as Megan and Baxter squabbled and whined on those endless days when the rain drummed on the roof and the windows steamed. Six weeks of catching water in a bowl as that rain dripped and ran through the cracked skylight. Six weeks of the baby's sometimes whimpered, sometimes fierce teething complaints.

*Six weeks ...*

And they were still in this idiotic caravan. In this hateful forest.

Or at least, she and the children were.

# 8

# Truman: 8.55 a.m.

*So he couldn't help the big grin on his face, could he?*

It wasn't a bad life, all things considered, Truman Bird thought, lying propped up on the plump pillows of the soft, ample double bed, drawing contentedly on his first cigarette of the day, watching the heavy smoke curl slowly towards the ceiling as a slender shaft of morning light broke through a crack in the curtains.

Without leaving the bed, he could reach the leaded lattice window and he had pushed it half open on its stiff hinges to greet the day. The ivy that clung to the front of the building was alive with birdsong and in the distance he could hear a solitary car making its way along the winding country lane; he could follow its gear changes through the steep bends that had become so familiar to him over the last six weeks. The curtains stirred in the slightest of breezes. It was going to be a hot one.

No, it wasn't a bad life, he thought; a grin spreading across his face as he scratched at his unshaven chin.

OK, the head might be a bit delicate this morning, the mouth a bit dry, the throat a bit rough from the singing, the laughter and too many cigarettes. But it had been one hell of a night and so you couldn't complain, could you?

And OK, life hadn't always treated him kindly; like everyone he'd had his troubles, he'd had his spot of bother. Just for a moment back there, he had to admit, things didn't look too good, did they? But he'd been smart enough, you see, he'd seen it coming in time, he'd got out, he'd moved on.

That's what people didn't get, what they didn't understand.

They didn't understand that it was all about making sure you kept moving, making sure you watched where your feet landed, that when life knocked you down, you bounced right back up with a beer in your hand and a smile on your face.

To do that, of course, you had to keep your wits about you and you had to stay one step ahead.

He'd been good at that, hadn't he? Just look at him now.

And, obviously, you had to keep things separate, he thought. That was important. Keep it simple, keep it separate. That was where people went wrong. They let everything get wound together so that when you had to tug at just a bit of it, all you ended up with was a knot tightening like a noose around your neck. You had to keep it simple and keep it separate. That way, when you pulled at a single strand, bingo, it just came away with your hand. Simple. Clean. Sweet.

So he couldn't help the big grin on his face, could he? Surely no one could blame him for that. Or maybe they could. And if they did, well, sod them, that was their problem, not his.

And the other thing is, he thought, the grin growing wider, since what we seem to be doing here is running through the opening chapters of *Truman Bird's Essential Guide to the Lessons That Life Teaches You*, the *other* big lesson is that you have to resist saying no to Lady Luck – especially when she comes along, plonks herself on your lap, pushes her big tits into your chest and plants a ruby-red kiss on you. Even more so when she owned a nice little boozer in the country.

'What's your name, princess?' he'd said, as Gerry & the Pacemakers played on the jukebox in the background.

♫ *How do you do what you do to me . . . ?*

'Maud,' she said. 'But everyone calls me Doll.'

'Hello, Doll,' he said, flashing a smile. 'You're a bit of all right, aren't you?'

She had looked at him through heavy fluttering eyelashes. He could see that she liked what she saw; he had something of a young Cary Grant in him, someone had once said. He'd settle for that.

'You're not so dusty yourself,' she said.

He lay there now, drinking in the scent of her in the bed next to him.

'Chanel No. 5,' she said on that first night. 'If it was good enough for Marilyn, God rest her troubled soul, then it's good enough for me.'

Doll moved closer to him now; murmured something softly in her sleep.

When all was said and done, he thought, reaching out to

touch her platinum-blonde hair cascading across her pillow, you're only young once, aren't you? What was it they said? That was it. You've got to *carpe* the bloody *diem*! That was what it was all about. Seizing the day, making hay before the heavens opened and it all started pissing it down on you again. You've got to take what you can, while you can.

And it was a decent little boozer, Doll's pub, The Hare and Hounds.

He'd only been up this way to see an old National Service pal and to try to touch him for a few quid to tide him over for a few days. It hadn't worked out; it turned out Badger Brown was just as skint and in almost as big a fix as he was. In the end, the trip had left Truman even more out of pocket than he was before – what with the petrol and buying a drink or two for the Badger. They had reminisced briefly and mechanically about their square-bashing days at Catterick, they'd talked about the old crew – Starling, Heehaw, Ginger and Fitz – but both of them knew that the magic, the camaraderie, had long gone and when they parted, despite the jovial back-slapping and the hearty handshakes, they'd known that if they were ever to meet again it would only be by chance.

Truman had been in no hurry to get back; after all, there were any number of reasons why he had needed to make himself scarce in Brighton. As he made his slow, meandering way back south, he had come across The Hare and Hounds and had decided to pop in for just the one and a bite to eat.

If truth be told, he was feeling pretty low at that point so he thought he'd nurse a quiet pint for half an hour and just try to figure out what on earth to do next, try to get his mind round finding a way out of it all.

But then Doll had spotted him sitting in the corner looking glum, had landed on his lap and planted her vivid kiss. Later she had introduced him to one of her regulars who had just put this caravan at some place called Tabell Ghyll and suddenly, bingo, all his troubles seemed behind him. At least for a while.

Of course, he hadn't let on to Doll about Christie and the children; almost at once she'd made it clear that she would never go with a married man, would never take any man who belonged to someone else. She had her standards, Doll did. It was one of the things that Truman liked about her.

'Me? Married? Of course not,' he'd said. Not the marrying kind; or at least he hadn't met the right woman yet, he'd said with a twinkle in his eye. No, the caravan was for his sister and her kids, he'd told her. She'd had some trouble at home, husband was a bit of a drinker, and he was trying to help her out, blood being thicker than water and all that.

He was quick that way; quick with a story; quick on his feet.

'Truman Bird, you're such a sweet man,' Doll had said. 'Not like the rest of them. After just one thing, most of them are. Rotten bastards ...'

'It's nothing,' Truman said, a warm glow running through him. 'After all, family comes first, doesn't it?'

Keeping it separate, see. Keeping it simple.

And like it had been meant to happen, as if it had been something waiting there for him all along, everything had fallen into place and it was all done and dusted in a few hours after that.

It had been easy, easier even than he had dared to think it might be. A fast drive back down to Brighton, get Christie and the children packed in double quick time, a nice family outing in the sunshine, back up to the forest, a bit of a sing-song in the car with the kids on the way to keep them happy, drop them off all excited at the caravan, tell Christie that it broke his heart and he was so sorry and he'd make it up to her somehow but he couldn't stay with them, that he had to go away on business for a few days, that he would be back to see them as soon as he could, as often as he could – that was the plan that had instantly formed in his mind and that was exactly how it had worked out. Simple.

He had been back at The Hare and Hounds for opening time that evening and between Doll's sheets shortly after last orders.

# 9

# Truman: 9.02 a.m.

## *The smile left Truman's face*

Doll stirred again and turned to face him and her arm fell across his chest. Truman let it rest there, watched it rise and fall as he breathed, and then ran his fingertips idly along the soft white length of it.

No, it wasn't a bad life at all.

And, he thought, there was no need to feel guilty about it. No one was getting hurt here, were they? Because what the eyes don't see the heart doesn't grieve over. Christie and the children were having the time of their lives in the caravan just a few miles down the road and Doll had a smile on her face like she was the cat that had got all the cream and then some.

Keep it separate. And everyone's happy.

Of course, it couldn't go on for ever like this. He knew

that; he wasn't stupid. He couldn't have them in that caravan once the summer was over. But he'd worry about that when the time came, he'd find something else for them then. A small cottage, perhaps, just far enough away so he could split his time between Doll and Christie and still no one would be any the wiser.

And of course, he'd have to start to get some money coming in soon. In these last six weeks, Doll hadn't seemed to notice, or maybe she just didn't mind, the odd fiver going missing from the till. And that had kept him going; paid for his petrol, his cigarettes, the rent on the caravan, and the food that he had taken to Christie and the children every few days.

But a fiver here and there wasn't going to be nearly enough, was it? You're not a man without cash in your pocket; you're not a man without a nice motor, a good suit, a crisp white shirt, a shine on your shoes, money to stand a round of drinks for everyone wherever you were, presents for the wife and kids to keep everything sweet.

He would need money and he would need it fast.

It was like he was always trying to tell Christie, there was no point in waiting for it until you were old and past it, was there? No point in slogging your sad guts out eight hours or more a day, year after lousy year, earning a crust, hoping to save just enough to keep body and soul together for those few years between the day you retired and the day you found yourself standing there shaking hands with St Peter. St Peter or the other bloke.

The smile left Truman's face.

That was something that Christie just didn't get. She wanted him to have this steady job, with steady hours and steady money, and he'd tried it, hadn't he? He'd tried it when he was a kid and then he tried it again for her.

Mug's game.

After he'd left school at fourteen, his mum had found him a place as a junior in the new Gas Board offices on Park Lane in Croydon. He'd stayed three years and had seen all the men there, with their elbow patches and pipes, growing old together. Even those just back from the war and still wearing their brown double-breasted demob suits didn't seem to Truman to want anything more. They'd fought for King and country and now all they seemed to want to settle for was a quiet life, a couple of kids, a nice little house in the suburbs and a week at Butlins in the summer if they were lucky. It made no sense.

At lunchtime Truman would watch them as they'd open up their sandwich tins. They'd pick through their meat- or fish-paste sandwiches, and talk about their gardens or about the football. One day, just before he left, they'd started talking about what they'd do if they came up big on the pools or if Ernie came through for them.

They'd have a bigger house, a bigger garden, they said, a bit of a holiday, a new car perhaps.

'Of course, we'd carry on working,' they'd all said, all nodding together, like a row of those dogs you could get for the back window of your motor. 'We wouldn't want it to change us.'

Truman couldn't help it. He'd laughed out loud. No bloody idea, had they? Not a bloody clue.

'What's so funny?' they said.

'Nothing,' Truman had mumbled, stifling his laughter.

'So if you're so clever, sonny boy, what would you do if you suddenly came into money?'

He'd closed his eyes and he'd told them. He'd buy a bright red Jag, an XK120 with leather seats and chrome trim, he'd pick up a flash bird and he'd buy her furs and diamonds and perfume and he'd drive up West and they'd stay at the Ritz and drink champagne out of crystal and they'd eat caviar with silver spoons. He'd take her to Ascot and they'd mix with the toffs and then they'd fly to Paris for the afternoon and they'd go to the Moulin Rouge. The next day he'd hire a driver to take them to Monte Carlo and they'd play the tables through the night and then they'd lie in the sun sipping martinis all day.

When he paused and opened his eyes, he found that they'd snapped their lunch tins closed and gone back to their desks.

Losers, the lot of them.

Escaping from there, he'd worked up in the Smoke, in one of those shops selling musical instruments, just off Charing Cross Road.

Bent as a nine-bob note, the owner was; Truman had seen it at once. In the long and frequent breaks between customers, he would gaze adoringly as Truman messed around on the piano in the shop window, trying to teach himself to play jazz like Hank Jones. Day after day Truman would pick at the notes, cigarette dangling from his lower lip. It was fun for a while but it was never going to make him rich and Truman had put on his jacket and walked the day the proprietor had shyly joined him on the piano stool and put a tentative hand on his knee.

After National Service, and when he and Christie were first

married and he'd moved to her home town of Brighton, he'd worked in a bookie's on Western Road, calculating the odds. He had a head for figures and was good with the punters, but it hadn't lasted; he'd had a row with the boss about taking time off to go to the races and had stormed out, telling him where he could stick his poxy job.

Then he'd worked in the office of the local rag, the *Evening Argus*, in the circulation department, sorting out the daily van runs and the bundle sizes for the deliveries. But the money was rubbish and before long he'd walked out on that too.

After that and for the last few years, until not so very long ago, he'd sold insurance door-to-door in Brighton and down the road in Hove. And what with being tall, dark and – if not quite Hollywood then certainly British B-movie – handsome and what with his gift of the gab, he had been good at it; he was the top salesman in the region and they'd given him a prize, a watch with a gold bracelet, engraved with his name on the back.

He'd enjoyed it at first and, it had to be said, it had its perks, its side benefits: a few young widows, left lonely by the war and looking for comfort, looking for a bit of loving on a rainy afternoon. Well, it was there on a plate for him. It would have been rude to say no, wouldn't it? He still saw one or two of them from time to time.

Truman reached for the ashtray beside the bed and stubbed out his cigarette. Doll stirred once more beside him.

The money hadn't been bad and as jobs went it had been OK, but doing it day after day had slowly worn him down and as time had gone on he'd found himself spending more and more time in one pub or another and less and less knocking on doors.

Just as he was starting to wonder what to do next, he'd had a stroke of luck. The company changed their paperwork and he discovered that, bingo, there was a way to do a bit of a fiddle to keep the commission still rolling in without leaving his bar stool. He found that he could add new policies to existing customers without them knowing, could forge their signatures, and could make a few weekly payments on their behalf. As long as the upfront commission was greater than the weekly payments, and as long as he kept adding enough policies to keep the wheels turning, he was all right, everything was sweet.

Well, there was no real harm in it, was there? He'd worked hard for that company. It was only what he was worth, what he was due.

For a few months it had all been going along just fine and dandy but then the boss had got suspicious, had poked around a bit, had found out what he was up to and had sent him packing. It was only because the company had wanted to keep it quiet that they hadn't gone to the police.

# 10

# Truman: 9.13 a.m.

*Let's be honest, no man did, did he?*

Truman slid another cigarette from his packet, tapped the head of it on the windowsill to compact the tobacco, eased the warm weight of Doll's arm from his chest and stretched across her for his lighter.

So he'd tried it, this steady-job malarkey. And it wasn't for him.

Not that Christie knew that he wasn't still out there on the knocker, of course. As far as she was concerned, he was working all day every day and into the evenings. It suited him, the freedom this gave him. It allowed him all the time he needed – for a bit of fun with his lonely widows, for seeing Sally from The Salvation when she finished her lunchtime shift, for sharing a joke and a few beers with the lads in the bar at The Trumpeters, for playing the piano in the snug at The Young Pretender and for working up the idea.

The Big Idea. *His* big idea.

Or rather that stupid sod Bernie's big idea, he thought with sudden bitterness.

Supposed to make him a mint, it was, but instead it had landed him on Carey Street. Had cost him everything he had and much, much more.

But there was no point in dwelling on it. No point in getting yourself down. You had to try these things, didn't you? You had to give it a go. And he was young, he'd bounce back. Anyway, maybe it wasn't as bad as he thought, maybe there was something still there, something he could salvage.

And that was what today was all about, wasn't it? It might be a bit risky but he had to go back to see how things stood in Brighton, to get the lie of the land, to assess the damage. He had to see if anything could be rescued from the wreckage, to see if the dust had finally settled after six weeks.

And taking the boy with him was a stroke of genius.

When Christie had first suggested it, he had thought it was a bloody terrible idea. All he had done was to casually mention one day that he was thinking of going back down to Brighton, to the house, to check it out, to make sure that everything was OK, and then, bingo, she'd immediately pounced and said, 'Oh good, Baxter can go with you.'

Like she had been waiting for him to say it; as if she'd planned it all along.

What did she think he was supposed to do with the boy dragging along behind him, whining all day, throwing up in the back of the Wolseley? It was the last thing he needed when all he wanted was to get down there, have a quick look around, ask a few questions and then, if he had to, get the hell out as fast as he could.

But the more he had thought about it, the more he could

see how it might work; how the boy might be useful after all, how he might be a bit of insurance just in case he needed it. If he ran into someone he didn't mean to and things threatened to cut up rough, get out of hand, they'd back off if they saw he had a little nipper with him. You'd have to be a real psycho to have a go in front of a kid, wouldn't you?

And that wasn't what he was dealing with here. Some bother, perhaps; but not psycho stuff.

Taking the boy with him would help keep Christie off his back too. Every time he saw her now, he could feel her building up to asking him all those questions he didn't want to go anywhere near. That's why he was always in a hurry when he was with her; he was always 'Must dash, got to go, too busy to stop and talk, got to see a man about a dog,' that sort of thing. Taking the boy would give her a break, keep her sweet, buy him some time.

Of course, he would have to face her questions at some point, he knew that. So far he'd told her nothing about any of it.

But if he could hold out for just a little longer, something might just turn up, he could get some money rolling in and he might be able to come up with a whole better set of answers than the ones he had now.

With money in your pocket, see, you could make the truth whatever you wanted it to be.

Anyway, if he could just get used to the way the boy looked at him with his mother's eyes, maybe it wouldn't be so bad to spend some time with him. Maybe they could do that father-and-son thing you saw in those Yank films: become buddies, pals, go to the football, that sort of thing. It didn't seem all that likely to Truman but maybe that was the way it was

48

supposed to happen between fathers and their boys – not really being bothered with them when they were small, but slowly getting used to them being around and then spending some time with them when they got older. If it hadn't been for the war, maybe that would even have happened with *his* old man. Maybe he would have mellowed. Maybe they would have got on after all. It was possible, wasn't it?

It was different with his Megan, of course, different with his little princess. You couldn't help but have a smile on your face when you saw her. But, even having said that about Megan – and don't get him wrong, he wouldn't be without her for the world – the truth was that he had never really wanted children in the first place.

Let's be honest, no man did, did he?

He wanted children for her, of course, for Christie. So that she could stay at home and be a proper mother, a proper wife. But after that, it was down to her, wasn't it?

Truman stubbed out his cigarette and reached for his watch on the windowsill, feeling the pleasing weight of the gold bracelet. Be ready at ten o'clock sharp, he'd told the boy. It was going to be a long day and he didn't have time to hang around for him, he'd said.

But he'd wait, wouldn't he, the boy? Wasn't going anywhere without him, was he?

And, like so many nights at The Hare and Hounds, it had been one hell of a party yesterday, hadn't it?

So it would be a shame to rush away now, wouldn't it?

Truman gently nudged Doll awake and snuggled down into her.

# 11

# Strachan: 9.21 a.m.

*Not too dusty, he thought; all things considered*

Strachan was staring at his hands.

He had discovered that if he really concentrated on them, held them out in front of him as if he was looking for specks of dirt under his fingernails, he could stop the shaking for a while.

Not that you'd exactly call it shaking, he thought. That would be going too far, making too much of it. No, it was more a slight tremor; a tremor that only he knew about.

Best kept that way.

The floorboards creaked as he stooped forwards to the mirror on the chest of drawers and adjusted his red-and-yellow-striped silk tie; double Windsor, perfect. He picked up a clothes-brush and gave the broad pinstriped shoulders of his suit jacket one last brisk vigorous working over. Nice bit of cloth, it was; had it made up by that tailor in

Kemptown, a fair few years ago now, still looked good as new though.

Oh yes. Always spick. Always span. Always.

Strachan lifted the corner of the net curtain and peered out of the tall sash window of the bedsit; saw the sunlight bouncing off the listless sea. There were already shirtsleeved day-trippers setting up on the beach, fussing over the deckchairs so that Mum and Dad could sit side by side and watch the kids pick their way gingerly across the pebbles down to the water's edge. The air was filled with the baleful shrieks of the sleek seagulls, now hanging in the air above the shoreline, now swooping above the promenade.

He picked up a neatly folded handkerchief from the bedside table and dabbed at a bead of sweat on his forehead. A bit hot for the suit today, he thought. But there was no choice; it was what he always wore. It was how people recognised him for who he was.

Strachan. Just Strachan.

It suddenly came into his mind what his ma used to say to him. What was it exactly? 'You may not always be the best-looking man in the room,' she'd say to him, 'but you can always be the man looking his best.' That was it, that was what she used to say, fussing over him, reaching up on tiptoes to straighten his collar, way back, when he was Jack the lad going out on the town.

Too long ago now.

He turned to the mirror again, reached into his inside jacket pocket for his comb and ran it once more through his dark, slicked-back, Brylcreemed hair. Thinning a bit now, the odd strand of grey; but again, only he knew it.

He stood back to look at himself in the mirror. Not too

dusty, he thought; all things considered. He was still the big man and he hadn't let himself go. Not like some. He could still carry himself the way he used to; hadn't gone soft. Bit heavier in the face than he was, a few scars, a few more lines. But that was to be expected.

He hadn't lost it, you see, he could still mix it, he was still a player. More than that: he was still the best; the best in this town anyway. He was still the one Mr Smith turned to, the only one he really trusted.

He patted at the pockets of his jacket, patted them flat.

No giveaway bulges.

No fat wallet to spoil the line. Money clip in the back pocket took care of that.

No knives, no knuckles.

Job like this one, who fucking needs them? Strachan thought.

# 12

# Christie: 9.34 a.m.

## *It was true, he had overwhelmed her*

C hristie knelt on the worn carpeted floor of the caravan so that she could reach to raise the cushioned top of the bench seat to reveal the hidden storage box below. Quickly and precisely, she folded the children's sheets and small eiderdowns into quarters and then worked each in turn into the corners of the confined space. It was the only way she had discovered to make them all fit sufficiently well for her to be able to close the top on its broken hinge and nudge it back into position.

It was the same as everything in the caravan; it was cramped and threadbare and broken and ridiculous.

Outside, she could hear Megan's muffled voice as she sang in time to the swoosh of her skipping rope. Christie smiled; it was one of the songs she had taught her.

*'One, two, three, mother caught a flea,*
*Put it in the teapot and made a cup of tea.*
*The flea jumped out,*
*Mother gave a shout,*
*And in came Father with his shirt hanging out.'*

It was a rare moment of quiet for Christie during the day. The baby was contentedly in his carry-cot in the shade of the caravan; somewhere in the long grass Baxter would be making a camp.

Inside the caravan, the radio played softly. Still on her knees, Christie closed her eyes and allowed herself to be lifted and lulled for a moment. Roy Orbison was singing.

♫ *I'm falling, falling in love, falling in love with you . . .*

Not for the first time, Christie wondered whether she had ever truly loved him.

After all, it wasn't as if Truman had swept her off her feet. It wasn't that she had heard the violins start up and had gone head over heels for him the way they did in books and films. She hadn't exactly felt herself *falling, falling.*

She had wanted to, of course; she had wanted it to be like that. And there had been moments when she had almost convinced herself that she *was* falling, especially when he had made her laugh or when he sat at a piano and sang to her. And she had wanted *him* to love her. She was a little embarrassed to admit it, even now, even to herself; but more than being in love, what she had longed for then was the feeling of being loved by someone.

But mostly what she felt now, she thought, as she knelt

with her eyes still closed, trying to find just the right word for it, what she felt was that she had been *overwhelmed* by him. That he had been so relentless, that somehow he'd given her no choice.

Outside, the skipping rope tangled and Megan began again. '*One, two, three, mother caught a flea . . .*'

Christie got to her feet and began to gather up the children's scattered nightclothes.

To begin with it had been exciting to be with Truman, of course. To be wanted so much, to be pursued by a boy who was so tall and handsome; it was like nothing that had ever happened to her. And there had been times then when it had felt almost magical. When he put his arm around her shoulders to keep her safe as they crossed a road. When they walked back late through wet streets after dancing all night to the Syd Dean Orchestra at the Regent Ballroom and he suddenly stopped and waltzed her under the clock tower. When they held hands and tiptoed painfully across the pebbled beach, wincing and laughing all the way, to swim for the first time together in the sea.

Later she had enjoyed the admiring jealous glances of the other girls as she walked arm in arm with him along the seafront. They had looked good together, people said. And, of course, there had been some defiance in it too. Because she had known that her mother wouldn't approve, it had made her all the more determined to go out with him in the first place.


She had been just eighteen years old and queuing for an ice cream with her sisters outside the aquarium on the seafront in Brighton. Suddenly, as if from nowhere, he had been by her side and had started to talk to her. And once he had started there had been no stopping him. He had talked up a storm.

His attention had flattered her, made her blush. He was down from Croydon for the day and this was his last twenty-four hours of freedom, he told her. He was off to Catterick to do his National Service the very next morning and he couldn't face sitting down to eat a lonely last supper. Would she do this shy and unassuming young man the honour of joining him for fish and chips on the Palace Pier? It would keep a smile on his face through all the barren years ahead, he said; the memory of a fish-and-chip supper with the most beautiful girl in Brighton.

He went down on one knee to beg her.

'Come on, princess. How about it?' he said, with a lop-sided smile.

Her sisters, the twins, had stood there open-mouthed, already constructing in their minds the report that they would take back to their mother. It had been worth agreeing to go with him just for the expression on their faces. And there had been something about him that had made Christie think of her father; it was the way he talked, perhaps, the way he made her laugh.

After Christie had run from her mother in the kitchen that morning, she had cycled through the near-empty early-morning streets, feeling the renewing freshness of the breeze on her face.

She had still been able to hear her mother's laughter echoing in her head as she had pushed hard on her pedals and had slowly climbed the hill that went steeply up towards the Old Shoreham Road. Halfway up she had got off and walked the bike the rest of the way to the top to give herself the chance to gather her breath. One day she would have a bike with gears that worked, she had told herself.

Somehow, that resolutely practical thought had calmed her and by the time she reached the cemetery, she had put her mother as far out of her mind as she was able. She had a promise to keep. Nothing was going to spoil it. Nothing.

She closed her eyes. Remembered.

'Dance with me, Daddy,' she had said, tugging at his hands.

'To this?' he'd said, looking at the radiogram in mock disbelief.

♪ *I got a gal in Kalamazoo, don't want to boast but I know she's the toast of Kalamazoo . . .*

'Please dance, Daddy. It's Glenn Miller,' Christie had pleaded.

'I know what it is, young lady,' he'd said, laughing. 'But it's too fast for me. My old knees won't stand it.'

'Please, Daddy . . .' she'd said, ten years old and not taking no for an answer.

He'd sat her down on his lap and they'd listened to the music together. It had been bedtime and she had been a little sleepy despite herself.

'You know, I'm not much of a one for dancing, Christie,' he'd said.

'But I want you to dance with me,' she'd said sulkily.

'One day, perhaps,' he'd said.

'When?' she'd said, seizing her chance.

'One day,' he'd said, tapping her nose. It was a signal, it was time for bed.

'But when?' she'd demanded, not letting go.

'Tell you what,' he'd said. 'We'll dance on your wedding day. Will that do?'

She had nodded enthusiastically.

'Promise?' she'd said.

'Promise,' he'd said.

For a while they had settled back and listened to the rise and headlong tilt of the music.

'What shall we dance to, Daddy?' she had asked him as it came to an end.

'It would have to be something slow,' he'd said, pointing to his knees.

'One of Frank's?' she'd said.

'Sinatra?'

She'd nodded.

'Which one?' he'd said.

Christie had thought for a while.

'How about "Night and Day"?' she had finally said.

'Perfect,' he'd said. 'My favourite.'

Christie could have found her way through the paths between the graves to the far corner of the cemetery with her eyes closed; she had been there that often over the past seven years. This morning it had been just as well, so profoundly lost had she been in her thoughts. It had come almost as a surprise when she had found herself standing in the familiar spot beneath the old broken yew.

'Hello, Dad,' she said, reaching out to touch the headstone, pulling her hand away at once as she felt the small shock of the coldness of the marble. 'I've come to keep that promise,' she said, patting her hand at her mouth to try to check the tears.

She felt the first notes begin to swell inside her.

'Do you remember, Dad?' she said. 'Do you remember?'

♪ *Night and day, you are the one . . .*

Christie closed her eyes, wrapped her arms about her and swayed gently as the music played in her head and the tears finally ran.

When she was done, when the music had faded and she no longer moved with it, Christie gave a small embarrassed laugh as she tried to push at the tears with the heel of her hand. It was as if somehow he'd caught her out, caught her crying.

She could hear his voice.

'Perfect,' he'd said. 'My favourite.'

'Now off to bed, young lady, and sweet dreams,' he had said.

Christie had *such* dreams when she was young. She had been fourteen years old and had just left school when her father had been rushed late one winter's evening into the Royal Sussex with a heart attack. When he died that same night, she had thought her world would end. But those dreams and his voice deep in her head had somehow kept her going, had somehow seen her through. 'Don't be like me,' he had always told her: 'follow your dreams, wherever they take you.' And that, she had decided, was exactly what she would do. The war was finally over and suddenly anything seemed possible. She had been good at school, always near the top of the class; she would go to night classes, learn book-keeping, get a proper job, find her own place, move away, see something of the world and make something of herself.

But her mother wouldn't hear of any of it and had found her a position as a junior in the haberdashery department of Hannington's store on North Street.

'And very lucky to have it too,' she had said. 'Ungrateful girl.'

The morning that had begun with her mother's taunting laughter and continued with her tears at her father's graveside had hardly been a bride's typical preparation for a wedding.

At Hannington's, however, all that had changed. She had promised to call in to see everyone on her way to Jenny's.

When her mother had found her the job at Hannington's straight from school, she had hated the idea of working there. But she had stayed seven years with never a serious thought of leaving. It was a funny, creaking, old-fashioned place, with its tall glass cabinets, dark wooden counters and a faint but persistent smell of beeswax polish. It was a place that carried on as if it didn't know it was 1953 and the world had changed around it. But being there was like being part of a family, a big, warm, slightly eccentric family. Although Christie was reluctant to admit it, because she still hankered for something different, something more, she loved being part of that family.

This morning, from the moment she had walked on to the floor of the haberdashery department, she had been surrounded by chatter and laughter. Everyone was so pleased and excited to see her. Even Mr Bonfield had smiled and patted her lightly on the shoulder.

They'd had to be quick because a customer might have

come at any moment, but Mrs Ashmore had gathered everyone around. They had clubbed together to give her something old, something new, something borrowed and something blue, she had told Christie. Although, she had added, looking tellingly at Albert, the new apprentice, she was still waiting for some people to put their hands in their pockets and find something more than holes. Standing next to him, Mr Bonfield had aimed a soft playful admonishing punch to his arm, everyone had laughed and Albert had stared at the floor.

Something old was a locket given to Mrs Ashmore by her mother on her wedding day.

'I've no daughter of my own, Christie,' she'd said, brushing away a stray tear. 'I'd be so proud if you'd have it.'

Something new was a pair of silk stockings and a bottle of Miss Dior perfume; something borrowed was a pair of pearl earrings that Mrs Boult had worn on the day she had met her husband; something blue was a daring French garter that young Albert had been designated to present. This he had managed to do with a curious combination of swagger, scarlet blushes and minimal eye contact. He had then taken swift evasive action before Christie could reward him with a kiss on the cheek.

After the presentations, Mr Bonfield had led Christie to his small office and they sat facing each other across his desk.

'How long is it that have you been with us, Christine?' he said, taking his dark-rimmed spectacles from his nose and polishing them on a large white handkerchief.

'Seven years, Mr Bonfield,' she said, glancing at her watch, wondering whether she had time for this, wondering why he wanted to see her. 'And it's Christie, Mr Bonfield. Everyone calls me Christie.'

It was what her father had called her. She had adopted it after he had gone. It somehow kept him close.

Mr Bonfield carefully replaced his glasses, sat a little more upright in his chair and straightened the knot of his tie.

'I don't think we do nicknames at Hannington's, Christine,' he said. 'I think it best that we stick to the formalities, don't you?'

'Yes, Mr Bonfield,' she said.

'I've watched you very carefully over those years, Christine,' he said. 'And I have to say that I have been impressed. Most impressed. You are a popular girl. You have worked hard. You have done well.'

'Thank you, Mr Bonfield,' Christie said, smiling.

'So much so, Christine, that I think you're now ready to move on,' he said.

'Move on, Mr Bonfield?' she said, suddenly alarmed.

He raised his hands reassuringly.

'When you come back next week, Christine, we're going to see about that job in the office that you've always wanted. It won't be easy, of course. There will be much to learn, new responsibilities, you'll have to study, of course, go to night school, you might even need to go to college and ...'

Distantly, Christie was aware that Mr Bonfield was continuing to talk and that she was no longer listening.

Truman would be proud, she thought; her Dad would have been proud. So proud.

'Follow your dreams,' he had said.

And finally, it was happening. Finally they were starting to come true.

\*

It had been four years after she started at Hannington's that Truman had gone down on one knee to her in the queue for the aquarium. After that, and without ever quite being able to explain to herself why, she had found herself waiting for him during his National Service.

He had written all the time, long poetic letters, and one day he had told her that he loved her, that he would love her for ever, that she was his princess, his only princess. He could write as he could talk; like a storm.

And he had made her laugh. One morning she received seven postcards, each bearing a single boldly printed letter – *I L O E YO U*. The missing *V* arrived apologetically (*V. sorry!*) in the second post. The next day the first letter of every new paragraph spelled out her name. The day after, he wrote to say that he had shown her photograph to Badger, Starling and Fitz and they were all now head over heels in love with her: *Badger has his heart sett on you, Starling is all of a flutter, and Fitz has lost witz!*

Every day of leave that he had he would spend in Brighton, staying at a cheap boarding house in Upper Rock Gardens, walking her to work in the mornings, turning up in the haberdashery department unexpectedly during the day, pretending to be a customer, asking for knicker elastic, making her blush, making Mr Bonfield frown, making the other assistants giggle, walking her home when the store closed, taking her out every evening.

It was true, he *had* overwhelmed her; he hadn't given her a chance to say no.

'You do know ...' Jenny said as she removed the last roller from Christie's hair and picked a hairbrush from the jumble of make-up and tissues on the dressing-table top.

Christie had known Jenny her entire life. They had grown up living next door to each other; they had walked hand in hand to school on their first day; they had learned to swim in the sea side by side; they had gone arm in arm together to their first youth-club dance. Jenny was more of a sister to Christie than the twins had ever been. They had always been so much for each other, so much for their mother.

'Know what?' Christie said, smiling as she looked in the mirror at her friend standing behind her.

'That it's not too late,' Jenny said, looking away.

'Too late for what?' Christie said, the smile giving way to a small frown.

'It's not too late to say no,' Jenny said. 'It's not too late to change your mind ...'

After she had left Hannington's, Christie had cycled the mile to Queen's Park, to where Jenny now lived in a flat that was almost impossibly small but was proudly her own. Christie had jumped at Jenny's suggestion that she could get ready for the register office there rather than at home.

'To change my mind?' Christie said.

'To not go through with it,' Jenny said quietly.

'But why wouldn't I want to go through with it?' Christie said.

She thought she knew what was on Jenny's mind, but she pretended not to; she didn't want to put the words in her friend's mouth. Jenny shook her head and looked away.

'I know what it is, Jen,' Christie said, relenting. 'I know you've never really liked Truman ... You've never been sure about him.'

Placing the hairbrush back on the dressing table, Jenny

64

fished among the tissues for her packet of cigarettes. Taking one from the packet, she fished again for a box of matches.

'I just want you to be happy, Chris,' she said. 'That's all.'

'But I am,' Christie said, renewing her smile. 'I will be.'

Jenny lit her cigarette and looked into the reflection, directly into Christie's eye.

'Give us a puff,' Christie said, trying to avoid her friend's eye and looking for a way to change the subject.

However well-meaning Jenny was, nothing was going to be allowed to spoil this day.

'But you don't smoke!' Jenny said, scandalised. 'You've never smoked!'

'I know,' Christie laughed. 'But there's only an hour to go and I've never been more nervous about anything in my whole life.'

Jenny handed Christie her cigarette. Christie took the smallest puff, pulled a face, coughed and let go of the smoke.

'I don't mean to go on, Chris,' Jenny said. 'This will be the last time I say it, I promise.'

'What now, Jen?' Christie said.

She didn't want to hear it; she didn't want to hear anything else.

'Just tell me that you're sure he loves you.'

Christie looked at her friend uncertainly.

'He says he does,' she said.

'But are you sure?' Jenny said.

'How can you be sure, Jenny? How can anyone be sure?'

'I don't know ... A feeling, I guess.'

'Well,' Christie said, 'all I know for sure is that he says he loves me. And that's enough.'

'And you ... ?' Jenny said.

'Me?' Christie said.

'Are you sure you love him? Because if you're not sure, then it's not too late to change your mind.'

'I've told you, Jen ...'

Jenny put her hands on Christie's shoulders; put her head close to Christie's ear.

'But you have to be sure, Christie. You have to know that you truly love him.'

Outside Megan was skipping in time to a different song.

> *'Granny was in the kitchen*
> *doing a bit of stitching*
> *when in came a bogey man*
> *and pushed her out ...'*

Putting the children's clothes away, Christie went to the caravan door to check on the baby. She sat down on the step beside the carry-cot and straightened the light blanket that he had kicked away.

*But you have to be sure, Christie. You have to know that you truly love him.*

Christie remembered now that she hadn't answered Jenny that day. She hadn't known what to say.

And ten years later, if Jenny had been there, sitting next to her on the caravan step, and had asked the same question, Christie still wouldn't have known. She still wouldn't know for sure whether she had ever truly loved him.

# 13

# Baxter: 9.46 a.m.

## *He should have felt free*

The funny thing was, Baxter thought as he lay cocooned in the long grass, the warmth of the morning sun washing over him, his eyes closed against the brightness, the funny thing was that he didn't feel any better.

He had tried to think of something happy because that's what his mother always said to do whenever he fell over and hurt his leg or something. He had tried to think of the day in the woods when he and Soldier had been sitting on the wall and he had nudged Soldier with his elbow and Soldier had nudged him back. And then they both did it harder and faster until Soldier fell off and Baxter laughed. And then Soldier climbed back up and threw himself off again straight away in a big heap and then they both fell off together and didn't get up and just stayed there looking up at the sky. For ages.

It was the best happy day he could think of but it hadn't worked, he still felt the same.

As it had turned out, there had been no need for him to pretend to be sick and he didn't have to run away to hide in the woods. He hadn't even got as far as making the big serious speech that he had so carefully rehearsed in his head; that he had decided that he wouldn't go to Brighton after all and that it was only fair that Megan should go in his place. Because she was nine. And she could have an ice cream. Probably.

It had been very early in the morning and he was still in bed when his mother had come to him, had leaned over and had whispered with her hot breath into his ear that it was OK, that he didn't need to go with his father after all and that he should stop worrying and go back to sleep.

And he had. He had fallen asleep instantly, as if someone had thrown a switch or something. But when he woke up, he didn't feel any better. Not really.

He should have felt free, like this big solid weight thing had been lifted from him. He should have felt happy because now he could play all day and make camps and go into the woods and see Soldier or do whatever else he wanted.

And no one would stop him.

And it wouldn't be boys together.

But instead, the ticking continued inside and the key kept turning tighter and the sickness and the ache were still there in his stomach. But worse than before.

It was the same as at school when the teacher asked a question and you didn't know the answer and then he suddenly pointed to the boy next to you and you knew you were all right and safe. But still you had the feeling that you weren't. Not really.

It was like that and it felt as if something bad was still going to happen even though Baxter now knew that it wasn't. That it couldn't.

It was as though his mind had been told one thing but his body didn't believe it.

# 14

# Soldier: 10.03 a.m.

## *The father had not come*

From just after dawn Soldier had watched and waited. He had waited anxiously, impatiently at first as the sun had risen higher in the morning sky and as the soft morning dew had slowly lifted. Waiting for the boy to emerge, waiting for the father to arrive. Boys together.

He had heard the baby's fitful cry. He had seen the children push open the caravan door and come blinking into the light of the new day. He had watched the quick-footed girl as she picked up her rope and began to skip and sing. And he had watched as the pale boy had trailed through the tall grass before dropping to his knees and disappearing into it.

And he had watched as *she*, she had sat on the caravan step and fussed over the baby. He had seen the new slump in her shoulders, the new frown on her face.

Lulled now by the low dreamy murmur of a solitary bee working the late faded-yellow flowering of the gorse, he continued to watch from the warm embrace of the shadows beneath the beech tree.

The girl's voice carried across the clearing.

*'Granny was in the kitchen*
*doing a bit of stitching ...'*

He closed his eyes and heard it as a song sung long ago by voices joined together in a playground chorus. Girls jumped in, girls jumped out as a long rope turned. Some other time. Some other place.

From just after dawn Soldier had watched over the boy and had waited for the father.

But the father had not come. Perhaps he would not come.

# 15

# Christie: 10.14 a.m.

## *Suddenly it was perfect*

Christie straightened the cushions on the benches that ran either side of the drop-down table and retrieved Megan's book from where it had become wedged on the narrow shelf. She checked her watch and sighed.

He was late.

She might have guessed he would be late today. He was always late. Why should today be any different? As far as Christie could see, and she'd had ten years of marriage and three before that to see it, he had been late for pretty much everything in his life and there was no reason to think that he would change now.

He was always late.

He had been late that day she had gone all the way up from Brighton to King's Cross to meet him; he had been drinking with Badger, Starling and Fitz at the station in

72

Darlington where the Catterick bus had dropped them and he had missed his train.

He had been late when he was due to meet her mother for the first time; tea and cakes had been laid out in the parlour, the best china had been liberated from the oak dresser, and she, the twins and her mother had sat side by side in withering silence while the grandfather clock in the hall ticked the minutes away. Her mother had never forgiven him.

He had even been late at the register office at Brighton Town Hall. The registrar had been looking meaningfully at his watch with ever greater frequency when Truman had waltzed in, smelling of beer and cigarettes, with a smile on his face and seemingly without a care in the world.

Christie had waited, shivering with nerves, in the white lace shift dress that she had made herself. Mrs Ashmore had found the pattern and had set aside the fabric so that Christie could pay it off weekly; Mrs Boult had lent her the sewing machine.

'He's not coming,' Jenny had said, taking Christie's hands and rubbing them briskly to warm them.

'He'll be here,' Christie had said. 'He's always late.'

When Truman had finally walked in, flanked by Starling and Fitz, he had strolled over to Christie and had planted a cheery kiss on her cheek.

'Hello, princess,' he'd said. 'You look a million dollars.'

The registrar had begun at once and had galloped through the service to make up for lost time. There had only been a handful of them there. Fitz had been best man and had dropped the wedding ring; Jenny had been one of the witnesses.

Afterwards they had walked around the corner to The Trumpeters, where Truman had hired a small private upstairs room for the reception. There was a barrel of beer in the corner and a scant buffet arranged on the top of an old upright piano. The thin ham sandwiches, pallid sausages on sticks, cheese and pineapple chunks and Scotch eggs had disappeared almost at once: snatched up by more friends of Truman's as they arrived and made for the laughter around the beer barrel.

Jenny was Christie's only friend there. Truman had been insistent that he would only have Starling and Fitz with him and Christie had been shocked to see so many people coming through the door who she didn't know.

'This is too bad, Chris,' Jenny said, scowling across at Truman, surrounded by his friends.

They were standing together, each nursing a Babycham that was growing warm in the gathering heat of the small room.

'It's OK, Jen. He's just having a bit of fun,' Christie said, trying to hide her disappointment.

It was not meant to be this way. It was meant to be perfect.

Despite the warmth of the room, Christie shivered. She looked across to Truman and somehow caught his eye. He smiled his lopsided smile and pushed his way through the crowd of friends to come towards her.

Seeing him coming, Jenny gave Christie's hand a small squeeze and moved away.

'Having fun, princess?' Truman said.

'There's a lot of people ...' Christie said. 'I've only got one friend here.'

'Jenny?' Truman said, looking around for her. 'I've never liked her. Po-faced cow.'

'Truman!' Christie said, shocked. 'She's my best friend!'

Truman held his hands up in *faux* surrender.

'Don't take on, Christie,' he said. 'I just don't like her, that's all. Don't trust her.'

'Please don't, Truman. She's my friend,' Christie said.

'Don't worry about it,' Truman said. 'We'll talk about it later.'

A new shout of laughter went up around the beer barrel. Truman took Christie's hand.

'Come on over, princess,' he said. 'We're going to have a bit of a sing-song.'

He led her over to the piano. Seeing him coming, leading Christie by the hand, a raucous cheer went up from his friends.

He pulled the piano stool out, sat down and patted the space beside him for Christie to join him. He raised a hand and the laughter in the room fell away.

'This one ...' he said, 'this one is for my wife.'

The cheers went up again and only hushed when the first notes played.

'*Unforgettable,*' he sang, looking into her eyes, '*that's what you are ...* '

And suddenly, Christie thought, suddenly everything was the way it was meant to be. Despite her mother's cruelty and Jenny's doubts. Despite Truman being late and despite all his stupid friends.

Suddenly it *was* perfect.

*

75

When Truman had first suggested it, Christie had been shocked.

'Double quick at the register office and a few beers around the corner at The Trumpeters, what do you think, princess?' he'd said.

She had expected so much more. In the dream she had of being loved by someone, of being loved by Truman, she had seen a church wedding, bridesmaids, the cake, the confetti, the lot. She knew they didn't really have the money for it: the same as every couple starting out, they barely had two far-things to rub together. But that had been her dream and she was sure they could have managed somehow. Other couples did.

The more she had thought about it, though, the more she had been convinced that it was the right thing to do. Not to save the money but because she could glimpse a future with him that would be different, that would somehow be free of all those stifling affectations, all those silly pretensions and conventions that her mother had brought to her childhood. A wedding day like that was what her father would, with a sparkle in his eye, have called 'bohemian'. Or at least he would have done when out of earshot of his wife.

Yes, that was how they would get married and that was how she and Truman would live. They would live a *different* life, a modern life.

She could see it all.

She would finally be able to go to night classes and get on, just as she had always wanted to. Truman would find just the right job and, although they only had the bedsit to start with, one day they would have a house and there would be noth-ing old in it. Everything would be brand-new, everything would be just the latest thing and all the colours would be bright yellows and greens and blues. They would have the G Plan furniture she had seen in the window of Vokins, all of it in teak and ebony. They would have those bookshelves that seemed to float on the walls as if there was nothing holding them up. She would be able to fill them with all her books! The books that her mother had said were nothing but a dusty waste of space and that Christie had kept hidden in the cardboard box under her bed. They would have a leather cocktail cabinet in the corner stocked with different-coloured drinks from all around the world. They would have their own telephone, maybe even their own television. They would get home and every night they would talk. They would listen to music and read the newspapers. They might even go to the theatre. And they would save up and go on holidays. They would go to the Continent: people were doing that now, ordinary people, people like them. She'd seen it on the Pathé News at the cinema. And later they would have children, a boy and a girl, and they would all go out for special days and have these wonderful adventures together. As a family.

It was 1953, the world was changing, everyone said it was, and they would be part of it all. *She* would be part of it. And Truman would help her. She knew he would.

Truman was alone in the world. Whenever she had asked him about what it was like for him when he was growing up, when he was a boy, he'd always quickly tried to brush off her questions. It was too painful for him to talk about it, too difficult to revisit memories from that time. But, from the little he had told her, she knew that he'd been orphaned at the start of the war and that he'd been left with no choice but to make his own way, to find and follow his own path.

Although he was the same age as her, because of what had happened to him, because of what he'd been through, he seemed so much older. He knew so much more about the world than she did and Christie could rely on him to know how to do things.

Yes, she would be part of this different future and Truman would show her how.

When she was a girl, Christie had stood and watched one summer's evening as cars pulled up outside the Grand Hotel and ladies in furs and long ballgowns and gentlemen in dinner jackets had made their way arm in arm up the red-carpeted stairs and through the glass doors. Uniformed doormen had bowed to each new couple as they arrived.

Christie had never stayed in a hotel before and in her twenty-one years of life in Brighton she had never set foot in the Grand. It had remained in her imagination as a fairy-tale place of elegance and jewelled splendour beyond her reach.

It was dusk as she and Truman walked hand in hand from The Trumpeters along the seafront towards the hotel. The lights on the West Pier were coming on and Christie couldn't help feeling like Cinderella on her way to the ball. They were staying for one night at the Grand before they moved into their bedsit. Butterflies danced in her stomach; she squeezed Truman's hand, taking courage from him.

Suddenly she found she needed to talk, to distract herself. It wasn't just the thought of walking up those red-carpeted stairs; it was what was waiting for her beyond the hotel-room door when she was alone with Truman for the first time as his wife.

'Oh, I meant to tell you ...' she said.

'What's that, princess?' Truman said.

'Mr Bonfield says I can start working in the office when I go back,' she said excitedly. 'Isn't that wonderful news? It's what I've always dreamed of—'

Truman laughed. 'I reckon that Emmanuel Bonfield has always had a thing for you,' he said.

'It's not true!' Christie said, appalled.

'Yep,' Truman said. 'I reckon the old man fancies you, dirty bugger.'

Christie let go of Truman's hand and stopped walking.

'Please, Truman,' she said. 'Don't spoil it ... Not this ... It's what I've always wanted. I've worked so hard for it. I thought you'd be pleased for me. I thought you'd be proud.'

Truman took both of her hands in his.

'I'm always proud of you, princess,' he said soothingly. 'But I'm just saying—'

'No, Truman,' she said, once more letting go of his hands.

'Anyway,' he said, smiling. 'None of it matters now does it?'

She looked at him, not understanding.

'Why doesn't it matter?' she said.

'Because ...' he said, reaching across to her and gently tapping her nose with his forefinger, just like her father used to do to send her on her way to bed.

'Because what?' she said, mystified.

'Because you won't be staying at that poxy place for much longer, will you? Not now we're married.'

'But I don't understand, Truman,' Christie said.

'There's no buts about it, princess,' Truman said, decisively. 'You'll be giving your notice in next week. A wife's place is at home and that's all there is to it.'

'But—' she tried again.

He swung her around, hurt her wrist. And he had never hurt her before, not in all the time they'd been courting.

'I said no buts,' he said. 'And that's the end to it.'

While restlessly working through all those memories, studying all those snapshots, Christie had sometimes dwelled on the thought that the only choice, the only real decision, she had ever made for herself had been to go on that very first date with Truman. Before that her mother had decided everything; after that it had been Truman, Truman and then later, in a thousand ways every day, the children. And it had turned out, she thought, with a mixture of wonder, resentment and resignation, that her sole decision, made when she was just eighteen years old and knew no better, was the decision that had changed everything in her life.

Because of just that one thing, all this.

And one inevitable consequence, one early casualty of that decision, had been that the bold young Christie of her dreams, the Christie she had hoped to be, had been irretrievably lost.

Christie had run back along the hotel corridor from the bathroom, barefoot and in her dressing gown. She'd been sitting on the edge of the bath for so long that someone had knocked impatiently on the door and shouted at her. It was only when she had heard their footsteps retreating that she'd seized the opportunity and set off running.

She was slightly breathless when she pushed open the door and went back into their room. Truman was lying on the bed, legs crossed at the ankles. He was still dressed but the top buttons of his shirt were undone, revealing his white vest. He had a cigarette in one hand and the newspaper in the other. There was an ashtray balanced on the bed beside him.

'You've been a long time, princess,' he said, not looking up.

'I'm sorry,' she said, suddenly feeling tearful.

There must have been something in her voice. Truman put down the newspaper, moved the ashtray to one side and patted the bed next to him.

'Come on over here,' he said.

She went over to the bed, lay down next to him and put her head on his shoulder.

'It's a lovely room,' Christie said.

She had somehow expected that all the rooms would face the sea and they would each have one of those small wrought-iron balconies that you could step out on to and look up and see the stars. She had been disappointed to discover that their room was at the back of the hotel and that it was small, dingy and drab. She had sensed the disappointment in Truman too, the moment they had walked through the door. She wanted to reassure him.

'It'll do, I guess,' Truman said, grudgingly.

For a while neither of them spoke. Christie could feel the warmth of him; she closed her eyes and heard his voice. *Unforgettable*, he had sung to her. He had looked into her eyes as though there was no one else in the room, no one else in the world.

'When you sing, you're just like him,' Christie said dreamily.

'Like who, princess?' Truman said, reaching across to stub out his cigarette in the ashtray.

'Nat King Cole.'

Truman laughed. 'I hope not,' he said.

Christie raised her head a little to look at him.

'Why not?' she said.

'Because he's a darkie, isn't he?' Truman said.

Christie pulled away.

'Don't say that, Truman. He's lovely. Don't spoil it.'

Truman pulled her back to him.

'I'm just saying, that's all. Now stop all this talking and give me a kiss.'

It was happening too fast. She didn't want it to be this way.

'Don't you need to go to the bathroom first?' Christie said uncertainly.

'No, I'm fine,' Truman said.

As he kissed her, she could smell the beer and tobacco on him. He slid his hand to her breast beneath her dressing gown and then worked down to her hip, releasing the gown's knotted cord as he went.

'Truman ...' Christie said. 'I'm frightened.'

'Me too,' he said, running his hand from her hip to the top of her leg.

'Truman ... I don't know ...'

'Don't worry about it,' he said. 'Everything will be fine.'

He let go of her, rolled off the bed, stood up, unbuckled his trousers and let them drop to the floor.

'But—' Christie said as he climbed back close to her.

'I said don't worry,' Truman said.

'But shouldn't we take some precautions?' Christie said, as he moved his hands to her thighs. 'We don't want babies straight away, do we?'

Jenny had talked to her about precautions.

'No need,' Truman said, hoisting himself at once on top of her so that his weight bore down on her.

'No need,' he said. 'No one gets pregnant straight away.'

It had been like being picked up and carried by a whirlwind and everything in her life had changed. It had never been part of her dreams to marry young; but they had married the day after her twenty-first birthday. She had never dreamed of having children so soon; but Megan had arrived nine months after the wedding night and Baxter a year later.

Everything had changed and nothing was the way it was meant to be.

She had dreamed that she and Truman would build that different kind of life together; it was to be a modern marriage of equals. But almost from the beginning he had hardly ever been at home and, whenever he was, as soon as he walked through the door, he expected a meal on the table and to talk only about what he wanted to. He was the breadwinner, out in the world, and she was to be the little woman at home. That was how he saw it.

She had never intended being this stay-at-home wife; that was not the woman she was meant to be. But Truman had given her no option and looking after the children had soon filled every hour of every lonely day. And just when Megan and Baxter were old enough that she could begin to harbour a new small dream of finding a part-time job somewhere and having something of a life for herself, the baby had come along. And she had been trapped again.

That was what children did, she had quickly discovered. However much you might love them, however much joy they brought you, they filled your life and took away any choices you had left.


Later that night Christie had slipped quietly from the bed and run back along the corridor to the bathroom. For a long time she perched on the edge of the bath, trying to understand why she felt the way she did.

It wasn't that she was frightened any longer. In the end, Truman had been right; there had been nothing to worry about. Not really. And afterwards he had told her he loved her.

No, it wasn't that.

What she felt was this strange aching emptiness. And she didn't know why.

After all, she finally had what she had always wanted. For the first time in her life she had someone, someone who was hers.

For the first time she had someone who loved her.

And yet she had never felt so utterly alone.

# 16

# Christie: 10.27 a.m.

## *Stale and used*

In ten years together, she had never been able to understand it. Did he love her? Did he?

She couldn't work it out. For weeks he would all but ignore her. Day after day, he would arrive home late and barely speak. There would be months on end when he would come in and then storm out again as soon she or the children had said or done something to annoy him. The slightest thing would spark him off.

Then suddenly, when they were all sitting nervously waiting for him, when she could feel the anxiety eating away inside her, when she was expecting it to be the same as the day before and the day before that, he would fall through the door with presents and surprises for all of them. One Saturday he had turned up unexpectedly with a special doll – a new Barbie he'd bought no-questions-asked from someone he'd met in a pub – and a train set. All afternoon he had crawled about on the carpet putting the tracks together with Baxter and later he had sat Megan on his lap with her new doll and had made her laugh by talking in a high-pitched Barbie voice with an American accent. And they were all just so happy. It was impossible to imagine being any happier.

But as quickly as he had changed, he would change again. Baxter had begged for five more minutes when it was bedtime and Truman had shouted and had dragged him upstairs crying.

He could still surprise her by being romantic too. Not often now, but sometimes.

When he'd come home that day with the new car, he had insisted on taking her out for a drive. And she didn't even know he was thinking about getting a car; she didn't know they were in a position to afford one. They'd dropped the children off at her mother's and they'd driven into the countryside, just the two of them, and he'd found a pub. There was a piano in the corner and he'd sat down and had sung to her.

'*Love, love me do . . .*'

And all the time, he had looked her right in the eye. Just the way he did on their wedding day. As if there was no one else in the world.

But then as soon as they'd all got home, something had upset him and he'd shouted and the children had cried and he'd slammed out of the door again.

She didn't understand. Was she so difficult to love? She didn't understand why he had chased her with all that poetry and passion, pursued her like that and then, almost as soon as they were married, how he had changed. How he was never there but still didn't want her to go anywhere, to have any friends of her own, to have any life for herself.

She didn't understand any of it.

She didn't understand how he could live with his own children's fear of him, with all their tears; how he could shout at them, lash out at them, so that they shrank from him. All she knew, what she had quickly learned, was that she had to try to keep them quiet. Keep them away from him, keep them safe. Try to make sure they didn't do anything to upset him.

And she didn't understand how she could have lived with him for ten years, could have borne him three children and yet still know so little about him. Where he went when he was out all hours of day and night, what he did, who he saw.

Very quickly she had learned not to ask too many questions. That was part of the truth of it; questions had always provoked him.

And that was how it was that she and the children were stuck in this caravan in the middle of nowhere. Not knowing why they were there. Or for how much longer. Or what was going to happen to them next. Because she didn't ask questions. Because she hadn't dared to ask.


As Christie set about the washing-up after the children's breakfast, taking the dishes from the caravan's tiny sink and balancing them on what passed for a draining board, she could feel the irritation rising in her.

He was late.

Not that it really mattered if he was late today, of course, not now that she had told Baxter that he didn't have to go with his father, that he could stay with her here at the caravan, that he could continue to build his camp in the forest in the sunshine. Baxter was happy and no doubt Truman would be delighted too, not to have to take the boy with him.

It was only Christie who was left angry and disappointed.

Having dried the breakfast bowls and spoons and put them away in the small overhead cupboard, the one that always clicked back open as soon as you clicked it closed, she undid the catches and pushed at all of the windows on their stiff, complaining hinges. The air in the caravan was stale and used.

Later, when she went to fetch water from Mrs Chadney, she would try to remember to leave as many of the windows open as she could.

Stale and used, Christie thought. That was about right. That was how she felt now.

Stale and used.

# 17

# Soldier: 11.26 a.m.

## *Soldier had scrambled unsteadily to his feet*

The boy was suddenly up like a startled rabbit. Up and out of the tall grass and frozen for a moment. Not knowing which way to turn, what to do. Soldier imagined him fighting for breath, the panic rising inside him. He felt his own breath coming shorter, his chest tightening, the constriction in his throat.

The boy looked around and saw the man coming towards him from the caravan. He heard him calling his name, heard the anger in his voice as he shouted for him. And then, his instincts kicking in, he did the only thing he could do and dropped once more into the safety of his warm nest in the grass.

But it was too late. He had been seen.

The man started striding angrily across the broad clearing towards where the boy had fallen, to where he was hiding. And *she*, she was half running to catch him up, with the baby in her arms and the ponytailed girl taking stuttering hesitant steps by her side.

The man suddenly turned to face her. Perhaps he had heard her swift rustling footfall behind him; or perhaps she had called out his name to try to stop him. He turned, swung around and raised his clenched fist towards her.

She stopped. Held the girl's hand, as the man strode on and on towards the boy.

'Baxter! Baxter!' she called.

And as she called, she stood on tiptoes as if the few extra inches gained would help her locate her boy hidden in the grass before his father reached him or, failing that, would at least enable her voice to travel more quickly to him.

'Baxter!' she called. 'Baxter!'

Soldier could hear her voice clearly whereas the man's had been a muffled roar to him.

And having heard the plea in her voice, having decided what it meant, what it was asking him to do, the small fair-haired boy got to his feet. Slowly. Haltingly. Until his head and shoulders were finally just visible above the long breath-less grass.

He shielded his eyes against the beating light of the sun as his father strode towards him. He reached him, grabbed him by the arm, dragged him, half stumbling, half falling, back past his mother. Back past the caravan and then on to the car parked on the rough track.

With his free hand the man flung open a rear door, lifted the flailing boy in, threw him on to the back seat, and then kicked the door closed. He turned, shouted something at the woman that Soldier couldn't hear, and then, slamming the driver's door behind him, he drove off in a swirling cloud of dust.

For some moments, as the dust began to settle and the quiet sounds of the forest returned, the woman stood with her head bowed, her arm around the girl's shoulders and the baby still held to her. She then slowly turned and she and the girl walked towards the caravan and sat, side by side and in silence, in their familiar place on the step.

Stooped low in the feathery shade cast by the ferns on the edge of the wood, Soldier could feel the thickening heat of the day. It unlocked the rich heavy muskiness of the earth itself. He breathed deeply now. Calmer after the storm he had witnessed.

It had begun so differently.

He had waited longer than he had expected for the father to arrive but finally he had heard the car approaching, the tyres crunching on the stony sandy track. He had seen him climb out of the car with a wide smile on his face and had watched as the girl had run to greet him and then as he had reached down for her and scooped her up and hoisted her high on to his shoulders.

They had walked that way towards the caravan. He with his smile wide; the girl laughing, bouncing high on his shoulders.

For a moment in the warm drowsy shadows of the wood, Soldier had stopped watching and had found himself lost and wondering. Wondering how it would feel to have a child riding so proud, so high on your shoulders. Wondering how it must feel to be that child.

Soldier had not anticipated this. The sight of the smiling devoted father, the happy carefree child. This was not the picture that he had pieced together in his mind from what the boy had told him.

'I'm not frightened,' Baxter had said.

Soldier had heard the fear in his voice.

'Not really,' the boy said.

They were leaning against the wall and Baxter was kicking distractedly at a low tufted clump of grass, breaking the frail white roots as he scuffed at them with his toe.

'Because it's not always telling off and hitting and things,' he said.

Soldier could see that there was something more the boy wanted to say. He waited to hear it as a blackbird landed near by and as they both watched it boldly test the hard ground with its beak before hopping away into the undergrowth.

'There was this best day ever,' Baxter finally said. 'Daddy came home and I had a train set and Megan got a stupid doll and all afternoon we lay on the floor, just me and Daddy, putting the tracks together and then playing trains.'

Baxter looked up at Soldier, shielding his eyes against the sun.

'Well, he did most of the putting together,' he said. 'But that was all right because I didn't mind and he was better at it than me.'

He nodded to reassure Soldier that it really had been all right.

'It was Hornby Dublo Super Detail,' he said. 'And it was quite complicated.'

The blackbird reappeared but this time Baxter didn't stop to watch it.

'And it was quite sad too,' he said. 'Because when we were lying on our tummies together, Daddy told me that when he was a little boy *his* father never bought him any toys. Not ever.'

Soldier reached out and touched the boy on the shoulder. He let his hand rest there for a moment; pulling it away only when Baxter began to speak again.

'It *was* sad,' Baxter said. 'But it was the best day too.'

Baxter began to kick again at the grass, tearing the roots from the dark earth.

'It was the *only* best day,' he said.


Perhaps, Soldier thought, the boy had got it wrong. Perhaps the day would be good for him after all, like the playing-trains day. Just him and his father. Boys together.

Him and his father.

Another distant memory had stirred within Soldier.

*He was walking along a high-hedged winding country lane. It was decked with the palest yellow primroses and crisp white wood sorrel. They were walking side by side and there was a book in his father's hand. He could hear the birds sing. He could see the scattered clouds in the sky above. He could see the book in his father's hand. But he couldn't see his face. Couldn't see him. His father.*

For just that moment Soldier had felt again what it was to be near to him, to walk by his father's side. He had felt it with such intensity that it had forced his eyes to close.

Father and daughter had reached the caravan and, as Soldier's eyes blinked open, *she* had stepped out through the door to meet them, drying her hands on a tea-towel. With

93

the girl still balanced aloft, the father had managed to bend, to somehow lower himself enough to kiss his wife on the cheek. As he did so, Soldier, looking down across the gentle sweep of the sun-filled clearing, could see all three of them laugh.

They had chatted for a while in the shadow of the caravan, the girl still riding high. And then suddenly, suddenly the man had pulled the girl roughly from his shoulders. Reaching up with one hand. Tearing her away from him. Landing her heavily on the ground.

The girl stumbled, almost fell. Her mother reached out to catch her.

Something his wife had said must have angered him and the man's voice was raised and he had grabbed her by the arm and he was pointing now, jabbing his finger at his wife, inches from her face.

Soldier had scrambled unsteadily to his feet, a sudden jolting pain in his left knee betraying him.

No! No! No!

He had steadied himself against a tree. Readied himself to go crashing from the dark dense undergrowth. To send himself careering into the light, swooping down across the clearing.

His duty.

Lest violence and harm should come to her.

His duty.

To keep her safe.

But at that moment, the man had jerked away from her and gone striding from the caravan. He'd started to call angrily for the boy and Soldier had held back, staying in the shadows. Breathing hard.

Then the man had taken the boy and had gone.

Now, as Soldier continued to watch over them, mother and daughter were sitting silently pressed together on the low step of the caravan.

As he watched, words from some other place, some other time, came unbidden to his lips.

*Sunt lacrimae rerum.*

Soldier worked the words on his tongue; he could almost taste them, their bitter saltiness. He repeated them slowly, quietly to himself. In wonder.

*Sunt lacrimae rerum.*

The words had come as if from nowhere and yet somehow they were so utterly familiar.

*Sunt lacrimae rerum.*

There are tears. Tears at the heart of things.

And Soldier could feel them now. Wet on his face.

# 18

# Strachan: 11.30 a.m.

## *He glanced across at Strachan and blew him a mocking kiss*

Strachan eased himself into a seat at Jaconelli's cramped window table and raised his mug to his lips. As he did so, the slight trembling of his hand caused the milky coffee to slop.

Fuck it.

He used both hands to steady himself and looked around to see whether anyone had noticed. He was the only customer. He sat back and began his vigil.

Find him; sort it.

That's what Mr Smith had said; and to Strachan, Mr Smith's word was law.

If Strachan was honest, what Mr Smith had actually said was: 'This is most tiresome, Strachan darling. Find him, will you, my dear boy, and sort it all out for me, there's a love.'

Strachan admired Mr Smith, he had been loyal to

Strachan, good to him for too many years to remember now, he had taken care of him. But if there was one thing about him that he found difficult it was this, this ... this flamboyance.

He was ashamed to admit it, and he never would to Mr Smith himself, of course, but being with him made him feel uncomfortable. It always made him shift uneasily in his chair.

'He's pissed me off,' Mr Smith had said. 'He's played havoc with my karma.'

He had reached across and patted Strachan lightly on the knee as they had sat at the table at the back of the tea room.

'So be a love and find the odious little toerag for me and do whatever it is that you do to these appalling little shits.'

Find him; sort it. That's what Strachan had chosen to hear.

'Only do please spare me all the gruesome details,' Mr Smith said with an elaborate shudder, hand still on Strachan's knee. 'You know how delicate I am. My constitution simply won't stand it.'

Finally he had moved his hand away and had run his long bony fingers through his carefully ruffled shock of white hair.

Strachan had always been aware that whenever they sat together in the tea room, as they had done so often over the years, they made the most unlikely of couples. Next to the dapper bird-like Mr Smith in his pale safari suit and floppy red bow-tie, Strachan, perched on a small spindle chair and wrapping his large hands around a tiny bone-china teacup, felt oversized. Like some ungainly, dark-haired, dark-suited giant taking tea in a doll's house.

Three decades before, when they were both much younger

men, Strachan thought that they would have looked odd enough. As the years had passed and as Mr Smith's hair had turned whiter and his clothes and mannerisms more ostentatious, and as Strachan had filled out, had taken to wearing his pinstripe, he knew that the pairing must have looked ever more incongruous.

The grand Victorian tea room with its panelled walls and gilded ceiling, its white tablecloths and polished silver teaspoons, had always been Mr Smith's office. It was where they had met for the first time when twenty-year-old Strachan had a message to meet him pushed under the door of his bedsit.

New in town, Strachan had been working as muscle for some of the bookies at the dog track in Hove. As soon as he had walked through the door of the tea room that first time, he could see that Mr Smith was a big step up in class.

Mr Smith, it turned out, was a businessman who had his slender manicured fingers dipped in many different pies. Some of these pies were, he explained, hotter than others, hotter perhaps than they strictly should be, and from time to time he needed a man who could – how could he put it? – take care of business for him and his associates. He had heard that Strachan was such a man; a man who could handle himself, who could be trusted, be discreet.

The tea room was the only place they had ever met and Strachan had grown sufficiently accustomed to it over the years not to be entirely intimidated by the haughty condescension of the waitresses dressed in their severe long black lace-trimmed dresses and starched white aprons. Not that he would ever have chosen to go there alone; it wasn't his kind of place, he knew that he didn't belong there.

'Meet me at my office, darling. Usual time, usual table.'

That's what Mr Smith would say each time Strachan was called to the shared payphone in the dark airless hallway of the ground floor of the bedsits.

In all the years that he had lived there, Mr Smith was the only person who had ever rung Strachan at the bedsits and the truth was, and it was a truth Strachan was reluctant to confront, that those calls had become less frequent in recent years. When Strachan had asked around, he had been told that the word on the street was that Mr Smith had begun to turn elsewhere, that he had found another, younger man to call on. He had been told that the word was that his time was over, that he was on the way out. But he had refused to allow himself to believe it.

He had been loyal. Always loyal. He wouldn't just be cast aside.

In the last few years though, months had sometimes gone by between calls. From his room Strachan could hear the telephone ring below – and it would ring frequently during the day for one or another of the occupants of the six bedsits in the gloomy down-at-heel building. Every time it rang, he would stop whatever it was that he was doing in his room, he would stand close to his door, straining to hear, and he would find himself holding his breath, waiting for the shout up the stairs. Ninety-nine times in every hundred, the call would not be for him and he would turn away, another drip of disappointment finding its way into his veins.

When finally his turn came, and the call was for him, he would put on his jacket, straighten his tie and make his way down the three creaking flights of stairs. He would take care not to rush, not to appear too eager; breathing deeply, he would feel the adrenalin surge once more.

Oh yes. He was still there, still in the game.

'Any clues?' Strachan had said.

'About what, darling?' Mr Smith replied.

'About the toerag. Where I might find him . . . ?'

Mr Smith had told Strachan everything he knew.

'We know where he lives, of course – with his wife, who I'm sure will be the most dreadful creature, and three brats who are certain to be unutterably loathsome. But they're all long gone from there. I'm told that he drinks at The Trumpeters and at The Young Pretender among other places. And, oh yes, he's got something going on with a barmaid at The Salvation; Sally, her name is, a very pretty little thing, they tell me. Not to my taste though, needless to say, darling. And before all of this palaver, he used to work selling insurance. That's how I first came across him. Would you believe that he had the bare-faced cheek to knock on my door one evening and try to sell me some ghastly little policy?'

He patted Strachan's knee again.

'"Silly boy," I told him. "I've got all the insurance I need."'

At his window table in Jaconelli's, Strachan, with both hands, once more raised the coffee mug to his lips.

He had taken a slow stroll along the seafront from his bedsit, the swagger back in his stride. He was Strachan and he had to be seen. It was important to remind people, important not to be forgotten.

He was Strachan; still there, still in the game. Whatever they said.

Some of the older shopkeepers and café owners had nodded to him in polite greeting before turning away and hurrying about their business; a group of taxi drivers who were standing by their cars, sharing a joke, had fallen silent when they had seen him walking towards them and had parted like the Red Sea to let him through.

He was Strachan and this was what he had come to expect. Respect. It had been earned the hard way. He had the scars to prove it.

He had spent a few moments chatting about the weather with big Jimmy O'Hagan at his hot-dog stand, both of them sweating in the full glare of the sun. He had been too early for opening time at The Salvation and had decided to pass half an hour sitting at Jaconelli's window table, watching the road, hoping to be able to identify this Sally, the barmaid, on her way to work.

When he had arrived, the place had been empty but it had quickly filled and now the room was suddenly echoing with laughter and the jukebox had kicked into life, with Buddy Holly launching into 'Bo Diddley'.

♫ *Bo Diddley buy baby a diamond ring . . .*

With a scowl, Strachan turned away from the window and looked around him; he was the oldest person in the room by thirty years and the only one wearing a dark suit and tie. A leather-jacketed boy was standing at the jukebox; he looked at Strachan with a long challenging sneer before making his way to join his friends at a table near by. As he pulled out his chair to sit down, he glanced across at Strachan and blew him a mocking kiss.

Strachan reached for his handkerchief and dabbed at his forehead.

He's just a kid, he thought, not worth the trouble. Not worth it.

He looked around the café, taking in the young faces; he listened to the rhythm of their voices, to the unfamiliar jarring music of the jukebox.

These people, they didn't know him. They didn't know who he was, what he was.

More than that, he thought, they didn't care.

He felt old. Out of place. Out of time.

Another fucking place where he didn't belong.

# 19

# Baxter: 12 noon

## *Baxter didn't mind the lonely bit. Not really*

The car screeched and shuddered to a halt.

'Just sit here. Don't move and don't bloody touch anything. I won't be long,' he said.

The car door slammed behind him and Baxter watched as his father went striding across the car park towards the old ivy-clad building. Baxter didn't know where they were or why they had stopped but he could see that the building with its funny criss-cross windows was a pub; he peered up above the door and saw the sign, THE HARE AND HOUNDS. The big-eyed hare was standing up on its back legs, its front paws dangling like hands; from the distance a pack of brown-and-white dogs was closing in on it.

After all the shouting, after the angry roaring of the car as it hurtled along the track, and his father's cursing and his thumping of the steering wheel as he drove, it was suddenly quiet.

Baxter felt empty now; empty except for the clock thing that had started ticking inside him again.

It had stopped for a while as he was being dragged through the grass, as he was thrown into the car, as he had slid from side to side on the shiny leather of the back seat as his father swung fast around the bends of the winding country lane. But it had started again now.

Tick ... tick ... tick ... tick ...

It was hot in the car. All the windows were closed and his father hadn't sought out the shade of the nearby big oak tree, and where he was sitting, where he had been told not to move from, Baxter could feel the burning heat of the sun. He slowly turned the chrome handle on the car door to inch down the window; he opened it just a crack, watching all the while to see whether his father would return and catch him in the act.

He didn't know what had happened, why he was there. He wasn't supposed to be there, he wasn't supposed to be with his father, his mother had told him, had whispered to him, had promised him.

He wasn't meant to be there. He was meant to be in the woods building a camp or something with Soldier.

It was hot and a little lonely in the car.

But Baxter didn't mind the lonely bit. Not really.

## 20

# Truman: 12.01 p.m.

### *What he actually had was borrowed time and a dicky heart*

Truman paused in the low gabled doorway of The Hare and Hounds to collect himself, to calm himself. He took a series of deep breaths, filling his lungs, holding the air there for a long moment before slowly releasing it through his mouth. He straightened his tie, took a comb from his top pocket and ran it through his hair. None of it made him feel any better; he could still feel the tension in his aching shoulders, his hand was bruised from where he'd hit the steering wheel, his head was a dull throb and his mouth was dry and sour.

Stupid cow, he thought.

Look what she'd done to him; getting him into this state. Under his jacket, the back of his shirt was clinging to him, wrinkled and cold, wet with sweat. *Stupid, stupid cow!* Where did she get off talking to him like that? What made her think she could tell him what he could and couldn't do? Not take the boy? If he needed the boy with him, he was going to have the sodding boy with him. Simple as that; no argument. Who the hell did she think she was?

The curtains of the snug bar were still drawn from the night before; where they hung crookedly, failing to meet in the middle, a single shaft of dust-speckled sunlight broke through and illuminated the murkiness like a spotlight. At the bar itself, perched high on a wooden stool, a cigarette in her manicured hand, the smoke curling away to the yellowed beamed ceiling, Truman could see Doll holding court with a small huddle of the morning regulars; he recognised the faces of all the men standing in a semi-circle in front of her. Her hair was swept up into an elaborate lacquered beehive and she wore a crisp white blouse and a tight black skirt, both chosen to accentuate the promise of her curves; a string of over-sized red beads hung around her neck. She had undone the top three buttons of her blouse, and Truman could picture her in front of the long bedroom mirror unbuttoning them one by one, to give herself the plunging neckline that the beads served to emphasise.

'There's a sight for sore eyes, if ever I saw one,' Truman said from the shadows of the doorway.

Doll turned, peered short-sightedly into the gloom, gave a small squeal of delight and then hopped down from her stool and rushed breathlessly to greet him, her shiny red stiletto shoes clacking across the worn flagstones of the floor. Truman gathered her into his arms.

'Back so soon?' she said.

'Can't stay away from you, can I, princess?' Truman

replied, pulling her closer to him, nuzzling into her neck, breathing in her scent.

'Thought you were off down to the coast?' she said. 'Thought you had things to do down there?'

'Forgot my bloody keys, didn't I?' Truman said.

It was true, he had forgotten his house keys and had only realised as he'd turned from the rough track on to the country lane. With the palm of his hand, he'd thumped the steering wheel once more in frustration.

'Silly boy,' she said. 'Forget your head if it wasn't screwed on, wouldn't you?'

She wriggled teasingly in his arms; pushing herself into him.

'Seeing as you're here, you going to have a drink before you set off again?' she said.

'Don't see why not,' Truman said, glancing at his watch over Doll's shoulder. 'But better make it just a quick one though, I've got the boy in the car—'

The words were out of his mouth before he had time to think.

It was bloody Christie's fault; he couldn't get his head straight.

'The boy?' Doll said, her curiosity immediately aroused.

She pulled herself free from Truman's arms and went quickly to the window, twitching the worn blue velvet curtain to one side, straining to see the car.

'What boy?'

Keep it simple and keep it separate; that was the rule. It was supposed to be straight in, pick up the house keys, straight out and no need for Doll to know anything about the boy.

Bloody Christie.

'My ... my nephew,' Truman said, seeing a way through. 'My sister's nipper; you know, from the caravan.'

He smiled, feeling his head ease a little, the fluency starting to return.

'Thought I'd take him with me, buy him an ice cream at the seaside, that sort of thing. Thought it would give my sister a bit of a break to have one less on her hands. You know, she's been pretty down lately,' he said.

Doll snuggled back into his arms.

'Truman Bird, you're a wonderful man, do you know that?' she said.

'You might have mentioned it once or twice before,' he said.

'Don't you go getting big-headed on me now,' she said. 'Pint of the usual, is it?'

Truman nodded and, as Doll playfully bumped her way through her huddle of admirers to get behind the bar, he reached into his jacket pocket for his cigarettes and lighter. He flicked the lighter open, watched as the flame caught on the cigarette and took a long restoring drag. He looked at his watch again. Plenty of time, plenty. And the boy could wait, couldn't he? Wouldn't do him any harm, would it?

Behind the bar Doll pulled at the white porcelain pump handle, delivering Truman a frothing pint. Truman leaned on the counter, contentedly watching her at work.

He could see that Doll knew he was watching her and he could see too that she liked that, being looked at by a man, being watched. He wondered whether her Frank, God bless him, used to stand in this same spot and watch her in the same way. Her late husband's framed photograph still hung on the wall behind the bar; through the smeared and dusty glass you could see he had a grin on his face as if he was sitting with all the aces in his hand and he'd hit life's jackpot; you could almost hear him purring. Poor sap, Truman thought. Old Frankie thought he had it all but what he actually had was borrowed time and a dicky heart. Two years ago he'd passed on, Doll had told Truman with a tear in her eye as she sat on his lap on the night they met; keeled over and dropped dead in the cellar changing the barrels, she said.

Poor old Frank; lucky old Truman.

'Here, tell you what,' Doll said, looking up at him with a smile. 'Let's take a lemonade and some crisps out to that nephew of yours, shall we? I'd love to meet him.'

Bloody Christie and her stupid ideas. The boy wouldn't have been there if she hadn't suggested it in the first place.

'I'm not sure we've got the time, Doll,' Truman said, looking at his watch again, shrugging his shoulders, an expression of regret playing across his face.

'Nonsense!' Doll said. 'Hot day like this, got to be time enough to give a young boy a lemonade.'

Bloody Christie. Sometimes he wondered why he had ever married her.

# 21

# Baxter: 12.04 p.m.

## *Although he didn't know why,*
## *he felt a bit ashamed*

As Baxter looked again at the sign with the big frightened hare standing on its back legs and the dogs chasing, a woman with white piled-up hair and funny red shoes came out of the door below it and made her way towards him, tottering across the tarmac of the car park. She carried a glass in one hand and a cigarette in the other and she had a big smile on her face; it was one of those put-on smiles that Baxter had noticed that people did when they saw dogs or babies or people they didn't really like.

The car park was quite small, and although the woman seemed to be putting quite an effort into getting across it, she moved slowly because she couldn't walk very well. At first, Baxter thought there was something wrong with her legs but then he saw that it was because of her shoes and because her skirt was so tight around her knees. As if they were tied together.

Behind her, his father was walking very slowly, he was a bit slouched and his hands were buried in his trouser pockets. And that wasn't fair because he had once shouted at Baxter not to walk in exactly the same way. His father had a cigarette hanging from his mouth and Baxter decided he didn't look very happy even though he had been to the pub.

The woman finally got to the car and signalled to him to wind his window down, making small quick circles with her cigarette hand.

He glanced behind her at his father for permission; Truman made the same small circles with his hand but more slowly than she did and he wasn't smiling like she was. The woman couldn't see this because she was staring so hard at Baxter with her big put-on smile.

Baxter inched the window down, all the time looking at the woman, who kept beaming in encouragement as if he was a baby or stupid or something.

'Hello, dear,' she said, bending down as the window opened. 'What's your name then?'

Baxter looked to his father behind her; Truman nodded.

'Baxter,' he said quietly.

'That's a funny name for a boy, isn't it?' she said.

Baxter decided he didn't like her. She smelled of perfume and powder and cigarettes and she couldn't walk properly.

'My name's Doll,' she said. 'And I suppose that's a bit of a funny name too.'

Doll leaned as far she could through the window; she looked at him intently, sniffed at the warm air. Baxter found himself backing away, shuffling his bottom across the leather seat.

'I'm not going to bite you, silly!' she said, laughing a bit.

She stood, straightened herself and turned to his father.

'He's hot in there, bless him,' she said. 'Look, he's all flushed; it's baking in that car. What were you thinking of, Truman, leaving him like that? You should be ashamed of yourself.'

His father leaned forwards, put his head close to hers at the window.

'I thought I told you to open all the windows,' he said to Baxter. 'You were supposed to let some air in, you silly sausage.'

He'd never said silly sausage before, Baxter thought. Not to him anyway. And it wasn't true; he didn't say about the windows.

'Going to the seaside, are you?' Doll said, her head still close to his father's. 'You're a very lucky boy,' she said. 'Wish I was off to the seaside on a scorcher of a day like this. Best place to be, the seaside, when it's as hot as this.'

Baxter didn't say anything and for a while neither did Doll or his father. They just stayed there, heads close together at the window.

'Here, I've got you something,' she finally said, carefully handing him the lemonade and the packet of crisps through the window.

'Say thank you,' his father said.

'Thank you,' Baxter said, his voice so small he could hardly hear it himself.

Doll stayed crouched down but his father stood up behind her again.

'Must be nice to have a day out with your Uncle Truman,' Doll said. 'He's a very kind uncle to take you, don't you think?'

Behind her, his father winked and put a finger to his lips.

Baxter didn't understand what she meant but he understood his father. He said nothing.

'Doesn't say much, does he?' Doll said, turning to his father, shielding her eyes against the sun. 'Shy little thing, isn't he?'

'They've been through a lot, the whole family,' his father said, smiling now. 'With his dad and everything. It's made the boy a bit on the silent side. It's not surprising really.'

'Poor scrap,' Doll said.

She leaned through the window and gave Baxter a big red lipstick kiss on his cheek; he could smell her sweet-stale powdery smell.

'Bye-bye, Baxter,' she said. 'You be a good boy for your Uncle Truman and come and see me again soon.'

Baxter didn't say anything as Doll turned to make her teetering way back across the treacherous car park, leaning heavily now on his father's arm, looking up at him and laughing at something he had said as if it was the funniest thing she had ever heard. Baxter could feel the kiss lingering slick and damp and cold on his cheek, like it was the liquid trail left by a garden slug. As soon as he thought it was safe, that she wouldn't look back and catch him, he rubbed fiercely at it. The more he rubbed the more he succeeded in spreading the violent smudge on his cheek; he then rubbed at the frown on his forehead and transferred a streak of lurid red.

When Doll reached the gabled pub doorway, still supported on his father's arm, she turned and waved to Baxter with both hands. She crouched down low to make herself as small as him; she smiled her big smile at Baxter and she screwed up her eyes at the same time.

Baxter didn't wave back at her but he didn't think she could see anyway with her eyes like that. He thought her hair looked funny because it was so tall and stiff and bigger than her head; he thought he would ask his mother about it when he got back to the caravan, why Doll would have hair so big. Then there was the lipstick, the red shoes and the tight skirt; he thought he would ask her about all of them. His mum would probably know Doll anyway.

Although he didn't know what Doll meant with all that business about Uncle Truman, although he thought that she must somehow have made a mistake, there was something about her, about what had happened and about what she had said to him, that made him feel even more sad than he was before.

More sad and more alone.

And there was something else he felt.

Although he didn't know why, he felt a bit ashamed.

It was as if something really bad had happened; as if he had done something really bad.

He shifted on the leather seat of the car, glanced up at the sign above the doorway, saw the hare looking down at him with his big knowing eyes, and took a sip of the lemonade Doll had given him. It was warm and sickly sweet.

# 22

# Strachan: 12.22 p.m.

## *Almost casually, Strachan swayed to one side*

S trachan had been standing at the long polished mahogany
bar at The Salvation for twenty minutes; pint glass in
hand, he had watched Sally as she worked, watched the
spark in her as she greeted each new customer with a smile,
her easy way as she chatted and joked with them, watched
her as she lifted the hatch on the counter just enough to be
able to shimmy through, and then as she moved busily
around the room, collecting empty glasses and wiping the
sticky spills and rings from the tables.

He had watched her as she stopped to talk to the two elderly men sitting together at a corner table; with their flat caps
set firmly on their heads despite the heat of the day, they were
the only other drinkers still in the bar. Now, as she made her
way back behind the bar, his eyes never left her.

Every now and then it had seemed to him that she had
looked over to him, had caught his eye and had then looked

quickly, shyly away. For a time he resisted the thought, what it might mean; but he found it coming back to him, seductively, insidiously. Perhaps she had. Maybe she had. Why not, it wasn't impossible. After all, there had been a time when he would have been able to catch and to hold the eye of any barmaid in Brighton. He could have anyone he wanted back then. Anyone. And, for a time, he did.

But only Shirley had been worth anything, Strachan thought, and she'd wanted him to give it all up and settle down. But he couldn't give it up. What else would he have done? And one day he had got back to the bedsit and the clothes she kept in the wardrobe were no longer there. That had cut him up pretty bad and after that he'd decided he was better off on his own.

Best that way. In his line of work. Safer too.

Even so, he couldn't keep his eyes from her. This one, this Sally, she was special, he could see that, anyone could see that; nothing flash, nothing brassy or tarty. Must be twenty years younger than him, looked a bit like that Audrey Hepburn, he thought.

Special.

He shrugged off the thought. Who was he kidding? You are who and what you are and you can't change it. Simple as that.

He was Strachan, just Strachan. Always alone. Start thinking any other way and you forget, lose concentration, get careless. You get hurt.

The pub door swung open and, from behind the counter where she was now standing drying and polishing freshly washed glasses, Sally immediately looked up. Strachan saw the frown settle on her face and the sudden tense hunch of her shoulders.

116

'Not you, Danny,' she said wearily. 'Please, not in here, not today. You know you're barred . . .'

Strachan followed her eyes. A tall, thick-set man leaned heavily against the frame of the door, the sunlight bright behind him.

'Come on, Danny, please,' Sally said. 'We don't want any trouble now, do we? Why don't you be a good boy and just go home and sleep it off?'

The man stepped unsteadily into the room; he held a bottle by the neck in his left hand.

Seeing him, the two elderly men scurried through the open door, leaving their half-full glasses on their table. Danny watched them go.

'Come on, Danny, there's a good boy,' Sally pleaded.

'Barred!' he roared at her, rocking forwards as he did so, the spit flecking from his mouth. 'No fucker bars me.'

Oh yes, Strachan thought. Time to play. This one's for me.

He put his glass carefully down on the bar top and took a step towards the man. He calmly straightened his tie, tugged gently at his shirt cuffs, easing them down a fraction from his jacket sleeves.

'Now that, Danny boy, is no way to talk to a lady,' he said evenly. 'I think you need to watch your tongue, sunshine.'

The man swung around, bottle in hand, and looked Strachan up and down; scornfully he took in the suit, the immaculate white shirt, the silk tie.

'Who the fuck are you?' he slurred, raising the bottle towards Strachan's face. 'This is none of your fucking business, so just fuck off out of it, ponce!'

Strachan took another step towards him; he stood eye to eye with him now, close enough to smell the alcohol, sour on

117

the man's breath, and the distant reek of stale urine and vomit on his clothes.

'That's very disappointing, Danny boy,' he said. 'Very disappointing.'

His voice was clipped and measured. A monotone cut through with menace.

'That's very disappointing indeed,' he said. 'You see, I asked you nicely. I asked you to watch your tongue—'

'What the—?' Danny tried to interrupt.

But Strachan raised a finger to his lips. Silenced him.

'But you've disappointed me, Danny. And now I'm going to have to teach you a lesson. Because I don't like people to disappoint me. Never have.'

It was a speech he had made many times before.

'And because you've disappointed me, Danny, I'm going to have to hurt you. Because that's the way it works.'

Danny stood looking at Strachan, uncomprehending, momentarily stunned, swaying slightly, bottle in hand, trying to absorb what Strachan had just said to him.

Finally he found his voice.

'*Disappointed?*' he bellowed. 'What the fuck are you talking about? Disappointed? I'll fucking give you disappointed—'

It was all over in an instant.

Still holding the bottle by the neck, Danny smashed it down on a tabletop, and then swiped upwards angrily towards Strachan's face with the jagged broken glass.

Almost nonchalantly, almost casually, Strachan swayed to one side, caught the flailing arm with his left hand and, jolting it backwards, sent the broken bottle skittling across the floor. With his right he then landed two sharp thudding blows in rapid succession; one to Danny's guts to double him over and, stepping back, one to his jaw as he buckled. Danny went down like a broken wheezing bull in a slaughterhouse.

Strachan stepped back, straightened his tie once more, pulled at his cuffs. He flexed his fist, rubbed briefly at the knuckles of his right hand, and then reached for his handkerchief and, not for the first time that day, dabbed a bead of sweat from his forehead. He returned to the bar now, picked up his glass and met Sally's gaze.

Behind him, Danny tried to haul himself upright, fell backwards and sent a table crashing to the floor; trying again, he half staggered, half crawled to the door and then disappeared out into the light. A few seconds later, the two old men crept back into the room, looking nervously around to assess the damage. They went back to their table and silently, simultaneously, they lifted their glasses and swallowed noisily.

'Is that how you always deal with things, is it?' Sally said to Strachan, nodding towards where Danny had gone down.

'Pretty much,' Strachan said impassively, taking a sip from his glass. 'It's always worked for me.'

'There are other ways, you know,' Sally said crossly. 'I was dealing with it; I didn't need your help.'

'Dealing with it?' Strachan said. He couldn't help the sarcasm in his voice and he instantly regretted it; she would think less of him and, despite everything he kept telling himself, he found that this somehow mattered.

Forget it. He was just Strachan. Always alone.

'I would have talked him into going and no one would have got hurt,' Sally said. 'It's always worked before.'

Strachan considered this for a moment.

'Better my way,' he said, taking another sip of his drink. 'My way, he doesn't come back.'

Sally went through the hatch on the counter and picked up the table and rearranged the scattered chairs. From a tall cupboard cut into the dark panelling in the corner of the room she collected a dustpan and brush and then bent to sweep up the broken glass. As Strachan watched her, Sally looked up, caught his eye and then turned quickly away. There was no mistaking it this time, the look, what it meant, where it was taking them.

Returning behind the bar, she went back to polishing the glasses but moved a little closer to him.

'You're new here, aren't you?' Strachan said.

'Not that new,' Sally said. 'I've been here about a year; came down from the Smoke.'

No more small talk, Strachan. She's twenty years younger. Remember, *who* you are. *What* you are.

'Whereabouts exactly?' he said, falling straight back into it.

'Whitechapel way,' she said. 'In the end there was nothing for me up there, nothing to keep me there. Thought I'd like to live by the sea for a while ...'

'And do you?' Strachan said.

'Do I what?'

'Do you like living by the sea?'

'I hardly ever see it,' she said with a thin, disillusioned smile. 'I seem to spend every waking hour working in this dump.'

Strachan looked around the room, seeing as if for the first time the shabby battered tables and chairs, the scuffed parquet flooring, the peeling red flock paper on the walls. Outside, the streets bustled with trippers, down from London for the day on the *Brighton Belle*; money in their pockets, burning a hole, determined to have a good time. In their thousands they came to wander arm in arm on the piers, they came to ooh and ahh, to play the slot machines, to have their fortunes read, to ride the ghost train. They came to eat candyfloss and ice cream and to sit on the pebbly beach in the sunshine. They came for their cod and chips with bread and butter on the side and a cup of tea. They came for a good drink and a bit of a sing-song in a pub on the seafront or in The Lanes. None of them came to The Salvation.

He breathed deeply, forcing himself to focus.

'Do you know who I am?' he finally said.

Sally looked up at him, met his eye and held it. Her eyes were grey-green; he couldn't remember the last time he had noticed the colour of a woman's eyes.

'You're Strachan, aren't you?' she said.

'That's right, lady,' he said softly. 'Strachan. Just Strachan.'

Despite himself, Strachan couldn't help the small rush of pleasure that came with the discovery that she knew who he was. Not that Sally would have guessed it, of course. Another man, a younger man perhaps, might not have been able to help himself, might have had to look away for a moment of private embarrassed delight, might even have blushed; Strachan, however, continued to meet her grey-green gaze.

'You know a lot for someone who's new in town,' he said.

'I keep my ear to the ground,' she said. 'I hear people talking.'

'Oh yes?' Strachan said. 'And what do they say, these people?'

'They say that it's not a good idea to get on the wrong side of you,' she said.

Strachan smiled.

'I don't like to be disappointed,' he said. 'I don't like people to disappoint me.'

Even now, he couldn't help the threat in his voice, couldn't quite eliminate it completely.

'So I see,' Sally said, laughing nervously, looking to where Danny had gone crashing to the floor.

'So what brings you here, Strachan?' she said playfully.

There *was* no mistaking this, Strachan thought; there *was* something going on here, something between them.

'You do,' Strachan said a little throatily, leaning towards her, relishing the sudden intimacy of the moment.

'Oh yes?' Sally said, lowering her eyes, touching her hair, smoothing it into place. 'Why's that?'

Fuck it, Strachan thought.

He knew that whatever he said next would shatter everything.

Fuck it.

'I want to talk to you about your boyfriend,' he said, hearing the menacing edge return fully to his voice.

Behind the counter, Sally took a step backwards, a step away from him; she picked up a glass and started polishing it vigorously.

'I haven't got a boyfriend,' she said, her eyes no longer meeting Strachan's.

'Truman,' Strachan said. 'Truman Bird.'

'What about him?' Sally said.

'Your boyfriend, Truman. I need to know where he is. I need to find him.'

'What's that to do with me?'

'Don't mess me around,' Strachan said. 'Don't disappoint me, Sally.'

She looked up at his sudden first use of her name.

'I haven't seen him for six weeks or more,' she said. 'He just disappeared on me one day.'

'Where to?' Strachan said.

'I don't know,' she said. 'I told you, he just disappeared.'

Strachan had listened to too many lies over too many years not to know the truth when he heard it. He was hearing it now; she didn't know where Truman was.

'Well, if he *un*-disappears, if he comes back, I want you to call me,' Strachan said. 'Understand?'

Sally placed the polished glass upside-down on the shelf; she said nothing.

'Call me at this number,' Strachan said.

He picked up a beer mat and wrote down the telephone number at the bedsits. No one had ever called him there; only Mr Smith.

'Leave a message with someone if I'm not there.'

Strachan sensed that however afraid of him he might make her, she wouldn't call him; she was too loyal, too true.

'What do you want him for?' she asked anxiously. 'What's Truman done? Is he in trouble?'

'An associate of mine wants me to visit him, wants me to have a friendly word . . . ' he said.

He picked up his glass, drained the last of the now-warm beer, and started to walk towards the door; he could feel Sally's eyes on his back. He stopped and turned to face her once more.

'It's right then, what people say?' he said. 'He *is* your boyfriend?'

Sally shrugged.

'Funny,' Strachan said. 'I didn't have you down as that kind of girl ...'

'What kind of girl?' she said.

'Carrying on with a married man.'

It hit her like a slap; he could see that, he could see her wince and reel.

'*Married?*' Sally said. 'He told me—'

'Married, three kids,' Strachan interrupted her, landing the blows.

Slap. Slap. Slap.

'Children ...' Sally almost whispered in disbelief. '*Children?*'

Her face was ashen now; she looked small, somehow defeated.

'How do I know you're not lying?' she said despairingly. 'How do I know you're not just making it all up?'

Strachan straightened his tie, adjusted his cuffs once more.

'Because I'm Strachan,' he said, and he couldn't prevent the pride or the snarl in his voice. 'Ask around, lady. People will tell you: Strachan never lies.'

He could see her fighting the tears in her eyes.

'Call me if he shows up,' he said.

Sally nodded.

# 23

# Christie: 12.24 p.m.

## *She moved about on her stick like a broken-winged crow*

It had become a familiar ritual over the past six weeks. Christie would empty the last of the water into saucepans in the caravan; she had learned that since every drop had to be carried, it was precious and not to be wasted. She would then lift the big box-like plastic water carrier into the wheelbarrow that Mrs Chadney had grudgingly lent to them and, with the baby in her arms, she and Megan would walk side by side along the shady unmade lane. Baxter would push the barrow; it was light and he would race ahead, swerving it around the potholes, making the guttural high-revving noises of an imagined engine and of vicious squealing brakes and cornering tyres. Christie and Megan, walking sedately behind, would watch Baxter and then exchange knowing womanly glances.

It was one of Christie's favourite times, especially with the sun shining and the light dappling through the overhanging branches. In truth, in these six weeks there had been more grey, cool, rainy days than there had been days of light and warmth; it had been as if the relentless winter earlier in the year would not finally let go its grip. But whenever Christie thought of this walk with the children, in her mind the sun was shining. They were away from the caravan, and that alone was enough to make her heart lift a little; they were together and Megan and Baxter were happy. Despite their destination it always felt like an adventure.

The journey back, of course, was more difficult. The water carrier was full and the wheelbarrow would wallow under its weight; Baxter could no longer push it alone. He would try so hard, straining with every ounce of strength his small body could summon, but as they walked on, however slowly they walked, he would fall further and further behind. Christie would then hand the baby to Megan and would hurry back to Baxter to help to push. They would catch up with Megan, and Christie would take the baby again. A few hundred yards later she would have to return to help Baxter once more. It was slow and painful and when they finally rounded the last bend she was glad to see the caravan in the clearing.

It was the only time she ever was, she thought.

The return journey was also made in the shadow invariably cast by Mrs Chadney. Christie had come to rely on her entirely for water and for other things that Truman never thought to bring. Over the weeks Mrs Chadney had provided her with washing powder, pegs for the clothes line, disinfectant, a bucket and a mop. Christie didn't know what she would have done without her.

But all of it came at a price.

There was no point in pretending otherwise: Christie was afraid of Mrs Chadney; and to the children she was the stuff of nightmares. To Megan and Baxter, the way she looked was terrifying enough; she moved about on her stick like a broken-winged crow, crooked, bent, ancient and dressed entirely in black. To them she was the wicked witch of the forest made real; whenever they met her they were reduced to wide-eyed silence. But to Christie it was her anger that was most frightening; the wild, spitting, venomous cursing rage she carried with her at all times.

There was something in Mrs Chadney's contemptuous scorn, in her cruelty, that reminded Christie of her mother; it diminished her and turned her into an inadequate clumsy tongue-tied child again. But Christie could sense something more; that there was some terrible violence that had been done to her, some great hurt in her that made her scratch and claw at anyone who came near.

On the morning after Truman had first dropped them at the caravan, Christie and the children had set off down the lane. They were going exploring, Christie had told Megan and Baxter as they peered uncertainly out of the caravan door. But the truth was that she had needed to know that she was not entirely alone there, that there were houses near by, maybe a village, perhaps even a small shop. They walked what must have been a mile down the lane and all they could find was a solitary stone cottage, with a handsome gabled wooden porch, standing proudly where the lane ended and a narrow grassy bridleway began.

Christie had knocked on the door and she and the children had waited under the porch. As she waited, she had looked around and had admired the meticulously worked garden, the bright colourful flowerbeds lining the path, and she had seen the neat stack of newly chopped logs against the wall. Inside she had heard a strange shuffling scraping noise as someone approached the door. Suddenly the door had been flung open and the three of them – she, Megan and Baxter – had taken an involuntary step backwards.

Leaning heavily on her stick, Mrs Chadney had glowered at them.

'What?' she had screeched, her face distorted by rage.

It had been like that every time since. Christie had no choice but to summon up the courage to go there every few days for water. And it was in desperation that she had asked for what she needed to keep the children's clothes washed and the caravan clean. Each time, Mrs Chadney had cursed her violently, terrifyingly, but in the end had always given Christie what she needed. She had thrown the bucket and the mop at them and every time she had slammed the door in their faces as soon as they were done. But she had given them what Christie had asked for and had refused all thanks and all offers of payment.

Had she not had enough in her own life to puzzle about, Mrs Chadney was a mystery that Christie would like to have solved. She wondered where all the anger came from; what it was in her life that made her that way. She wondered about her history, whether she had always lived there alone. More prosaically, she wondered how she survived on her own so far into the woods, far from anywhere, from anyone. She wondered how she managed to keep the house and garden so immaculately maintained. She wondered too how she chopped and stacked those logs.

One day she had asked Truman if he had heard anything about her from whoever it was who owned the caravan. That was how Christie learned her name.

'Madwoman who lives up the lane?' Truman had said, scaring the children even more. 'That'll be Mrs Chadney; nasty piece of work, apparently. They say she'd eat you alive as soon as look at you ... Best keep away, princess.'


Today there was no joy in the walk to Mrs Chadney's cottage; there was no Baxter to race ahead with the barrow and it was uncomfortably hot and still. Megan pushed the wheelbarrow in silence, her eyes still red from the tears she had shed as she had sat beside Christie on the caravan step. There had been nothing Christie could say that would console her. One minute she had been riding high on her father's shoulders, the next she had been dumped to the ground and her brother had been dragged from the clearing and thrown into the car while her father had all the time screamed threats and abuse at her mother. There had been nothing that could be said, there were no words. Christie had just held her as Megan fought for air, until the sobs subsided.

There *were* no words, Christie thought as they trudged along the lane.

There never had been words that could forgive or explain.


He was sitting on the stairs as she had pushed open the front door.

'Where have you been?' he yelled at her before she could even take the key from the lock.

'Don't, Truman . . .' she said.

In the early months, after the wedding, she had told him that she wanted to visit friends, girls she had grown up with, girls she didn't want to lose touch with. She thought she might see them from time to time, she'd said, have an occasional evening out with them, go to the cinema or maybe see a show at the Hippodrome, or perhaps just have a walk along the front.

But it had never happened. Every time she had arranged to meet up with someone, Truman had erupted into a jealous rage.

She had been so frightened and confused at first. He would sulk. He would beg. He would shout and swear.

Confronted by this, every time she had given in and cancelled at the last minute.

But this time, in a small act of defiance and desperation, she had gone anyway; she had gone with Jenny to the Astoria to see *Rear Window* with Jimmy Stewart and Grace Kelly. It had been lovely. They had walked home arm in arm and laughing, giggling under the stars, like the schoolgirls they used to be.

He stood up, loomed over her.

'I asked you a question,' he roared.

She closed the door behind her.

'I've been with Jenny,' she said quietly. 'To the pictures.'

'Liar!' he screamed, his face so close to hers that she could feel flecks of spit hit her.

She pushed past him, ran up the stairs to the bedsit.

'Bloody lying bitch!' he shouted, thundering up the stairs behind her.

He slammed the door.

She hadn't been with Jenny, he yelled. She'd been with another man.

No, no, Truman, it wasn't true, she'd said.

Liar, he'd screamed again, his face twisted in anger.

She was a lying, cheating whore.

A tramp, a lying whore.

She'd been with another man.

Who was he?

Who was he?

Who was he?

He'd kill the bastard. Who was he?

Over and over.

He pushed her to the floor, knelt over her. He raised his hand, went to hit her, to slap her, to punch her.

At the last moment he had pulled back, just enough in control of himself to stop his fist inches from her face.

He got up, picked up a dining chair, smashed it against the wall. She cowered in the corner on the floor. He made as if to kick her and then turned and slammed out of the door.

He didn't come back until the following evening and when he did he brought chocolates and flowers.

He never talked about it. Never apologised. Just handed over the chocolates and the flowers and later took her into his arms. As if nothing had happened.

She should have left him then.

But they had only been married a few months and, by the time he'd come back with the chocolates and the flowers, she'd managed to convince herself that everyone deserved a second chance. And he was only like this because he loved her, wasn't he? If he didn't love her, he wouldn't have been so jealous. And where would she have gone? She would never have been able to face her mother's told-you-so sneer. And anyway, Megan was on the way.

She was worried about Baxter; Baxter and his father, just the two of them together. She had been sure that no harm would come to her boy, but now she no longer felt so certain.

It had, of course, been her ridiculous idea in the first place, her dream that father and son would spend time together, get to know each other, become close. Her fairy story. Not that she had expected Truman to go along with it with any enthusiasm. At first he had seemed so set against the idea, so why did it suddenly matter so much to him now? But then again, if it did now matter so much, then surely he wouldn't hurt the boy, would he? Surely he would take care of him. Surely he would keep him safe.

But to drag his own son, to throw him ... How could he do such a thing? And to treat Megan like that ...

In her arms, the baby spluttered, screwed up his eyes and let out a wail of discontent that echoed along the tree-lined lane. Christie rocked him gently as she walked until the cries gradually ceased.

But at least she now knew what they had to do, she thought. There was no decision to make, no discussion to be had. What had happened that morning had finally confirmed it in her mind. They simply couldn't go on like this.

For the children's sake, she and Truman had to try to find a way to make a new beginning. They had already left it far too long. *She* had left it too long. They needed to sit down together and talk about it, to sort out whatever it was that

132

was wrong between them. He wouldn't want to, he would be angry, he would shout and threaten; but this time she was determined. She would find the strength from somewhere.

And it had to start with leaving this awful place and going home. Whatever it took, whatever Truman might say to the contrary, they were going home.

Tomorrow, she and the children were going home.

# 24

# Truman: 12.25 p.m.

## 'Love, Love Me Do ...'

It was a game they played. Someone would shout out the name of a song or they would hum just a fragment of a tune or they would say 'What about that one that goes ...?' and Truman, sitting there as they huddled beerily around him, sitting at the piano keyboard, squinting through the stinging smoke of the cigarette he held in his mouth, would immediately begin to pick it out, one note at a time.

He had that kind of ear; he could hear a tune once and then play it, improvise around it, make it his own. From 'Colonel Bogey' to the Beatles, from Cole Porter to Billy J. Kramer, from Eddie Cochran to Count Basie, it was all the same to him. As his audience hushed, he would begin one-handed, slowly, note by note, and then he would start to build it, nurture it, make the music swell, and finally he would stomp it out until the whole pub was swaying and rocking and singing along with it. It was the best feeling, the best of all, nothing could come close. He loved being right there at the centre of it, he loved making the voices come together, and he loved the way the music stopped his mind.

And everyone needed to do that once in a while, didn't they? There was no harm in it. Everyone needed just to lose themselves in something, to stop everything in their head.

Three things did it for Truman. A warm belly full of beer, better still if it had been washed down with whisky chasers; that final moment in a new woman's arms, her breasts crushed beneath him, her legs wrapped hard around him; and the music. And right now, he thought, right now there was no question about it; the best of all was the music.

Before Doll and the others had cajoled him into playing, into picking up where they had reluctantly left off at closing time the night before, he couldn't fully shake Christie and the boy from his mind. They wouldn't leave him alone, they had nagged at him – the boy sat there in the car with his eyes like an accusation, Christie's imagined reproachful look. Why couldn't they just let him alone?

But now Doll was standing by his side, her hand on his shoulder, and the music was flowing from his fingers and the whole pub was singing along. At the end of a particularly raucous 'The Night Has a Thousand Eyes', a cheer went up.

'Don't you forget that boy out there,' Doll whispered to him, bending down close to his ear.

'Just one more, Doll, and then I'll be on my way,' Truman said reluctantly, remembering.

'Last one,' he shouted, although he could feel that his heart wasn't quite in it now. 'What's it to be then?'

'"Love Me Do",' someone yelled from the back of the room.

Not waiting for any other suggestions, Truman looked Doll in the eye, smiled and launched straight into it.

'*Love, love me do ...*' they sang.

But Truman wasn't listening now; he was playing the notes but he wasn't listening.

He'd make another call, he thought, on the way down to Brighton. After all, it wasn't far out of his way, just a bit of a detour and he had the time, so he could be in and out and the boy could stay in the car, couldn't he? And it would help to keep things sweet there, wouldn't it? It would be one less thing, at least.

Big finale and then he'd be on his way.

'*... love me do.*'

But if he was to do that, make that visit, to keep it sweet, he'd need to show some money, wouldn't he? He couldn't go there with nothing. That would be far too difficult, far too much to explain. No, if he couldn't get the cash, he wouldn't go.

'Here, Doll,' Truman said, standing at the bar, downing the last of his beer. 'You couldn't lend us a few quid, could you?'

Doll looked at him with a smile.

'Of course, love,' she said without hesitation. 'What do you need?'

Truman calculated what he would need, calculated again what was the most he could ask her for, what he could get away with.

'Haven't got fifty, have you?' he said, trying to keep it casual.

Doll's smile disappeared.

'*Fifty?*' she said. 'That's half a week's takings.'

136

Maybe he'd got it wrong; maybe it was too much.

'Only until this evening,' he said. 'I'll be flush by then, you'll see.'

'It's an awful lot, Truman, you sure you need that much?' Doll said.

'Got some business on the way to Brighton,' he said matter-of-factly. 'But if it's too much . . .'

Doll looked at him; the smile returning.

'No, no, it's OK,' she said. 'And later on, I'll take my interest in kind . . .'

Truman laughed and grabbed her by the waist.

'You sure you don't want your interest now? I'm more than happy to pay in advance,' he said.

'You haven't got time, lover boy,' she said. 'And anyway, you've got your nephew sitting outside in the car.'

Sitting there like a bloody accusation, Truman thought, letting go of Doll's waist.

# 25

# Soldier: 12.43 p.m.

## *A small frown had settled on his brow*

With every step along the way, he took care to stay back, to stay far enough behind them, low beneath the tall screen of ferns.

Still wearing his long dark coat despite the cloying heat of the day, Soldier shuffled along the thin path that now dipped and then climbed along the ridge of the steep wooded bank that ran haphazardly alongside the lane. However slowly they walked and, without the boy racing ahead, mother and daughter walked so much more wearily than he had seen before, he hung back. He stayed back; watching, to keep her safe; watching over their plodding heavy-hearted progress towards the cottage.

The girl was pushing the wheelbarrow and *she* was carrying the baby in her arms. As he watched, Soldier could see that her head was bowed and that she was being carried somewhere far away in her thoughts.

The ache in Soldier's knee dizzied him. His head reeled and swam with the pain, with the heat. From time to time he would stop to rest against the great trunk of one of the twisted broken oak trees that clung to the bank.

He closed his eyes against the stinging of the sweat that ran down his face.

'What's your name?' the boy had said, unafraid.

It had been on the third day of watching that the boy had caught him there, had come at him stealthily from behind, found him crouched low at the very edge of the wood above the clearing. Soldier had somehow not seen him leave the caravan, had not seen him enter the woods and circle around, playing his explorer's game.

The black dog had been beside Soldier. It ran off, crashing into the undergrowth.

'What's your name?' the boy said.

Soldier's fingers had fumbled towards the frayed name tag that was sewn to the lapel of his coat. It had been handwritten long ago, and over the years the crude block-capitals lettering had been almost bleached out by the sun and washed away by the rain.

'*Soldier*?' the boy said, his face screwed up in disbelief. 'Nobody's called Soldier.'

There had been a long pause as Soldier had considered what the boy had said. The words had worked on his lips and had repeated inside him.

*Nobody's called Soldier. Soldier's called nobody. Called nobody.*

They had gone on spinning and ricocheting through him.

All the while the boy had looked down at him, unwavering and bold. Finally Soldier had shrugged apologetically, not knowing how else to answer, crouching low, trying to quieten the ricocheting words and break free of them.

'But what's your *real* name?' the boy said.

Again Soldier had shrugged. Ashamed.

A small frown had settled on his brow but in the end the pale fair-haired boy had accepted Soldier's silence as an answer.

'Were you a proper soldier? A soldier in the war?' he said.

Soldier had managed to nod. That much he knew to be true; that much at least, he imagined, must be true.

'Did you kill anyone?' the boy said.

Soldier said nothing; he had no answer.

The boy had looked down at him as he stayed uncomfortably low amongst the ferns, the brambles, the sparse and scraggy gorse.

'You don't say very much, do you?' he said to him.

There had been another long pause as the boy had studied him, as if calculating whether to venture anything more.

'And you do look a bit funny . . .' he finally said. 'And not very clean, if you don't mind me saying so.'

Soldier had looked at his clothes. Tattered. Muddied. Had held out his hands. Had studied his fingernails. Long. Yellowed. Broken. Blackened.

He had looked back to the boy. Uncertain. The boy had nodded as if to reassure him that it was indeed true.

'My name's Baxter Bird,' he said. 'I live in Brighton. Where do you come from?'

*

Where *do* you come from?

Long ago this had been the question that Soldier would ask of himself. Repeatedly, obsessively, fearfully.

Sleepless at dawn in his shelter, he would hear the wood pigeon's echoing calls. He would hear the woodpecker's rattle in the distance and he would lie awake and listen to the taunting creaks and groans of the branches in the canopy of the trees above.

Every sound had been like a question.

What was it that had happened to him? How could it be that his eyes had opened one morning and he had found himself here, alone in the woods? Found himself filthy, bloodied and torn, in a long coat and with a crippled knee. And before that, nothing.

Sometimes a question would come singly to him and would stay with him all day. Sometimes a rush would come at once. Why? Who? What? When? His head would ache with trying to find answers, trying to remember, to recall anything. Anything. Why could he not remember?

But it was as if his mind had been wiped clean like a slate. And the forest had long ago grown tired of asking him questions to which there were no answers.


Confronted by the boy, looking up at him as he still crouched low, Soldier once more wanted to find answers. For the boy, he wanted answers.

Where *was* he from?

The black dog was back, nuzzling at him. Sniffing at him. Pushing at him.

Where *was* he from?

Finally, Soldier had replied in the only way he could. With a slow abashed shake of the head and another hesitant shrug of the shoulders.

He glanced up at Baxter and could see him carefully absorbing this. Could see him weighing it in his mind, considering it for what it was, what it was worth. And then, as if satisfied, moving on.

'What are you doing in the woods? Are you playing a game?' Baxter had said, bending down low beside him, joining Soldier amidst the welcoming tangle of undergrowth on the forest floor.

'Can it be our secret game?' Baxter had said.

## 26

# Baxter: 1.22 p.m.

## *He hunkered down, lower in his seat*

'Best keep it to ourselves,' his father had said as they pulled out of the car park of The Hare and Hounds and turned back on to the road.

'It can be our secret. Like a game.'

Now, through the tall metal railings of a park, Baxter could see four boys playing in the bright sunshine high on a silvery slide; he could see it was a special game by the way they each did something different every time they slid down. One held his arms stretched wide as if he was flying, the next lay flat on his back, the third covered his eyes with his hands like a blindfold and the final boy, small, ginger-haired and reckless, plunged down head-first on his stomach. Even through the car window, Baxter could hear their shrieks of laughter echoing across the park.

It was better to be sitting here, better to be able to watch these boys playing, than to be outside the pub with just the sign with the big hare to look at. It was better as long as they didn't see him, of course.

If they did, if they did see him in the car looking at them, he knew they would come over and point at him through the window. And he knew that what would happen next was that they would all shout at him and demand to know what he thought he was doing, looking at them, staring at them. He knew all of this would happen because that was what the bigger boys did that time in the playground at school. He was just watching them because it was quite interesting and they came over and started pointing at him, started jabbing at him with their fingers, started shouting at him.

Baxter slumped lower in his seat so that if the boys at the top of the slide were to glance over at the car all they would see would be the top of his head.

He was in the front seat of the car now.

That was how he knew that although they had driven to another place after the pub, it definitely wasn't Brighton. They had come to a junction in the road and from his front seat Baxter had seen quite clearly the finger of the road sign that pointed the way to Brighton. As the car pulled away in the opposite direction, Baxter had looked at his father, wondering whether he should say something, whether he should tell him that he had taken the wrong turning. In the end though he had decided it was best not to say anything in case his father got angry again.

*

'What you doing back there, sport?' his father had said with a big smile when he came out of the pub. And he had never said 'sport' before, Baxter thought. Not to him, anyway.

'Come and sit here in the front with me,' he said. 'It's much better in the front.'

'Everything all right, sport?' his father said, still with a big lopsided smile, as he helped Baxter to climb over the seats.

'Looks like you've been up to no good,' he said, laughing a bit, pointing. 'You've got lipstick on your cheek and on your forehead.'

Baxter had really wanted to ask him about the music he had heard coming from the pub, about the piano and the singing, but instead he had looked out of the side window, away from his father, rubbing feverishly at the blotches of lipstick.

'By the way . . . ' his father said as he turned the key in the ignition. 'It's probably best not to say anything to your mum.'

Baxter had turned to look at his father.

'About *Auntie* Doll and the pub, I mean,' his father said. 'Only, your mum, she doesn't really like her, you see. She doesn't really get on with Auntie Doll,' his father said, glancing across at him as he manoeuvred the car out on to the open road.

'It's a shame really because Auntie Doll's a nice lady, isn't she?' he said. 'Even though she gets a bit confused about uncles and stuff . . . '

Baxter didn't say anything because Doll had hair bigger than her head and she couldn't walk properly.

'But they fell out years ago, you see. There was this big argument and it was all your mother's fault,' his father said. 'That's why she doesn't like to talk about it. Understand?'

Baxter didn't understand.

'You know what women can be like.'

Baxter didn't know.

'No, we'd best keep it to ourselves,' his father said. 'It can be our secret. Like a game.'

After the junction with the road sign, his father had driven on, not seeming to mind that they were going in the wrong direction. Finally he had pulled over and had left Baxter in the car next to the park. Baxter thought the place where they now were might be called Crawley because there was a poster on the railings that said something about a circus coming there.

'Won't be long. Just got to see a man about a dog,' his father had said as he slammed the car door.


At the top of the slide, the small ginger-haired boy paused and just for a moment Baxter was sure that he would look towards the car, would look directly at him, would see him and that it would all begin.

And it would be worse because of the lipstick on his cheek and on his forehead.

He could feel it still, the ticking. Growing louder now.

Tick ... tick ... tick ... tick ... tick ...

He hunkered down, lower in his seat.

Making himself so small that he was very nearly invisible.

## 27

# Christie: 1.23 p.m.

### *Christie could feel a chill creep over her*

Heads lowered, hot, leaden-footed and lost in their solitary thoughts, Christie and Megan finally rounded the last bend of the lane. Almost at the same moment they raised their eyes and, at the sight of the caravan hunched in the clearing, mother and nine-year-old daughter turned to each other with the same smile of encouragement. They had made it.

Christie had pushed the wheelbarrow back along the rough and pitted lane from Mrs Chadney's cottage, the water slopping loudly from side to side in the plastic container. Megan had carried the baby, rocking him, hushing him, murmuring softly to him just as she had seen her mother do a hundred times. All the way they had walked in near-silence; their only exchanges had been that every so often Christie would ask Megan if she was OK and Megan would reply with a small brave nod.

Christie's arms and back ached from pushing the barrow but what had kept her going, what had sustained her was that tomorrow there would be taps, taps in her own house, taps that you turned to make the miraculous water endlessly flow. Tomorrow there would be hot water without the need to boil a kettle; tomorrow there would be a bath. Her resolve that there would be no more of this ridiculous fetching of water had helped her to keep putting one plodding foot in front of the other. They *were* going home. Tomorrow. They were going home and, whatever the difficulties that had to be faced, she and Truman would look them squarely in the eye and start to put their lives back together again. That same resolve had for once also made her immune to Mrs Chadney's anger – that and the fact that she was still too numbed by the events of the morning to allow anything Mrs Chadney might say to upset her.

Despite the now-suffocating heat of the day, Christie could feel a chill creep over her as she closed her eyes and saw again her son being dragged from the long grass and thrown into the car. She whispered a prayer for Baxter; a prayer to Truman, a prayer laced with the suggestion of a threat.

Don't you dare ... Don't you *dare* hurt him ...

It was what she had said the first time.

'NO!' Christie screamed, coming back through the kitchen door. She had only left them alone for a minute. Maybe two.

'NO!'

Truman turned towards her, one hand still raised above his

head, the other holding Baxter roughly by his shoulder. He was two years old. He hadn't meant to spill the milk on his father's shoes.

'NO!' Christie screamed again. Megan was suddenly beside her, grabbing at her leg, clinging hard.

As Truman turned, the boy shook under his hand, his head a froth of blond curls.

Christie could hear the raw shake in her voice.

'Don't you dare ... Don't you *dare* hurt him ...'

Truman's face was twisted in anger.

'Stay out of it!' he yelled.

But Christie bent to scoop Megan up into her arms and went towards him.

'Back off!' Truman shouted.

Christie didn't stop. Couldn't stop. But she wasn't quick enough. Truman's hand came crashing down on Baxter's nappied backside. The force of it lifting him from the ground.

A second later Christie was there, on her knees, catching him before he fell, holding him close in one arm, the other wrapped fiercely around Megan.

Truman pushed past her and a moment later she heard the front door rattle and slam behind him.

He was gone. They were safe.

They had stayed that way for some time. Christie on her knees on the cold lino of the kitchen floor, a child in each arm and those arms aching with the unquenchable need to hold them, their three wet faces pressed tightly together.


Still she struggled to make sense of it; still she tried to explain it to herself. How could Truman be this way?

Perhaps it *was* because he was an orphan. Maybe it *was* as simple as that after all.

Her thoughts had taken her this way many times over the years; they followed a well-trodden path. Because Truman had lost both his parents when he was so young, that would explain why he was the way he was with his own children. He didn't know what it was to be in a family, how to behave around children. He didn't know any better.

*Don't you dare hurt him ... Don't you dare ... Keep him safe ... Just keep my boy safe ...*

It was no excuse, nothing could excuse him; but maybe that *was* it, or at least part of it. And perhaps it could also explain why he got so angry with her and with the children. Because deep down he felt abandoned. Because his parents had left him, alone and so young. It was the sort of thing she'd read about in books; the hero scarred by some unspeakable loss, unable to escape his past.

And perhaps all of this was something else they would need to try to talk about. He wouldn't like it, but in talking about it she just knew she would find a way to help him. She was sure she would.

In this new beginning of theirs. When they got home.

# 28

# Truman: 1.23 p.m.

## *Anyway, he'd inadvertently killed her off, hadn't he?*

'Is that you, Eric?' she called out, an anxious, wavering note in her voice. Truman winced; no one else called him Eric, not now, not for a long time.

From the kitchen, she must have heard his key turning in the latch.

'Yeah, it's only me, Mum,' Truman said.

He picked up her post from the hall table, flicked through the envelopes and, finding nothing to interest him, tossed them to one side.

The windowless hallway was gloomy, ugly and worn; the passage of time had long ago drained the colour from the heavy floral wallpaper hung by a previous occupier and the carpet was scuffed and threadbare. Clinging to the walls and wedged uncomfortably into corners, the bulky mahogany furniture looked ill at ease in these surroundings. It had been second-hand and all they could afford when Truman's newly-wed parents had excitedly bought it more than thirty years before, but it had fitted handsomely enough into their high-ceilinged terraced home on the outskirts of Croydon. Here, in the cramped Crawley council flat where his mother had lived for the past ten years, it looked exactly what it was: an ungainly dark relic of another time, another place.

Truman walked into the kitchen, knowing that he would find her where he always did, sitting at the blue Formica-topped table, nursing a freshly brewed cup of tea, with the *Daily Express* spread out in front of her.

'Kettle's just boiled,' she said as he bent and pecked at her cheek.

'No, I'm all right, Mum,' Truman said. 'Can't stay long.'

'Always in a hurry,' she said sourly.

Truman picked up the paper and scanned the headlines: Gary Sobers had scored a century at Headingley the previous week, another spy had defected to Russia, and they were still going on about the speech that Kennedy had given in Berlin a fortnight ago. '*Ich bin ein Berliner*'? *Ich bin* just another smarmy smart-arsed Yank, more like.

'Such a nice young man,' his mother said, seeing what he was reading.

'Who's that then, princess?' Truman said.

'That President Kennedy,' she said, and Truman could hear the accusation in her voice.

Truman knew the words she had left unspoken. Here she was all alone in the world and her days were long and lonely and her own son, her *only* son, could only find time to visit once in a while when the moon was blue and when he did he was in such a tearing rush that he wouldn't even sit down and have a cup of tea with her. Meanwhile, and on the other hand, you could be absolutely sure that that nice young President Kennedy, busy as he was, what with a whole country to run and everything, you could be sure that he wouldn't dream of treating his dear old mother that way, would he? *He* would find time to sit down and have a cup of tea, you could bet your sweet life on it. Because everyone knew about the Kennedy family, how close they were, didn't they?

'And he's got such a nice young wife . . .' she said.

Another accusation.

'And children,' she said. 'Grandchildren for his mother . . .'

Truman had to smile. That again, always the same, never gave it a rest, did she? You had to hand it to her.

'I've told you, Mum,' he said. 'I haven't met the right girl yet.'

Keep it separate, see; keep it simple.

'Seems to me you never will,' she said.


Well, she didn't need to know about Christie and the kids, did she? And at the same time, there was certainly no need for Christie to know about her. That way there could be none of that mother- and daughter-in-law stuff, getting together behind his back, gossiping about him, spreading their poison, talking about him, about what he was up to, about the way he was, the way he had always been, sticking the knife in, running him down.

Anyway, he'd inadvertently killed her off, hadn't he?

He hadn't meant to. It had just sort of happened.

And when Christie had seemed to like it so much, that he

was alone in the world, that he was an orphan, he couldn't then disappoint her, could he?

He could see it in her eyes when he'd told her all that time ago, could see her melt a bit. It was on his first leave, back from Catterick, and she'd been going on and on about her own family and how she had lost her father just a few years before.

'Same with me,' he'd said, looking for a new way into her heart, breathing in her scent, looking for a way to get his hand inside her blouse.

'Mum and Dad were both ... both taken when I was just little,' he'd said.

'Oh, Truman,' she'd said. 'I'm so sorry.'

Of course, when he'd said it he wasn't to know that he was going to end up marrying her. He couldn't have foreseen that, could he? And once he'd said it, he couldn't very well take it back. He couldn't dig them up, exhume them, as it were, couldn't resurrect them from their graves and introduce them to her over a nice cup of tea.

He and Christie had been sitting on a wooden bench, side by side and holding hands, in one of those ornate painted shelters on Brighton seafront as the wind ripped at the sea and the rain went sideways past them.

'My dad ... He didn't come back from the war,' he had said to her, feeling the need to elaborate.

And that bit had been true, hadn't it? Of course, his father hadn't died or anything like that; he just didn't come back. The truth was that he'd found some fancy French piece and had just buggered off. Came back to Blighty when the fighting was all done, got demobbed and went straight back over to her. Shacked up with her somewhere near Boulogne. He didn't even bother coming home. Just wrote letters to both of them, Truman and his mum. Good riddance is what Truman had thought. But it had broken his mother's heart, and her spirit.

'And what about your mother?' Christie had said, so quietly, so tenderly; eighteen years old, barely been kissed, and struggling for the right words.

'How did she ... how was she ... taken?' she said.

Truman had said nothing, had just sat there shaking his head, as if it was all too painful to talk about.

OK, so in all honesty he did feel a bit of a louse about it at the time, didn't he? It had felt a bit low, a bit shabby, killing his old mum and dad off like that. But he'd soon got over it and it had all turned out for the best.

Yep, it had worked out well for ten years or more now.

And, of course, there was also this 'Eric' business. He'd never told anyone, not his mother at the time or Christie later, about changing his name by deed poll. There was no need to. It was nobody's business but his. Had he told his mother, there would have been tears and protestations and she would have gone on and on at him and would never have let go of it. Had he told Christie she might have thought he was some kind of a phoney and she might have asked all sorts of questions about what had made him want to change it and why he had chosen 'Truman'. He could hardly have told her the truth, could he? He could hardly tell her that he had always thought that he'd never felt like an Eric; that 'Eric' lacked the stature, the necessary pizzazz, the chutzpah, for a man like him, a man who was going places. And he could hardly tell her that he had just seen 'Truman' on the spine of a book in a Brighton shop window on the day that he first met her and liked the sound of it. The first time he'd tried it out for size was on her on that day, and then he'd adopted it when he went up to Catterick and he'd had the legal business done as soon as he'd turned twenty-one.

So for more than ten years now he had been both Eric and Truman.

And that was just fine.

'It's good you've come, Eric,' his mother said. 'I've been so worried. I've been at my wits' end.'

'What about, princess?' Truman said, knowing full well.

'I've been worried about the money I gave you. About the "*investment*".'

Truman could hear that the word was uncomfortable, unfamiliar on her lips. It had been his word when he had explained the whole scheme to her, or at least the little that she needed to know, and she had no choice but to borrow it now.

'Safe as houses, it is,' Truman said. 'Best thing you've ever done.'

'But it's all I've got, Eric,' she said. 'I was thinking it might be better back in the Post Office after all ...'

'Nonsense,' Truman said. 'It's like I told you before, there's absolutely nothing to worry about.'

His mother looked up at him; he could see the uncertainty, the pleading in her eyes.

'But it was months ago when I took the money out and gave it to you and I haven't heard a word from you since. I haven't even seen you,' she said.

'I know, Mum. But I've been busy,' Truman said. 'Busy

156

working on the investment.' He rested a consoling hand on her shoulder. 'And anyway, that's what I've come to see you about today, isn't it?' he said. 'That and to make sure you're all right, of course.'

'I haven't been able to sleep,' she said. 'I've been so worried. I was going to come and try to find you in Brighton – only I haven't got an address. My own son and I haven't even got an address!'

'It's all right, Mum. Don't go getting yourself upset now,' Truman said.

'I thought it might all be lost, all my life savings gone, and then what would I do? I'd just have my pension to get by on.'

'It's not lost, Mum,' Truman said. 'In fact I've got good news for you. I've got your first interest payment here with me now ...'

He reached into the inside breast pocket of his jacket, pulled out his wallet with a flourish, removed the crisp notes that Doll had handed him less than an hour before, and waved them like a seductive fan in front of her.

'You invested five hundred pounds – and here's fifty back for you in just a few months!' he said, like a showman. 'That's more interest than you'd get in a whole year in a bank!'

His mother looked up at him; her eyes wide now.

'And my five hundred? It's still there ... wherever it is?' she said suspiciously. 'Still *invested*?'

'Of course it is, princess!' he said. 'Of course it is!'

'So that means that I've now got five hundred and fifty pounds?' she said uncertainly.

'That's right!' Truman said, and as he handed her the fan of notes, he could see all the doubt fall away from her.

'Oh, Eric, that's wonderful!' she said, counting out the notes one by one. 'You're such a clever boy.'

Truman let her count for a while.

'Of course . . .' he eventually said. 'Of course, the smart thing to do would be to plough it straight back in . . .'

She stopped counting and looked up at him again.

'Back in?' she said.

'Back into the investment . . . That's what the big boys would do, of course. That's how they get to *be* big boys. Rolling in it, they are.'

'Put the fifty back in?'

'That's right. Put the fifty straight back in and that way you get to earn even more in the future,' he said. 'In a few months you could have more than six hundred pounds . . .'

His mother put all the notes down on the table.

'*Six* hundred?' she said. 'That would be lovely.'

'Of course, it has to be your decision,' he said. 'I can only tell you what other people would do.'

'But if you think it's best, Eric,' she said. 'Then what I'll do is the ploughing-back thing. I'll be one of the big boys!'

She scooped the money up, held it for one last moment and then handed it back to Truman.

'That's the spirit, princess, one of the big boys,' Truman said, slotting the money back into the folds of his wallet.

'And I'll tell you what,' he said. 'I'll give the address of where I'm staying at the moment. Just in case you get worried again and want to talk about it. You can drop me a line there and I'll come and see you right away.'

He took a biro from his jacket pocket and wrote the address of The Hare and Hounds in the margin of the newspaper.

'Are you sure you won't have that cup of tea, Eric?' his mother said. 'You could stay a while and we could have a chat ...'

'Sorry, Mum,' Truman said, glancing at his watch. 'I've really got to go.'

He could see that she looked a little crestfallen at that. But she rallied bravely.

'You do know, don't you, Eric?' his mother said, as he bent to give her a goodbye kiss.

'What's that, princess?' Truman said.

'That I'm so very, very proud of you,' she said.

# 29

# Strachan: 1.25 p.m.

## *Strachan laughed in the man's face*

In the full numbing glare of the early-afternoon sun, the small round man's spectacles slipped slowly down his nose; he pushed them back up and shifted awkwardly on the wooden bench of the shelter. It was a place where young lovers came to hold hands, where elderly couples sat silently with their memories and watched the endless rolling and breaking of the sea. It was not a place for a middle-aged insurance broker in a starched collar, morning-coat, waistcoat and pinstripe trousers.

'You know, I really don't have time for this, Mr ... Mr ...?' the man said, pushing the heavy black-framed glasses back up his nose, tugging hotly at his starched shirt collar.

Strachan could see that he was not a man who was accustomed to being outdoors. He was a man who was made for spending his waking hours behind a polished desk in a small dimly lit office, tracing down the columns of leather-bound ledgers with his stubby finger and then sifting through the closely typed pages of the dense files of policies that landed regularly and with a gratifying thud in his in-tray. This meeting in the shelter on the seafront had discomfited him; he was a man out of place, out of time.

'Strachan,' he said. 'Just Strachan.'

'As I told you on the telephone, *Mr* Strachan,' the man said tetchily, asserting his authority, 'as I told you, and I can only repeat it now, I am *not* at liberty to discuss our mutual friend Mr Truman Bird or, for that matter, any other former employees of the company. To do so really would be most irregular.'

The promenade was thronging with day-trippers; wave after cheery wave of them passed by the shelter, all intent on making the absolute most of their day out by the sea. Strachan watched as a harassed young mother negotiated the crowds with a pushchair; her daughter, with her head of Shirley Temple curls, looked up at her with a dripping ice-cream cone in her hand. His eyes then fixed on and followed a group of three teenage girls as they sauntered by, heads high, giggling, gossiping, arms interlinked, on their way to the West Pier; one of them had something of the look of Sally, something of her sparkle.

'But you were *most* insistent . . .' the man said.

'I don't like to be disappointed,' Strachan said, turning to him, unsmiling, the edge unmistakable in his voice.

The man looked at him sharply, quizzically, hearing the same menacing tone that he had heard on the telephone; the menace that had convinced him that it would after all be wise to leave the safety and security of his office and come to this unlikely and unwelcome rendezvous.

161

'That's as may be, Mr Strachan—' he said.

'*Strachan*. Just Strachan.'

'That's as may be,' the man continued, more nervously now. 'But disappointed or not I am afraid I really can't help you with your enquiries.'

Strachan sat back on the wooden bench, cupped his hands behind his head and gazed out to sea; the sunlight bounced and glistened on the water; three ships moved slowly across the far horizon, their shapes reduced by the distance to grey and distant smudges.

'Let's get this straight,' he said evenly. 'It works like this. I'm going to ask you questions and you, you're going to tell me everything you know. Everything about that toerag Truman Bird.'

'No, really I—' the man began, pushing at his glasses once more.

His eyes still fixed on the horizon, Strachan slowly raised a finger to his lips to silence him.

'You're going to tell me,' he said. 'And that way, you see, I won't be disappointed.'

He could feel the man tensing beside him.

'And because I won't be disappointed,' he continued, 'that means that I won't have to hurt you.'

'*Hurt* me?' the man said, alarmed now.

'Hurt you. Hurt your wife . . .' Strachan said, turning to him now.

'My wife?' the man said, instinctively grabbing at the wedding ring on his finger. 'Are you . . . are you threatening me, Mr Strachan?

Strachan leaned closer to him, close enough that the man would have his breath on his face as spoke.

'I fucking told you,' he snarled. 'The name's *Strachan*.'

'But—'

'No buts. It's simple. You tell me and you can go back to your boring little life. You don't tell me and I will hurt you. I will hurt you in ways that you can't even begin to imagine. I will make sure that your life will never be the same again. Understand?'

'But the police—'

Strachan laughed in the man's face.

'You need to know something, my fat friend,' he said. 'You need to know that the man I work for and the local coppers understand each other. He's made sure of that over the years, looked after them. They're like this, they are.'

He raised his hand to show the man his snugly crossed fingers.

'So they let him and they let *me* go about our business. No questions asked.'

The man looked about him helplessly.

'It's the way it works, sunshine. So stop fucking me around, and just tell me what I need to know,' Strachan said, a sudden icy weariness now accompanying the menace.

The man removed his glasses, pulled a spotted silk handkerchief from his trouser pocket and began to wipe furiously at the thick lenses.

'I don't know what it is that I can tell you,' he finally said. 'Your friend Truman Bird left my employment some time ago now—'

'You gave him the boot?' Strachan interrupted.

'I had occasion to terminate his employment, yes,' the man said.

'Had his fingers in the till, did he?'

'Let's just say, he proved to be less than reliable—'

'What else?' Strachan said, aggressively cutting across him again.

'What?' the man said, startled.

'What else can you tell me about him?'

'Nothing really,' he said. 'I checked through his file this morning after your telephone call and there is very little there. I have his home address, of course ...'

'No use to me, he's long gone,' Strachan said.

'I have his next of kin ...'

'His wife?'

'Was he married?' the man said, surprised. 'I didn't know that. How extraordinary. No, he gave his next of kin as his mother.'

'His mother?' Strachan said, interested now. 'Got an address, have we?'

The man nodded, fumbled in the fob pocket of his waistcoat and handed Strachan a slip of paper. He had come prepared, Strachan thought. He'd come knowing his own weakness, his lack of resolve, knowing that his nerve would fail.

He took the slip and read the hastily scribbled name and address.

'Looks like I'm going to be taking a drive up to Crawley later this afternoon,' he said with a smile.

Strachan offered his open palm and could sense the relief course through the man as he went to accept what he thought would be a handshake and an escape back to his office, his desk, to the life he knew and understood. But instead of the expected handshake, Strachan reached across to the man's face and, with a hand that no longer trembled, slowly, softly, tauntingly patted him on his flushed cheek.

Oh yes.

*There are other ways, you know*, Sally had said.

She didn't understand; she didn't know the half of it.

'There,' Strachan said with a smile that was closer to a sneer. 'That wasn't so fucking difficult after all, was it?'

# 30

# Soldier: 1.32 p.m.

## *Because of that. All this*

Mother and daughter were finally back at the caravan. They were safe and Soldier was able to rest. But he could find no peace. Questions that he thought he had put to rest long ago had suddenly reared up to taunt him again. Now, as he looked down and across the clearing, it was all the years that had gone by that worked at him. They clawed at him feverishly.

How many years?

How many years had there been since he came to this place? How many years had passed when it had been all he could do to simply stay alive each day? To fight off illness when it came. To try to keep himself warm and dry. To scratch and forage for food. To rise in the morning to the forest dawn, to wash sleep away in a forest stream and then to walk the paths of his forgotten corner of the forest alone.

His head ached and swam from trying to remember, from trying to account for all the summers that had gone by.

It felt as if he had grown old here.

But he couldn't remember how or when he had first come to be there.

There was a picture in his mind.

*He was stumbling, falling, half dead. He was dragging himself across heathland, desolate and sparse. He was stumbling along a tangled wooded trail. Falling. Falling. Falling into a warm bed of bracken. He was waking to a harsh voice, to the sun on his face. To a harsh voice calling . . .*

Sitting far into the shadows, with his back against the crumbling fallen trunk of a once towering beech, Soldier held the thought, fragile in his mind. He nursed it.

Another picture came.

*He was in a shallow muddy hole, gulping warm gritty water from a pristine mug. Above him the air thundered and sang. Thundered. Sang.*

And then, the connection. The old connection between these two dislocated memories; the only connection he had ever been able to make. It was the point he always reached, the only small sense he had ever been able to find.

Because of that. All this.

Because he had been there, he was here. He was here in the forest because he had been there in that shallow hole.

*Above him the air thundered and sang. Close by a shell exploded.*

Before, he had been whole. After, he was in the forest with the black dog and the slate of his mind wiped almost clean.

The world lurched, rushed, eddied. Soldier tried to steady himself; he closed his eyes, exhausted, done.

Once more the words came.

*Sunt lacrimae rerum.*

Again.

*Sunt lacrimae rerum.*

There are tears. Tears at the heart of things.

Soldier fought to keep his eyes open, forced himself to look down and across the clearing.

*She* had come out of the caravan and had called to the girl. They had taken a blanket and small plates of food into the long grass and were now sitting eating a silent desultory meal.

He should be watching, watching over them. Lest violence and harm should come.

Their guardian angel.

He should be watching over them. He should be watching.

Finally Soldier slept.

# 31

# Truman: 2.28 p.m.

## *He could read her like a book, could read them all*

Truman paused in the doorway of The Salvation to light a cigarette; the smoke snaked stinging into his eyes as he did so. Behind the bar, Sally was reaching high to a narrow ledge to return the prized pewter pot of one of the regulars to its usual resting place.

She was quite a looker, his Sal, standing there on tiptoes, stretching up like that, Truman thought.

She was younger than Doll, of course, and that alone was enough to make her special, all that spring and newness in her; but she didn't have everything that Doll had, did she? She didn't have that playfulness, that come-to-my-bed knowingness.

And that, of course, was part of the wonder of it, part of the excitement. That they were so different. They were so very different but, although of course they would never know it, they had one important thing in common. They were both his. Truman couldn't prevent the smile that crept on to his face at the thought of it.

Both his.

The truth of it was that any man would look at his Sally and think she was a real cracker, a proper bobby dazzler, would be bowled over by her, and then would look at Doll and fall head over heels and backwards.

And yet Truman, he had them both, didn't he?

He tried to picture them there side by side behind that bar – his Doll, his Sal. Now *that* would be something a bit special; his Doll, his Sal, standing side by side, eyes flashing, him knowing, them not.

'Hello, princess,' he called to her from the doorway.

At the sound of his voice, Sally started to turn towards him and then, obviously thinking better of it, immediately spun away again. Truman smiled to himself; he could read her like a book, could read them all, couldn't he?

It made him laugh because underneath everything they were all the same. They had to show him that they were mad with him, didn't they? None of them really meant it, not for long anyway, but they had to do it, it was all part of the game. And this time he couldn't really blame her. After all, he'd done a Harry Houdini on her, he'd just done this big vanishing trick on her, gone missing in action. But give her time, a few laughs, a couple of drinks and a bit of sweet talk and she'd come round. They all did in the end.

He shouldn't have been there at all, of course. Get to the house, straight in, straight out, get the lie of the land, no messing around, that was the plan. But as he had driven towards Brighton he could feel the idea grabbing hold of him. He couldn't resist it. Just a quick one at The Salvation, see his Sal, start mending the broken bridges, a bit of billing, a bit of cooing, and, if the coast was clear, maybe he'd pop back down again the next week and take her out on the town and show her a good time.

The boy had slept in the car, curled up like some bloody cat on the floor in the passenger seat footwell, he was. All the way down from Crawley he'd slept like that. Not that Truman was complaining because at least it had meant he hadn't been staring up at him with those eyes of his.

Behind the wheel of the Wolseley, as he had passed the giant stone pylons that marked the far boundary of Brighton, Truman had found himself shuddering at the thought of it, the thought of the boy's eyes staring up at him. Shifting in his seat, he had reached into his pocket for a cigarette and lit it with a flick of his lighter.

People had always said that the boy looked like him, a real chip off the old block they said, but Truman couldn't see it, never had been able to. All he could see, all he had ever been able to see from when the boy was just a nipper sitting in his cot, was the way that he gazed up at him with those bloody eyes, his mother's eyes.

Questioning him. Accusing him.

Poor little sod, it wasn't his fault. He couldn't help it, could he? But the truth was that it made it hard for Truman to bring himself to even look at him. It put him on edge, made him feel uncomfortable just being around the boy.

*

'Come on, princess,' Truman said to Sally as he walked towards the bar. 'Give us a smile . . .'

Of course, the name didn't help either. All right, it had been his idea in the first place to call him Baxter but now it just grated on him, it reminded him of another scheme that should have delivered big. Should have, but didn't.

It had been worth a punt at the time though. No one else in the family had even talked to that tight-fisted, miserable old sod Fred Baxter for years. Everyone knew that old Uncle Fred was worth a packet and, with no family of his own, all that dough would have to go somewhere when he finally popped his socks, wouldn't it? So Truman had started dropping around from time to time, taking a bottle of something for him or a few cigars. Then, when the boy was born, he'd made this big thing of naming him after him.

Christie had hated the idea at first, had wanted to call him after her own father or something, but he'd won her round by coming out with this sob story of how Uncle Fred had helped him after his parents had gone and he'd been left all alone in the world.

For a moment he'd almost believed it himself.

'All right then,' she'd said in the end. 'But not Fred.'

'Alfred?' he'd said.

'No,' she'd said.

'What about Baxter then?' Truman had said.

And all of that had been for what? For nothing, for another big fat zero. It turned out that the miserable old bastard had left every penny to some busybody do-gooding charity that helped starving children somewhere on the other side of the world. Didn't he know that charity was supposed to begin at home?

Still, at the time it had been worth the punt. Nothing ventured and all that.

When he had reached the town centre, Truman decided that he should park the Wolseley far away from prying eyes. After all, you couldn't be too careful. He didn't know who might be watching out for him and the car was a real giveaway: not many people had a motor and fewer still a brand-new Wolseley.

In the shadowy back streets of the North Laine, he had found a space on some rough ground at the back of an abandoned lock-up. He had managed to get out of the car and close the door without waking the boy and had then walked briskly, zigzagging his way towards the seafront and The Salvation, through the maze of narrow sun-filled streets and dark alleyways that made up The Lanes.

'Come on, Sal,' he said. 'I know I've been away for a bit but I'm back now, so give us a smile ...'

Sally kept her back turned to him, her hands resting on the polished shelf where the glasses were stacked and lined up in neat gleaming rows. Her head was slightly lowered, as if she was deep in thought, as if she was preparing herself for something.

He could see the long curve of her neck. Nice.

'You've no idea how much I've missed you, princess,' he said.

Slowly she began to turn towards him.

Bingo! There you go, you see.

Read them like a book every time.

# 32

# Baxter: 2.28 p.m.

## *The man reached the car and hammered on Baxter's window*

The boy with the ginger hair had stood at the top of the slide, laughing, taunting, pointing, and Baxter had slipped further down into the car, had curled further down into its inviting depths, into the protective shadows of its footwell. There, in the carpeted, cosseting warmth, his eyes had suddenly become heavy and although he had tried to keep them open, had tried as hard as he could, it had been no good.

He had dreamed that he was lost and alone on a small ship on the rolling, tossing vastness of the seas; he had dreamed of the rhythmic swaying of the tall grass, of an ancient hare with rheumy eyes, unable to run any more, unable to move; he had dreamed of the dogs baying in the near distance. He could feel the hare's heart, thrumming like an engine, beating as if it was his own. He could feel the hare's fear in the tightness of his chest, in the sickness of his stomach. Now the sea, now the grass, now the hare; like a carousel spinning faster. Now the sea, now the grass, now the hare, now the dogs, now the playground. And now the baying boys coming towards him; closing in on him. And he was lost again in the tall swaying grass, unable to run any more, unable to move. Now the dogs, now the boys. Closing in.

Baxter blinked open his eyes.

Pulling himself up on to the shiny leather of the car seat, stretching, rubbing the sleep from his eyes, he looked out through the side window. The ginger-haired boy had gone, the park had gone, the blinding sunlight of the day had gone. In their place was a gloomy threatening street and, as if he was still asleep and the dream was now a different kind of nightmare, there was a tall thin man with a half-drunk bottle in his hand, stumbling towards him, stumbling over the broken bricks and abandoned flints of the rough ground.

The man reached the car and hammered on Baxter's window. His face was a violent red, his eyes glassy, his cheeks sunken, his teeth were yellowed, decayed and broken.

Baxter recoiled from him and turned away as the man banged at the glass with his clenched fist and shouted madly, incomprehensibly.

Baxter didn't know where he was, how he had got here, who this man was, what he was saying.

He remembered the lipstick smudged on his face like a mark of shame and rubbed at it again.

And he could feel it once more. Inside him.

Tick ... tick ... tick ... tick ... tick ...

# 33

# Truman: 2.29 p.m.

## *The collar of his shirt was wet with sweat*

As she turned, there was something in her face that Truman hadn't seen before, something he didn't recognise, something that had changed.

Standing either side of the bar, they looked at one another; he with an uneasy smile locked on his face, she deadpan. For a while they said nothing as he tried to work out what was going on, what had happened. This was not about him going missing for a few weeks, this was something more. Much more.

'Hello, princess,' he finally said; gently, hoping to see her soften.

She stared him straight in the eye as if she was looking for something she had missed in all the times she had looked at him before. He looked away, tapped the ash from his cigarette, watched it fall to the floor.

'Someone's been here looking for you,' she said.

The coldness in her voice cut into him.

'Oh yes?' Truman said, disconcerted, thrown as much by the way she was with him as by this news that he didn't want to hear.

'Been asking questions, he has,' Sally said, still meeting his eye.

Questions?

He shouldn't have come back. It meant they were after him, after what he owed them. Who else would be asking questions?

'Friend of mine, was it?' Truman said as lightly as he could manage.

Sally's reply was a derisive snort.

'Name of Strachan,' she said. 'Know him, do you?'

Strachan? The name meant something, rang a distant bell somewhere.

'Can't say I've ever met the fella,' Truman said.

'You'd remember if you had,' she said, with just the hint of a smile.

Truman's mind was working overtime. He had to get out, get away, but he also had to know what this Strachan had said.

'What is it, princess? What's wrong?' he said. 'I know I disappeared on you, but it was work, you see, I had no choice ...'

'He said you were married,' Sally said.

So that was it.

'Said you had children.'

Not a problem.

'Me? Married?' Truman said, the smile relaxing now. 'Not me, Sal. He must have had me confused with someone else.'

Sally leaned forwards, leaned towards him across the bar as she had on previous occasions. Back then it had been to greet him with a kiss.

'He said you were MARRIED!' she almost spat at him.

Truman was suddenly aware that the collar of his shirt was wet with sweat. He reached for it now, tugged his tie loose, opened his top button.

'Honestly, Sal. This Strachan bloke's got it all wrong,' he said. 'You've got to believe me. Why would you take his word and not mine?'

She leaned closer to him, her eyes widening with something close to pity and contempt.

'Because he's Strachan,' she hissed.

## 34

# Baxter: 2.35 p.m.

### *Suddenly the red-faced man wasn't by the car any more*

The red-faced, broken-toothed man was still banging on the car window and shouting something that Baxter didn't understand. His words were all slurred and he had a thick accent and anyway Baxter was trying hard to look the other way, as if by not looking at the man he would make himself somehow invisible. He was trying but it wasn't always working because, despite everything he kept telling himself, every so often he found that he had to take just a quick terrifying look at him. It was as if he had no choice because the man's face kept drawing him back.

And then suddenly there were two voices and one of them Baxter recognised and *could* understand.

'Oi, you! Get your poxy hands off my motor!'

And then suddenly the red-faced man wasn't by the car

any more and was instead crumpled against the wall of the lock-up. He looked comical. Almost.

'Filthy bloody drunk!' his father shouted as he got into the car and slammed the door. 'That'll teach him to put his filthy hands all over my car.'

And he had taught him, Baxter thought, keeping his eyes fixed on the man slumped against the wall as the car reversed out of its parking space and pulled quickly away along the shadowy road. His father had taught the man a kind of a lesson. But Baxter wondered how much of it he would remember when he woke up.

# 35

# Truman: 2.36 p.m.

## *He felt better for it, for the hurt that he had caused the man*

That showed him though, didn't it? That showed that you don't mess with Truman Bird. That showed the poxy drunk. That showed the bastard.

Truman was breathing hard.

That showed them all. All of them.

Mess with Truman Bird and that's what you get.

He'd never been in a fight before, had never hit anyone, not even up in Catterick, far too canny for that. Mug's game, fighting. But that showed he could, didn't it? Showed he could take care of himself. If he had to.

Truman was breathing hard, breathing hard from running through The Lanes back from The Salvation, from lifting the drunk away from the car and then sending him crashing against the wall, from the triumphant rush of adrenalin.

He felt better for it, for the hurt that he had caused the man.

The man had been surprisingly light, as though he was worn away and there was almost nothing left of him under his dirt-stained, threadbare clothes. If that had surprised Truman, what surprised him more was that the set of his face hadn't changed as he had grabbed him by the lapels, lifted and then thrown him. It was what was missing in his face that Truman had noticed most; there was no shock, no surprise, no question, no fear. Nothing. Throughout it all he wore the same slack-mouthed, unseeing expression; he was still wearing it when he was lying in a broken heap at the foot of the wall.

But he'd showed him, hadn't he?

And the same thing would happen to this Strachan bastard if he stuck his nose any further into his business. Snooping around like that, asking questions, upsetting Sally, queering his pitch.

Never mind though. She'd come round in the end; just take a bit longer, that's all.

Under his jacket Truman could feel his shirt clinging wet to his body. It was so damned hot today, too hot for all this chasing-around nonsense. It would be good to get back to The Hare and Hounds, have a bath, a quiet drink and a laugh with Doll. He shifted uncomfortably in his seat, reached for his cigarettes and lighter.

Strachan? Strachan? He just couldn't place the name. Somewhere, he'd heard it a long time ago.

Anyway, it didn't matter who he was, the important thing was that this Strachan was out there asking questions. Truman had already got his answer, he'd found out what he needed to know; it meant that they weren't going to let it go, they wanted what he owed them. And that meant that he had to get to the house, pick up the stuff that bloody Christie and the children wanted and then get the hell out of there once and for all.

Christie and the children. Christie and the children?

Slowly Truman became aware that he was not alone in the car.

The boy. He'd forgotten he had the boy with him, and he would have seen everything, would have seen him running up to the car, fighting with the drunk, everything.

Another bloody thing to explain to Christie.

'All right, sport?' Truman said to Baxter with a fixed smile.

The boy looked up at him from the passenger seat with his mother's accusing eyes.

# 36

# Strachan: 2.36 p.m.

*Strachan had kept out of it;
it wasn't his fight*

When the telephone rang far below in the hallway of the bedsits, Strachan was sitting in the single armchair by the tall sash window. For some reason he had found himself thinking about the war. Not the war that everyone else still talked about all the time; *his* war.

He had returned home to collect the keys for the car that Mr Smith made available to him for times like this, the car that sat waiting in the garage off Western Road, polished, fuelled and ready for the afternoon's journey to Crawley. As he had searched for the keys in the bedside cabinet, from nowhere a sudden wave of tiredness had drawn him towards the chair in the sunlight.

Strachan had held his hands out in front of him. There it was again, the fucking trembling.

He had sat back in the chair and closed his eyes and played through the morning's events in his mind: the taxi drivers parting for him as he walked along the front, the kid playing the jukebox in Jaconelli's, the drunk in The Salvation, Sally, the small round man in his morning-coat and pinstripe trousers in the seafront shelter, the pat of the man's flabby cheek. And then he had found himself catapulted back.

It was February 1946 and he could hear that racket, the tin mugs being rattled furiously on bars, he could hear the stamping of heavy boots on the wooden floor, he could smell the choking acrid smell of burning wood and rubber.

Stupid tossers.

They were all banged up in the glasshouse in Aldershot and a whole gang of them had decided that enough was enough and had set about wrecking the place, piling up the furniture and the mattresses, setting fire to it.

Strachan had kept out of it; it wasn't his fight.

One of them, a big man with tattoos who fancied himself a bit with his fists, had come over to him as he'd sat alone on the floor amidst the din and the chaos, with his back against the wall of one of the association rooms. He'd come over and had a real go at him, jabbing at him with his finger, giving him all sorts of mouth for not joining in. Strachan had said nothing.

Oh yes. Time to play, he'd thought.

Slowly he got to his feet. He took a step forwards and floored him with a left to the guts and a right to the side of the head as he went down.

They were pretty much the same punches he'd thrown an hour or so earlier at The Salvation; that was it, that must have been what had brought it to his mind.

With the big man out cold on the floor, Strachan had sat back down again against the wall. They had left him alone after that. When the Army Fire Service had burst through the door a day later, their hoses trained on those who had rejoiced in smashing the place up, who hours before had been beating their chests, full of boasts and bravado, and who were now soaked and shivering and cowering in a corner, they had found Strachan still sat alone and silent with his back against the wall.

And what did any of it achieve? It just kept all of them locked up for even longer, that's all it did, made the war even longer for all of them.

They had a point, of course; no one should have to live like that: single-man cells, each occupied by three men, living like animals. Couldn't move in the place without ending up with your face in someone's stinking armpit, couldn't escape the stench of the place. Five hundred of them must have been banged up in there and the place had been built for a third of that. They had a point; but wrecking the place was never going to change anything.

That wasn't Strachan's way.

It had been not long before VE Day that he'd been sent to the glasshouse that time. Went down for a year for clattering an officer: jumped-up little shit had tried to get him to clean the latrines. Strachan? Clean bogs? It just wasn't going to happen.

That was the way that he'd spent most of the war years, of course, in and out of one army nick or another. For going

186

AWOL, for refusing to obey orders, for decking a succession of officers.

He never did see any action. Not that that worried him. It wasn't his fight.

After that he had finally made it back home, home to Brighton. In his ill-fitting demob suit, he had arranged to meet Mr Smith in the tea room with the panelled walls and gilded ceiling. Sipping daintily from a bone-china cup, Mr Smith had told him how the war had been good to him, how he was now into everything; into nightclubs, casinos, hotels, property. He had been glad to welcome Strachan back to his fold. He had work for him, he said. Plenty of work.

When things got difficult Mr Smith would call on Strachan. And Strachan would sort it. Strachan would always sort it. Sometimes with his fists. Sometimes with just a word. Sometimes, when people got to know who he was, what he was capable of, all it needed was a look.

Those were the days. Not like now with scabby kids blowing kisses at him from the jukebox.

Fucking little bastard.

Someone was calling his name.

'Strachan! *Strachan!*'

He hauled himself out of the armchair and made his way to the door.

'What is it?' he growled.

'There's a phone call for you.'

As he made his way downstairs, he ran through what little news he had for Mr Smith: some progress, to be sure, but he was still some way from finding this Truman. He was an impatient man, Mr Smith; he liked things dealt with quickly and cleanly.

Strachan picked up the receiver that had been left dangling on its curled cord from the payphone.

'Hello, Mr Smith,' Strachan said.

'*What?*'

It was a woman's voice.

'I'm sorry,' Strachan said, thrown for a moment. No one but Mr Smith ever called him.

'It's Sally,' the voice said.

'Sally, from The Salvation,' she said, as if he might have forgotten.

'Sally?' Strachan said, his heart at once beating faster.

'He's been here,' Sally said. 'Truman was here just now, he's just left. I promised you ... I promised I would call.'

'Yes,' Strachan said, his mind frozen, not knowing what else to say. 'Thank you.'

There was a silence that lasted seconds but felt much longer.

'Did he say where he was heading?' Strachan finally said.

'Afraid not,' she said. 'Look, I must go ... '

'Yes,' he said.

'Sorry I couldn't help more,' Sally said.

'Don't worry,' he said. 'I'll find him.'

He replaced the receiver on its bracket, shook his head to clear it.

*I'll find him.*

As if he was doing it for her, for Sally.

*I'll find him for you.*

And he would find him, because he knew where this Truman joker would be.

188

If he was in Brighton after all this time, he would be sure to go home at some point. After six weeks away, anyone would. They couldn't resist.

Perhaps he wouldn't have to go to visit this sorry fucker's mother after all.

# 37

# Christie: 2.40 p.m.

## *There must have been something in her voice that betrayed her*

C hristie had retrieved the large battered leather suitcase from where she had stored it beneath the caravan. She'd had to lie flat on her stomach and wriggle forwards into the shadowed coolness until she could reach it with her fingertips and inch it towards her. In the six weeks it had been there, during the days of rain and in the morning mists, the leather had soaked up moisture like blotting paper. It was open now and drying out in the sun in the long grass.

Inside the caravan, Christie sorted through the children's clothes, folding them for packing once the case was fully dry. She would have to decide what they would all wear and she would have to find time to clean the caravan before they left. She knew she would need to be ready to go at any time the following day. Once she had spoken to him about going home, Truman's reaction would be unpredictable. He was as likely to make them leave at dawn as he was to put it off until the end of the day.

As she folded the last of Megan's dresses, and despite her anxiety about Baxter, Christie couldn't help but feel a rush of excitement.

Tomorrow they would be home. At last they would be home.

And she would never have to set her eyes on this place again.


The first night had been the worst.

When they arrived in the forest, Truman had pushed open the caravan door, stuck his head briefly inside, pronounced it perfect, and had then climbed into his car and disappeared almost at once in a cloud of dust.

Standing outside the caravan as the car retreated along the lane, Christie had felt momentarily defeated. Megan and Baxter were gazing up at her, both of them tired and hungry. She had a baby in her arms and a suitcase at her feet that she could hardly lift. And the light of the day was beginning to fade. What was she to do?

Finally, she had forced a smile and had stepped inside – only to be sent immediately rushing out again by an over-powering smell of mildewed dampness. Handing the baby to Megan, she had taken a deep breath, plunged back in and forced open the small windows on their reluctant hinges to let the odour of decay out and the fresh air in.

Ushering the children inside, she had tried to make them excited about the adventure of staying in a caravan. But there must have been something in her voice that betrayed her because Megan and Baxter had just looked up at her in wide-eyed disbelief.

She had then made a decision about the suitcase: it could stay where it was outside the caravan until the morning. Going back out and clicking open its locks, she had retrieved the children's nightclothes and their toothbrushes. As she did so, from inside the caravan she had heard the baby's sudden howl of complaint. Before anything else, he would have to be changed and fed.

'I'm hungry,' Baxter said as he waited for her to finish. There was the whine of tiredness in his voice.

'Me too,' Megan chimed in wearily.

Christie had found a large tin of spaghetti in the cardboard box of provisions they had brought with them from the house and had cut jaggedly into it with an opener she had discovered in a small drawer. Like everything she touched in the caravan, the tin opener didn't feel quite clean. It had a disconcerting patina of years of neglect following on from previous sticky-handed use.

For the next half an hour, Christie had tried to light the Calor gas ring. She simply hadn't been able to work out how to make the gas flow. In the end, she had admitted defeat and they had eaten the spaghetti cold; Megan pushing it disgust-edly around her plate, Baxter loudly announcing at frequent intervals to the sharp-elbowed annoyance of his sister that cold spaghetti was the very best thing in the whole wide world ever. While they were eating and squabbling, Christie had sat on the caravan step as the sun disappeared behind the trees at the edge of the clearing. She had suddenly been tired beyond imagining.

When the children were done, she had taken the plates outside and had left them by the step: they too could wait until morning. Then, to noisy protests, she had rubbed briskly at Megan and Baxter with a flannel in front of the sink that was scarcely bigger than a soup bowl and had made them clean their teeth and put on their pyjamas.

Finally, too tired to work out how to put the beds together, she had thrown all the cushions and seat covers on the floor and they had snuggled down together in the darkness under a solitary grey blanket that she had found in a storage chest beneath one of the bench seats. Something about that darkness and the lumpy unfamiliarity of their place on the floor had reduced their exchanges to whispers. She had started to tell them a story, her voice hushed.

'Once upon a time, deep in the forest ...'

The children had moved closer to her still; Megan to one side, Baxter to the other. Within seconds and with the story only just begun, they had been asleep. Christie had felt the soft warm press of them against her. At her feet, the baby was in his carry-cot.

As the children slept, Christie had listened anxiously to the sounds of the forest night, her eyes heavy with tiredness. She and the children had begun the day in their own home on the steep hill that led down to the sea. It was to be a summer's day like any other. They had ended it lying on the floor of a musty, broken-down caravan in a place where the branches of the trees creaked and groaned and the grass hissed as every breath of breeze ran through it.

It was difficult to come to terms with, she thought, as her eyes had slowly come to a close. But that too would have to wait until tomorrow. Like the suitcase and the Calor gas and the dirty dishes. She was too tired to think about any of it now.

And then, finally, she too had fallen into sleep.


Emerging from the caravan, shading her eyes against the light, Christie went to turn the suitcase so that the sun would continue to work on it.

She exchanged smiles with Megan, checked on the baby in his carry-cot in the shade of the caravan and looked at her watch. By now, Truman and Baxter would be in Brighton. At that very moment they were probably at the house and Baxter would be in his room, happily gathering toys to bring back with him.

She could picture it; and in this picture she had created, everything was all right and Baxter was safe. He was in his room, excitedly surrounded by all his favourite toys. And his father was at the foot of the stairs perhaps, cheerfully calling up to him, asking him to hurry up.

# 38

# Truman: 2.58 p.m.

## *He could see clearly what it was that was different*

Truman could sense it as soon as he pulled the car up in front of the house. It wasn't anything obvious, there was nothing he could quite put his finger on. But there was no mistaking it; something was out of place, something was different, something had changed.

OK, he was on edge already, what with the business with Sally and then the drunk, but suddenly now, suddenly he could feel everything ratchet up tight inside him.

Come on, Truman, he said to himself. You've got to get a grip, old son, you've got to cool down, you've got to relax.

'You coming in with me, sport?' he said to Baxter.

After all, that was the idea, wasn't it? To have the boy with him as a bit of insurance, to stop the possibility of any psycho nonsense.

The gate clicked behind them. The boy almost leapt out of his skin.

'For Christ's sake, Baxter! You scared me half to death!'

It was as if the boy could sense it too, whatever it was; so strung up, so jumpy, like a bloody jack-in-a-box, he was.

It was as Truman put the key in the lock that he saw that the front window had been forced open. Someone had been at it with a crowbar or a jemmy.

Someone had been there. At the house.

Someone was there still?

Strachan?

Truman turned the key, pushed the door open, suddenly as nervous as a cat. He stayed rooted to the doorstep, with the boy at his side, as the door creaked and swung slowly on its hinges.

He pulled the boy closer to him.

And then, when the door had fully opened, he could see clearly what it was that was different, what it was that had changed.

'Jesus H. Christ . . .' he whispered.

# 39

# Baxter: 2.59 p.m.

## *Like a mouse asking questions of a mountain*

A part from the plastic toy soldier there was nothing, nothing there at all; everything had gone. And the soldier shouldn't have been there anyway, it didn't belong there in the middle of the floor of the hallway, and someone had trodden on it, crushed it under their heel so that one of its legs was broken at the knee.

'Jesus H. Christ . . . ' his father said again.

With the door fully open, swung right back on its hinges like it never had been before, like his mother would never have allowed it to be, Baxter could see all the things that weren't there.

The picture of the dog with the sad face and its head held to one side that had always hung on the wall opposite the door was gone; the chair that you sat on so that your wellington boots could be pulled off because they were too hard to do on your own was gone; the mat to wipe your feet when it was raining or you'd been walking on the grass in the park, the thick soft rug you weren't supposed to step on with your outside shoes, the shiny brass hooks to hang your coat, the table for the red and yellow vase, the vase itself. All gone.

Through the door to the lounge, Baxter could see it was the same. No big blue settee with the white antimacassars draped over the back, no armchairs, no low wooden coffee table with the slatted shelf underneath for newspapers and magazines, no polished sideboard with its lace doily and framed photographs of him and Megan when they were babies, no carpet. Nothing. Just bare boards and empty walls.

As he looked around him, Baxter noticed that the staircase from the hallway had no carpet either; it was as if someone had ripped it from the treads of the stairs, torn it away so that there were just tufts of brown thread on the protruding heads of the black tacks that had once pinned it down. Until then he hadn't known that there were these black tacks that pinned carpets down.

Baxter could feel his father close to him, breathing hard, could feel his hand resting heavily on his shoulder. It made him uncomfortable. He took a step over the threshold and into the hallway, leaving his father standing there, freeing himself from him. He stopped where the doormat should have been, uncertain for a moment, and then stepped for- wards again, bent down and picked up the toy soldier, examined its damaged leg, and put it carefully into the pocket of his short trousers.

His father still stood on the doorstep and Baxter turned to look at him; he needed to have it explained to him what had happened, to be told that there was a simple reason for everything that wasn't there, and that it was all right really, everything was all right, and there was nothing to worry about.

'What . . . ?' he began to say.

But his father didn't look at him, he just kept staring straight ahead in a way that Baxter hadn't seen anyone stare, as if he was in the kind of a trance they talked about in storybooks. Hypnotised or something.

At the foot of the stairs, Baxter paused to look more closely at the tufted tacks that had held the carpet in place. He then started to climb, but the stairs didn't feel like the same ones that he had climbed so many times before, they looked and felt so very different that it was almost as if he had come to the wrong house.

'Don't run on the stairs!' his mother would call to him as he scampered up to his room as soon as he got home from school.

He didn't run now, in fact he found himself climbing more slowly than he ever had, unsure as to what would be there when he got to the top. It wasn't that he was afraid, that wasn't what made him climb so slowly – in fact from the moment the front door had swung open there had been only this empty feeling inside him where the ticking and the sickness was before. It was more that he felt that he shouldn't be there, that it was wrong to be there, that he was trespassing in this strange empty house. The house even sounded different. At each step that he took, he could hear the noise his shoes made on the floorboards, echoing through the emptiness, and that made him want to stamp harder, to find out if he could make it echo more. After he had taken three loud clomping steps, he remembered that his father was in the doorway and thought that at any minute he would shout at him to stop. But still his father didn't move, so Baxter carried on, slowly stamping to the top.

On the landing, he could see that it was the same.

Every bedroom door but his had been thrown open and everything was gone. Even the light bulbs had been taken and the flexes dangled forlorn and foolish from the ceilings. In the high top corner of his parents' room, behind where the big dark wardrobe had always stood, a broken cobweb hung, covered in thick, powdery dust.

Baxter hesitated for a moment before the closed door to his room. Why was *his* door pulled to while everyone else's was wide open? Could it be that everything that was his was still there, untouched, magically in place, just as it had been left? Baxter closed his eyes and felt a thrill of guilty anticipation; the bed under the window would be neatly made, the wicker toybox with the Dinky cars would be pushed against the wall, his reading books would still be on their shelf, the locomotive of the Hornby train set would still be standing at the station on the floor, the station master would still have his flag raised and his whistle in his pursed lips, the khaki-clad soldiers would be still fighting their desert battles on the top of the small desk in the corner, just one of their comrades missing in action and now in Baxter's pocket.

He slowly turned the doorknob and pushed at the door. And as he opened his eyes he could see that it was true. His dream *was* true – or was at least true in part.

Almost everything that had ever been important to him *had* been left behind. The bed, the chest of drawers, the small desk were gone, but the books, the soldiers, the toybox, the train set were all there. They were all there, scattered on the floor. All there, ripped apart, shattered, flattened, broken, crushed underfoot. It was as if some pernicious whirlwind had whipped through his room, destroying everything, leaving nothing intact.

Baxter stepped into the room and a shard of plastic from what was once the station master's office crunched under his foot. He reached down, ran his questioning fingers across the broken plastic, left it where it was; he picked up a page torn from a book, read a few words, let it fall back to the floor. The emptiness was back inside him. He felt betrayed; everyone else's things had just gone, had just disappeared, but everything that he treasured had been singled out and been reduced to this. It wasn't fair. It wasn't fair in a way that he couldn't find words for.

Downstairs a door suddenly slammed. The house shook.

Baxter picked his way out of his room, over the debris and back to the landing. Below, he could hear a voice, a voice he didn't recognise. He tiptoed to the banister and there he could hear the low rumble of the voice more distinctly.

There was a dull thud, like the noise the man with the bottle made when he hit the wall.

Baxter crept down the stairs, hugging the banister all the way. When he reached the hall, he could see there was someone in the lounge, a large man in a dark suit, and he was holding his father to the wall where the glass cabinet with his mother's best china teaset used to be.

There was blood running from a cut below his father's eye.

'Fucking pretty boy,' the man said, his teeth clenched. 'Not so fucking pretty now, are we?'

Baxter stood in the doorway, unseen. He didn't understand what the man was saying or why he held his father like that.

'Who – who are you?' his father managed to say to the man.

The man still held him there against the wall, held him high with both hands so that his father had to stand almost on tiptoes to support himself. His head was slumped to one side and the blood trickled down his cheek and on down his neck. It gathered in a dark stain on his collar.

'Me?' the man said, almost spitting his words into his father's face. 'I'm Strachan.'

'What – what do you want?' his father said, and Baxter could hear that his voice was thick with something that sounded like fear.

'I've been looking for you,' Strachan said, jerking his father angrily, higher against the wall.

'I've been wanting to have a word,' he said.

'What . . . what about?' his father asked.

'Oh, I think you know, sunshine,' Strachan said, jerking him again. 'I think you know very well . . .'

Baxter's father coughed, choked.

'No,' he finally said. 'I don't know.'

Baxter wondered why that didn't sound right, why it didn't sound true.

Strachan pulled Truman away from the wall and then slammed him back into it; Baxter watched as his father's head bounced and then rolled against the wallpaper.

'You disappoint me, Mr Bird,' Strachan said. 'And I don't like to be disappointed.'

'What do you want?' Truman gasped. 'I don't understand.'

'Then I'll make it simple for you, shall I?' Strachan said. 'You see, you've upset an associate of mine. Fucked up his karma or something, you have, and he's not happy with you—'

The man sent Baxter's father crashing into the wall again.

'So he asked me to have a word ...'

And again.

'A friendly word ...'

And again.

'A word about what you owe him ...'

And again.

'About the five thousand you borrowed from him ...'

And again.

'About the payments you haven't made ...'

And again.

'About disappearing on him ...'

And once more.

'So *now* do you understand, toerag?' Strachan said.

Baxter's father nodded. Or, more accurately, he raised his head just a fraction and then let it loll forwards again.

In the momentary silence that followed, Baxter took a small but decisive step into the room.

Still he had the empty feeling inside. It was sort of empty and sad at the same time. And somehow because of this, and because his father was being held against the wall, and because of everything that wasn't there, because everything was different, he didn't feel afraid and it wasn't like he was doing it at all. It was as if someone else was stepping into the room. Not him.

'Why have all my toys been smashed?' he said.

He was startled to hear his voice ringing out so clearly in

the bare room. The man turned, still holding Baxter's father aloft.

'What the ... ?' he started to say.

Baxter looked up at him; he felt very small against this man, like a mouse asking questions of a mountain.

'Why have my toys been smashed up?' he said again, a hush now in his voice.

'And where have all our things gone?'

# 40

## Strachan: 3.09 p.m.

### *Strachan looked at the boy's tiny hand*

The boy stood in the middle of the room, small and bony thin, pale as death, hair so fair that it was a rich creamy white, eyes as big as saucers and deep as water.

Strachan released his grip, let go of Truman, let him fall sagging to his knees, heard the heave of his breath, saw him struggle to his feet, watched him stagger towards the door.

He couldn't lift a finger to stop him; not with the kid standing there like that, watching him, paralysing him.

'My toys are upstairs, all smashed,' the boy explained to Strachan. 'Would you like to see them?'

The boy held out his hand towards him, as if to lead him, as if to take him there.

Strachan looked at the boy's tiny hand, looked down at his own swollen ham fists, the skin of his knuckles raw and broken from the blow he had struck Truman.

Slowly he shook his head.

He thought he'd seen everything, but not this. Not this.

Truman came back from the door, grabbed the boy by the arm, dragged him behind him.

The front door slammed and still Strachan stood there, shaking his head; he was aware of his own breath now, coming fast, aware too of the clammy sweat on his forehead. He reached in his pocket for his handkerchief, dabbed at it.

Maybe I am getting too old for all of this, he thought.

Outside the Wolseley spluttered, kicked into life, pulled away up the hill with a sharp squeal of rubber on the hot tarmac.

Fuck it.

# 41

# Truman: 3:33 p.m.

## *This was his chance, he knew it*

Truman yanked at the rear-view mirror, twisted it towards him to inspect the damage to his face; as he took his eyes off the road, the car twitched and swerved unnervingly. He was out of Brighton now and driving fast, too fast.

Slow down, Truman old son. Slow down.

The blood had almost stopped running and had begun to dry on his face. He fumbled for a handkerchief in his trouser pocket, licked a corner of it wet and rubbed at his cheek and then at his neck. He checked again in the mirror, taking greater care this time to focus sufficiently on the road. As satisfied as he could be, he swung the mirror back into place.

It wasn't so bad. He'd have a proper shiner later, as well as the cut. But he could explain it away, couldn't he? To Doll, even to Christie, come to that. He could make some crack about it. Daft bugger walked into a door. That sort of thing.

But the house, Christ almighty, the house!

The bastards, they had taken everything; *everything*. How was he going to explain *that* to Christie?

OK, so he owed him, Mr Smith, he owed him the five thousand. That was true enough. But he didn't need to do *that*. He didn't need to have the house stripped of *everything*.

It would have all gone to be sold, wouldn't it? Every last stick of furniture, everything he had worked for, sweated for. Well, maybe not sweated for exactly, but even the last shirt off his back; all of it was gone. That would be it though, wouldn't it? It would have all been taken to be sold against what he owed. What would it have made? A grand? No, not that much. A few hundred? Not enough, not nearly enough.

*Christ almighty.*

Truman thumped at the steering wheel with the palm of his hand; he felt again the tenderness of the bruising from when he had hit the wheel in anger earlier in the day.

*Christ almighty.*

And who would have believed it of him, that Mr Smith? He'd thought it would be safe to touch him for the money. Thought that if things didn't quite work out with the Big Idea, then what the hell. What was an old queen like him going to do about it? Truman would be able to manage him, wouldn't he? Who would have guessed he would turn out so bloody vindictive?

And who would have thought he would know that Strachan?

Truman shuddered. Evil bastard, that one. Never would be too soon to meet up with him again.

Although, come to think of it, if he did run into Strachan again, perhaps he'd suggest he should have one of his '*friendly words*' with Bernie. He was the one who Strachan should be after. After all, it was his bloody stupid idea in the first place, wasn't it?

Bloody Bernie. *Bloody sodding bastard Bernie!*

Truman hit the steering wheel again, more tentatively this time.

Bloody Bernie and his Big Idea.


It had all started one long liquid March lunchtime at The Trumpeters. Outside the wind had rattled at the windows, the sea churned and crashed and the rain bounced on the pavements; inside Truman was holding court. They had been talking about that 'Spend, spend, spend' pools winner, that Viv Nicholson, who was in the newspapers again.

'Another new car,' Bernie had said, tutting, pointing to the photograph.

'Seven quid a week at some sweet factory, that was what she was on before,' Sid said. 'Now look at her, a hundred and fifty grand in the bank and spending it like bloody water, as if it's going out of fashion.'

'Lucky cow,' Walter said. 'Shopping at Harrods, new motor every six months . . .'

'Do the pools yourself, do you, Truman?' Sid said.

'Not me,' Truman said. 'Mug's game. No point in leaving it all down to Lady Luck and eight score-draws, is there? Me, I'm going to make it on my own.'

'Oh yeah,' Sid said, incredulously. 'How you going to do that then?'

'By using this,' Truman said, tapping his head.

'Oh yeah?' Bernie said sarcastically.

'All I need,' Truman said, 'all I need is just the one big idea, *the* Big Idea. Just you watch me. One big idea and that'll be me, living the high life, the life of Riley . . .'

They all laughed and lifted their mocking glasses to salute him. All except Bernie.

'It's not a problem, you know,' Bernie had said to him quietly, as he got another round in.

'Not a problem?' Truman said.

'The Big Idea,' Bernie said. 'I've got it for you, if you're up for it.'

It was simple, he'd said; him and his mates at the golf course were all at it. What you did was buy up some knackered old property off the seafront cheap, you knocked it into bedsits and then let it out to those students from the new university. No need to worry too much if it was a bit of a doss-house, cracks in the walls, dodgy plumbing, paper hanging off with the damp; the way they lived, those students, they didn't care, did they? Money for old rope, it was, he said. Spend a few quid up front and then all you had to do was sit back and watch it all roll in. In clover, you were, he said. Easy.

Of course it meant you needed that bit of money up front to make money, Bernie had said.

'That's always the catch,' Truman had said, raising his glass. 'To them that's got and all that . . .'

But just five grand would do it, Bernie had said, just five grand would get him started. And, if Truman was interested, he knew just the property. It had just come on to the market, next door to one of his.

Truman barely had five pounds in his wallet, let alone five thousand, but he'd gone with Bernie to look at the house anyway: a big old Regency white-stuccoed barn of a place with the plaster hanging off the walls and ceiling. It had stood empty for years.

'Make you a small fortune, this place,' Bernie said. 'Interested?'

'You bet,' Truman had replied.

But five thousand? He could no more lay his hands on that than fly to the moon.

Five thousand . . .

Back at The Trumpeters, sitting on a bar stool with a pint and a chaser in front of him, he kept going over it in his mind. This was his chance, he knew it.

Since the war he'd seen people all around him making it big, people like Bernie. It was as if all his life the world had been run by these tired old men, these sad old bastards. You saw them everywhere. They were the bank managers and the solicitors and the teachers and all the rest. They were everywhere. They ran all the businesses; the local council; they ran the bloody country itself. And they'd run it into the ground, hadn't they? And they'd taken it into one bloody war after another. But now their time was coming to an end, they were finished, it was over. It was all changing and there was going to be a different kind of tomorrow where you didn't need to be some stuck-up toff to get ahead. He could feel it, *everyone* could feel it, and he wanted to grab his slice of it. Just like Bernie had.

All he needed was the five thousand for his ticket for a seat at the table. Five thousand and he'd never have to worry again; five thousand and he'd be in clover; five thousand . . .

And then, bingo, it had come to him.

Mr Smith had come gracefully leaping, pirouetting into his mind. Mr Smith, *of course*. He'd filed him away, you see, Mr Smith, filed him away that time he'd knocked on his door trying to flog him insurance, because he'd thought he might somehow come in handy one day.

Mr Smith just might be the answer. After all, with a house like that, he must be worth a few bob. No harm in asking, was there?

And like it was all meant, as if it was all there waiting for him all along, it had turned out that Mr Smith *was* only too keen to help. Yes, of course, he'd be happy to lend the cash to such a smart, good-looking and ambitious young man as Truman. Truman would have to come back to sign some papers, of course, *frightfully dull and nothing to trouble your pretty head about*, and he'd have to agree to pay just the *teensiest weensiest* amount of interest every week, if that was agreeable.

OK, the interest rate had seemed a bit steep, and maybe that should have set the old alarm bells ringing; and Mr Smith had said something about not letting him down or he would regret it, regret it for the rest of his life, in ways that he couldn't begin to imagine. But by then Truman had the five thousand burning in his pocket and he wasn't really listening, was he? He just signed the papers and was out through the door grinning like a cat.

That had been some night: champagne and Guinness and fat Havanas all round. And he'd shown Sally one hell of a good time, hadn't he? He'd bought her jewellery from one of those fancy shops in The Lanes, a gold necklace, pearl earrings, and he'd presented them to her as they strolled along the Palace Pier at close to midnight with the moon full and the light bouncing and rolling on the water.

Some night.

'Oh, it's too much, Truman,' Sally had said. 'I can't possibly take it, it's too much.'

'Course you can, princess,' Truman said, with a smile like he'd found the key to the Bank of England. 'This is what it's going to be like from now on.'

The next day he treated himself: new motor, smart new suit. After all, he reasoned, if you're going to do this, you've got to do it right; you've got to look the part, haven't you? You've got to be the part.

But then when he'd looked again at the money in his wallet he could see that, after the jewellery, the Wolseley, the clothes, the gifts for Christie and the children to keep things sweet at home, the five thousand had quickly become three and a half.

'How's it going, Truman?' Bernie had asked.

'Never better,' Truman had said.

Three and a half ... Still, that was more than enough for the deposit on the house, wasn't it? And he could find the rest somehow, couldn't he? Something was sure to turn up, wasn't it?

But once he'd handed over the deposit, made the first few weekly interest payments to Mr Smith and bought a few more rounds at The Trumpeters, he'd found that the money was all but gone. Five thousand, blown in less than three months. It was then that he'd 'borrowed' the five hundred from his mother to buy a little more time. But when he'd run through that as well, he could see that none of it was going to happen; none of it, not the house, the students, the money rolling in, the life of Riley he'd promised himself.

Bloody Bernie!

It was all spiralling down, spiralling away from Truman.

There was nothing for it, he'd thought, he'd have to go to see his brief and get the deposit on the house back. At least then he'd have some cash to live on while he worked out what to do next.

His solicitor had peered at him over his half-moon reading glasses, his brow wrinkling into a disbelieving frown.

'But I'm rather afraid that it doesn't quite work that way, Mr Bird,' he said.

'Don't mess me around,' Truman said impatiently, feeling like he needed a drink. 'I need the dough.'

The solicitor had dismissively shuffled the papers on his desk into an orderly pile.

He'd spelled it out as if to a child.

'But if you are unable to complete on the purchase of the property, Mr Bird, the *dough*, as you insist on calling it, is irredeemably lost. That being the nature of a *non-refundable* deposit,' he said.

Pompous git.

After that, he'd gone to see Mr Smith, to explain that he couldn't make the payments for a while, that he needed more time.

'But my darling boy,' Mr Smith had said, still with his genial smile. 'You obviously don't understand. There can be absolutely no question of you not paying what you owe me, *when* you owe me.

'I thought I'd spelled that out to you, I thought I'd made that crystal clear to you.

'How could you possibly have failed to comprehend?

'I told you, dear boy, that if you once let me down, you

would regret it. I would make sure you regret it, every day for the rest of your shitty little life.'

After that he'd known there was nothing for it; he'd have to get out for a while, he'd have to vanish and somehow take the family with him, let the dust settle and then come back and see what could be salvaged.

Give him some time and the old boy would calm down, wouldn't he? He was upset, Mr Smith, that was understandable, but in the end he'd drop all this 'regret it for the rest of your life' business. And then maybe the student house would somehow still be there and waiting and maybe it would still be possible, if he could just find the money from somewhere else.

And it had been then, just when he needed a way out, a way through, that Doll had landed in his lap at The Hare and Hounds and everything had suddenly come up smelling of roses.

But the truth was, of course, that none of it was down to chance, was it? He'd made his own luck, hadn't he? Because he'd been on his toes, you see. He'd seen it coming in time and got out. He'd moved on. He'd been smart enough; stayed one step ahead.

But he hadn't reckoned on *this*, had he? *Couldn't* have reckoned on this. Everything gone. *Everything*. And then that psycho Strachan bursting into the house like that, out of nowhere.

Truman flinched at the memory of it. He fumbled in his jacket pocket for his cigarettes, tapped one from the packet.

That was it, damn it! Sally must have told him.

Of course she had. How else would that Strachan have known that he'd be there? She must have picked the phone up to him as soon as Truman was out of the door at The Salvation. Who would have believed she'd do a thing like that? You couldn't make it up, could you? His girl, *his* Sally, ratting him up to some psycho bastard. And after all he'd done for her. All that jewellery he'd given her, spent hundreds on her, and then she sets that headcase on him? That was the thanks he got for treating her so well, was it? That was the thanks for showing her all those good times?

Yeah, Sally must have told Strachan.

Fancy him, did she?

Saw her next meal ticket, did she?

Ungrateful cow.

Sally must have told him that he was back in town and that madman had guessed that he would go to the house. And after that he'd come straight round there, grabbed him, smacked him in the face, threatened him with who-knew-what.

And the boy, the boy had seen it all.

*Bloody Christie.*

Why couldn't she keep her big nose out of his business? Insisting he took the boy with him. It was all her bloody stupid idea. Bloody Christie; always interfering.


Truman saw a lay-by ahead and pulled over. The heat of the day hit him as soon as he opened the car door. He got out, walked round to the passenger door, flung it open.

'Get out!' he shouted at Baxter.

The boy looked at him, stunned, fearful. Looked up at him with those eyes, but didn't move.

'I said, GET OUT!'

He reached into the car and pulled Baxter from his seat.

He bent down, grabbed him by both arms, shook him so his head bobbed like a broken doll.

'Now listen to me,' he said, still shaking him. 'You saw nothing. Understand? NOTHING.'

He gripped him tightly, shook him again and again; the boy too shocked to cry out.

'YOU SAW NOTHING. YOU SAY NOTHING. NOT TO YOUR BLOODY MOTHER. NOT TO ANYONE.'

Truman held the boy still now, leaned in to him, leaned close to him. He could see the smudged red lipstick on his face, Doll's lipstick, echoing the smear of blood on his own.

'*Not one bloody word.*'

He let go of Baxter, saw him stumble and fall against the car. Still he didn't cry.

Bloody Christie.

# 42

# Christie: 4.20 p.m.

## *They had been woven together like this from the beginning*

It was too hot to be inside the caravan; it was too hot to be anywhere. Christie sat on the step, the baby in the carry-cot beside her. Megan was lying on the blanket in the long grass near by, re-reading a favourite book. From time to time she would look up anxiously and across at Christie and smile. The smile would be returned and, reassured, comforted, Megan would go back to the pages of her book. They had spent much of the afternoon like this since fetching the water: Christie sitting on the low step, waiting for Baxter to come back to her, Megan reading. Christie had sorted the clothes ready for packing and had lifted the suitcase into the caravan. They had tried to eat, but neither of them had any appetite.

The heat now was stifling, suffocating. Summer clouds that had begun the day so benignly were now beginning to grow mountainously. The day would not end without a storm.

Christie looked up and across the clearing towards the woods. From the beginning, from that first morning when she had pushed open the caravan door and peered out across the great sway of grass, these dark woods had left Christie ill at ease. There had been something about them that seemed to bear down on her; something that served to unnerve her even more than the circumstances of her being there in the first place had already unnerved her.

Truman had dumped her and the children here, had all but abandoned them, and now the great oaks and haughty beeches loomed about her and sneered. It was as if they had eyes that followed her; she felt self-conscious under their unblinking gaze. It was as if, too, the canopied darkness below their weighted boughs held mysteries too terrifying to give voice to.

How could she keep the children safe in such a place? How could she herself be safe?

The rational part of Christie knew she was being fanciful, knew that there was nothing to fear from the forest. But she was so diminished and tired that it was difficult to cling entirely to the rational for long.

Whenever Baxter had disappeared into those woods to play, she had felt the fear unfurling cold inside her. She had wanted to call after him, to call him back to her, but she heard her father's low calm reassuring voice telling her that it was all right. That she must not worry so. That young boys were born to run and play in woods. That he would be safe.

He would be safe. Safer than he was now, perhaps. Safer than wherever he was with his father at that moment.

*Don't you hurt my boy ... Don't you lay a finger on one hair of his head ...*

Once more she looked across to Megan and smiled. This time their roles were reversed and she saw that the smile she got in return was meant to reassure and comfort *her*. Her nine-year-old daughter was telling her not to worry, that everything would be fine. Telling her with a smile.

They had been woven together like this from the beginning, Christie thought. Mother and daughter. They were of the same cloth and, because of that, so much of what passed between them could be left unspoken. Each mirrored look, every shared smile, every questioning eyebrow raised, every fretful frown served only to bind them closer still.

Megan was lying on her stomach as she read, her chin resting on her hand. Restlessly she swung her legs in the warm air as she turned another page.

When Christie was a girl, she had been restless too; her head had been full of all those dreams and plans. What would Megan's dreams be, she wondered? When she was older, when it was time for her to leave school or leave home, what would her brave and beautiful girl want from her life? She was so quick and bright, she might go on to college and do the things that Christie had always promised herself she would do. She was so gentle and caring, perhaps she would become a nurse. Or even a doctor. Nothing was impossible. Nothing would be beyond her.

But whatever it was, it didn't matter. As long as it was what Megan wanted; as long as it wasn't someone else deciding for her.

And whatever her dreams were, there was one thing that

Christie was certain of. They were not going to be taken away from her. Christie would make sure of that.

Follow your dreams, her father had told her. Well, it hadn't worked out like that for her but for Megan it would. On that Christie was determined. Nothing would be allowed to get in her daughter's way. No one would be allowed to steal her dreams one by one.


When the doctor had confirmed what she already knew, Christie had tried to summon a smile. But she hadn't been able to manage it. She had felt guilty about that. After all, it wasn't the baby's fault. He hadn't asked to be brought into the world.

'Congratulations, Mrs Bird,' the doctor had said.

From her reaction, or rather from the lack of it, he must have known that something was wrong. She hadn't been able to look him in the eye.

Later that day she had walked along the seafront from the Palace Pier towards Hove Lawns, trying to come to terms with it. She had been glad the afternoon was blustery; she liked the way it buffeted her, the way she had to lean slightly into it. She had wanted this physical effort. She felt it would somehow help to rid her of the deadening weight that all at once she felt she was carrying.

As she had battled into the wind, she had only one thought: Why now? Why did a baby have to come along just when she was allowing herself to dream again?

The wind had whipped at her raincoat, tugged at her beret. She had leaned more steeply into it and clamped the beret to her head with one hand.

And it wasn't even as if it had been that much of a dream. With Megan and Baxter both at school, all she had begun to hope for was a part-time job somewhere. A little money of her own. Friends at work, perhaps. It hadn't been so very much to wish for.

She had turned towards the sea and had stood against the cast-iron railings to watch the waves heave and then break and hiss and foam.

But there was no point, she had tried to tell herself. No point in feeling sorry for herself. She would just have to get on with it, make the best of it. There was no choice. And anyway, she was sure to be all right once she got used to the idea. She just had to give herself some time. In any case, she couldn't stay unhappy for long when there would be another child to love and to hold, could she? No, she had to pull herself together.

She had turned again to walk further along the esplanade. The wind was blowing harder now and she had forgotten to hold on to her beret. A sudden gust had plucked it from her head and had sent it spinning away, back in the direction from which she had just walked.

Glad of the distraction, she had set off running after it. The wind had pushed hard at her from behind, making her feel light and unsteady; it had propelled her onwards. But it had been no good. The faster she had run, the more the wind had mischievously picked up and carried the beret further from her reach.

From behind she had heard the heavy thump of footsteps. Someone else was running. A man. She had slowed her pace and in a moment he had been past her and had swooped down to retrieve the errant beret.

'Yours, I believe,' he said, bowing low.

He was a courtier returning a lace handkerchief she had let drop carelessly from her hand.

Without thinking Christie had replied with a small curtsey.

'Why thank you, kind sir,' she had said laughing, suddenly sixteen again.

He was pink and breathless from running, his hair ruffled. He asked her to join him for a cup of tea at a nearby café.

''Tis the reward I claim,' he said. 'For my chivalrous deed . . .'

To her astonishment, she had agreed.

In the café they had sat at a table with a sticky wooden top and had drunk bitter tea from chipped blue mugs and he had asked one question after another. What was her name? Where was she from? Who was her favourite film star? What was the best book she had ever read? If she could go anywhere in the world where would that be? It was like nothing ever before. Here was this person, this stranger, who wanted to know everything about her.

And Christie had found herself telling him. Everything. Or at least everything about herself when she was a girl, leaving school, full of dreams and possibilities.

'And now?' he said.

She had paused, suddenly self-conscious, suddenly aware of how much she had been caught up and carried by the excitement of the moment. Like her beret in the wind. Suddenly embarrassed by how much she had talked.

'Now?' he said again, to encourage her.

She had replied with a shake of her head. What was there to say about now, she thought? And whatever the moment had been, it had passed. She had said too much already.

He had asked to see her again.

Once more she had answered with a small shake of her head. And this time she had picked up her handbag and had run from the café.

She had wondered about him often since and about what might have happened if she had seen him again. He had said his name was Sean. The stranger she had shared her dreams with.

Sitting alone on the step of the caravan, Christie watched the woods as they watched her.

But it wasn't just her dreams that had been lost, she thought. It wasn't just the Christie she was *meant* to be; it was everything she was, everything about her. Little by little, drip by drip, it felt as if it had all been taken away.

Perhaps it had been in that first blast of Truman's possessive rage that she had begun to lose herself. Or perhaps it had been in all those later countless acts of denial, in all those questions she had chosen not to ask, in all the answers she had been too fearful to seek out. Or maybe it had been in all the times when she had said to herself that it was enough, enough to just try to hold everything together, for her sake, for the sake of the children. That nothing else mattered. That everything else could wait. Or perhaps the truth was more simple still: that she had lost herself in that very first moment of wrapping her arms about Megan and Baxter on the kitchen floor. Holding them close to her. To keep them safe.

Whatever it was, whenever it was, she blamed herself. For allowing him to make her feel so worthless. For making her forget who she was, who she was meant to be.

She had lacked courage. All those questions she had chosen not to ask.

She had been so proud of him for holding on to the insurance job, for working so hard, for winning the watch. She had told him that she was proud. But she hadn't dared to ask him about the new car, how they could afford it, where the money had suddenly come from.

She had been proud too of the home that she had been able to create. He earned the money and she made the home. It wasn't the home that she had dreamed of, with bright colours and everything new; they'd had to make do with a rented house and second-hand furniture. None the less, she had told him that she was proud. But she hadn't asked him about the new clothes, the expensive toys for the children.

It was true, she had lacked courage. About that and so much more.

She hadn't mentioned the stories her sisters had gleefully told her one day when they turned up unexpectedly on her doorstep. The stories of seeing him walking on the pier next to another woman at close to midnight. She didn't trust herself to even think about that.

And she hadn't asked him why they were here, in this caravan, in a clearing in a forest that watched her every move.


The air hung heavily and Christie tried to fan herself with her hand. Inside the caravan, the radio softly played and Jim Reeves silkily crooned.

♫ *Welcome to my world* ...

Her new resolve, what was it again? Oh yes, that was it.

Tomorrow they were going to leave this place. And from somewhere she would find the strength. She always did.

Tomorrow they were going home and whatever the difficulties, she and Truman would start again. For the sake of the children, if nothing else. That was it, wasn't it? That was always it. For the sake of the children. The children defined her now, and that was all there was and maybe that should be enough.

Christie closed her eyes and felt the warmth of the sun wash over her. Tomorrow they were going home. And the forest would no longer watch her.

# 43

# Soldier: 4.20 p.m.

## *Everyone she had ever loved had been taken*

Soldier carried the garden tools back to the potting shed:
the sharp-pointed trowel with the worn wooden handle,
the ancient heavy shears with the blades he had honed and
oiled at each passing season, the rusted pitted rake that had
always rattled loose in its shaft. With elaborate care, he
gathered the clippings, the prunings, the heavy dead heads of
the pale soft-scented yellow roses from the garden path and
carried them to the compost heap at the back of the cottage.
He then swept the path with the besom broom he had made
himself: the stout pole of hazel, the bristles of tender birch
twigs. It felt pleasing to his hand.

The black dog stayed outside. Sniffing at the gate.

In the distance a crow cawed.

He looked up, stretched to his full height, arching his
back to ease the ache that had settled there, felt the sun on
his face and, squinting against the brightness, saw the clouds

collecting above. There may be a storm approaching but there was peace here; there always had been. Today the hour spent in the garden had quietened the chaotic tumble of thoughts that clawed at his mind.

From time to time as Soldier went about his work, he could see the fierce twitch of the curtain at the window. He knew he was being watched and this made him more careful still, more self-consciously deliberate in all his movements.

It was their ritual.

He would spend an hour or so tending her flowerbeds, working the vegetable plot, clearing her path in the winter, or chopping the logs for the fire. Mrs Chadney meanwhile would stand behind the closed window and curse.

When he was done he would find a small parcel of vegetables on the back step. Every so often he would discover that they were wrapped in an article of clothing. There would be a shirt to replace the one that had worn ragged and thin on him, or a knitted vest, or thick coarse socks against the cold, or a pair of cord trousers, stouter in the waist and shorter in the leg than Soldier needed.

They had all belonged to another man.

And he was long gone.

Soldier knew that this was the reason for the violence of her anger, her consuming hatred; she had whispered it bitterly to him one day many years before. She cursed at him, as she cursed at the world for this man having been taken from her. Her strong quiet man.

And more than that, so much more than that; she railed at

Soldier as she railed at the world. For taking *them* too. Her sons, her two glorious roaring boys.

Every one of them was gone, she'd said. First the two booming fair-haired boys who had filled the cottage with their deep-voiced laughter and who would pick her up and twirl her around until she felt dizzy and young. And then the shy modest man who would look on and smile.

Everyone she had ever loved had been taken, she'd said. Everyone who had ever loved her had been lost. Her boys, one to Dunkirk and one to Arnhem. And then, after that second telegram, her husband to despair. To the noose, far into the forest.

Soldier carried the hiss of her bitter whispering voice with him whenever he was near to her. It helped him to make sense of the uneasy contract that had grown up between them.

It had begun with that voice.

It was her harsh voice that he had first heard, of course; it was she who had found him broken, half dead in the woods. He had known this and then not known it through the days, the weeks, the fog of years that had followed. Knowing it now; not knowing it then. She had found him and had nursed him as if he were her own. She had saved him. She had given him his name, had sewn it to his lapel.

Later, when he was strong enough and when he had retreated further into the forest, he had resolved to return each day to tend her garden. And her payment to him, for what he had chosen to do for her, was to stand at the window and curse him for what he was. For what he had been.

A soldier. Like one of those who took her sons.

She cursed him and then she left food and clothes for him. That too was because of what he was.

One of those who were taken, someone else's son.


It had been more difficult to find time to tend the garden during the weeks that *she* had been there in the caravan in the clearing. Not that he had defaulted on the contract for a single day. But he had found it so very hard to abandon her and the children, to leave them there in the clearing, unwatched.

His duty. Lest violence and harm should come to them, should be visited upon them.

Each day he would leave it until he knew he could leave it no longer. He would leave it until the sun began to sink low. And yet still he would hesitate.

The black dog would grow restless. Would press itself against him.

Pulled one way, pulled the other, torn between his two duties, finally Soldier would set off along the rising dipping path that bordered the road. But, even then, he would turn and go back. Turn and go back. Over and over.

But today had been different. In the heat of the afternoon, and after the numbing brutal fury of the morning, after the taking of the boy, and after the long listless walk to the cottage for water, mother and daughter had barely moved from their place on the caravan step. It was as if something had been spent, something had been exhausted. And Soldier had found that he had been able to leave them there, safe in the clearing.

But the boy? What had become of the boy?

Anxiety gripped at him once more.

After that first time, when he had surprised him on the edge of the wood, Baxter had sought Soldier out and had come to him every day. Sometimes they would sit silently together, knocking their heels against the wall close to Soldier's shelter in the woods. At other times the boy would walk beside him and ask him urgent insistent questions. How to build a camp, or catch a rabbit, or set a fire. And, when Soldier knew what it was that was being asked of him, he would crouch low and try to show him.

One morning they had lit a fire, even though the day was warm. For hours the boy had fetched dry twigs and leaves to feed it, had watched it as it crackled and spat, had prodded at it with a long charred stick.

It was then that Baxter had sat with him and had spoken haltingly of the games he liked to play. Of the other boys in the playground. Of his mother. His sister. Of the dreams he had in the long haunted hours of the night.

Then one day he had talked of going home. With his father. Just the two of them. Boys together.

'I'm not frightened,' Baxter had said.

Soldier had heard the fear in his voice.

'Not really,' the boy said.

Soldier knew he must get back; he had to be there when Baxter returned. His duty.

He hurried now to the back step to collect what Mrs Chadney had chosen to leave for him that day. On the chipped blue Willow pattern dinner plate that she had always used, he found two weighty carrots, three potatoes and a generous handful of green beans. Beneath the plate there was a flawlessly folded, crisp white collarless shirt.

It was not what he had expected. Not what he wanted. Not today.

Soldier bent to take the vegetables and pushed them into his coat pockets. He bent again, carefully moved the plate to the side of the step, and reached to pick up the shirt. He hesitated. It was too clean, too perfect. His hands fluttered uncertainly above it. He straightened and scratched feverishly at his beard.

How could he hurry to the clearing and carry it with him? Perfect. Clean.

He bent once more and tried to reach for the shirt. Again his fluttering hands stopped short.

It was no good. He couldn't take it. Not today. Soldier moved back from the step, turned and then went quickly around the cottage and along the garden path. Once through the gate, he clambered limping up the bank towards the narrow twisting track that led back to the clearing.

He took care not to look back.

But behind him he imagined the shirt being discovered abandoned on the step and a new ferocious, accusing twitch of the curtain.

## 44

# Baxter: 4.32 p.m.

### *He knew that the people in the cars must be looking at him*

There were a lot of things that worried Baxter. Things that were eating away at him like worms inside his tummy. Mostly they were questions about things that had happened and things that he didn't understand. But the first and most immediate worry, he understood only too well.

The first and the most urgent thing was that he felt sick, clammy and sick. And the more he worried about feeling sick, the sicker he felt. The car was going fast, lurching in and out of the bends, weaving and dodging erratically through the gaps between slower cars, riding the rolling camber of the road. However hard he tried, and he had tried very hard, Baxter knew that he couldn't stop the sick feeling growing inside him.

He was worried too about telling his father that he felt

sick, that he needed him to stop, soon, to pull over, now. His father was talking to himself, muttering something to himself, over and over, and sometimes he would punch at the steering wheel. Baxter pulled his eyes away from the pitching, wallowing road ahead and stole a sideways glance at him. A new thin trail of blood had started from the open cut on his father's cheek.

'I'm going to be sick,' he said quietly.

'*What?*' his father said.

'I'm going to be sick,' Baxter said, putting his hand to his mouth.

'*Jesus Christ!*' his father yelled, jerking the car off the road, mounting the grass verge in a cloud of dust, juddering to a halt.

Baxter pushed the door open, leaned out, vomited.

'*Get out, you stupid boy! Get the hell out!*' his father shouted.

Baxter climbed groggily from the car. He stood alone on the verge by the roadside, bent over, waiting for the sickness to overwhelm him again as passing cars whooshed by. He knew that the people in the cars must be looking at him, talking about him. He made himself retch again, anxious now that his father was waiting for him, impatient to be on the road. He retched and nothing came, there was just emptiness inside him, a sort of hollow feeling.

'I think I'm going to be all right now,' he told his father as he stepped carefully back into the car.

His father reached across him and slammed Baxter's door shut.

'Damn it, Baxter, if you feel sick again, you tell me,' his father said. 'I'm not having you throw up in here.'

Baxter felt ashamed; he felt that he had let his father down.

As his father manoeuvred the car away from the verge, Baxter wasn't sure why but suddenly he remembered about Soldier and about the bee and magic.

One day they had gone to a place where there were ferns that were so tall they came over Baxter's head even when he stood up, like big green umbrellas. It had been Baxter's idea to go inside because he was exploring and wanted to see whether he could make a camp.

Baxter went first, on his hands and knees. Soldier followed and because he was bigger and because of his bad leg it was quite difficult for him; but he crawled in after Baxter anyway. Inside it smelled like hay, heavy and warm and soft all at the same time, and the earth was black and crumbly. When they got to the middle there was an opening big enough that they could sit with the giant fronds of the ferns making a roof above them. But it wasn't quite a roof because there were gaps and you could see still the sky through it. It was the best camp ever.

Baxter had carried a plastic bag all the way and when he was crawling that had been quite difficult too. After they had been sitting for a while in the camp, he opened the bag and took out the jam sandwiches that his mother had made for him so that he could be an explorer and not have to go back for lunch. As he handed one of the sandwiches to Soldier, the jam ran down his fingers. He licked it away. Strawberry.

It was then that the bee came.

Baxter didn't want Soldier to know that he wasn't very

brave about bees. But he couldn't help it because it kept coming back, dive-bombing him, trying to get his sandwich or get to where his fingers were sticky. He tried to bat it away, swish it away with the plastic bag. But every time he swished at it, it just came back again, buzzing louder.

'Get it off me!' Baxter finally yelled.

And it was then that it had been like magic.

Because then Soldier reached out really fast with his hand like he was punching at something only he could see. And he caught the bee, snatched it from the air. One moment it was buzzing around, dive-bombing and everything, and the next it was in his hand. Then Soldier smiled a kind of smile and put his other hand on top of the bee hand and cupped them both together and the bee was still inside but it didn't buzz or sting or anything. And then Soldier did his smile again and brought his cupped hands up to his mouth and he blew softly into them. And then, when he opened his hands, the bee sort of looked at him for a second as if it was thinking about something, like it was a bit confused. And then it went slowly up in the air and just quietly flew away. Like it was sleepy or something. It went up and through the roof of the ferns where there was a gap. And it didn't come back. Not ever.

It *was* like magic.

And instead of feeling a bit ashamed that he hadn't been brave, Baxter had looked at Soldier and had felt as if he wanted to cry. Because of the magic. Because he was so happy.


They drove on in silence, his father taking the road more deliberately and glancing at Baxter distrustfully from time to time. Baxter stared straight ahead, feeling his father's eyes on him, feeling the worries start again like worms in his stomach.

Swaying nightmarishly into his mind came the man with the yellow broken teeth who had landed against the wall after his father had thrown him. Baxter's worry about *him* was that he might still be there, where he had been thrown, and that no one would find him and come to help him, that he would still be there when it got dark and night came. And at the same time he was worried too that someone *would* find him, but would only stand and point and laugh.

Like the boys on the slide. Had they seen him? Seen him curled up like a cat, asleep in the car? Did they come over and point and pull faces and laugh? He felt a new sense of shame creep tingling over him.

Baxter tried to concentrate only on the road ahead of him but as soon as he tried to stop his mind, to stop thinking about the things that had happened, he realised that he felt hungry, empty, hollowed out. He had only had the crisps and the lemonade. He couldn't ever remember having gone so long without anything to eat. That was quite a big worry now. That he felt hungry, thirsty, and sick. And whether he should say something about it.

And there was something else. When he was sure his father's eyes were on the road, Baxter felt gingerly for the upper part of first his left arm and then his right. His arms were tender and aching there, where his father had gripped him so tightly when he shook him and shouted about not saying anything. He was worried that when he had to take his shirt off to go to bed, his arms would be red and his mother would see them and perhaps be angry with him for upsetting his father or that she would ask him questions or something.

She might ask him about the house and he knew that he mustn't tell her, that he wasn't allowed to tell her. He couldn't say to her or to Megan that it was all empty, that everything had gone, as though it wasn't their house at all, as if they had never really been there. And what did it mean, it being empty like that? He didn't understand what it meant and he wanted to ask someone about that, he wanted someone to explain. He had asked the big man in the suit who had come to the house but his father had pulled him away before the man had the chance to say anything.

He was worried that he would dream about that man and he thought the man might come looking for him. What if that were true, what if he *did* come looking for him? Where would he hide? Where would they all hide? Him, Megan, his mother. In the tall grass? In the woods? Under the caravan? Yes, under the caravan where the suitcase was, that's where they would hide.

He was worried too that he had done something wrong and that was why they had singled him out, picked on him; why they had smashed his things and left them there on the floor in the house. And he wondered what it was that he could have done wrong. And he wondered too why a single soldier had fallen in the hall.

Baxter reached his hand inside his pocket, felt the broken soldier there. Safe.

So many different things had happened. Things that he didn't understand. Things like meeting the woman with the hair that was too big for her head, the one who couldn't walk very well, the one his father said that his mother had argued with a long time ago. The one who had reached inside the car and kissed him, leaving the smudge of lipstick.

And at that moment Baxter was worried most of all about that. About the lipstick smudged on his face.

# 45

# Strachan: 4.52 p.m.

## *Strachan heard his own mother's voice*

S trachan rattled at the letterbox, called her name.

All the doors to the flats, uniformly painted in an unwholesome bottle green, faced on to the gloomy concrete-covered walkway. Despite, or maybe because of, the perpetual half-light some of the residents had made an effort to make this space their own and had tried to disguise the stains where over the years rainwater had pooled and run on the concrete. There were small stone or terracotta planters with thin geraniums spindling towards the distant sunlight, there were neat rubber-backed HOME SWEET HOME doormats, and there were white plastic containers for milk bottles with black arrows pointing jauntily towards the number of pints to be delivered. But mostly there was just the gloom and a lingering smell of stale urine and bleach.

Further along the walkway a woman in a floral headscarf and apron stood on her doorstep with a cigarette in her hand. She watched Strachan as he reached again for the letterbox.

'Mrs Bird,' he called out.

He heard a muffled reply from inside.

'You'll have to shout louder,' the woman told him. 'She's a bit Mutt and Jeff . . . '

'*Mrs Bird, I've come to talk about your son*,' Strachan shouted.

There was a fumbling at the Yale lock; the door opened a crack, held by a chrome security chain. Lean on it and you'd be through in a moment, Strachan thought.

'Mrs Bird, I've come to talk to you about your son,' he said.

She peered up at him, small, frail and unsure.

'About Eric?' she said.

'About Truman,' Strachan corrected her.

'*Truman?*' she said, screwing her face up in puzzlement, in derision. 'I don't know no Truman.'

Strachan checked the number on the door.

'You are Mrs Bird?' he said.

She nodded.

'And you have a son? A son who lives in Brighton?'

'Yes,' she said, smiling now, condescendingly. 'But you've got his name wrong, dear. He's *Eric*; he's not this "Truman" you keep going on about. Do I look like a woman who would call any son of mine some poncey Yank name like Truman?'

Strachan couldn't help but smile; he saw his own mother standing there, chiding him.

'No, Mrs Bird, you most certainly do not,' he said respectfully.

'Well then,' she said, as if that settled it.

The woman on the doorstep further along the walkway cocked her head to one side, straining to hear every word.

'I was wondering, Mrs Bird,' Strachan said, trying again, more softly now, more confidentially. 'I was wondering whether you might have time for a bit of a chat about your boy. About *Eric*.'

She looked up at him uncertainly; said nothing.

'Over a cup of tea, perhaps?' Strachan said.

He was Ali Baba at the mouth of the cave; he had found the magic words.

'Oh, that would be lovely,' she said, closing the door just enough to free the security chain.

'He was here earlier today, Eric was,' she said, opening the door wide to invite Strachan in. 'But he didn't have time to stop long. He's always rush-rush-rush that boy.'

'Oh, that's a shame,' Strachan said. 'A son should always find time for his mother.'

Mrs Bird looked at him approvingly.

'Won't you come in, Mr ...?' she said.

'The name's Strachan. Just Strachan,' he replied.

'Won't you come in, Mr Strachan?'

'No, it's Strachan. Just Strachan,' he said as she led the way through her cramped hallway.

'What was that, dear?' Mrs Bird said, cupping a hand to her ear.

'No, nothing,' Strachan said, trailing behind her, suddenly feeling foolish, like a child again. 'It doesn't matter.'

The hall was like the walkway outside; it was gloomy and worn. The heavy dark-wood furniture wasn't at home there; it belonged to another time and an altogether grander house. The kitchen though was bright and welcoming.

'Have you lived here long, Mrs Bird?' Strachan said as she busied herself with the kettle at the sink.

'Too long,' she said, looking about her, scowling. 'If truth be told, it's not where I'd choose to be, Mr Strachan. There's some terrible types around here, you know.'

Strachan heard his own mother's voice, he could close his eyes and see her standing there, giving him what-for, setting the world to rights, telling him her troubles; 'Still, mustn't grumble,' she would always add.

'Still, mustn't grumble,' Mrs Bird said brightly, pouring the hot water into the brown teapot and covering it with a knitted cosy.

'It's not such a bad life, as long as you don't weaken,' she added.

'But your son,' Strachan said. 'You see him often, of course ...'

'Eric?' she said, nodding towards a silver-framed photograph on the sideboard.

There Truman was, a few years younger but unmistakably himself, the picture of innocence, the dutiful son smilingly watching over his mother. So what was it with this 'Eric' business?

'I see him once in a blue moon,' she said, unable to stop her voice betraying the bitterness. 'But he's so busy, you see ...'

'But you see his wife, of course?' Strachan said. 'You see the grandchildren? That must be nice for you. Three of them, aren't there?'

'Grandchildren? Hah!' she said, setting cups and saucers heavily on the table. 'I'm afraid you've got him confused with someone else, Mr Strachan,' she said. 'My Eric reckons he's not the marrying kind. Says he hasn't found the right girl yet. Too busy sowing his wild oats, if you ask me. Just like his father was before him.'

Not married? What was it with this joker? If it wasn't for the fact that there he was on the sideboard in black and white, as large as life and laughing at them, Strachan would have thought he had come to the wrong place.

Mrs Bird poured the tea into her best china cups and with a flourish added a dash of milk from the matching jug.

'Sugar?' she said to Strachan.

He shook his head.

'I'm sweet enough already,' he said as lightly as he could, although even then he couldn't help the edge of menace creeping back into his voice. He could hear it there himself and regretted it at once.

Mrs Bird looked up at him from her tea, a question suddenly in her eyes.

'How is it you know my Eric then?' she said.

'Oh, I don't really. I've only run into him the once,' he said, enjoying the truth of it. 'He's a friend of a friend of mine, you see. And my friend asked me to look him up, to have a quiet word with him about something.'

Mrs Bird glowed with delight.

'Oh, it's nice that my Eric has got friends. I've never met any of them before though ... Even when he was a boy, he never brought anyone home.'

'It's a lovely cuppa, Mrs Bird,' Strachan said, changing the subject.

'You've got to warm the pot, dear,' she said, accepting the compliment with a smile. 'That's the secret.'

'You don't know where I can get hold of Tru— of *Eric*, do you, Mrs Bird? Only my friend is quite anxious that I catch up with him soon.'

'As a matter of fact, I do,' she said proudly. 'He gave me his new address just this morning. He's staying at some pub or other at the moment – it's not that very far away from here and it's called ... Let me see ... Oh, yes, that's it: The Hare and Hounds.'

She handed Strachan the newspaper where Truman had written in the margin. Strachan took a biro from his jacket pocket and a slip of paper from his wallet and, with the pen sitting uneasily in his big hand, laboriously copied the address. He returned the newspaper to Mrs Bird.

'Are you from Scotland, Mr Strachan?' she said.

'You can still tell?' Strachan said. 'I thought the accent had gone, I've been down here so long.'

'I can hear it just a bit, dear,' she said. 'I like a Scots accent. Like that young Andy Stewart on the telly, the one in the kilt.'

She started to hum 'A Scottish Soldier' and then broke off with a girlish embarrassed laugh as she realised that Strachan was watching her.

'Do you mind if I ask you a personal question, Mr Strachan?' she said. 'Do you still have your mother, dear?'

The question hit Strachan like a blow from nowhere, a blow below the belt; it surprised him how much it hurt.

Remember why you're here, Strachan.

Find him; sort it.

No more of this talk. No more.

He flexed his shoulders, closed his eyes. And saw his mother standing on tiptoes in front of him.

It was no good. He would have to answer her.

'I'm afraid I lost her a very long time ago, Mrs Bird,' he said shakily, recovering himself just enough, realising that he had never spoken of it to anyone before. 'I was just a young man at the time. It was why I moved away, why I came down south.'

'Oh, I'm so sorry to hear that,' she said.

And Strachan could swear that her eyes filled as she said it, as if the loss were her own.

'It's been lovely chatting with you, Mrs Bird,' he said. 'But I guess I'd better be on my way.'

'It's been so nice meeting one of my Eric's friends, Mr Strachan.'

She led him back through the hallway to the front door.

'You know, he's a good boy really, my Eric,' she said proudly. 'Did I tell you he's taking care of all my money? He's invested it, he has. He says he's going to make me rich.'

Strachan could feel the anger surge inside him.

It was one thing to try to rip Mr Smith off; but to do *this*? To his own mother?

To lie to her, to lie about everything – about what he called himself, about his wife, about *her* grandchildren. And to take her money. How could he do that?

*The toerag.*

For just a moment, Strachan considered whether he should tell her the truth about Truman, about her precious son; but even as the thought went through his mind, he knew he couldn't do it. He couldn't be the one to break her heart. It would surely be broken soon enough without him.

*The fucking little toerag.*

Truman was going to pay for this.

First Sally.
*I'll find him for you.*
Now this.
Oh yes, Strachan would make sure he paid. And paid big.
He wouldn't know what had fucking hit him.

# 46

# Truman: 4.55 p.m.

*Just wear a big smile and treat
the truth like a stranger*

Truman turned the key in the ignition to silence the thrum and throb of the Wolseley's engine. He had pulled over into the dense shadow of a tall twisting oak tree at the beginning of the lane that led to the clearing; he needed a moment to collect himself, just to draw breath, just to get it all straight enough in his mind. He got out of the car, found a grassy patch of the roadside verge to perch on and reached into his jacket pocket for his cigarettes and lighter. Even in the shade of the tree, he could feel the day's heat wrapping itself stickily about him.

What a bastard of a day it had turned out to be.

He fished the blood-stained handkerchief from his pocket and dabbed charily at the cut on his cheek. The thin trickle of blood had stopped running but the cut was sore and open. The sharp stinging from the wound was matched by the low pulsing headache of earlier in the day which had returned to nag at him; he felt wrung out, spent, exhausted. He sat back against the raised knuckles of the tentacled roots of the oak tree and closed his eyes.

Come on, Truman old son, you can do this. You can *always* do this.

Take a deep breath, keep it simple and do what you always do. Just wear a big smile and treat the truth like a stranger.

Who was it had said that to him? His mother, of course, who else? *Don't treat the truth like a stranger.* That was it, that's what she had always said when he was growing up, wagging her finger at him when he stretched a story, embroidered it, made it work for him. What she didn't know, had never known, was that he couldn't have got through it otherwise. It was only being quick with those stories that many a time had kept him out of trouble with his father. They'd got him out of all sorts of scrapes at school too, hadn't they?

All that finger-wagging, couldn't have had it more wrong, could she?

Wear a big smile and *make sure* that you treat the truth like a stranger: that was the Truman Bird way. It had served him well enough, had always worked for him before, hadn't it? It had certainly always worked with Christie for all these years. Had her eating out of his hand.

She'd want to know why he hadn't brought the stuff she'd asked for from the house, of course. Well the boy got sick, didn't he? Too many ice creams, probably. Or maybe it was the candyfloss or the ride on the carousel by the pier or perhaps it was the go on the bumper cars. And that was how Truman had ended up with the cut on his face, wasn't it? Walked into the open car door when the boy was feeling a bit poorly. Rushing round to help the boy, he was, not thinking of anything else and like a dope he went smack into the door. No, it wasn't the boy's fault. You couldn't blame the kid for getting sick, could you? Yes, it hurt like buggery when he did it but it wasn't too bad now; he'd live. His own fault. Daft bugger. No need to worry about it though, Christie. It'll be OK, honestly princess. It'll soon heal up. Yes, maybe it will leave a bit of a scar. But it'll be OK. Honestly.

Simple.

You've got to make what you've got, what you've been handed, work for you, see? Strachan had planted one on him, had given him the cut and now, bingo, the cut would get him off the hook with Christie.

And the boy wouldn't dare say anything different. Truman had taken care of that, put the fear of God in him. And even if the boy did say something, then so what? Who was she going to believe? Was she going to take the boy's word over his? Not likely, was it?

With his eyes still closed, Truman could feel Christie's cool, tender touch as she bathed his face, dressed his wound, tutted and fussed over him. For a moment, he wanted no woman but her. He could feel her in his arms, feel her body pressed against him, pressed into him.

He shook the thought away; he needed to focus.

The trickier stuff could wait. It could wait for another day. She'd be so busy fretting over the cut that she wouldn't ask about anything else, not today. Later, he'd figure out a story about why they couldn't ever go back to the house and what had happened to their things. A fire? A break-in? Something like that.

Simple.

And as long as he steered well clear of Brighton, kept out of that Strachan's way, he was home free. Then what? Then he would run The Hare and Hounds with Doll and they would have a rare old time of it. Once the summer was over, he would find a cottage in the woods somewhere far enough away for Christie and kids. And then sometimes he'd be with Doll and sometimes with Christie. Not too dusty, was it?

That was it. He'd got it straight now. Sorted.

Truman opened his eyes and the smile returned to his face.

After all, you *had* to smile, didn't you? Because there always was an answer, if you put your mind to it, if you thought about it enough. It was all about staying one step ahead. And it was about making sure that when life knocked you down, you bounced right back up waving a two-fingered salute and laughing in its face. It was about using your head, see, looking for the angles, *working* the angles, finding a way round, finding a way through. There always was a way and that was what people didn't get, the mugs; that was what they didn't understand. And when you did find that way through, it suddenly didn't seem such a bad life after all. So you had no choice *but* to smile.

Truman ground his cigarette out on the tree root, flicked the stub to send it spiralling into the hedgerow beyond the oak, stood up and slapped at the seat of his trousers to beat the dust of the verge away.

The pain in his head had eased. He climbed back into the car, sliding behind the steering wheel across the leather seat, and turned the key in the ignition.

'All right, sport?' he said to Baxter.

# 47

# Soldier: 5.18 p.m.

## *Soldier could hear it for himself now*

They must have heard the car approaching before Soldier did.

Watching drowsy-eyed from his place at the edge of the wood, lulled once more to the brink of sleep by the sultry torpid warmth, he snapped awake when he saw the girl sit suddenly upright in the grass; when he saw her mother, saw *her* tense and get quickly to her feet, glance to the carry-cot to check on the sleeping child, smooth her dress; saw her hands go involuntarily to touch her hair, to confirm the perfect curl of it.

She beckoned urgently to her daughter, with both hands palm upwards. The girl dropped her book and ran lightly to her. She stooped to flick the girl's fringe from her eyes and to straighten her wayward ponytail. The girl looked up at her, asking her silent questions.

Is it him? Will everything be all right?

And the mother smiled and bent towards her once more to kiss her on the forehead. For just a moment she held the child to her with a promise.

Everything's OK; everything will be fine.

Soldier could hear it for himself now, the crunch and spit of the tyres on the stony road. He could see it, the flurry of dust rising from between the trees in the near distance. He was coming. It was time.

He struggled to his feet, cursing the pain shooting from his knee. As the car at last emerged, trailing a low billowing cloud of dust behind it, mother and daughter turned to face the track.

Soldier held his breath, felt the thump of his heart.

# 48

# Christie: 5.19 p.m.

### *Her body ached; she wanted to go to him, her son*

The car had left that morning with an angry slamming of doors, a throttled roar of its engine, a vicious squeal of tyres and brakes, and in an almost impenetrable fog of kicked-up dust. In contrast now its return along the lane was sedate, almost stately.

There was something in this contrast that unsettled Christie; something disquieting, almost menacing that made her pull Megan even closer to her. The car moved towards them along the lane so slowly, so calmly that its progress somehow taunted her, mocked her new resolve.

Megan looked up at her mother once more for reassurance and Christie, her eyes never leaving the road, replied with a gentle squeeze of the girl's shoulder.

Everything's OK; everything will be fine.

As the car neared, her eyes strained to seek Baxter out. She could see him now, could make out his shape, small and low in the front seat, but could not see his face. One look at his face, one look into his eyes, and she would know how he was, what his day had been. Her body ached; she wanted to go to him, her son, to run to the car, pull open the door, sweep him up in her arms, hold him, rock him, her baby. But some new uncertainty, some new hesitation, held her back, rooted her.

The car finally emerged into the sunlight from the shadow of the trees and reached the grassy edge of the clearing. It was crawling so slowly towards them now that the trail of dust behind had reduced to just a low powdery swirl from the back tyres.

The car rocked gently to a standstill. She could see Truman quite clearly, or could at least see his head turn to say something to the boy. She felt the knot of anxiety tighten in her stomach.

# 49

# Truman: 5.21 p.m.

### *He put his hand on Baxter's shoulder to propel him forwards*

'Remember what I told you, sport?' Truman said.

The boy said nothing. He just stared straight ahead towards where his mother and sister were standing side by side near the caravan. The sun was low enough in the sky now to cast lengthening shadows and Baxter was squinting into the dazzle of it to try to make out their faces.

Truman turned to him, irritated by the boy's silence. As he did so, he suddenly saw him, as if for the first time that day.

'What on *earth* ... ?' he said.

How come he hadn't noticed before?

What on earth did the boy look like? How the hell did he get in that state? He looked as if he'd dragged himself through the proverbial backwards and then bloody forwards again for good measure, the little sod. His clothes hung on him like crumpled rags; his hair stood up in short ugly tufts;

his face was ghostly white, and that made the scarlet smudges of lipstick on his cheek and forehead stand out even more; his eyes were red and puffy. How was Truman going to explain all this to Christie? *Damn it!* As if he didn't have enough to worry about? OK, the boy had slept a bit in the car, hadn't he? And, of course, and as usual, he'd thrown up beside the road. But even so, he must have worked pretty bloody hard to get into that state, mustn't he? It was right what they said, wasn't it? You couldn't turn your back on them for a moment. The little sods.

But stay cool, Truman, old son. Stay cool.

No point in getting wound up, was there? There was nothing to be done about it now. And anyway, it was hardly *his* fault. He couldn't be held responsible, could he?

'Remember what I said?' Truman said, more harshly.

Baxter nodded.

Truman twisted the rear-view mirror towards himself for a final time. He practised his smile; he took his comb from his pocket and ran it through his hair; he straightened his tie. He couldn't resist gently prodding at the wound on his face; he winced as he did so, sucked at the air.

He stepped out of the car, closed the door behind him and, with the wide smile now fixed on his face, he took a few jaunty steps towards Christie and Megan.

It took him those few steps to realise that the boy wasn't with him; he was still sitting sullenly in the car.

The smile falling instantly away, Truman walked back to the Wolseley, grabbed at the handle and pulled open the passenger door.

'For Christ's sake, Baxter ...' he said.

He made as if to pull him from the car but there was

something in the way the boy was sitting, the way he wouldn't look at him, the way he was trying to make himself so small, that suddenly made Truman's heart lurch. It was as if he knew how the boy felt, *remembered* how he felt from when he was a nipper himself. From whenever his own dad gave him a hard time.

But this was no time to be going soft, was it? He didn't have time for any of that now. He pushed the thought away from him. It had taken him by surprise, that was all.

'Just get a bloody move on, will you?' he said. 'I haven't got all day.'

Without meeting his father's eye, Baxter slowly slid to his feet from the leather seat. Truman pulled him away from the car and then pushed the door firmly closed behind. He put his hand on Baxter's shoulder to propel him forwards and side by side they slowly began to make their way over the flattened grass that led across the clearing to the caravan.

The smile was back on Truman's face and when he was sure that Megan would be able to see him clearly enough, he let go of Baxter, went down on one knee, spread his arms wide, and invited her to run to him as she had that morning.

Megan didn't move; she just inched closer to her mother's legs.

It was Baxter who ran.

It was Baxter who ran, ran like the wind, ran like a hare.

It was Baxter who ran past the caravan and went crashing through the long grass towards the forest beyond.

# 50

# Soldier: 5.23 p.m.

## *As the small boy ran, Soldier clung to the trunk of a great oak*

As the small boy ran, zigzagging erratically along faint trails through the long grass; as he ran past his mother, past his sister and on towards the darkness of the woods; as he stumbled and fell, stumbled and fell again and then picked himself up once more and ran; as he looked back over his shoulder to see if he was being followed and bent double to catch his breath and to clutch at the sudden stitch-like pain in his side; as the small boy ran, Soldier clung to the trunk of a great oak, looked down across the clearing and watched and urged him onwards.

Run, Baxter, run!

Throw your head back and run like the rushing wind. Run like the hare pursued. Run like there's no tomorrow. As if the hounds of hell are on your tail, snapping at your heels. Grow wings on your feet and run, Baxter. Run! Run like the messenger. Run like the spirits. Run like a demon. Run like fury. Like fire. Run through the tall grass whipping at your legs.

Run!

Run to the forest, where the tree roots writhe like serpents, where the nettles sting, where the brambles claw. Run until your lungs burst, until your head swims, until your chest heaves. Run, boy, run! Until you can run no more.

Run, Baxter, run.

Run to the forest.

*Run to me ...*

Soldier had never felt so desperate. So exhilarated. So proud.

# 51

# Baxter: 5.25 p.m.

### *He didn't want to cry, so he ran*

Baxter didn't know exactly what it was that had made him run. But once he started, he knew he couldn't stop.

It wasn't anything that he had planned, or even thought about. It wasn't that he had sat in the car thinking that he would run away or anything like that. He wasn't even sure now that he *was* running away. It was just that one minute he was there slowly walking next to his father and then the next minute his legs had taken him off. Only it wasn't his legs, not really. It was more about something to do with crying, or rather something to do with *not* crying. It was because his body somehow told him that if he didn't run, he would cry. And he didn't want to cry, so he ran.

It was something like that anyway.

Baxter stopped, bent over. He had a pain in his side, a stitch, he was hot and he felt a bit sick again. As he bent he could see that his shoes were scuffed and his knees were grass-stained and grazed from where he had tripped and fallen, not once but twice. It was very difficult to run through the long grass. He looked back to where his mother and Megan were standing and to where he had left his father. He saw that his father hadn't moved. No one had moved. His mother had her hand up shielding her eyes: he thought he heard her call his name. He set off again. He was going more slowly, but he was still running.

It wasn't anything that had happened during the day that had made him want to cry. Not really. It wasn't the lipstick or because he had to hide from the boys on the slide or from the man with the broken teeth and the bottle. It wasn't going to the house and seeing his things broken and nothing else there or seeing that big man who was angry with his father. It wasn't even because his father had stopped the car and had shaken him and shouted or because he had been sick by the road and people had seen.

It wasn't any of those things.

What made him want to cry was when his father went down on one knee and beckoned to Megan to come to him.

That's what made tears start to come.

Because his father had never gone down on one knee to ask him to run. His father had never scooped him up in his arms and twirled him around and held him like he did with Megan. Not that he could remember anyway.

Baxter felt ashamed because it wasn't Megan's fault. It wasn't her fault that she was the favourite. And he felt ashamed too in another way he couldn't explain properly; he felt ashamed that despite all the bad things that had happened, despite the way his father had been with him, shaking him and shouting and everything, he still wanted him to pick him up and twirl him.

He stopped again. The woods were getting closer. He looked back for a final time. Still no one had moved. He knew they were all watching him and he felt ashamed at that too, that he had made them watch him.

And it wasn't that he had really thought of running to Soldier. It was only when he started to run that he thought that was where he would go, that was where he would have to go. Not because he wanted to especially, but because there was nowhere else.

He wasn't even exactly sure that he liked Soldier very much all the time. He looked funny and he didn't remember anything, not even his name, and that was very peculiar. He was very tall and thin and his clothes didn't fit and he cried quite a lot and his hair and beard were long and grey and wild. He didn't smell very nice either and he talked to himself. No, that wasn't right; he didn't exactly talk to himself. He talked to things around him, to the woods, to the trees, sometimes to the things that lived in the trees. He would see a squirrel climbing or hear a bird singing or a woodpecker tapping and he would talk away to it for ages. Only it wasn't exactly talking; it was more like muttering or mumbling. Like you weren't supposed to do in school.

And he had a limp. But that wasn't his fault.

And he thought he had a dog. But he didn't.

But it wasn't that he *dis*liked him either. He had been a soldier in the war and that was good, just knowing that. And they could sit together on his wall and they didn't have to say

263

anything and sometimes that was the very best thing ever, not having to say anything. And other times he would listen as Baxter talked on and on about all sorts of things and that was good too, having someone to listen. And he could do magic with bees and he had a really excellent camp. A secret camp built into the bank beside the stream and camouflaged so that you wouldn't even know it was there.

Baxter plunged into the woods. After the sunlight of the clearing, it was suddenly dark. The brambles clawed at him as he ran along the trail, his feet slapping and thumping on the dry hollow-sounding ground. The tree roots, twisting like snakes, jumped out at him. A crow cawed a guttural greeting and flapped darkly away deeper into the forest.

But Baxter wasn't afraid.

Suddenly he wanted nothing more than to just sit on a wall. To sit there and not have to say anything.

# 52

# Christie: 5.27 p.m.

## *Perhaps they had found each other on the dodgems*

It was only when Baxter disappeared into the woods that Christie found that she could move again. Until then she had called to him, over and over and with increasing desperation, but had found her feet firmly rooted to the spot. When she finally pulled her eyes away from the path that Baxter had taken into the woods, she discovered that none of them had moved. She, Megan and Truman were exactly where they were when Baxter had shocked them into this strange paralysis by taking flight. Ridiculously, Truman was still on one knee like some thwarted suitor; his arms were no longer outstretched, the smile had vanished. As Christie looked towards him, he climbed slowly to his feet and reached into his jacket pocket for his cigarettes.

'Let him go, Christie,' he called to her, hunched over,

lighting his cigarette, sending a thin trail of smoke sky-wards.

*Let him go?* But he'd gone already. Her boy had fled like a bewildered fawn through the tall grass and vanished into those dark forbidding woods. *Let him go?*

'But what . . . ?' she said, anxiously, struggling to make sense of it, her hands towards Truman, raised in a question.

'Don't worry about it, princess,' Truman said, walking towards her now, the smile beginning to return.

'He'll be fine,' he said. 'He's just had a bit of a day of it, that's all.'

'A bit of a day?' Christie said, apprehensively.

'Car-sick,' Truman said. 'Ice cream, candyfloss, dodgems, car-sick. You know what he's like.'

They were less than a yard apart now; Megan came close to Christie again, pressed her body fiercely against her.

'What's happened to your face?' Christie said softly, seeing the cut, reaching out despite herself to brush it with her fin-gertips.

Truman flinched, pulled his head away.

'It's nothing,' he said. 'Just an accident.'

'But how . . . ?' Christie said, reaching out gingerly towards it again.

'Walked into the car door when the boy was throwing up,' Truman said, pulling away from her touch, but more slowly, almost playfully, this time. 'My fault. I was just trying to get to him to help him. Stupid.'

'Oh, Truman . . .' Christie said, and there was real ten-derness in her voice.

*Father and son.*

'And you went on the dodgems?' she said with wonder.

'Yeah, well, you know ...' Truman said, looking down, looking away, affecting embarrassment.

*Just boys together.*


What had happened that morning wasn't forgotten, wasn't forgiven. How could it be? How could it ever be? But perhaps somehow in some unlikely way everything had turned out for the best after all. Perhaps at some unsuspecting moment during the day, when the anger had abated, a father had found his son and a son had found his father. Perhaps they had found each other on the dodgems, in a joyous laughter-filled head-on collision.

Was that too naïve? Was that too much a dream, a fairy tale, too much to hope for?

A spluttering cry from the carry-cot announced that the baby was awake. Christie went to him, picked him up, rocked him, hushed him. As she did so, Truman bent down again to Megan, cocked his head to one side in a comic apology, matched her growing smile with a lopsided one of his own, and wrapped her in his arms. The girl snuggled into him.

This was all so much better than Christie had hoped for, better than she had dared to hope. This was her moment; there would never be a better one.

'Truman ... ?' she said.

'Yes, princess?' he said, swaying Megan gently from side to side.

'We need to talk ...'

'What about, babe?' he said, tickling at Megan's waist, making her giggle, making her try to push his hand away, making her squirm.

267

'About us ... ' Christie said.

'Us?' Truman said, giggling along with Megan.

'About home,' Christie said.

Truman pulled Megan to him, drew deeply on his cigarette.

'Home?' he said, suspiciously.

'About *going* home,' she said, quietly, determinedly. 'Going home, tomorrow.'

'*Tomorrow?*' he said. 'I don't understand.'

'We need to go home, Truman,' she said; plaintively now, she couldn't help herself. 'I don't know why we can't just go home.'

'You want to go home? You want to leave all this?' he said, looking towards the caravan, the clearing, the woods beyond.

He saw something there that Christie didn't see. That was it; that must be it, or at least part of it. He didn't understand what it was like being there, living there, how tired she was, how worn down she was by it. He didn't understand.

'After I've *paid* for all this for you and the kids?' he said. 'Working day and night ... '

'It's time,' Christie said.

Truman let go of Megan and got to his feet.

'OK, princess,' he said, a note of bitterness suddenly in his voice. 'We'll have to talk about it.'

'Now?' Christie said, suddenly uncertain.

'Later, when we're alone,' he said, dropping the stub of his cigarette, grinding it into the grass with the sole of his shoe.

'Later?' Christie said.

'*Later,*' Truman said firmly, conclusively. 'Because first I'm going into those woods to try to find that bloody boy of yours.'

Christie watched him as he strode off, following the same trail that Baxter had taken. She watched him as he walked, hands thrust into his trouser pockets, and as he made his way to the opening into the woods. She saw him pause and reach for his cigarettes again.

She hoped that he might turn and wave to her and Megan before he stepped into the darkness of the trees.

He didn't.

## 53

# Strachan: 5.54 p.m.

## *They came roaring at him, charging at him*

Strachan felt good, being back behind the wheel again. Before today, before the drive to Crawley and now the short journey across country to The Hare and Hounds, it had been a long while. There had been a time, of course, when he would have been out and about taking care of different bits of business several times a week. In the years just after the war, as Mr Smith's interests had begun to expand still further, as he had begun to dip his fingers into other people's pies along the coast, Strachan had got to know every twist and turn and every hill and hollow of the road from as far west as Southampton to as far east as Hastings.

Those were the days, the best days. People knew who he was back then, people who mattered; there were no pimply leather-jacketed jokers blowing kisses at him from a jukebox back then. They wouldn't have fucking dared.

There was one time, and some people still talked about it

all these years after, when Mr Smith had asked him to pop over and have a friendly word with the owner of a rival nightclub, to smooth things out between them.

As he drove now, following the road that snaked through the forest towards The Hare and Hounds, Strachan smiled as the memory of it played through his mind as it had done a hundred times before.

In Portsmouth, it was. Not far from the docks. Mr Smith had only recently opened this swanky new place there and, like everything that Mr Smith touched, it looked as though it was going to be a proper little goldmine. Mr Smith could do glamour, he could do glitz, and in those ration-book make-do-and-mend years, when times were still tough, that was just what people wanted. Anyway, the owner of this other club had been threatening to cut up a bit rough, had started to put the pressure on, claiming he was losing business to Mr Smith's new place. So Strachan set off to pay him a visit, to have a 'friendly chat'. He went there alone, of course. Only ever worked alone. Best that way. He got to this club, run-down place it was, sticky lino, peeling paint, that sort of thing, and in he walked, on his own, as casual as you like but as watchful as a cat. What greeted him there wasn't anyone in the mood for a chat. Standing at the bar was the slimy toerag who owned the club and four of his muscle, the ones who usually worked the door at night. Dressed for duty they were, dinner jackets, frilly white shirts, bow-ties, knuckles, the lot.

Hello, Strachan thought, time to play.

They didn't even let him open his mouth to say his piece.

As soon as he came through the door they just went at him. One of them with a baseball bat. So what did Strachan do? He didn't just cut and run like anyone else would. No, Strachan took them on. He grabbed the bat as it was swung at him by this big fat ugly bastard with a broken nose and a moustache. He wrenched it from him and then, with two swings of it, he laid out the ugly bastard and one of his friends. Laid them clean out, he did; they went down like dead men, went down like Jersey Joe Walcott to Rocky Marciano. The other two heavies were a bit more wary after that and the slimeball owner started backing away to the door. The heavies circled Strachan as he stood there with the bat raised and a smile on his face, like Babe Ruth eyeing up another home run. In the end they came roaring at him, charging at him, both together, two bulls rushing a gate, and all hell broke loose. There was blood and guts everywhere and, in truth, at the end of it some of the blood and a couple of broken teeth belonged to Strachan. But when it was done it was Strachan who walked out of the club – or rather it was Strachan who staggered back to his car, fumbled to turn the key in the ignition and then just about managed to drive back to Brighton. And it was the four heavies who were left slumped unconscious amongst the broken glass, the smashed chairs, the upended tables, the swill of blood and cheap whisky. As for the club owner, he was nowhere to be seen and the word was that after that he never showed his face in Portsmouth again.

That was the very best of the best of days. After that he was cock of the walk.

And it got better.

A week later he had a visit from two of Ronnie and

Reggie's people. They brought a message from the twins; they'd heard about what had happened in Portsmouth and wanted Strachan to move up to the Smoke and join their crew. Strachan, his left eye swollen and closed, stitches still holding his right ear in place, the bruising to his ribs still making it painful to take even the shallowest of breaths, had managed to smile. The Krays; there was no higher accolade. He told them he was flattered, told them that he would think about it, he shook their hands.

But he never went, of course. His loyalty to Mr Smith would never have allowed it.

Strachan had kept the baseball bat, originally as a memento of that day. But there had been plenty of times when it had come into its own in the years that had followed. He started to take it with him on certain jobs and always it felt good in his hand; somehow it made him feel like the man he was, like the man he had become. It made him feel untouchable, invincible. Over the years it had opened a few more heads, rearranged a few more jaws, loosened a few more teeth, it had spilled blood; but mostly when some would-be hard-case saw the bat in his hand they would remember the story of that day in Portsmouth and they would just back down, back away.

The legend of that bat became part of the legend that was Strachan.

Long ago. Too long ago.

Many had been the times in recent years when Strachan had snapped to, catching himself daydreaming in the chair by the bedsit window; he had been lost in the past, remembering how it had all been, and the bat was on his lap and he was stroking it like a cat.

He'd brought it along for the ride today, for old times' sake. It was on the passenger seat next to him.

Ahead of him, on a steep bend in the road, Strachan could see an ivy-clad pub. The sign that hung in front of it showed a large hare standing on its hind legs and a pack of baying dogs beyond.

And now Mr Smith had turned elsewhere, or so people said. He'd turned to someone younger, fitter, stronger. Prettier, people said. Despite himself, Strachan had to smile. Prettier wouldn't be difficult.

Strachan pulled into the pub car park and silenced the engine. There were no other cars there and he had parked in the shade of a sprawling oak tree; despite the lateness of the afternoon hour and the clouds gathering above, it was still stiflingly hot. For a moment he sat there, his mind dwelling on what had gone before, finding it hard to turn to what would come next. For that moment he felt every one of his fifty-one years.

What was he about? At his age, still chasing around the countryside after some loser like this Truman? Perhaps Mr Smith was right. Perhaps it *was* work for a younger man.

He held out his hands in front of him and watched the slight tremor. He couldn't concentrate hard enough to make it stop.

Fuck it.

Strachan heaved himself out of the car; in his familiar ritual, he smoothed the creases away from his jacket, he tugged at his shirt cuffs, he adjusted his tie. Always spick, always span. Always.

He walked over to the latticed window and peered through a gap in the curtains into the lounge bar. Nothing. The pub was empty, abandoned after the lunchtime rush, not yet made ready for the evening session. He checked his watch; another thirty-five minutes until opening time. He wasn't going to wait around that long. He stepped back from the building to see whether there were signs of life at the windows above.

He went to the door and hammered on it with his fist. Nothing.

He pounded at it again; the dark-varnished oak door rattled on its wrought-iron hinges.

'Hey!' came a voice from above, an irritated woman's voice. 'What's all the bloody racket down there?' she shouted. 'Can't you see we're shut?'

Strachan backed away from the doorway, looked up, shielding his eyes from the sun. At the open window, leaning forwards top-heavily, peering down short-sightedly, was a woman with blonde hair piled high and a string of large red beads at her plunging neckline.

She had to be the landlady, Strachan thought, catching a heavy waft of her musky perfume. Dolled up that way, she couldn't be anyone else.

'I'm looking for someone,' he called up to her.

'Well, whoever it is, sweetheart, they're not here,' she said.

'I'm looking for Eric,' Strachan shouted, squinting up into the sun.

'Eric? There's no Erics here. I don't even know any Erics,' she said, making to close the window, signalling the end of the conversation.

'Wait,' Strachan corrected himself. 'I'm looking for Truman ... Truman Bird.'

The woman opened the window fully and leaned forwards again.

'Truman?' she said.

Strachan nodded.

'*My* Truman?'

*Her* Truman? This guy beggared belief; a wife and three kids somewhere, Sally at The Salvation, and now this.

Strachan nodded again.

'Well, why didn't you say so?' she said. 'Hang on and I'll be right down.'

As he waited for her to make her way downstairs, Strachan remained exactly where he was, head tilted upwards, face towards the sun. He closed his eyes, letting the warmth wash over him, feeling it creep into him. It had been quite a day. It took the clatter of the door's great iron bolts being released to jerk him back to the moment.

'Come in, sweetheart, come in,' she said, swinging the door back, beckoning him in out of the light.

As she held the door open for him, Strachan could see her clearly for the first time; she was quite a woman, one glance told you that, one glance would tell anyone that. Not like Sally, of course; a few years older, the curves a bit fuller, the make-up heavier, but quite something. This Truman, this Eric, he could certainly pick them.

'Now then,' she said, closing the door and turning to him with a smile. 'My name's Doll. How can I help you, sweetheart?'

'I'm looking for Truman,' Strachan said again.

'Friend of his, are you?' she said.

'Friend of a friend,' Strachan said. 'He asked me to look him up.'

'And you are . . . ?' Doll said.

'I'm Strachan,' he said. 'Just Strachan.'

'Well, Strachan,' Doll said, getting it immediately, 'I'm afraid Truman's not here right now. He's gone down to the coast today, on some business or other. He'll be back some time this evening though. You're welcome to wait, if you want.'

She started to make her way busily around behind the bar, quickly wiping it down, squaring up the beer mats and towels. By the practised, automatic way she went about it, Strachan could see that she had done it countless times before. He could tell from the way she moved that she knew he was watching her; he could see she was used to that too, liked it, being watched.

'And you and him are . . . ?' Strachan said.

'Me and him, sweetheart, are none of your business,' Doll said, with a smile meant to tell Strachan everything, a smile that said she had a secret to share, that Truman was hers and that she was possessive and proud.

'You got business with him, have you?' she said.

'Business?' Strachan said.

'Business,' she said. 'With my Truman.'

*My Truman*. Strachan studied her for a moment; how could a woman like her be taken in by this scum? Like Sally, like his own mother.

'Business,' he said, hearing it in his voice once more, the deadpan threat. 'Yes, you could say that.'

Doll was walking busily behind the bar, her high heels clipping lightly on the stone floor, both hands full, fingers wrapped around the clutch of handles of empty dimpled beer mugs she had collected from the draining board. She heard it too, in his voice, the menace, the threat. She put the glasses on the counter.

'What sort of business?' she said suspiciously.

'Oh, the usual sort,' he said. 'Money business.'

'Oh yes?' she said.

'He owes my friend,' he said. 'He owes him big.'

Strachan could see the disappointment in her; Truman was not quite the man she had imagined. He could see the small drop and droop of her shoulders, the slight bow of her head. He could see that his words had taken something from her, some of the wind from her sails. She leaned back against the bar.

'How much?' Doll said.

He could see her bracing herself for the worst.

'Five,' he said.

'Five *hundred*?' she said, the shock there in the upwards flick of her eyes.

'Five *thousand*,' Strachan said with heavy emphasis.

He could see her flinch, see her fighting for her usual composure. She was a class act, this Doll.

'*Five . . . thousand*?' she asked, needing the confirmation.

Strachan nodded.

'Here,' Doll said, suddenly seeing it all, recognising Strachan for what he was, realising why he was there, 'there's not going to be any trouble, is there?'

'No trouble,' Strachan said.

No trouble at all.

'You known him long, have you?' he said.

'About six weeks, that's all,' Doll said, her voice trailing away. 'I didn't know he was in any bother.'

No bother.

'So it's just him staying here, is it?' he said.

'Of course,' she said. 'Who else would it be?'

Strachan wondered whether his words would have the same effect on her as they had on Sally earlier in the day. He calculated they would.

'I thought his wife might be with him, perhaps?'

Doll looked at him, her eyes flashing.

'He's not married, sweetheart.' Her voice a spiced cocktail of defiance and doubt. 'I don't have anything to do with married men. Never have.'

Strachan met her eye.

'Married,' he said.

Doll shook her head, still not prepared to accept it.

'Married,' he said again. 'Three kids.'

She accepted it now, in the defeated weary slump of her body.

The fucking toerag.

'One of these kids . . .' she said. 'Is he a little scrap of a thing, fair-haired, pale like a ghost, big blue eyes?'

Strachan nodded.

'The lousy no-good bastard,' she said. 'He told me that was his nephew.'

'He told you what?' Strachan said, not understanding.

'Nothing,' Doll said. 'It doesn't matter. But I think I know where you'll find the family.'

'Where's that?' Strachan said.

'At a place called Tabell Ghyll. Back down the road a mile or so, there's a track off to the right, follow it through the forest down to a clearing, there should be a caravan there . . .'

Her voice faded to nothing and she stood now with her back against the bar, her eyes closed. Strachan sensed there would be no tears, not now, certainly not in front of him. If there were to be tears, they would come later, come alone, perhaps in the empty sleepless hours, in the lonely void before dawn. Now there would be anger; he could see it in the set of her face.

'I don't suppose he's left anything here? Any cash?' Strachan said.

'I lent him fifty this morning,' Doll said, her voice small.

'That's the last you'll see of that, I'm afraid,' Strachan said. 'He's even robbed his own mother.'

She closed her eyes again, absorbing this latest blow.

'Follow me,' she finally said with a new determination in her voice.

Doll set off, stilettos clacking on the flagstones. She led the way to the back of the bar, through a door marked PRIVATE, up a narrow staircase that creaked under Strachan's weight, across a beamed and crooked landing and into the bedroom. The smell of her perfume hung in the air.

'Get it down,' she barked at Strachan, pointing to a small brown leather suitcase on top of a wardrobe.

Strachan reached up, brought the suitcase down and dutifully placed it on the bed.

He then backed into the doorway and stood and watched as she flung open the doors of the wardrobe, yanked shirts, a jacket and trousers from their hangers and threw them in a chaotic heap on to the bed. He watched as she went to a chest at the foot of the bed, pulled out a drawer and emptied socks and underwear on to the pile. And he watched as she opened the top drawer of the chest and took out a large pair of scissors – the kind of gleaming razor-sharp shears that his mother had used for dressmaking so long ago.

In a controlled frenzy of rage, Doll then set about the pile of clothes. She cursed, chopped, sliced and scythed at them. She swore and tore at the shirts; she cut and then hacked at the back of the jacket; with the flashing blades of the shears she slashed at the trousers. In a few tumultuous, exultant minutes she reduced them all to rags. She threw the scissors down on the bed, gathered up the rags and crammed them into the suitcase. Breathing hard, she rammed the lid down and forced the locks closed.

She looked up at Strachan, her eyes gleaming and triumphant now.

He was right; she was a class act.

'Take that to him,' she said, pointing at the suitcase.

She snatched up the scissors from the bed, brandished them.

'And tell him from me . . .'

Strachan picked up the suitcase and smiled, enjoying the moment.

'What shall I tell him, Doll?' he said.

'Tell him,' she spat, holding the shears in front of her, rapidly opening and closing the blades, snipping away like a gardener attacking a nettle patch, 'tell him that if I ever set my eyes on him again, I swear I'll cut his fucking balls off!'

Strachan winced. Any man would have done.

He turned and made his way back down the narrow stairway, suitcase in hand. The screech from above made him flinch again.

'*I'll cut his fucking balls off and feed them to the cat!*'

## 54

# Truman: 6.05 p.m.

*He had that to thank him for, the little sod*

Truman had found the trunk of a fallen tree on which to sit, to put his feet up and rest. And like it was meant, as if it was there waiting for him all along, he had found it no more than twenty-five yards from the entrance to the woods. It was perfect. It was close to the path, close enough to the clearing and yet was hidden from view by a dense tangle of brambles and a tall, gently swaying stand of feathery ferns; Christie and Megan weren't able to see him from the caravan and, although he in turn couldn't see them, he would certainly hear them coming if they decided to follow him into the forest on Baxter's trail. The trunk of the tree had been worn smooth and had been silvered by the seasons and it had the slightest hint of an indentation that formed an ideal contoured seat. Better still, Truman found he could lean back and there, at just the right spot, at just the right angle, was the stump of a bough that supported his back and allowed him to put his feet up, crossed at the ankles. In easy reach, a hollowed knot on the trunk served as an ashtray. Dappled sunlight played through the overhanging branches of a neighbouring beech tree.

Truman closed his eyes and breathed in the warmth.

Well, there was no point in breaking your neck, was there? No point chasing about in the woods like something demented looking for the idiot boy. In any case, it would be looking for a needle in the proverbial: the boy could be anywhere out there. And if he didn't want to be found, if he wanted to go off like that, playing silly buggers hiding in the woods, that was up to him. That was his lookout. Anyway, chances were that he had already found his tearful way back to the caravan, back to his mother's loving arms. Chances were that he had scared himself half to death among these twisting overgrown paths and had headed back, tail between his legs.

The way it worked was like this. If it turned out that he *had* gone back, it was obvious that Truman must have missed him. There he had been, dutiful father, thrashing about in the undergrowth, desperately searching the depths of the forest, calling for his lost son, calling his name over and over, and somehow he'd missed him. More than possible, wasn't it? And if Baxter *hadn't* wandered back to the caravan, if it turned out he was still out there somewhere, well, Truman had searched high and low, had worn himself out with worry and had done his best. No father could have done more, could he?

Either way, no one would ever know that he had been able to spend a pleasant hour or so dozing in the sunshine. Either way, no one would be any the wiser.

And anyhow, he could hardly be blamed. It wasn't his fault that he wasn't much of a one for the great outdoors. Now, give him a stool at the bar of any boozer in the world and he'd feel right at home; or, for that matter, give him a stool at any piano in any boozer in the world and he'd be there with a smile on his face and as happy as Larry. But not out here, tramping the woods. That wasn't his game, was it?

Truman tapped at his cigarette, flicking the ash into his improvised ashtray. He leaned back again against the stump of the bough, drew hungrily on the cigarette, puckered his lips and sent a perfect ring of smoke drifting up into the branches of the tree.

But at least Baxter's disappearing trick had got him off the hook with Christie. He had that to thank him for, the little sod; that and this hour or so in the sun, of course.

You see, by the time he got back to the caravan, it would be far too late to talk. He'd make sure of that. I'm sorry, love, it's too late now, Christie. Truth is, what with one thing and another, it's been quite a day, princess; let's talk about this going-home business tomorrow, shall we? Let's sleep on it, see how we all feel in the morning. Let's see what tomorrow brings.

Only he wouldn't go to the caravan tomorrow, would he? He'd be too busy, away on business, something like that. He'd lie low for a bit, let it all blow over. And then, in a few weeks, there would be that burglary or that fire down at the house in Brighton and, bingo, he'd then be in the clear to start to look for a cottage somewhere for Christie and the kids.

Truman opened his eyes and looked at his watch. Plenty of time. He took the watch from his wrist, felt the weight of its gold bracelet as he jiggled it in his hand. He turned the watch over and studied the inscription. Smiling, he returned it to his wrist.

Of course, there was one thing, one small fly in the otherwise perfect ointment. If Baxter *wasn't* back at the caravan when Truman finally decided to call it a day, when he finally decided it was time to make his way back there, if the boy was still out there somewhere wandering in the woods, he wouldn't be able to just leave, would he? Back at The Hare and Hounds there would be a pint on the bar and a cuddle from Doll waiting for him but he'd have to hang around until the boy finally showed up.

Selfish little sod.

Truman touched the wound on his cheek once more, felt the tenderness of the bruising.

It *had* been quite a day, hadn't it? A bastard of a day.

But it was almost done now.

An hour or so with his feet up here. And then he was home free.

Truman settled back and closed his eyes again.

A faint breeze suddenly stirred.

Perfect.

## 55

# Soldier: 6.08 p.m.

### *He felt foolish, crestfallen, crushed*

The magpie had landed near by, had glanced up at Soldier and had laughed. It had been that hoarse cackling, the magpie's cocksure rattling laughter, that had first told Soldier that maybe he was wrong. That maybe after all he had got it wrong and the boy would not come running to him there where he waited, crouched low beneath the outstretched branches of the beech tree on the ragged edge of the woods.

Despite the magpie's laughter, Soldier had continued to wait. Fearful that should he stir from his place even for a moment, the boy would at once appear, would come scrambling anxiously through the ferns and would find him gone.

Finally the forest itself had seemed to lose patience with him. A rustle of leaves high in the trees, caught by the shimmering rush of a sudden warm breeze, had whispered to him. Had told him that he should heed the magpie's call.

All at once Soldier had felt foolish. Crouching there and waiting on the edge of the woods for a boy who did not come. He felt foolish, crestfallen, crushed.

The magpie had called again, more distantly now but still sleek and derisive.

Soldier had taken one last long look down across the clearing to where *she* was still standing with her arm about the ponytailed girl. To where they stood stock-still. Stunned and watching for the father. Expecting him at any time to emerge from the woods with the small boy safely at his side.

But Soldier knew he would not come. He knew they would have long to wait and that the father would return to them alone.

Soldier knew this because he had watched as Truman had settled himself into the embrace of the stricken tree, closed his eyes and blown his smoke rings to the heavens.

Taking care not to disturb him, not to attract his attention, staying low, pausing often to nurse the pain that shot through his knee, Soldier had crept away from his hiding place on the edge of the clearing. He had retreated into the woods and had made his way back towards the sanctuary that was his shelter.

*Sunt lacrimae rerum.*

Again his lips had worked at the words.

*Sunt lacrimae rerum.*

And again.

The words had run through him to the rhythm of his walk.

\*

287

He was hungry and tired and as he stumbled homewards, the black dog panting and eager by his side, he fought the constant prick of tears at his eyes.

It was then that he found him.

The boy was sitting on the flint wall with his head bowed and he was gently, softly knocking his heels. Hearing Soldier's shuffling approach, Baxter looked up. He said nothing. And at once, as if ashamed, he looked down again. He swung his legs faster, knocked his heels harder against the flints.

Soldier found tears clouding his eyes as he joined the boy on the wall. He sat a little apart from him and he too bowed his head. He bowed his head to make himself smaller and to hide his tears.

There had been nothing said between them and just that one glance exchanged.

After they had sat in silence for some time, Soldier watched from the corner of his eye as the boy searched his pocket and pulled out something that looked small and grey and plastic.

For a moment Baxter studied the object intently. Then, still with his head bowed and his eyes fixed on the forest floor, still without turning towards him and still without a word being spoken, he reached out his hand and passed it to Soldier.

It was as if the forest held its breath.

Uncertainly, Soldier found himself drawn towards the object. He stretched out his hand. Accepted it from the boy and locked his long bony fingers carefully about it. He looked down at his closed hand and saw it somehow as if it wasn't his own; surprised to see the grimed skin of his fingers, the fingernails yellowed, blackened, broken.

Slowly, one by one, he lifted his fingers. In the palm of his hand he found a small grey plastic toy soldier. It carried a rifle. Wore a backpack and a helmet. One of its legs was broken at the knee.

The black dog came closer. Sniffed at it.

Soldier looked at the small toy with wonder. He turned it about. Over and over. He ran his fingers over its every surface. He held it up to catch the sunlight. He weighed it in his hand. Finally, reluctantly, he made to hand it back to the boy.

Still looking downwards, Baxter shook his head.

'It's for you,' he said quietly.

Soldier didn't understand. He held the toy out urgently to the boy. Thrusting it at him as if to say, 'It's yours. Take it . . . take it.'

The boy shook his head again. And it was then that the realisation took hold in Soldier that it was a gift. That it was to be his. Truly his.

He looked to the boy for a final confirmation. Baxter shook his head once more. Soldier then fumbled in the pocket of his long coat, found a frayed scrap of rag, and wrapped it with meticulous care about the small plastic toy.

The boy looked up.

Soldier could feel his eyes on him as he gently pushed the wrapped parcel securely into his coat pocket. It was then that Soldier saw that Baxter's face was vividly blotched with red. On his cheek. On his forehead. He saw too that the boy's hair was spiked and dishevelled. That his eyes were puffy.

Soldier eased himself from the wall. He patted gently at his coat pocket to know that the parcel was safely there. Then, with a rapid bird-like flapping movement of both hands, he beckoned to Baxter to follow him.

The boy dropped from the wall and followed Soldier as he limped and shambled along the worn path that led a short distance down to the fast-running stream. Elsewhere, the stream meandered lazily through woods. But where Soldier led, the water shimmied and danced in the sunlight over a cascade of smooth pale pebbles.

Below the fall of pebbles, where the small torrent had collected in a shallow clear pool, Soldier bent stiffly down and scooped the cool water up into his hands and splashed it to his face. He signalled to the boy to join him, to do the same. He then stepped back to allow him through to the water's edge.

Soldier watched over Baxter as he knelt low beside the pool, as he rubbed the water vigorously into his face as if trying to rid himself of some terrible stain, and as he smoothed and patted at his unruly hair.

As he watched, the boy's short sleeves shot up his arms and Soldier flinched as he saw what looked like ugly red and purple marks.

His duty. To keep him safe. Lest violence and harm.

Still kneeling, the boy turned to Soldier; he looked up and smiled. Soldier's hands went urgently, questioningly to his own arms, to where the marks would have been had they been his.

The smile went from the boy's face. He looked away from Soldier, down once more into the still clear water, and he pulled at his sleeves.

Somewhere in the charged stillness of the woods, the magpie called once more. Above, a startled flight of starlings hurried by.

The storm was approaching. Soldier knew that it would not be long now.

## 56

# Christie: 6.52 p.m.

### *Perhaps they were out there*
### *in the woods talking*

C hristie had been glad that it had been Truman who had
followed Baxter into the woods; who had chosen to go
looking for the boy after he had run off like that. Despite her
fears of the forest she would have gone after him herself, of
course, but Truman had set off at once and without bidding.
The fact that he did so, the *way* that he did so, seemed to
confirm the new relationship that had sprung up between
father and son during their day of dodgems.

Who would have thought that Truman would take the boy
on the dodgems? She was so proud of him, somehow proud
of them both.

It was such a shame that the boy had got sick and had then
been so upset about it. And she had been disappointed not to
have been able to finish the discussion about going home.
Going home *tomorrow*. But she consoled herself with the

thought that they would be able to settle that once Truman had come back with the boy.

Perhaps he would bring Baxter back, Christie thought, riding high on his shoulders? Just like he had brought Megan back once before.



On the bus they had sat at the very front of the top deck. Christie was beside Baxter, Megan next to Truman. As soon as they set off, Truman nudged and tickled Megan and Baxter looked across and laughed. As the bus neared the first corner, they all pretended to drive. Each of them holding an invisible steering wheel, all of them following Truman's lead and reaching for an imaginary gear lever. As they approached the next stop they leaned back, pushing hard at four unseen brake pedals, and made the squealing noise of tyres on tarmac.

It was to be a treat for Megan's sixth birthday. They were off to the fairground at The Level.

Truman hadn't wanted to go by bus: he would always rather have walked than be seen having to take public transport. In truth, Truman hadn't wanted to go at all – but Megan and Christie had somehow combined to gently cajole him into it. He had turned up late and they'd had to rush.

Christie was surprised by the crowds at The Level and she immediately picked Baxter up and carried him; Truman held Megan's hand as she skipped beside him.

'What first?' he said.

'Helter-skelter!' Megan shouted.

'Skelter!' Baxter echoed.

When they got there, the queue to collect the mats was long and Truman let go of Megan's hand to light a cigarette.

Christie meanwhile, still with five-year-old Baxter heavily on her hip, was pointing out the giant Ferris wheel that was slowly turning in the sky, the dizzying spin of the waltzers, the bobbing painted horses on the carousel, the stand where you fished for yellow plastic ducks and the man selling swirls of candyfloss.

She turned to Megan to make sure she had seen the candyfloss too. She wasn't there.

'Where's Megan?' Christie said, fear instantly gripping at her.

'What?' Truman said, turning lazily towards her, the cigarette dangling from his mouth.

'Megan?' Christie said, fighting to control her voice. 'Where is she?'

Truman looked about him and shrugged.

'How the hell should I know?' he said.

'She's gone!' Christie shouted at him. 'Megan's gone!'

Truman took the cigarette from his mouth, threw it to the ground and crushed it under his foot.

'Stupid bloody woman,' he said. 'Can't even look after your own bloody children. Not for a minute—'

Christie ignored him. 'Take Baxter,' she said, trying to hand him across. 'I'll find her.'

Truman pushed Baxter away.

'No you bloody won't,' he said. 'I'll go.'

Hands thrust into his pockets, he stomped off and quickly disappeared into the thick of the crowd. Christie held fast to Baxter and turned and turned again as she scanned every child's face in the crowd.

Minutes passed and the fear settled like a sickness in her stomach.

It was Baxter who saw them first.

'Megan,' he said, pointing.

Riding high on her father's swaggering shoulders, Megan was laughing as she carried a pink sugared cloud in each hand. Returning in triumph, Truman had bent to allow Megan to hand over Baxter's candyfloss.

After that, Megan had been fine and Truman had carried on as the father ostentatiously devoted to his daughter. But Christie hadn't been able to shake off the feeling of dread all afternoon. And later Baxter had been sick on the swing-boats.

For some long time after Baxter had run off and Truman had followed him, she and Megan had stood together watching the opening to the woods. It had been as if they were held suspended in a trance and only when the baby cried for her had the spell finally been broken. Now mother and daughter were sitting in their familiar favourite spot on the caravan step and Christie was holding the baby in her arms.

Yes, she had been glad that Truman had gone after the boy but now her anxiety was mounting once again. They had been gone for a very long time now, much longer than she might have expected.

Every few minutes Christie glanced at the watch on her wrist.

Perhaps Baxter had fallen? Perhaps he was hurt? Maybe he had run so far into the woods that Truman couldn't find him? He could be lost and hurt.

'Where *are* they, Mummy?' Megan said, sensing the tension in her mother.

'Everything's fine,' Christie said, giving her a squeeze. 'They'll be back soon, you'll see.'

Perhaps they were out there in the woods talking? Perhaps that was it. Or maybe Baxter was showing Truman his camp? Yes, that would be it. There was nothing to worry about. Nothing.

She looked towards the sky; a new anxiety. The scurrying of a flight of birds and the closeness of the air confirmed to her what she had sensed earlier in the day: there was a storm approaching. Would Truman and Baxter be back in time, before the storm broke about them?

*Was that them?* Could she hear something? Could she hear them coming?

Christie sat upright, straining to hear, to hear anything at all in the heavy stillness. In the distance she finally caught the low rumble of a car starting slowly down the lane. Megan heard it too; she looked up at her mother with questions in her eyes.

They were questions Christie could not answer.

Who was it? Why now?

In all the weeks that they had been there, only Truman had driven up and down that dusty lane.

The approach now of a stranger only added to Christie's urgent unease.

# 57

# Strachan: 7.10 p.m.

## *Like an avenging fucking angel, he was*

As Doll had said it would be, it had been easy enough for Strachan to find his way the few twisting tree-lined miles back along the corkscrewing country road to the turning of the lane that led to the clearing. Strachan couldn't be certain that he would find the toerag Truman at this caravan that Doll had talked about, but it took him one step nearer, that much was for sure. He was close now, very close; close to finally collecting, to making Truman pay.

And boy, was he was going to make this joker pay. He was going to pay for all of it.

He was going to make him pay for having him chase around the countryside like this. He was going to pay for the money he owed Mr Smith, of course. And more than that he was going to pay for what he had done to Sally and then to Doll, and for all the lies he had told his own mother, for what he had taken from her. Most of all for that.

Strachan shifted in his seat, gripped the steering wheel tighter.

Yes, most of all for that.

Somehow through the course of the day all of this had become Strachan's responsibility; it had become his duty, his purpose, to extract payment on behalf of all of them. He had taken it upon himself and to each one of them in turn he had made the same unspoken promise.

How the fuck did that happen?

Like an avenging fucking angel, he was; like a fucking knight in shining armour.

As he swung the car on to the dusty potholed track, the brown leather suitcase full of Truman's sliced and tattered clothes slid across the back seat and thumped against the passenger door.

You had to hand it to that Doll; a touch of real class there.

As Strachan lurched the car slowly along the lane, he could see ahead that the long dark shadows cast by the tunnel of overhanging trees gave way to sudden sunlight. It must be the clearing. And, yes, there was a car parked beside what looked like a great grassy rolling meadow.

Truman's car.

Time to play.

Strachan pulled to a halt in the shadows of the trees, taking care to angle his car so that there was no space for another to pass, making sure that he blocked the lane entirely. This time Truman was not getting away from him, boy or no boy, this time he was going nowhere.

He climbed out of his car and went through his ritualistic

sleeve-tugging and tie-straightening and walked towards the evening sunlight of the clearing. There, sure enough, just where Doll had said it would be, was a small caravan that looked half submerged in the middle of the tall grass. It was a squat, ugly, old-fashioned van, the kind you saw parked up in lay-bys selling mugs of scalding strong tea and doorstep sandwiches to truck drivers; it was certainly not the kind of place anyone would want to stay in for too long.

Standing not far from the caravan there was a dark-haired woman wearing a light summer dress; even from this distance, and despite having to squint into the sun, Strachan had a sense of how slight, how young, how vulnerable she looked. A slip of a thing, Strachan's mother would have called her tenderly, approvingly. Beside her was a young ponytailed girl who was unmistakably her daughter; they stood close together as Strachan made his way towards them.

He looked about for the father and the boy. They were nowhere to be seen.

Didn't Mr Smith say three children?

A baby's brief gurgling cry answered the question.

# 58

## Christie: 7.11 p.m.

### *It was difficult to imagine anyone belonging there less*

There was something in the way the man was dressed, in the deliberate and careful way that he pulled at the cuffs of first his suit jacket and then his shirt, in the way that he adjusted his tie, twitched his wide shoulders and jutted his chin; there was something in all of this that made Christie shudder and almost want to laugh aloud at the same time.

He was so out of place there, he didn't belong there. It was difficult to imagine anyone belonging there less. There was something so utterly incongruous, almost laughable, in this heavy-suited, slick-haired, thick-set man suddenly appearing on the dusty lane that led to the clearing.

He started to walk towards them and, just as she had somehow feared it would be, it was clearly there: the controlled swagger, the powerful solid roll of the shoulders, the menace. Every step he took towards her, towards her and Megan, seemed a threat.

Any thought of laughter died in her.

Christie watched as he paused, reached into his pocket for a handkerchief and dabbed at his forehead. The sun was lower in the sky, the long day was drawing slowly to an end, but the heat was still adhesive.

Perhaps he was lost. Perhaps he had taken a wrong turning and had now stopped to ask her for directions. That would explain why he had parked like that, across the lane, ready to turn. Yes, that would be it.

'Mrs Bird?' he called out to her as he walked towards them.

He wasn't lost.

'Mrs Bird?' he called again.

Christie pulled Megan closer.

# 59

# Strachan: 7.13 p.m.

## *She didn't know. How could she not know?*

Strachan shouted to her again as he drew near. Christie didn't answer; he could see that she held herself tense, could see that she had braced herself against him.

'Mrs Bird?' he said once more, the edge now in his voice, irritated by her silence.

She had her arm around the girl's shoulder, pulling her tightly to her.

'Mrs Bird, I'm trying to find your husband,' he said. 'I'm trying to find Truman.'

She looked up at him and Strachan could see her face clearly for the first time; her eyes drew him in with a question and then flashed defiance. Another stunner, another heartbreaker. How the fuck did this Truman do it? A wife like this, Sally, Doll – any one of them would be enough for any man. And with a woman like this at home, why the fuck was he playing away anyway?

'He's not here,' Christie said, her voice strained and hushed.

Strachan turned and pointed to Truman's car.

'Well, he can't be too far away can he, Mrs Bird?' he said. 'Be back soon, will he?'

Why was he speaking like that? He'd started to sound like the Old Bill, as if he was Dixon of fucking Dock Green. Ridiculous.

'We don't know when he'll be back,' Christie said, looking down at Megan.

'He's in the woods,' the girl said.

'The woods?' Strachan said, looking up from her and across the clearing to the edge of the forest.

'Why's he in the woods?' he said.

He could see how reluctant Christie was to explain. She didn't want to say anything more to him than she had to, she wanted rid of him, she wanted the ground to open up and swallow him whole.

'He's out there looking for our son, for Baxter. He was a bit upset. He ran off into the woods.'

Strachan nodded, he understood, he could picture it, the boy getting back here, running from his father, taking off on his toes to the woods. Made sense.

'Because of what had happened to his things,' he said in confirmation, almost to himself. 'At the house.'

Christie frowned, gripped her daughter's shoulder ever more tightly. He could see the shock running through her. The girl looked up at her mother and could see it too.

'The house?' Christie said. 'What about the house?'

She didn't know. How could she not know? She didn't know that she'd lost everything that she ever had, that the home she had made for her children had gone. Every cup. Every saucer. Every pot. Every pan.

'You've been to *our* house?' Christie said.

Leave it, Strachan. Leave that for now. Move on.

'Mrs Bird, do you know who I am?' he said. 'Do you know why I'm here?'

She shook her head, confused now.

'You live in Brighton, yes?' he said, as if to a child.

She nodded.

'Lived there long, have you?'

'All my life. Born and bred,' Christie said. 'But I don't understand ...'

He smiled; a smile that he knew would look almost a sneer to her. He couldn't help it.

'If you know Brighton, lady, then you know me, you know who I am,' he said evenly. 'You'll know my name, at least ...'

Her eyes narrowed. She was dazed, confused, he could see that.

'Why would I know your name?' she said.

'Because I'm Strachan,' he said softly.

# 60

# Christie: 7.14 p.m.

*'The money?' she said, bewildered.*
*'What money?'*

Growing up she had heard the name; everyone had heard the name. The boys used to brag and bully at the school gates.

'I'm going to do you!' one would yell, jabbing an accusing finger in a fat boy's face. 'I'm going to do you just like Strachan!'

Everyone knew the name.

'Leave me alone,' someone else would plead. 'Leave me alone or I'll get Strachan on you.'

Even her father had talked about him.

'I hear that Strachan's been up to no good again,' he said, putting the newspaper down, sucking at his pipe. 'Talking about it at work today, they were. Put two in hospital this time, they say. Don't know how he gets away with it.'

Yes, back then everyone knew who Strachan was; you

couldn't grow up in Brighton and not know. And now he was there, larger than life and pulling at his cuffs again, he was there in the clearing. He had come for Truman, for her, for her and the children.

'Why are you here, Mr Strachan?' Christie managed to say.

Almost in a whisper, Strachan replied. 'It's Strachan,' he said. 'Just Strachan.'

It was as if all her nightmares were suddenly standing in front of her.

'But what do you want with Truman? Why are you here?' she said.

'Why am I here?' he said, his lips curling back in a quick grin. 'I'm here for the money, of course.'

'The money?' she said, bewildered. 'What money?'

Christie could see the way that Strachan looked at her now, with what she imagined was an expression as close to pity as he was capable of.

# 61

# Strachan: 7.17 p.m.

## *It was the way she closed her eyes that suddenly got to him*

You didn't know whether to laugh or cry, Strachan thought. She didn't have a clue. Not a fucking clue. Well, it wasn't for him to worry about that. He wasn't about to go pussyfooting around now, trying to spare her finer feelings. He didn't have the time or, in truth, any inclination for that. But all the same he would have preferred it if the young girl, the daughter, wasn't there staring up at him like that.

He looked down at the girl and Christie got the message.

'Go inside the caravan, Megan,' she said, pushing her gently away.

'But Mummy ...' the girl said pleadingly.

'No buts, please,' Christie said. 'You read your book for a while and I'll come for you soon, I promise. You can put the radio on if you want.'

Christie and Strachan watched in silence as Megan

trudged towards the caravan, as she slowly climbed the step, lingered for a moment and then finally disappeared inside. They heard the click of the radio and the fizz and hiss of static as she tuned it to another station. Billy J. Kramer's muffled voice came drifting chirpily through the open door.

♪ *Listen, do you want to know a secret?* ...

'What money?' Christie said again.

She really didn't know.

'The five thousand,' he said.

It was the way she closed her eyes that suddenly got to him. It was the way that she closed her eyes and then wrapped her arms about her, clinging to herself as if to keep herself safe, to keep herself from falling apart.

'Five *thousand*?' she said.

Strachan knew he should have pitied her. But as he stood there sweating and uncomfortable in his pinstripe suit, weary from the day, tired of chasing around like a teenager, tired of all of it, he realised that what he felt for her was anger.

She had no idea about any of it.

How could she not know? Had she been walking around with her eyes closed? Her ears closed? What had she been playing at all these years? She wasn't stupid, he could see that. So why hadn't she known what her own lousy husband was up to?

'He borrowed it. From a friend of mine,' Strachan said. 'It was for the property, for the students.'

'The *students*?' she said.

She was like a fucking parrot.

'For the bedsits,' he said.

307

She shook her head. Not a clue.

'My friend wants what's owed to him,' he said. 'I've come to collect.'

He realised that he was angry *on behalf of* Sally and then Doll, for the way Truman had treated them, but he was angry *with* her. And he knew that wasn't right, of course. If anyone had been hurt here, it was her. But why had she let it happen? *How* had she? If she'd had her eyes open she could have stopped it. She deserved whatever she had coming.

She looked up at him; all the defiance had gone from her now.

'You said something about the house?' Christie said. 'You said something happened at the house?'

Strachan raised his fist, examined it carefully, rubbed at his knuckles.

'I was there today. Introduced myself to that husband of yours,' he said, the beginnings of a grin curling on his lips again.

He could see that she understood.

'His face? You did that to him?'

Strachan's grin grew wider.

'Not the car door then?' Christie said.

'I don't know anything about any car door, lady,' Strachan said.

He saw that Christie shivered despite the warmth.

'But you said something about Baxter . . . about my son? About his things?' she said.

So she wanted to hear it all? OK, if that was what she wanted that was fine by him.

'The boy was upset. All his things had been smashed up.'

'*Smashed?*'

The fucking parrot was back.

'Listen, lady, you've got to understand something,' Strachan said. 'Your toerag husband borrowed this five grand from my friend. Borrowed it and then just buggered off. So my friend is none too happy about this. Understandable really. Under the circumstances.'

Christie said nothing.

'So, being unhappy, he calls me. Asks me to find the piece of garbage who owes him. To have a friendly word. And at the same time he calls another friend of his and asks *him* to pay a visit to your house—'

'*My house?*'

'So he pays a visit and he looks around and then he takes everything he can find. Towards the debt. Towards what's owed. He takes the lot, he clears the house. Every pot. Every pan. Everything.'

'*Everything?*' Christie said. 'You mean it's all gone? We've got nothing left? He took *everything*?'

Her eyes, those eyes, were filled with tears now but she was determined to hold them there, determined not to let them flow, he could see that. She was a fighter, he had to give her that much.

'Everything, lady,' Strachan said. 'Everything except in your son's room. Your son's things he just smashed.'

'But why?'

Strachan shrugged his shoulders.

'It's like a calling card, it's like a message,' he said. 'It's like saying that we're going to hurt you. You and yours. And we're going to keep hurting you until we have what's owed.'

'And Baxter? He found all of his things smashed?' Christie said.

Strachan nodded.

'Oh my poor boy ...' she said.

Her hands went to her mouth; she looked up and towards the wood, scanning the trees that edged the clearing, trying to penetrate the darkness beyond. Strachan's eyes followed hers.

'You see them?' he said.

Christie didn't reply. Her eyes closed again, as if she was trying to digest it, to take it all in.


'Everything gone?' she finally said. 'And you're still after us?'

'After *him*,' Strachan said.

'But how did you know where we were?'

'I've been busy,' he said, the flicker of a grin returning.

'Busy?'

'Busy talking to a lot of people who know your husband,' Strachan said. 'First of all I had a chat with his old boss – the one who fired him for being on the fiddle.'

'Fired him? But he still works ...'

She didn't even know that? How could she not know that?

'Then I talked to Sally.'

'But I don't know anyone called Sally,' she said.

'You wouldn't, lady,' he laughed. 'She's the barmaid from The Salvation that he's been seeing for months now.'

He watched to see how she took the blow, watched the flinch, the recoil, watched to see how she absorbed it, steadied herself.

'I don't understand ...' she started to say.

310

But he could see that she did, he could see that she understood only too well.

'And this Sally was the one who knew we were here?' Christie said.

'No,' Strachan said. 'She didn't know about you and the children. Didn't know you existed. She wouldn't have had anything to do with him if she had.'

It felt good to be talking about Sally, to set the record right about her.

'So how . . . ?'

'So after Sally, I went to see your Truman's mother . . .'

He watched again to see how this blow landed, watched the wince, the juddering shock, the colour draining from her, the stunned questioning look on her face. This hurt. This hurt much more than finding out about Sally. This was a greater betrayal.

'But Truman's an orphan, he told me . . .'

It was all she could manage.

'Well that would be news to the nice little old lady in Crawley who gave me a cup of tea this afternoon.'

Again she shook her head, as if she was somehow clearing her mind, trying to get it straight. He carried on.

'The one who's got his photo on her sideboard, who calls him her son and whose money he's now stolen.'

'He's taken *her* money?'

Strachan reached into his pocket for his wallet. From it he took the slip of paper that Truman's boss had handed to him.

'Why does that surprise you, lady?' he said. 'Why would anyone be surprised that this Truman character was capable of stealing from his own sweet mother?'

He handed her the slip of paper.

'Here,' he said. 'Here's her address. You can send her a Christmas card.'

Christie took the slip from him, stared at the address as if she needed confirmation that this wasn't all some new cruel invention.

'But why has she never wanted to meet me or the children?' she said. 'Why has she never wanted to see her own grandchildren?'

She still didn't really get it. Still didn't see all of it.

'Because she's another one who didn't know you existed, lady,' Strachan said, slowly, deliberately.

Christie frowned, shook her head.

'I don't understand . . . If she didn't know we existed, how could she know that we were here?' she said.

'She didn't. She gave me Truman's latest address. It was Doll who knew you were here.'

'*Doll?*'

'The woman Truman's been shacked up with while you've been stuck in this dump.' He pointed towards the caravan.

'She runs The Hare and Hounds a couple of miles back down the road.'

Another blow struck; Christie rocked a little unsteadily on her feet. She covered her ears, she didn't want to know, she wanted to block it all out now. But she wasn't getting away with that. Strachan raised his voice to make sure that she would still be able to hear.

'Quite something, our Doll,' he said.

Christie uncovered her ears at once, glanced towards the caravan, fearing that Megan would hear.

Strachan lowered his voice once more.

'Needless to say, this Doll didn't know about you or the kids either. He told her you were his sister or something. Anyway, she's sent a special gift for your Truman.'

'A gift?'

'You'll see,' he said. 'Oh, and she sent a message too . . .'

'I don't want to know,' Christie said, her voice thin and pinched.

Strachan ignored her.

'She said that if she ever clapped eyes on him again, she'd cut off his balls and feed them to the cat.'

He laughed; he was enjoying this.

Christie said nothing. She was looking in the direction of the woods again but her eyes were empty, unfocused, and Strachan knew that she looked without seeing.

'Lady, you've a lot to think about,' he said. 'Tell you what, I'll wait in the car for the toerag to come back. And when he does, maybe you can take the nippers off somewhere while I have a *friendly chat* with him . . . ?'

He turned away from her and as he did so the baby let out a sudden anguished whimper from the carry-cot.

The sound of the baby's cry broke Christie's trance.

'Hush, little Truman, hush,' she said, hurrying to the carry-cot, reaching in and lifting the baby to her.

Strachan couldn't help it; he couldn't help the growl of laughter that gathered in his throat.

'What was that you called him?' he said.

Christie looked up from the baby.

'Truman,' she said. 'We named him after his father.'

Strachan laughed again.

'Then,' he said, reaching for his handkerchief, dabbing at his brow, the rumble of laughter lifting his shoulders, making his whole body shake. 'Then you shouldn't have called him Truman, should you?'

'*What?*' Christie said, looking bewildered again. 'Why not?'

Strachan dabbed again at his brow, swallowed a rising gulp of laughter.

'Because that's not the lying bastard's name.'

'*What?*' Christie repeated, holding the baby more closely to her.

It was too much. It was all too much.

'Because the toerag's real name,' Strachan said, fighting for air, fighting for the words, 'his real name . . . is *Eric*.'

'*What?*' Christie said again.

'You should have called the baby *Eric*,' Strachan said, the laughter dying now as quickly as it had arrived.

He took a step towards her, he leaned in to her and felt the gentle press on his chest of her arms holding the baby; his face was near enough to hers to feel the warmth of her breath.

'You should have fucking called him Eric,' he whispered.

## 62

# Christie: 7.43 p.m.

*Everything had been hacked and*
*shredded and peeled away*

Once, as a child, Christie had stood and watched a butcher as he worked. It had been a very long time ago, when she could have been no more than seven years old, but the memory had stayed vividly with her. She could still smell the sawdust fresh on the floorboards, could feel the chill of the tiled shop wall that she rested against, could see the straw boater perched on the back of his head, could see him yet wiping his great hands on his blue-and-white-striped apron.

She had stood there for what seemed an age while her mother had chatted conspiratorially to a neighbour in the queue at the counter. She had stood and watched as he chopped and hacked and peeled at the deep red flesh, as he pulled at it, eased it from the shockingly white bone; watched him leave a few raw streaks of tattered flesh and stretched stringy sinew behind.

That was how she felt now; as if everything had been hacked and shredded and peeled away from her.

When the butcher was done, he had smiled and winked at her and she had shrunk away from him. Strachan had laughed, had put his face close to hers, had sneered and she had shrunk from him too with the same revulsion.

Despite that, and despite all that Strachan had told her, despite everything that had been taken from her as each new lie had been laid bare, as each new blow had fallen, what troubled her most was that Baxter had still not returned.

Where was Baxter? Where *was* he?

He had been gone now for more than two hours, a small boy lost in the woods, and what had given her comfort before – that his father was out there looking for him – now only added to her anxiety.

*Where was he?*

But they had ridden dodgems and eaten candyfloss, so surely Truman would find him, surely he would keep him safe and bring him back riding on his shoulders?

She was sitting once more on the step of the caravan, the baby in one arm, the other holding Megan close. She felt worn, tired, empty, raw, anxious.

*Where was he?*

From time to time fragments of what Strachan had told her ran through her mind. Not an orphan; a mother there for him all along, a photograph on her sideboard. Sacked. Sacked for being on the fiddle, was that what Strachan had said? Five thousand pounds. Five *thousand* pounds. Sally didn't know – *Sally*? Doll had a message for him, had a gift for him. For Truman. You should have called him Eric. Eric. Every pot. Every pan. Everything. Gone. Everything but

316

Baxter's things. And they were smashed. A calling card, a message.

Only now, piecing it together, did she confront the fact that everything in her life had been a lie.

She had lived through all of it for all these years, she had lived through all the jealous rages, keeping the children safe, she had put up with the threats, the abuse, the not-knowing, the being afraid to ask. She had steered a course through all of it for the sake of the family, to keep them together, for the sake of the children.

For what?

For a lie.

She could find nothing now that was true except for the children. Baxter, alone and wandering in the forest; Megan by her side, looking up at her with such fearful unanswerable questions in her eyes; the baby held tightly to her. They were the only truth.

Where was he? Where was her boy?

And where would they go now? No going home tomorrow now. No home to go to.

Worse still was that Strachan was still there, leaning against his car, waiting, waiting for Truman. What was she to do? Should she warn Truman when he returned? Should she tell him to run, to hide? But why would she? Why would she help this man who had betrayed her so utterly?

She hadn't even known his real name.

She remembered, at the very beginning, how her heart had softened as he told her that both his parents had been lost. And if there had been this Sally and this Doll, there would surely have been others through the years, there *must* have been others. How could she have been so stupid, so blind?

So, so stupid . . .

It was over now.

Finished.

Whatever it was, whatever it had been, it was over. Only at that moment did she know it.

While Strachan had been talking, while Christie had been trying to absorb each new shock, she hadn't faced it. But now she had got there. There was no other way, no decision to be made. It was over, her marriage was over.

It wasn't because of Sally or Doll or the others; in some way they seemed the least of it. It wasn't that she felt anger towards Truman, or bitterness; it was too soon for that. Anger was a luxury she couldn't afford; it was an indulgence, when she had the children to worry about. It was that she felt nothing for him; everything had been a lie; she didn't know him, she didn't want to know him.

They would still leave in the morning, she and the children. They couldn't stay there any longer. But how would she care for them? Where would she take them? They had no money, nowhere to go.

Christie closed her eyes and tried to think.

It would have to be back to Brighton, to her mother's pursed lips and told-you-so scorn. There was no other option.

Christie shivered at the thought and Megan nudged closer to her as if to keep her warm.

*Where was he?*

And where was Truman?

# 63

# Truman: 8.05 p.m.

## *She couldn't even be bothered to give him a bit of a wave*

Still lying with his feet up in the cradled embrace of his fallen tree, Truman arched his back and stretched and yawned expansively. Slowly flickering his eyes open, he reached between the lower buttons of his shirt with a crooked index finger and scratched lazily at his stomach. It had done him a power of good, this couple of hours dozing in the sun. Properly recharged the old batteries, it had. He yawned again. After all, a man needed a bit of time to himself. Deserved it, didn't he, with all the rushing about he'd done today?

Truman looked at his watch; it was later than he'd thought. He'd better make a move soon. Better go and check if the boy had found his way back to his mother, back to the caravan. Probably had his tea and was already tucked up in bed, wasn't he? Little sod.

A quick chat to Christie – 'Looked high and low for him I did, the little rascal, worried sick I was, see you tomorrow, princess,' that sort of thing – and then, bingo, he could be out of there and on his way back to Doll and The Hare and Hounds and a pint of special quicker than you could say Jack Robinson.

But after today it had to be back to normal, Truman old son. It had to be back to living by the rules, *his* rules. Back to keeping it simple, keeping it separate. It had all got a bit complicated, a bit out of hand today. It had been a close call, too close for comfort, what with having the boy in tow and meeting Doll and then coming face to face with that bastard Strachan. He should never have had the boy with him.

Bloody Christie and her bloody stupid ideas.

But if the kid kept shtum, it was no problem. And he would, wouldn't he? He'd made sure of that.

Truman swung his legs round and sat upright on the tree trunk. He flexed his shoulders, rotated them slowly, easing away the slight stiffness that had settled there as he slept. He took the comb from his top pocket and ran it through his hair. He stretched again, less extravagantly this time, and then fished in his jacket pocket for his cigarettes and lighter.

He flipped open the cigarette packet. Nearly out; definitely time to be on the move.

Lighting a cigarette, he looked slowly around him. The kid wouldn't have been stupid enough to run off far into these woods, would he? With the web of paths, the fallen trees, the dense ferns, the impenetrable banks of brambles, he could be lost for hours out there if he had, could be lost forever. It gave him the creeps just thinking about it. And if that wasn't bad enough, there was a storm on its way, Truman was sure of it, he could feel it hanging in the air. No, he wouldn't still be out there, the boy; he'd be back at the caravan.

Truman stubbed out his cigarette, thrust his hands into his trouser pockets and made his way slowly towards the gap in the trees that led to the clearing. Once he was out in the open, he'd have to get a shift on, move a bit sharpish, show a bit more urgency.

At the opening he took a deep breath and then a step out into the evening sunlight of the clearing. He saw Christie at once, sitting as she always seemed to be on that step by the caravan, Megan by her side. The boy was nowhere to be seen. He was right; Baxter must already be inside, safely tucked up in bed. Truman could almost taste that first pint, fancied that he could almost smell Doll's perfume as he wrapped her into his arms, heard her voice tutting and fussing over his black eye and the cut to his face. He stood with the entrance to the woods behind him and waved to Christie. She got to her feet as soon as she saw him, but she didn't wave back.

That was a bit rich, wasn't it? He'd been gone all this time, looking for that precious son of hers, and she couldn't even be bothered to give him a bit of a wave.

He set off across the clearing, striding out now, raising an arm to wave from time to time. Neither Christie nor Megan waved in return.

As soon as he was near enough to be heard he called out to Christie.

'All right, princess?'

She looked hunched, ashen, haunted; despite the warmth

of the evening, she had a white cardigan on now, pulling it tightly about her.

'All right, princess?' he said again, more uncertainly, as he got nearer, fixing a reassuring smile to his face.

'You haven't found him,' Christie said.

It wasn't an accusation, it was a statement of fact, but there was an edge of desperation in her voice, a barely subdued panic, he could hear it. Shielding her eyes against the sun, still holding Megan close, she scanned the edge of the woods once more.

'You mean he's not back?' Truman said. 'I thought I must have missed him, I thought he would have found his way back.'

Along with the surge of irritation that ran through him, the irritation that he couldn't be off and on his way to The Hare and Hounds, there was a small rush of anxiety too. This wasn't good, was it? The boy had been gone a long time now, too long.

'I looked everywhere, I did. Hunted high and low,' he said. Even to him it sounded lame now, phoney.

'You'll have to go back,' Christie said, not looking at him. 'You've got to keep trying to find him. He's out there somewhere ...'

Truman plunged his hands into his pockets, looked to the ground and kicked at the grass.

'There's no point, princess,' he said sullenly. 'I'll never find him out there. Those woods are a nightmare, they go for miles. I nearly got lost myself.'

'But you've got to go back,' she said.

'I'm not going anywhere, Christie. Trust me, he'll be all right. He'll be back before dark, I'm sure of it,' Truman said.

She turned to him now; he expected to see the flash of accusation in her eyes, expected to see the fear for her lost boy, the panic. Instead there was nothing, nothing there at all. Her eyes seemed sunken, dead; not like his Christie's eyes at all.

'What is it, princess?' Truman said gently.

He reached out his hand, reached out to softly brush her cheek with his fingertips.

She pulled away from him, drew Megan more closely to her.

'Don't touch me,' Christie said, her voice dead now. 'Don't you ever try to touch me or my children again.'

'*What?*' Truman said, with a nervous laugh. 'What's happened? I don't understand.'

She knew something. Somehow she knew. No problem, though: whatever it was, he'd talk her round.

'I don't want you anywhere near any of us,' she said.

'*What?*'

What did she know? How did she know?

'I want you to find my son and then I want you gone from our lives for good,' she said.

Truman could feel the heavy stillness of the evening like he never had before, could hear the unnatural silence, could feel the sun's warmth creeping on his back; suddenly he was more awake, more aware, more alert than he had ever been.

'You've got a visitor,' Christie said, turning from him, looking back up along the lane.

Truman could see him now, lolling against the bonnet of his car, watching them. There was a smile on his face; Truman could swear there was a smile on his face.

Strachan.

*Sodding* Strachan.

'What's he said to upset you?' Truman said soothingly. 'What's he been telling you, princess?'

More to the point, how did he get here? How the hell did he find them here?

'He's told me everything,' Christie said.

Truman tried to laugh again, to laugh it off, but the laughter choked in his throat.


Out of nowhere, out of the far distance there was a juddering crash and a low reverberating roar of thunder that shattered the stillness. The storm was beginning to break far away over the forest. The clearing itself was still filled with dazzling late-evening light, but the clouds that had been gathering slowly throughout the afternoon were now banked dark and steep behind them to the east beyond the road. Above the woods where Truman had dozed, the sky was reddening as the sun suddenly began its dip towards the horizon.

Truman looked to the reddening sky, looked back towards Christie.

'Whatever it is he's told you isn't right. You can't believe any of it, princess. You can't believe a word he says,' he said. 'He's a loony, a psycho . . .'

It was just like he always said; you had to keep it simple, keep it separate. Otherwise everything got wound together and soon it was a knot tightening like a noose.

'He's told me *everything*,' Christie said again.

He felt the tug of the knot at his neck.

'No, princess. Whatever it is, I can explain—'

There was another mighty muffled crash and roar. A little closer this time.

Christie looked up at him and there was something in her eyes now, something new, something he had not seen there before. It was the same thing he had seen in Sally's eyes earlier in the day.

Contempt.

'I don't want to hear any of it,' Christie said. 'It's over, don't you understand? I know everything I need to know.'

'But princess,' he cooed, reaching out to her once more. 'It's Truman, princess! You know me; you can trust me. It's your Truman.'

She pulled away again. Now there was anger.

'But it's not *my* Truman,' she said, her face twisted into a sneer. 'It's not *Truman* at all, is it?'

'What?' he said.

'It's *Eric*,' Christie hissed.

Eric?

How the . . . ?

# 64

## Strachan: 8.14 p.m.

*'Here, toerag!' he shouted. 'I've
got something for you'*

Strachan leaned against the bonnet of his car, watching.
There was no rush. He could take his time. Enjoy it.

Even with the storm surely coming this way, there was
time enough to let that bastard Truman dangle awhile, to let
him squirm, let him suffer a few moments longer. It was no
more than the toerag deserved.

Behind him, beyond the dusty potholed road, the distant
sky suddenly lit up like a thousand tremoring flashbulbs
going off. Strachan counted out the seconds until the next
crashing mountainous rumble of thunder finally came. Sure
enough, it was still some way off, it had some miles to
travel yet; but it would be quite something when it finally
arrived.

He held out his hands in front of him; steady as a fucking
rock.

Strachan smiled as he saw Truman glance anxiously towards him once more.

Time to play.

From the passenger seat of the car he picked up the baseball bat; he weighed it in his hand, patted it in his palm, enjoying the meaty smack of it. It felt good, like it was meant; just as it always had. From the rear seat he collected the leather suitcase, the one that Doll had stuffed with Truman's shredded clothes.

He was going to enjoy this. Oh yes.

Slowly, baseball bat in one hand, suitcase in the other, he began to walk towards the caravan, towards where Truman, Christie and the girl were standing. At first Christie still held the girl closely to her but as he started to get nearer to them he could see that she had looked up, that she had seen him approaching and that she was now urgently propelling Megan once more towards the open door of the caravan.

'Go inside, Megan, please,' he heard her plead.

Good. Better that way. Better that the girl wasn't there to see it.

The girl disappeared inside the caravan, lingering as she had before for just a moment on the step.

Still slowly, almost casually, strolling towards them, Strachan lifted the baseball bat to point towards Truman.

The sky flashed, flickered behind him.

'Here, toerag!' he shouted. 'I've got something for you.'

Another low booming clap of thunder rolled away in the distance.

Truman stood his ground but it wasn't courage that kept him there, Strachan could see that; he was close enough to see it all now, the blank fear in Truman's eyes that fixed him to the spot.

Strachan threw the suitcase towards Truman; it scythed and skidded through the grass and stopped at his feet.

'Open it, lover boy!' Strachan barked.

Still Truman didn't move.

'Open it, I said!'

As Truman fell to his knees and fumbled with the locks, Strachan turned to look at Christie. He wanted to see how she was enjoying this spectacle of her lying git of a husband brought to this: scared gutless and on his knees. She was standing with her back to the caravan watching Truman as he scrabbled frantically at the suitcase; her white cardigan was pulled about her; her hand was to her open mouth; her eyes were wide.

Finally Truman had the suitcase open. One by one he lifted the slashed and tattered remnants of his clothes. On his face he wore a look of utter bewilderment, the bewilderment of the innocent victim.

'Present from Doll,' Strachan said, with a laugh. 'When she found out you had a wife and kids ...'

Truman said nothing; wearing the same stunned, wronged expression, he just kept picking through the contents of the suitcase. He didn't even turn to look up at Christie.

Another searing bolt of lightning lit up the sky; more brightly this time, coming closer.

'I've come for what's owed,' Strachan said.

Still on his knees, looking down into the suitcase, Truman gave a small helpless shrug.

The thunder broke, rolled, echoed.

'For the five thousand,' Strachan said.

Finally Truman looked up.

'I haven't got it,' he said, his voice pitifully quiet.

He turned to Christie.

'I haven't got it, princess,' he said, as if at last it needed to be explained to her, as if at least something needed to be explained to her. 'It's gone, you see. All of it.'

Strachan took a step towards where Truman knelt. He lifted the baseball bat, pointed it towards him again.

'Don't disappoint me, toerag,' he said. 'You know I don't like to be disappointed.'

Truman raised his hand to his face, touched the cut below his eye. He remembered.

'But I don't—' he started to say.

'I'll take the car,' Strachan said, cutting across him.

'What . . . ?'

'Give me the keys!' Strachan said.

'*What?*'

'Give me the fucking car keys!'

The sky lit up once more as Truman took the keys from his jacket pocket. He looked at them longingly, lovingly, as if there was nothing in this life that could be more precious to him. For one last time, he held them in his clenched hand and then, finally managing to part with them, he threw them towards Strachan.

As Strachan bent to retrieve them from the long grass he felt a twinge to his back. It was enough to remind him. Too old for this game; too old to be chasing around after the likes of this sorry loser. It was time to get this over with now, time to get it done.

'And the watch,' he said.

Back at the house, pinning Truman to the wall, he'd noticed the watch with its heavy gold bracelet. It would be worth a few quid. It all helped; it was all grist to Mr Smith's mill.

Truman looked up at him, helpless, defeated.

'Please, no . . .' he said.

'The watch, loser!' Strachan said, twitching the baseball bat closer to Truman's face.

Truman took the watch from his wrist, held it as he had held the car keys, tightly and to himself, held it out towards Christie as if to show how unfair this world was, how everything was being taken from him, and then tossed it lightly into the grass at Strachan's feet.

Behind and above him, high in the sky, there was another vivid electric flash as once more Strachan stooped to pick it up. The pain tweaked at his back again.

'And I'll have the fifty,' he said.

Another low shattering rumble.

'The fifty . . . ?' Truman said.

'Doll's fifty,' Strachan said. 'The fifty she gave you this morning.'

Dejectedly, Truman reached once more into his jacket pocket. From his wallet he took out the crisp notes that Doll had handed to him in The Hare and Hounds, the same fifty his mother had briefly and delightedly held. He flung the notes at Strachan's feet.

Strachan collected them with his free hand, never letting the baseball bat drop for a moment.

'Get up!' he said to Truman. 'Now!'

*

Truman hauled himself slowly to his feet. He looked as if nothing more could be done to him, he looked for all the world as if nothing worse could happen.

He was wrong.

With a rapid short-armed swing, Strachan sent the clubbed end of the bat thudding into Truman's stomach. It knocked the wind from Truman, lifted him an inch from the ground, folded him and then sank him once more to his knees.

'That's for your mother,' Strachan said, taking a deep breath.

He raised the bat again, preparing himself. The next one would be for Sally and the one after for Doll.

'NO!' Christie screamed.

Strachan stopped mid-swing, looked at her as the heavens flashed again.

'My boy is MISSING,' she shouted at him, bending almost double to launch the words towards him. 'He's out THERE!'

She was pointing wildly towards the woods, jabbing her finger at them accusingly as if the gnarled and malevolent oaks themselves had reached out with their claw-like branches and snatched him, taken him.

'He's out THERE! He's all alone. And the two of you . . . the two of you . . . you're doing THIS!?'

Strachan dropped the baseball bat. He was breathing hard now. Suddenly and from nowhere he felt reduced, ridiculous and old.

It wasn't that he gave a toss about the boy, her son. He didn't; what was the kid to him? What did it matter to him if he'd gone walkabout for a few hours? No, it was this woman's violent hurt that made his own small anger on behalf of Truman's mother, on behalf of Sally and Doll, feel so inadequate, so manufactured, so fucking pointless.

It was that and the sight of the girl watching him from the open door of the caravan with her eyes wide like her mother's and tears rolling down her cheeks and the baby in her arms.

Fuck it.

Strachan held both hands out in front of him and it was there again, it was unmistakable, it was there for all to see.

# 65

# Christie: 8.25 p.m.

## *The world swam and rushed and the sound roared back*

For what seemed to Christie like long moments, everything had slowed down. Truman had managed to struggle to his feet once more; he was still fighting for breath, trying to straighten himself, clutching at his stomach where the baseball bat had struck. Strachan had dropped the bat and was standing a little apart from him and, for reasons that Christie couldn't understand, couldn't make sense of however much she tried, he was holding his hands in front of him and staring at them as though somehow they didn't belong to him, as though he had just discovered that they had a life independent of him. The sky above him to the east flickered and flashed once again but miraculously the clearing itself still gloried in the golden glow and the long summer shadows of the last light of the day. To the west, above the woods that had taken Baxter, that held him still, Christie could see that the sun would disappear very soon now from the unfeasibly red-streaked sky.

It *was* as if everything had slowed down. After Christie had shouted and screamed at Strachan to stop, it was as if *she* had somehow made the world go slow.

It was what she had seen sometimes in films: like when a volcano was about to erupt or a giant wave about to break over an island and they slowed the film down so much that you could see everything, every boil and run of lava, every fleck of spray, every fleeing face. You could see every last little thing. It was like that suddenly. And Christie felt that she was part of that everything, part of that everything going slowly. Part of it and yet apart. Because there was something else. She could see every last little thing and yet at the same time it seemed to be all so far away, so very distant. It was far away and the world was turning slowly and it was quiet, so quiet that Christie heard and yet somehow didn't hear the muted hollow crash of the thunder; she heard and yet didn't hear Truman's choking, rasping gasps for breath.

It was in the midst of this everything-going-so-slowly that Christie turned towards the caravan and saw that at the open door, bathed in the glowing golden evening light, a small ponytailed girl was standing and she was rocking a baby in her arms. It made Christie smile to see this girl, so young, so sure, so wide-eyed and pretty, with the baby held so tenderly.

But something was wrong. There were tears in the girl's eyes.

The world swam and rushed and the sound roared back to Christie's ears. She steadied herself against the faintness that had been about to overtake her. Unsure as to whether she could yet trust herself to move, she called to Megan.

'OK?'

The girl nodded; her practised nod of reassurance.

Christie pulled her cardigan about her, feeling a sudden chill. At that moment something caused her to look up once again towards the woods. Was that movement there? Did she see something there? She shielded her eyes once more against the sun. There *was* someone there. At the very edge of the clearing, against the dark shadows of the woods, she could just make out the silhouetted shape of what looked like a man, a tall man in what appeared to be a long coat. And then suddenly beside him there was a smaller shape. Was that a boy's shape?

Still uncertain, Christie took a few tentative, questioning steps towards the wood. Was it him? Could it be Baxter? After a few more steps, she made up her mind. It *had* to be Baxter.

She stopped to kick off her shoes.

And then she started to run.

She ran steadily at first, still not fully trusting that the faintness had completely passed, but soon she discovered that the running restored her. It felt good to run; it felt like an escape, like freedom. She ran more quickly now, feeling the still-warm air on her face, the tall grass brushing against her legs, the bounce of the cushioned earth beneath her feet. With her long, strong, confident stride she followed the track beaten through the grass, the track where Baxter had stumbled and run, stumbled and run, the track that Truman had followed. She ran on and on until she was close enough to see him quite clearly.

It *was* him! He was with someone, but it *was* Baxter.

Now, now she forced herself on, now she ran as fast as her legs would carry her. With her head thrown back and her hair flowing, she felt that she was running like the wind itself. And now as she ran she reached out her arms towards him, for Baxter, for her son, beseeching him to come to her. Because there was an ache in her arms that only her lost boy could ease.

# 66

# Soldier: 8.26 p.m.

*It was only then that he felt the
boy's hand slip into his*

I t was at that moment that Soldier thought his heart
would finally break. To see her running like that. Running through the tall grass towards him. And he thought that
through all the weeks of watching, perhaps he had been
wrong, that he had got it wrong.

He thought that perhaps, all this time, *she* had been waiting for him, *she* had been watching over him and now, finally,
she was coming to him. Coming for him. To take him from
this place.

It was only then that he felt the boy's hand slip into his.

And he remembered.

Soldier had never felt a child's hand in his before, or at
least he had no memory of it, and he wasn't sure what he
should make of it now. The boy's hand felt so warm and new

that it startled him and made him ashamed of the coarseness of his own.

The boy looked up at him, as if to reassure him.

Soldier took another step forwards into the clearing, further into the evening light. His heart was racing and in his head a thousand broken thoughts swirled and swam. But somehow, somehow through it, he remembered why he was there.

He had watched over her, her and the children. His duty, lest harm should come to them. Their grizzled angel. And now he was to deliver the boy safely back.

Ahead of them, beyond the clearing, beyond the road, over the far forest and the rolling scrubby heathland, the sky flashed a deadening white. Long seconds later the thunder broke once more. Everything else was silence now. The approaching storm had stilled all the forest voices.

## 67

# Christie: 8.28 p.m.

### *He carried the smell of decay about him, heavy, rank, fetid*

Some yards short of where they were standing, Baxter and the man, side by side and hand in hand, Christie stopped running.

She had felt elated and relieved as she had run, but now a new profound tiredness had suddenly hit her and, to her shame, somewhere within that tiredness there was hurt too. Despite her outstretched arms, Baxter had not run to her.

Tired, hurt, relieved, disappointed, Christie dropped to her knees and hugged Baxter close to her. Only now did the ache in her arms begin to stop. It would never finally go though, never finally leave her, that ache, she knew that. Once a mother had held her child, it would be with her always.

'Where have you been, Baxter?' Christie said, holding him close, holding his head against her shoulder, feeling the silky touch of his hair. 'I've been so worried.'

Baxter wriggled free from her arms.

'I've been with Soldier,' he said, taking Soldier's hand again. 'I've been at his camp. He's my friend.'

Still on her knees, Christie looked up at the tall gaunt man with wild, darting, fearful eyes who stood beside Baxter. Against the reddening sky, with his frizzled hair tumbling to his shoulders and his long grey messy tangle of a beard, he had the look of an Old Testament prophet, like Elijah bringing fire down from the sky. At first glance, the long dark coat added to this illusion, flowing as it did like a desert robe; but as Christie looked more closely, she could see that the coat was worn frayed and thin, that it was encrusted with countless years of dirt and grime and that it hung from his shoulders like a rag. One surviving button dangled forlornly on a single cotton thread and with the coat falling open Christie could see that the man's blackened trousers were gathered and tied at the waist with string and that they finished some way above his ankles, above his scuffed, broken-laced boots.

Christie looked at Soldier with the rising horror of a child's nightmare. She wanted to look away, but she couldn't pull her eyes from him. In all her fears about what might have happened to Baxter, lost in the woods, she could not have imagined this; she could not have imagined him being out there with this strange and terrible creature.

And then the smell hit her. He carried the smell of decay about him, heavy, rank, fetid and unwholesome.

Christie got to her feet and took a step backwards; her hand went to cover her mouth, to cover her nose.

340

'He washes in the stream but he does still smell a little bit,' Baxter said by way of explanation.

'But you do get used to it after a while,' he added. 'Sort of.'

The man still held Baxter's hand in his own; he was saying something softly, over and over, in a low droning mumble. Baxter looked up at him proprietorially, as if he was at once both troubled and proud.

'And he sort of talks to himself all the time. And I think he talks to other things as well. But I don't think he knows he does. Not really,' Baxter said.

Another jagged flash of lightning, another sonorous boom of thunder.

Christie twisted to look towards the storm and then turned quickly back to Baxter and to the man beside him.

'We need to be going,' she said to Soldier.

Despite the revulsion towards him that had risen up in her, she felt she needed to acknowledge him and in doing so to thank him in some way for bringing Baxter safely back to her.

'The storm,' she said. 'It's coming this way.'

Soldier carried on with his low repetitive mumble, his face without expression, his eyes darting shyly, feverishly.

'I think you should say goodbye to your friend now,' Christie said to Baxter.

Baxter shook his head; not defiantly, more pleadingly.

'I want him to come too,' he said.

'No, Baxter …' Christie started to say, looking up in horror once more at Soldier.

'I want to show him the caravan,' Baxter said. 'Please.'

Another quickfire flash, another threatening roar. Closer; it was coming closer. They would have to move soon.

'Very well,' Christie said. 'But not for long – and we must go now.'

Baxter tugged gently at Soldier's hand and they set off walking across the clearing, walking as if into the footsteps of their impossibly long, improbably stretched shadows as the storm crackled and fizzed, crashed and echoed in the sky ahead of them.

Baxter and Soldier walked hand in hand and, walking a little apart from them, Christie couldn't help but feel another small ridiculous stab of hurt. As if sensing this, Baxter reached for her hand. The hurt faded just a little.

# 68

# Truman: 8.36 p.m.

## *He took a succession of greedy gulping breaths*

Truman hadn't seen Christie kick off her shoes and start to run; he had been still bent almost double at the time, fighting for the breath that Strachan had forced from his body when he had smacked him with the baseball bat. Inch by inch and painfully, and still wheezing shallowly like some asthmatic old man fighting his way up a hill, Truman had finally managed to straighten himself and open his eyes. It was only then that he had seen Christie running towards the woods along the zigzagging trail through the long grass of the clearing. With one hand still clutched to his stomach where the blow had landed and the other shielding his eyes against the blindingly low sun, he had tried to work out what the hell she was doing, why the hell she was running across the clearing like that. Finally he could just make them out, the two figures dark against the woods. One of them must be her precious Baxter come back to her. The little sod.

Bloody Christie. You couldn't make her up, could you?

Here he was, fighting for his life against this madman Strachan. Here he was, having had everything taken away from him, everything *stolen* from him – his car, his watch, everything. Here he was, at the very end of his tether and instead of helping him, instead of making sure he was all right, where was his beloved wife, where was Christie? She was off, skipping through the grass like some bloody schoolgirl, as if she hadn't a bloody care in the whole bloody world. That's where.

Still barely trusting himself to breathe, Truman had watched as Christie had slowed to a walk, as she had reached the two figures, as she had fallen to her knees and taken Baxter into her arms.

And another thing.

She'd taken her time back there, hadn't she? She'd taken her time to finally find her voice and yell to stop the psycho. She could have put a stop to it all before that, couldn't she? She could at least have screamed at Strachan *before* he'd laid into him with the baseball bat. Unless, of course, she'd wanted Strachan to hit him. Unless she wanted Strachan to hurt him. Yes, that was it, that must have been it! She must have been enjoying it, watching him being hurt, watching him suffer that way. Bloody *enjoying* it, she was.

Bloody Christie! Like he said: you couldn't make her up, could you?

Clutching at his stomach, Truman had turned and looked towards Strachan. Was he going to come at him again, now Christie wasn't there? Was he going to have another go? For reasons that Truman couldn't make any sense of, Strachan was standing there, not far from the caravan, staring at his hands. The baseball bat was at his feet.

'I'll be back tomorrow,' Strachan had finally said, his eyes still fixed on his hands.

What? He'd come back tomorrow? Well, if he did, Truman for one wouldn't be there. Not bloody likely.

'I'll be back tomorrow. For the car,' Strachan said.

He had at last finished examining his hands. Looking directly at Truman, he had gone through a routine of flexing his shoulders, adjusting his tie, pulling at the cuffs of his shirt sleeves, pulling himself fully upright. But it didn't look as though his heart was really in it and instead of making him look composed, instead of making him look menacing, it just made him seem fidgety and agitated.

Just for an instant Truman wondered what he had been so scared of.

'I'll be back tomorrow, so make sure that fucking car is still there,' Strachan had said.

Scooping up the baseball bat by its fat clubbed end, he had pointed the shaft towards Truman as a final reminder before setting off slowly, heavily, back to his own car, the car that he had so carefully parked across the lane beneath the canopy of trees. The driver's door had slammed closed, the ignition had turned and fired and Strachan had manoeuvred his way back along the lane.

Good riddance.

It was only when the car had disappeared in a spiralling cloud of dust that Truman had finally allowed himself to breathe. He took a succession of greedy gulping breaths, like a thirsty man glugging down great reviving draughts of water. Feeling at least partly restored, he looked back across the clearing to the woods. Christie and the boy were walking towards him and there was someone with them. They were all walking hand in hand, as if all three of them were off to some bloody picnic.

The sun was sinking to the horizon now and as the three figures walked, their giant pinched shadows extended far in front of them. Another burst of lightning lit up the darkening sky. A mighty crack and growl of thunder quickly followed.

The storm. Truman had forgotten about the storm. Somehow until that moment he had not been aware of the lightning, had not heard the distant thunder. Now it was almost upon them.

'Jesus H. Christ ...'

That was all he bloody needed, Truman thought. One minute he's lying there in a tree in the sunshine and he's dreaming of that first pint of the evening at The Hare and Hounds, dreaming of Doll, of nuzzling into her neck, of breathing in her musky scent, of pulling her hard against him, of the silkiness of her dress, of the rustle of her stockings, and life could hardly have been much sweeter. The next, bingo, everything has gone arse over tit and backwards and he's got nothing, nothing but a black eye, a pain burning where his guts once were and a suitcase full of sliced-up clothes. He's got nothing and nowhere and now, as if all that wasn't enough, all hell was about to break loose and it was going to rain and storm like there was no tomorrow.

Instinctively Truman's eyes went towards the only shelter there was, the caravan. Even that was barred to him. In the doorway, Megan stood holding the baby. Both of them were crying; Megan a shivering whimper, the baby a vigorous wail.

Even his Megan had turned against him now.

And one more thing.

*None* of this would have happened if it hadn't been for them, for Christie and the bloody boy, would it? It was all down to them. All of it. If it hadn't been for them, if it hadn't been for the boy running off like that, he would have been away from there hours ago. He'd have been out of their way before that Strachan had got there. He'd have been away scot-free and he'd still have the car, he'd still have his watch, he'd still have the fifty in his pocket. He might even have got to his clothes before Doll did.

Doll? You couldn't trust anyone, could you? She'd ratted him up to Strachan; just as Sally had done earlier in the day. You treat people right and they end up doing you down; there was no justice, was there? And she didn't need to do that to his clothes. That was just vindictive. That was just plain nasty. And not content with that, not content with taking it out on his shirts and the crotch of his trousers, *then* she'd sent that bastard Strachan after him. He didn't deserve that. All he was guilty of was showing her a good time, wasn't it?

He was piecing it together now.

So Doll had sent Strachan to the clearing, but the mystery was how Strachan had got to Doll in the first place. No one knew about Doll. No one knew about The Hare and Hounds, about the good thing he had going there. No one even knew the place existed. No one except— His mother! His own mother, she was the only one that knew, he'd given her the bloody address that morning, just to keep her sweet, to stop her moaning at him all the bloody time, and Strachan must have somehow tracked her down, Christ alone knew how. And she'd shopped him! His own mother!

They were much closer now, Christie, Baxter and the stranger, all still walking hand in hand. Despite the long shadows and the rapidly fading light, Truman could now see him quite clearly.

'Jesus H. Christ . . . !'

Christie had found some filthy old tramp, or Baxter had. Whoever had found him, they were bringing him back to the caravan like he was some long-lost brother. What the hell were they bringing him back there for? Holding his bloody hand, the boy was! And the man, the tramp, he scarcely looked human at all. He was just this stomach-churning yellowing bag of bones and hair wrapped in rags.

'Who the hell are you?' Truman called to him.

Jesus Christ. He smelled like death.

'He doesn't talk,' Baxter said, still holding his hand. 'His name is Soldier. He's my friend.'

The sky lit up once more; thunder raged and bellowed; a sudden gusting breeze scurried across the tall grass. They were standing in front of Truman now; all three of them in a line. Christie and Baxter looked up briefly to follow the progress of the storm; the tramp just stood there, muttering to himself, his downcast eyes moving restlessly.

'I'm not talking to you, boy,' Truman said to Baxter, pointing at him. 'I'll deal with *you* later.'

Truman turned again to Soldier. 'I said, who the hell are you?'

Christie took a step forwards, a step towards him.

'No, Truman,' she said. 'You have no place here.'

Stunned, Truman took a pace backwards.

'*No place?*' he shouted at her.

Christie ignored his question, ignored the shout of anger. That wouldn't have happened before, Truman thought. It was as if something was suddenly different in her.

She spoke quietly, evenly, quickly.

'This man is Baxter's friend. I think he lives somewhere in the woods. Baxter is going to say goodbye to him. He is leaving now—'

'*No place?*' Truman yelled again.

The slow blink of her eyes told him that he'd got to her this time. This time she couldn't find it in herself to ignore him.

'It's over, Truman. I told you before. It's over,' she said.

She sounded like she meant it. But just keep her talking and that would soon change.

'Don't you realise I've lost everything, everything?' he said disconsolately.

Christie nodded; Truman could see that she was reluctant to say anything more. It was a game, really. It was all a game.

'But I did it for you, princess,' he said. 'For you and for the kids. Everything I did was for you ...'

If he could just keep her talking, she'd come round. That was the game. She'd have to get angry first, of course. She'd have to get that out of the way, get it out of her system, that was only to be expected. But slowly and surely she'd come round, wouldn't she? Wouldn't she?

'Your mother, Sally, Doll? They were for *me*?' Christie said.

She couldn't help herself, see; she couldn't help being drawn in.

'They've got nothing to do with it, princess. Forget about them; I can explain all that. Honestly I can. All I was trying to do was to give you and the kids the best of everything. That's why I borrowed the money.'

Christie looked up at him and suddenly Truman could see it in her eyes. The look, exactly as it was before, the steely contempt.

He knew then that he'd been kidding himself. He could try to keep her talking all day; he could sweet-talk her and promise her the earth, the moon, the sun, the stars, and none of it would make a blind bit of difference. It had all gone too far for that. Thanks to that bastard Strachan.

'I don't want to hear any more,' she said. 'I've told you, I don't want to hear any of it.'

It wasn't just her eyes; he could hear the determination in her voice too. Something *had* changed in her. Instead of breaking her up, what Strachan had told her had somehow made her stronger.

'We're going inside now and I want you to leave,' she said.

Baxter let go of Soldier's hand and Christie started to usher him towards the caravan door.

Leave? It might have gone too far, but he wasn't having that.

'*Leave?*' he said, looking around him, arms outstretched, palms upwards as if to catch the first few drops of rain when they came. 'But where will I go? Where?'

'I don't know, Truman,' Christie said wearily. 'And I don't care. We're going inside now.'

350

It was too much, too much to take; something snapped inside him.

She didn't care! She didn't bloody care! Who the hell did she think she was? She'd just walk off and leave him there, would she? Leave him with nowhere to go. Leave him with nothing. After everything he'd done for her. Well, he'd see about that.

Truman took two quick strides forwards, grabbed Baxter by the arm and dragged him away from Christie.

'You're going nowhere!' he shouted at her, jabbing his finger, shaking with the anger that was now pounding through him, dangling the boy in one hand.

'Not before I deal with this little sod, you're not!' he said.

'NO, DADDY!' Megan screamed from the door of the caravan.

'NO!' Christie cried out.

He'd cost him everything, that boy. Everything. Him with those bloody eyes looking at him.

'I'll teach you to run off, you little sod!'

He grabbed Baxter with both hands and shook him, shook him hard, just as he had shaken him by the roadside earlier in the day, shook him like a broken doll. He then raised his open hand, held it high, poised, momentarily frozen in time, ready to bring it crashing down.

'I'll knock the living daylights out of you!'

# 69

## Soldier: 8.42 p.m.

### *It ran from his bony finger and dripped on Truman's face*

Everything seemed to happen at once; as if everything had been waiting to come together in that one moment. It was at that moment that the sun finally dropped below the horizon, draining the last light from the clearing; that lightning forked and crackled and fractured the now-darkened sky directly above; that a shattering cannon-roar of thunder shook the earth itself; that the breeze that had scurried lightly through the long grass became a howling rush of wind; and that the hammering rain began to fall in a torrent.

And it was in that same moment that Soldier stepped forwards.

As Soldier stepped forwards, as he strode confidently the few paces towards Truman with his long coat billowing and flapping behind him in the wind, he looked upwards and he closed his eyes, he clenched his fists and raised them high.

Suddenly it was as if the storm was meant for him.

The lightning lit up the smile stretched on his face. The artillery crash of the thunder had ceased the querulous babble in his head. While the tempest raged, all was still within him.

It was as if he was suddenly at the very eye of the storm.

It was more than that.

It was as if he was conducting it. Lifting it. Urging it. Forcing it ever onwards. Carrying it towards its crescendo. Riding it like a wave, a wave of sound and fury.

It was even more than that. It was something that made Soldier want to shout with laughter.

It was as if he had *become* the storm itself. He *was* the storm. He commanded it, it ran through him.

Seeing him coming, seeing him striding towards him while the storm broke around him, Truman recoiled from Soldier.

He shrank from him, tried to step back and away and, in doing so, he slipped, stumbled, toppled and fell backwards. As he fell, he let go of the boy.

'Who the hell are you ..?' Truman shouted up at him, lying flat on his back in the long grass.

Soldier answered him with an agonising roar. He answered and his voice was thunder. He shook his fists and lightning scorched the sky.

Freed from his father's grasp, Baxter ran the few yards to his mother.

Truman was at Soldier's feet, squirming in the tall grass. Towering above him, fists still raised high, the gaping smile still fixed to his face, Soldier opened his eyes wide and watched as the boy clung hard and fiercely to his mother. He watched as the wild wind and the pummelling rain beat at them.

'*What the ...?*' Truman managed to splutter, trying to push himself backwards, slithering through the grass and away from Soldier.

Soldier leaned over Truman as the sky lit up above him once more. He looked down, lowered his arms, unclenched his fists and pointed a long accusing finger towards him. Rainwater ran from Soldier's brow, from his cheeks, from his nose, from his matted hair and beard. It ran from his bony finger and dripped on Truman's face.

Truman desperately shook the water away, as if it were acid that burned into him.

'You're a bloody headcase, that's what you are!' Truman said, still trying to force himself backwards and away from Soldier.

'You need bloody locking up, you do!' he said, finally struggling to his feet and backing away as quickly as he could.

Soldier bent and picked up the suitcase that Truman had left open in the grass. He swung it by the handle and threw it towards him. The suitcase arced as if in slow motion, scattering Truman's shredded clothes to the mercy of the storm. It landed with a small hollow thud and skidded into Truman's shins.

Hopping first on one leg and then the other, Truman rubbed at his shins. He then picked up the empty suitcase.

'You'll pay for this!' he shouted at Soldier, at Christie, at Megan and Baxter, through a curtain of hurtling rain. '*You'll all bloody pay for this!*'

Soldier once more raised his bony finger. As if to send Truman finally on his way.

Seeing Truman slipping and stumbling towards the lane,

Christie grabbed Baxter by the hand and pulled him towards the caravan.

Soldier heard the caravan door click to a close.


The storm was passing quickly now. It was gone from him and the black dog was once more by his side, rubbing its liquid flanks against his legs. The rain was falling steadily but its sting had diminished. Thunder grumbled and growled in the distance. And the last faint flicker of lightning briefly illuminated the woods that bordered the clearing.

It was over.

# 70

# Baxter: 8.45 p.m.

## *He didn't understand what she meant*

Inside the caravan everyone was holding each other and they were all crying. Megan was crying softly, the baby loudly, his mother silently. Everyone was crying except Baxter. And he didn't want to. Not really.

Baxter and Megan were standing side by side and Christie was kneeling on the floor in front of them. She was trying to dry Megan's tears, first with her fingers and then with the heel of her hand, trying to somehow push them away and rub them dry at the same time. She did the same with her own tears and she then put her hand to Baxter's face. But he was just wet from the rain, he didn't have any tears. Not really.

'You're soaked to the skin,' she said to him, with a sudden small wild laugh as she shivered in her own wet clothes.

Baxter didn't say anything. Through the caravan windows

that were quickly steaming up, he could see Soldier still standing in the rain outside, still pointing in the direction that he had sent Baxter's father.

'You must be tired,' his mother said. 'And you must be hungry?'

Baxter may have been a little tired but he wasn't hungry.

'I had some food that Soldier made,' he said.

After Baxter had tried to wash the stain of Doll's lip-stick from his face, Soldier had added the vegetables that Mrs Chadney had given him to a saucepan of leftover stew. Baxter and Soldier had then sat by the fire and watched the pan bubble. Baxter hadn't been sure what the few pieces of grey meat were in the stew, and he wasn't sure that his mother would have thought that everything was really clean enough to cook with and then eat from, but the stew had tasted much better than he thought it would and he had never sat by a fire and eaten from a saucepan before.

Once they had eaten, Soldier sluiced the pan in the stream and they had then sat side by side just watching how the water shimmied and eddied and ran over the small dam of pebbles. Finally, reluctantly, Baxter had broken the spell, had broken the silence and said that he should go back to the caravan. He didn't want to, but he thought his mother might have started to get worried. Probably.

'Was the food good?' his mother said with a big smile.

'Sort of,' Baxter replied.

'And you had candyfloss in Brighton,' she said.

Baxter frowned.

'And you went on the dodgems,' she said.

He didn't understand what she meant.

'And there's a red mark on your cheek,' his mother said gently. 'And there's another on your forehead.'

Although his father had told him not to, Baxter wondered whether he should after all ask his mother about the woman called Doll, about her piled-up hair, about her skirt that meant she couldn't walk properly, about her lipstick and everything. And he wondered whether now would be a good time to ask her.

He wondered too whether he should say anything else, whether he should tell her about the house that wasn't like their house any more because of everything that wasn't there. He thought perhaps that she might be able to tell him why his things had been all smashed up while everyone else's had just gone. He also wanted to tell her about the boys he had seen on the slide and about the man with the yellow broken teeth and the bottle who had banged on the car and who had landed against the wall. And he wanted to tell her about other things like the red marks on his arms or about sitting with Soldier and watching the stream and how a small bird had come down to drink.

Baxter wasn't sure exactly why but in the end he decided he wouldn't say anything about any of it. He wasn't sure why but in the end he decided he would never say anything about any of it at all.

His mother still knelt in front of Baxter and Megan; she put her arms around them both and pulled them in to her. Over her shoulder as she hugged him, as she rubbed and patted at his back to make him warm, Baxter could still just about see through the misted caravan window.

Soldier was still there in the rain and Baxter watched intently as he stood in a small pool of light that came from the caravan, the rain glistening on his face. Baxter watched as he reached into his coat pocket and as he pulled out and then unwrapped the rag that he had folded so carefully while they had sat together on the flint wall. He watched as Soldier peered into the rag and then as he held up the small toy soldier to check that it was safe. And he watched as he turned it in the light, as he weighed it in his hand, as if there was nothing more precious in the world, and as he ran his bony finger over its every surface.

Baxter was still watching as Soldier once more wrapped up his small parcel with such concentration and care, as he plunged it back into the depths of his pocket, and then finally as he limped slowly away into the darkness.

And it was then that Baxter thought that maybe he did want to cry a little after all.

# THE FOLLOWING DAY

# 71

# Truman

*Like a lover saying a sad farewell*
*with a last gentle caress*

Truman was up with the lark. And, bearing in mind what he'd been through the day before, considering everything that Christie, Sally, Doll and that psycho Strachan had tried to do to him, considering the mill they'd put him through, *and* considering he'd been set upon by some stinking lunatic in a storm, he felt pretty good.

For one thing, he'd slept much better than he thought he might. He'd thought he would be haunted by thoughts of Strachan coming at him swinging that bat. Or maybe of Soldier stepping out of the storm itself and looming over him like Christopher Lee or that Peter bloody Cushing. Or of the rainwater running off his blackened hand and burning into his face like drops of acid.

Instead, as he slid between the crisp white linen sheets of the soft single bed, he'd slipped off into an untroubled sleep almost as soon as his head had touched the pillow. He'd just about had time to think that it was difficult to beat, that soft seductive smell of fresh linen and that small tingling shock of the newness of the sheets on your skin, and that was him gone, out like a light.

And he'd eaten, of course: mutton stew and apple pie last night, and he'd helped himself to a bit of breakfast in the morning.

And then there were his clothes. His shirt was freshly laundered, his collar scrubbed, his suit had been dried, brushed and pressed back into shape and his shoes had the kind of glassy polish that only someone who had done their turn of National Service could hope to achieve. He may not have learned much about anything else in his time at Catterick, but he certainly came away knowing how to put the very devil of a shine on a pair of boots.

As he marched back along the lane towards the clearing, to where Christie and the kids were still asleep inside the caravan, there was almost a spring in Truman's step. The sun was up, the day was new and the only evidence that remained of the storm of the night before were a few scattered puddles where the potholes in the lane were particularly deep; it scarcely seemed possible to Truman that the land could have taken so much punishment, absorbed so much water and could then have recovered so entirely that it could almost be forgotten that the storm had passed that way.

Yes, all in all, he felt pretty good.

OK, so his stomach was sore as hell from where the baseball bat had hit, the cut on his face was still raw and tender and he boasted a shiner as if he'd gone the distance with the Big Bear, Sonny Liston. And OK, so that bastard Strachan had taken his car, his watch, everything that mattered to him. And OK, the suitcase he was swinging in his hand was empty and, yes, it was true that the only clothes he had were those that he stood in, but it wasn't all bad, was it? After all, no bones had been broken, had they? He still had his health. He was still smart enough to stay one step ahead of the rest. He'd bounce back. And the thirty pounds in his pocket helped, didn't it?

When he reached the clearing, Truman rested the empty suitcase on the ground; he plucked the comb from his breast pocket and ran it through his hair while he looked about him with a smile on his face.

His shredded clothes had been left where they had fallen as the suitcase had flown through the air; they were lying in the long grass in sad sodden pools. Truman rammed the comb back into his pocket and the smile fell at once from his face.

If someone had been there at that moment to tap him on the shoulder and ask, he would have had to admit that it had taken some of the wind out of his sails, that it had brought him up a bit short, the sight of his clothes like that. As it was he stood there alone and let a wave of bitterness break over him. And who could blame him for that? Because you would have thought she would have picked them up. That wouldn't have been too much to ask, would it? All right, they were no use for anything but rags now, but you'd have thought she might have shown a bit of decency, a bit of respect, a bit of pity.

Bloody Christie.

The Wolseley was still there, of course, parked just where he had left it. He ran his hand over the curve of its bonnet, like a lover saying a sad farewell with a last gentle caress of the face.

He turned back to face the caravan. For just a moment he was tempted by the idea of striding across the clearing and knocking sorrowfully on the door. He played with the thought that something might come out of his saying some big tearful goodbye to them, that by laying it on thick he might make them realise what they would be missing once he was gone from their lives. But as quickly as the thought had come, it was gone.

Sod them. Sod her, sod Christie.

He'd done everything he could for them, hadn't he, and what had he got in return? A door slammed in his face, that's what he'd got. A door slammed in his face when he'd nowhere to go and no way of getting there, in the dead of night in the pouring rain after that headcase, that filthy tramp, that 'Soldier', had attacked him. He could have had a gun, that Soldier; he could have had a knife. Truman could have been left for dead, for all they bloody cared. So sod them; he didn't need them. For the time being, he was better off on his own.

Truman took a final long look at the caravan, picked up the empty suitcase, and set off walking briskly again, along the lane towards the road. The more he walked, the more the bitterness passed, the more his step remembered its spring.

Because, like he said, it wasn't all bad.

He'd had some fun, had more than a few laughs, sat at the old Joanna with the crowd at The Hare and Hounds. And he'd had a good time with Sally and with Doll. Any man would envy him that, wouldn't they? And no one had been seriously hurt. He'd shown them a good time; he'd been good to them, to all of them. And Christie would come round in the end. She just needed time. He'd smooth it all over with her; he'd make it all sweet. Anyway, she'd find out soon enough. She'd soon learn how hard it was to get by, without him. She'd come running back in the end, wouldn't she?

Wouldn't she?

Truman was glad when he rounded the final bend and the end of the lane at last came into sight. He had been surprised how much longer the lane seemed on foot than in a car. After a while his pace had gradually slowed to little more than an amble and the suitcase, empty as it was, had grown heavier in his hand with each step he took. Along the way he had come to the view that, where the canopy of trees over the lane parted from time to time to let the light flood in, the sun was unnecessarily bright for a man who had been knocked about as much as he had in the past twenty-four hours. He had also decided that the birds made one hell of a needless racket at that time in the morning. And he had decided that what he wanted above everything else and with an urgency that nagged at him, what he needed more than anything in the world, was a cigarette.

He'd had his last cigarette just before turning in the night before; usually he would have had his first of the day in bed before he got up. By instinct, by habit, that morning the first thing he had done was to reach for his cigarette packet. Finding it empty he had screwed it to a ball and tossed it into the corner of the tiny cottage room. It had rolled under the big old heavy wardrobe where his newly pressed suit hung. She probably wouldn't find it for years under there, he'd thought.

The thought of the cottage took his mind briefly away from the need for a cigarette.

It had been a gamble, of course, turning that way, walking that way down the lane towards the cottage, stumbling and splashing through the flooded potholes and the treacherous puddles in the dark. Most people wouldn't have done it; most people would have tried to struggle back the greater distance to the main road. But that's where he was different, see. That's how he stayed ahead of the game. He took risks and this one had paid off handsomely.

And they'd been wrong about her. Christie, Doll, the bloke in the pub who had rented him the caravan, they'd all been wrong about Mrs Chadney. She wasn't that bad, was she? After all, he'd turned up there in the pitch black, in the pouring rain, with nowhere else to go and nothing in his pocket and he'd hammered on her door and had come up with some cock-and-bull story about his car breaking down and she'd taken him in.

All right, she hadn't been happy about it at first or, in truth, at any time later, and she certainly had a bit of a tongue on her. That was for sure. A bit of a nasty temper too; she could curse and swear with the best of them. But she had a heart made of pure gold. When you came to think of it, she'd done more for him than his own family had, hadn't she? More than his own wife, without a shadow of doubt.

No, she was all right, Mrs Chadney: she'd taken him in and he wouldn't hear a word against her.

And that hadn't been all. Not only had she taken him in, she'd lent him some old clothes while his own had dried on the back of a chair in front of the stove; she'd fed him and she'd made him a mug of strong steaming tea; she'd scrubbed the blood from the collar of his shirt; she'd shown him how to work the old heavy iron; she'd rummaged around for some ancient boot polish and brushes; she'd boiled the water so that he could wash and bathe the cut to his face; she'd found an old cut-throat razor and a strop to sharpen it on so that he could have a shave; she'd made up a bed in the spare room with fresh sheets.

OK, she may have grumbled about it, she may have ranted and sworn as she shuffled about the cottage on her stick, she may have done all of it while cursing non-stop under her breath, she may even have spat in disgust into the kitchen sink at one point, but she did it, didn't she? She did all that for a stranger who turned up in the dead of night looking like he'd been dragged through a hedge both backwards and then forwards again for good measure and who had a cut on his face and blood on his collar.

And even that wasn't all. She'd also told him something about the headcase who had attacked him, that Soldier.

'Do you know what, princess?' Truman had said to her while he worked at the kitchen table at the shine on his shoes.

She hadn't replied; she had just kept scrubbing at his collar over the kitchen sink.

'Do you know what, I thought I saw someone tonight . . .' he'd said.

'Saw someone?' she'd hissed, looking up.

'As I was coming along the lane,' he'd said. 'I thought I saw this old tramp. Long hair, long white beard, big dark coat, lit up by the lightning, he was.'

She had stopped scrubbing, rested the collar in the sink and turned to him.

'You seen him?'

'I think so,' Truman had said.

'No one ever sees him,' she said. 'Only me.'

'But who is he?' Truman said.

'That'll be Soldier you seen,' Mrs Chadney said.

'But who is he?' Truman had said. 'I thought he might be in trouble, out on a night like this. I thought he might need some help.'

'He don't need no help, bloody stinking fool,' she said. 'Lives out in the woods, he does. Got some kind of shelter place on the far side of Tabell Ghyll.'

'You know him though?' Truman had said.

'Know him?' she'd laughed. 'It was me that found him. Came across him half dead in the woods, years ago now, it was. Nursed him, I did; brought him back to life. I even gave him his ruddy name; had to call him something so I called him what he was, a bloody soldier—'

It was then that she had spat in the sink.

'But I should have left him out there, should have left him where he was.'

'Why's that, princess?' Truman had said soothingly.

'Because he's soft in the ruddy head, that's why,' she said angrily. 'He don't know who he is or where he come from; I never heard him say a single bloody word you could make sense of. I even put a label on him, I did. I hoped someone would find him and take him away.'

'But no one ever did?' Truman said.

Mrs Chadney shook her head.

'He keeps coming back here,' she said sadly. 'Does my garden. Bloody fool.'

She picked up the collar from the sink.

'I reckon they blowed his senses clean away, they did,' she said, the anger still in her voice.

'Who did?' Truman said.

'Back in the war,' she said. 'They must have blowed him to bits and blowed his senses away too. He'd be better off dead—'

She spat again.

'It ain't right,' she said, as if to herself. 'It ain't right why he should live and others be taken.'

Truman wasn't sure what she meant by that, and he had a sense that there was something more that she wanted to talk about, but he didn't have time for an old woman's reminiscences so he went back to working on the shine of his boots.

No, Truman wouldn't hear a word against her, Mrs Chadney. He'd always remember her, always be grateful.

And she wouldn't miss it, would she, Mrs Chadney?

She wouldn't miss the thirty. After all, what did she need the money for at her age? What was she going to spend it on out there in the woods? It had probably sat in that tea caddy on the top shelf of the dresser for years. She had probably forgotten all about it. She probably wouldn't even know it had gone.

When Truman finally reached the road, he put the smile back on his face and stuck out an optimistic thumb to the first car that passed. Bingo; the driver pulled to a stop a few yards in front of him.

'Where to?' the man shouted to him, winding down his window.

'What's the first town on your way?' Truman said.

'Well there's Forest Row not far away ...'

'That'll do, thanks.'

Truman climbed into the car and threw the suitcase on to the back seat.

'That's some shiner,' the man said approvingly, pointing to Truman's eye.

'Spot of bother with somebody's husband,' Truman said with a laugh.

'Oh, I see, like that, is it?' the man replied, joining the laughter.

He was a large round-faced man with a neat moustache; he wore a tweed jacket and a matching flat cap. Truman guessed he must have been RAF.

'Here, mate, you haven't got a cigarette, have you?' Truman said.

The man took a packet from the dashboard and tossed it towards Truman.

'Help yourself,' he said with a smile.

Truman did help himself. While the man concentrated on negotiating the bends in the road, Truman took three cigarettes from the packet. In the same motion with which he searched for his lighter, he then dropped two of them into his jacket pocket. For later; to keep him going.

Truman relaxed now, back into the passenger seat; he drew on the cigarette, held the smoke in his lungs, and then slowly released it.

He was off, he was on his way. He had a call to make, a score to settle and after that it was pastures new for him.

He had an idea that he might give Margate a try; he'd heard good things about it, heard there may be opportunities for a man like him, opportunities to make it big quickly. It would be a shame to leave Brighton, of course. It was his kind of town, the kind of town that woke up late and with a sore head on a Sunday morning, the kind of town that knew how to let its hair down and have a good time, how to have a right old knees-up. Still, it couldn't be helped, could it? And maybe once the dust had settled, he might get back there one day.

'Where in Forest Row can I drop you?' the man said.

'Is there a phone box?' Truman said with a smile.

It would be best to do it anonymously, he thought. After all, there was no need to give a name. A name would only complicate things. The Old Bill would still follow up on it, with or without a name. They had no choice; they couldn't turn a deaf ear to a report of a dangerous lunatic on the loose in the woods, could they? They couldn't turn a blind eye to a madman who lived rough out there, not far from the clearing at Tabell Ghyll where a nice young family were staying in a caravan. They couldn't ignore a madman with a knife.

Truman closed his eyes and took another long drag on his cigarette.

No, it wasn't such a bad life at all, was it?

# 72

# Strachan

*Strachan had something else
in mind for the fifty*

In the time it had taken to leave the clearing and arrive
back in Brighton, Strachan had made three decisions. And
the first had been the most difficult.

It was over, finished. *He* was finished.

Not that he had been able to admit it to himself right
away; it hadn't been that simple.

At first he'd not been able to put it into words. To begin
with, and from the moment when Truman's wife had
screamed at him to stop and he'd dropped the baseball bat at
his feet, he'd been like some fucking zombie, not able to put
*anything* into words.

It had only been later, after he'd driven as if in a trance
some way back along the lane away from the clearing, after
a blanket of darkness had wrapped itself suddenly around the
car and had sent him scrabbling at the dashboard for the

headlights, after it had started coming down cats and dogs and the rain had begun bouncing off the bonnet and the windscreen; it had only been when the lane had flooded and had turned instantly into a rutted, potholed lake that Strachan had finally snapped to, had jerked back to life.

And that's when the words had come.

It was over. Finished.

That was him done; that was him out of it. All of it.

The truth was that he had known from the moment he'd dropped the baseball bat that he couldn't do it any more, that he didn't want to do it any more. For one thing, it had all felt so pointless, so completely fucking ridiculous: a man of his age carrying on like that, carrying on like some teenage hoodlum while that boy was out there lost in the woods. That was part of it. But there was something else. There was a bigger truth: he'd realised that, however long he stood there and however hard he stared at his hands, he wouldn't be able to stop the shaking. Not this time, he wouldn't. He'd known that there was no going on like this; there was no possible way back from that. How could he do what he did and be like that? How could he be Strachan and have the fucking shakes?

It was over.

He had been so numbed, so out of it, so tired and through with all of it, he almost hadn't even bothered to bend down and pick up the baseball bat. What he had felt like doing was just walking away and leaving it there, his precious bat, this thing that had been so much part of him. But he'd still had some pride. He was still Strachan. He wasn't going to let that toerag Truman see what was going on. So somehow he'd pulled himself upright, pulled himself together; he'd tugged at his cuffs, smartened himself up; he'd waved the bat at Truman; and then somehow he'd made it back to his car.

It was over. He would tell Mr Smith tomorrow and he could send someone else to fetch Truman's car. He could send his new pretty boy.

By the time Strachan had driven far out of the reach of the storm and had passed the stone pylons on the last stretch of the road into Brighton, he had made his second decision. About the fifty.

Mr Smith could have the car and the watch and he already had the contents of the house. But Strachan had something else in mind for the fifty; it was destined for elsewhere. It wasn't like Strachan to conceal the truth from him but on this one occasion he reasoned that what Mr Smith's eye didn't see, his heart wouldn't grieve over.

By the time Strachan had climbed the echoing stairs of the bedsits and had wearily fumbled to turn his key in the lock of the door to his room, he had made the third decision. He would go back and see her the following morning. He would go back to see Sally.

The thought of it had brought a smile to his face.

Before first light, and unable to sleep any longer, he had risen, dressed and taken up his position in the armchair by the bedsit window. Awake through the small hours of the night, he had been left more certain about his first two decisions and less sure about the third. He had watched the day begin to dawn over another placid grey sea. He had heard the rattle and purr of the milk float and the bottles clinking on the steps. He had watched a solitary swimmer dance her way unevenly across the pebbles. Alone on the beach and close to the shore she had dropped her long black raincoat from her shoulders to reveal a startling red swimsuit. With one hand she had twisted and gathered up her shoulder-length blonde hair and with the other she had pulled on a floral rubber swimming cap. Then, dipping a toe, she had tested the temperature of the water. Gathering her courage, she had waded into the sea before finally plunging head-first into the gently rolling waves.

Fuck it. He *would* go to see Sally.

Still sitting in his chair, nursing a mug of tea, Strachan had then watched the seafront come to life. Across the road and beneath the arches cut into what was once the cliff face, the shutters had been unlocked and thrown open and the shops that had been hidden behind them through the night had begun to prepare for another day. Trestle tables had been carried out and set up on the promenade and straw sunhats were then piled high; children's rubber beach shoes, goggles and blue and black flippers were hung on metal hooks; beach balls were inflated; postcards were slotted into rotating stands; the plastic cloths on the tables of the beachside cafés were wiped down and carousels of sauce bottles and cruet sets were brought out; the owner of the whelk stall had shared a joke with the deckchair attendant, their laughter carrying across the road and upwards to the bedsit window. There had been a sense of expectation, the buzz of a new day beginning, the buzz of a summer weekend starting.

Before long the first Saturday trippers had begun to arrive, hand in hand or arm in arm, in their shirtsleeves and in their summer dresses, wearing their new dark glasses, with their pushchairs and their prams and their laughter. They had arrived on the early trains from London, had hurried from beneath the dark shadow of the canopied station and had expectantly thronged the sunlit high pavements along Queen's Road and West Street and down to King's Road and to the glistening sea beyond.

Finally, having run through the words a hundred times, having put it off for as long as he could, Strachan had hauled himself out of the chair and made his way heavily down to the payphone at the foot of the stairs. Feeling more nervous than at any time he could recall, and suddenly discovering a stammer that had never been there before, he had rung Mr Smith and had told him, tripping and falling over his words as though he was a schoolboy, that he had done his last job for him and that Truman's car needed collecting from the clearing at Tabell Ghyll.

Mr Smith had fluttered, fussed and clucked like an agitated hen. In equal measure he had expressed consternation, concern and dismay; although Strachan had a sense that he may also have detected something that sounded like relief amongst Mr Smith's fluffed-up protestations. Perhaps he too knew that it was time for Strachan to call it a day, that it was beyond time. Refusing to take no for an answer, Mr Smith had insisted that they should meet to talk it all through. He wanted to hear all about Strachan's plans for the future.

*Plans?* Strachan had thought. What fucking plans? He had no plans.

They should meet, Mr Smith had said, where they had always met, at his table at the panelled tea room, the tea room with the gilded ceiling and the starchy white-aproned waitresses. With a sinking heart, seeing in his mind's eye his swollen-knuckled ham fist wrapped once more around a

378

dainty bone-china teacup, Strachan had said that he would ring again in a few days to arrange a time and a date. He didn't know whether or not he would; he didn't know whether he could face it.

It was over. Best just let it go.

When he put the telephone down, his hands were clammy and they were shaking again.

It really was over.

It was shortly after noon when Strachan stepped through the front doorway of the bedsits and set off along the crowded pavement, picking his way through the oncoming tide of newly arrived trippers, to cover the few hundred yards along the seafront to The Salvation. After the creaking quietness of his room, the cheerful hubbub on the pavement and the sound of the cars, impatiently revving their engines while queuing along King's Road looking for somewhere to park, surprised him.

Seeing the postbox on the corner ahead of him, Strachan patted at the pocket of his suit jacket to make sure that the envelope he had carefully placed there was still safe. In the envelope was the fifty. Reaching the corner, Strachan took it from his pocket, checked the address for a last time, and dropped it into the postbox.

He had decided not to include a letter. He wouldn't have known what to say or how to say it. And that meant that she would never know who had sent it to her; and, of course, she would never think of Strachan.

Better that way.

She would know immediately that it hadn't come from the

toerag; she'd see at once that it wasn't his handwriting on the envelope. She would take her time and she'd open it while still puzzling over the handwriting and that was when she would find the neatly folded notes. She would count them out: ten, twenty, thirty, forty, fifty. And she would wonder whether there had been some mistake. She would check the envelope again. She would think that it wasn't really meant for her, she would think it couldn't possibly be right, that she didn't deserve it, this money from nowhere. But to Strachan's mind no one deserved it more; no one had a greater claim to it. It would land on her doormat on Monday morning and it was only right, wasn't it, after that thieving bastard had taken everything she had? It gave her something back at least. OK, it was Doll's money. But she'd get over it. Truman's mother needed it much more than she did.

On the doorstep of The Salvation, Strachan paused. He went through his ritual of straightening his tie, tugging at his cuffs, smoothing his hair.

Always spick, always span.

He took a deep breath and pushed the door open.

The bar was empty except for the same two old men in flat caps who were at the same table as the previous day. They glanced across at Strachan as he stepped into the room and nodded to him in recognition and greeting. Sally was behind the dark wooden counter, slowly, distractedly polishing a tall pint glass. Strachan could see that there was a pale faraway look on her face. It was only when he walked towards her and the door swung closed behind him that she glanced up and greeted him with a small faint smile.

'Sorry, I didn't see it was you,' she said as he reached the bar. 'Miles away, I was. Lost in my thoughts . . .'

'Penny for them?' Strachan said gently, resting his hands on the polished counter, standing just close enough to catch the breath of her perfume.

'Not even worth a penny,' she said, looking away, looking down, looking embarrassed. 'Just daydreaming, I suppose.'

For a moment silence settled between them; Strachan wasn't sure what to do next, what to say next, he wasn't sure any more whether he had anything to say at all. He felt like a lumbering, tongue-tied teenager. It was left to Sally to break the silence.

'So,' she said. 'What brings you back? You still after Truman?'

'No,' Strachan said. 'I found him.'

'And . . . ?'

'And we had that friendly conversation that I said we would. Two conversations, in fact.'

Sally looked up, looked him directly in the eye. She was checking for the truth.

'Did you . . . Did you hurt him?' she said.

Strachan never had been able to lie. He'd never had it in him.

'Only a little,' he said.

Sally winced, closed her eyes for a moment. Those grey-green eyes.

'Don't get me wrong, I never want to see him again,' she said, 'but I wouldn't want him to be hurt. I don't like to see anyone hurt.'

She raised the glass that she was polishing to Strachan in a question. Strachan shook his head; he didn't want a drink.

'So what next?' she said. He could hear the sarcasm in the lift of her voice. 'Someone else you've got to hunt down, is there?'

'I'm no longer in that game,' he said quietly. 'I packed it in.'

It felt strange to be telling her this. Like sharing an intimacy. It felt good.

'Why's that?' she said, her eyebrows dipping into a puzzled frown.

Strachan shrugged. She didn't need to know.

'So, what will you do now?' she said, reaching for another glass to polish.

He shrugged again. The silence settled once more. This time it was Strachan who broke it.

'Sally . . ?' he said. It felt good to say her name. It felt new, it made his heart beat faster.

She looked up from her polishing.

'Sally, I was wondering . . .'

'What?' she said.

Fuck it.

'Nothing,' he said.

She was smiling at him, her face was lit up with this enormous delighted smile, her eyes were dancing; she was almost laughing, he could see that.

'Look,' he said, starting again, realising at once that somehow he was starting in the wrong place.

'What?' she said.

Fuck it.

She *was* laughing now.

'Are you trying to ask me something, Strachan?' she managed to say.

He nodded.

'Are you trying to ask me out?' she said.

He steadied himself.

'I just thought we might walk along the front together,' he said. 'This afternoon, in the sunshine . . . After closing time.'

The laughter had stopped but the smile was still there.

'I'd love to,' she said. 'But only if you buy me an ice cream and promise that you'll take off that jacket and roll up your sleeves.'

He nodded again.

He felt he had to say something more; he had to at least try to explain.

'Sally, I know I'm too old for you, and—' he started to say.

She reached across the bar and put a finger to his lips.

'Let me tell you something,' she said.

With the tip of her finger still resting warm on his lips, Strachan didn't move. Hardly breathed.

'It's like Robert Mitchum and James Dean,' she said.

Strachan frowned. He didn't get it.

'Robert Mitchum?' he said. 'James Dean?'

She took pity on him.

'It's like this,' she said. 'I've spent my whole life looking for Robert Mitchum. But every single time I've ended up with some lousy James Dean.'

Sally picked up the tea-towel and went back to her polishing. She looked pleased with herself. Strachan grimaced, still trying to puzzle it out.

'What's so wrong with James Dean?' he finally said.

Her smile grew wider.

'It's the difference between men and boys,' she said. 'James

383

Dean will mess you around every time. Robert Mitchum will keep you safe.'

She was still smiling.

'And me, I'm . . . ?' Strachan said.

She put her finger briefly to his lips once more. He took the hint, stopped talking.

'Later?' he said.

'Later,' she said.

It was his turn to smile now.

'By the way . . .' she said as he started to turn to go. 'Just a thought . . .'

'What's that?' Strachan said.

'The brewery is looking for someone to take this dump on,' Sally said.

Strachan didn't understand.

'The previous landlord couldn't handle it, did a runner. It needs someone who could deal with the likes of that Danny you met yesterday. We get them all here. It needs sorting out.'

He understood now.

'They wouldn't give it to the likes of me,' he said.

'You never know,' Sally said. 'You must know someone. Someone who could pull a few strings, perhaps.'

Maybe he did. Maybe that cup of tea with Mr Smith might not be such a bad idea after all.

No, this was stupid.

'But I don't know anything about the trade,' he said.

'I could teach you.'

'You'd do that?' he said, disbelieving.

She nodded.

Fuck it. Maybe he *could* do it.

He looked around the room, saw again the shabby

battered tables and chairs, the scuffed parquet flooring, the peeling red flock paper on the walls. It would take some work, but it could be done.

Working for Mr Smith, he'd seen enough pubs, enough clubs over the years to know what was needed. It could be his place; a place where he belonged.

'So you might go for it then?' Sally said.

His eyes must have told her; she could read him like a book.

Strachan flexed his shoulders, he straightened his tie, he tugged gently at the cuffs of his shirt, easing them down a fraction from his jacket sleeves, his hand went to his slicked-back Brylcreemed hair, smoothing it into place.

'I'm going to think about it,' he said.

Wouldn't do any harm to just think about it, would it? Chances were that nothing would come of it, of course. Chances were that it would turn out to be just a pipe dream.

No.

Who was he kidding?

There *was* no point. There was no point in dreaming. It wasn't going to happen. You are what you are. So settle for what you've got, Strachan. Settle for a stroll along the front with your jacket off and your sleeves rolled up and Sally by your side.

As he walked towards the door, Strachan turned to wave farewell to Sally. His mind was made up. No more of the pipe dream.

But it was then that he saw it.

He looked back to Sally and there it was, just above her head, on that narrow shelf behind the bar where the regulars kept their pewter tankards.

It was the perfect spot for it. And he could picture it there. He could see it there now like it was meant. He could fucking see it.

And other people would see it there too, as soon as they walked in. And they would know, they would always know. They would know who he was. What he was. What he had been.

Strachan.

Just Strachan.

Oh yes, the baseball bat would look just fucking perfect there.

# 73

# Baxter

## *When the police arrived, Baxter was scything at the tall grass*

Baxter had been tired, so tired that he had been beyond knowing how tired he really was. Gradually, though, everything had stopped working, had fallen away from him and drifted to a stop and when it had all stopped he had found that he couldn't talk, couldn't think and couldn't keep his eyes from closing.

He remembered sitting on the narrow bench bed of the caravan; and, even though his eyes wouldn't stay open, he remembered his mother easing his shirt over his head and his hands getting a bit tangled in the sleeves; and he remembered her running her fingers over the red marks at the top of his arms; and he sort of remembered her tucking him in and kissing him lightly on the forehead. But he might have made that last bit up because that was what she did every night. So he might not have really remembered it at all. He might have just known that it had happened, because it always did.

It had only been in the early hours of morning, when the wood pigeon began calling a new day in the forest and Baxter's eyes had opened just enough to see the first silvery grey light of dawn, it had only been then that he had thought of Soldier striding towards his father through the storm, through the lightning and the thunder and the rain.

It had been funny how Soldier had been. One minute he was standing just like he always stood, sort of mostly looking at the ground and talking to himself quite a bit, and then all of a sudden he had looked almost tall, almost strong and almost brave. Almost as if he was a real soldier again. And just for a moment, just in that moment before his eyes had closed again and he was carried softly back to sleep, Baxter had wondered whether *some* of it might have been a dream.

When he had finally woken up properly, the caravan was full of bright sunlight and he could see that everyone else was already up and dressed and that they were being very quiet so as not to disturb him. His mother was by the open door jiggling baby Truman and making little noises for him, and Megan was reading her book by the window. For a while Baxter had pretended still to be asleep; he wasn't sure exactly why he did this, but it had felt good. It had somehow made him feel for a moment that he was the important one because they were all tiptoeing around him.

It was then, as he was lying there pretending to be asleep, that the thought had come to him that perhaps *all* of it had been a dream. Lying there, eyes half closed in the warmth of his bed, Baxter had wondered whether any of it had really happened. Perhaps he had dreamed her, the woman with the funny piled-up hair who couldn't walk properly. Perhaps he had dreamed the boys on the slide, the man with the bottle, the house where everything was gone, where his things were all smashed up. Perhaps that was why he was still in bed while everyone else was up, because he'd had so many dreams.

It was only when Baxter had rolled on to his side and felt the dull pain from the bruising at the tops of his arms that he had known for sure that it had all been real.

And the funny thing was that as soon as he had known it was all real, all true, the clock thing and the sick-feeling thing in his stomach had come back.

Tick ... tick ... tick ... tick ... tick ...

Baxter couldn't remember exactly at what point the ticking and sick feeling had stopped the day before but now it had come back just as it was before and it was a little strange because he couldn't think why it should be there at all. There was no reason for it. Not really.

When the police arrived, Baxter was scything at the tall grass with a long stick. He had been sent out to play while his mother cleaned the caravan for one last time.

Because he'd been thinking about his things at the house, and about all the other things that weren't there, he hadn't heard the car coming along the lane. It was only the slam of the door that made him look up and he was surprised to see two policemen climbing out of a pale blue Ford Anglia with white doors. On the roof of the car was a blue light.

Baxter was interested in policemen so he studied them closely.

One of the policemen was very tall, young and thin and the other wasn't; the other one was older, shorter, more round and he moved more slowly, like he had a bad back or something. As they both straightened the shiny-buttoned jackets of their uniforms, adjusted the truncheons on their belts and put their tall helmets on, tucking the tight straps under their chins, it made Baxter think of the Laurel and Hardy film that he and Megan had watched at the Duke of York's one Saturday morning. It made him think of that; but it didn't make him want to laugh. In fact it made him feel a bit sad and it made the ticking thing get a bit stronger.

'Hello, son, your daddy about is he?' the older, rounder one shouted to him.

Baxter shook his head.

The policeman looked across to the caravan and at that moment Christie appeared on the step, drying her hands on a tea-towel. The policemen walked towards the caravan and Baxter followed behind them.

'Good morning, ma'am,' the older one said, touching the brim of his helmet in a kind of salute. 'It's Mrs ... ?'

'Bird,' Christie said.

'Mrs Bird, we're very sorry to trouble you,' he said, with a friendly smile. 'Grand morning, isn't it?'

Christie nodded and kept drying her hands. Baxter could see that she had a kind of question on her face, a kind of worried question about why the policemen were there.

'One heck of a storm last night though, wasn't it?' he said.

The younger policeman stepped forwards impatiently.

'Mrs Bird, we've had a tip-off ...' he said.

He sounded excited, eager; he sounded like someone who

had never had a tip-off before and had certainly never used the words.

'Ahem,' the older, shorter policeman interrupted.

With his index finger he pointed to the three stripes on his arm.

'Sorry, Sarge,' the younger one said, looking at the ground, looking a bit apologetic.

'Mrs Bird, we've had a telephone call from a concerned member of the community,' the sergeant said.

He turned to the younger one with a long-suffering look of condescension; this was the way you did these things, this was the way police business was conducted.

'We've had a report about a man who might be living in the woods around here. A man who may possibly represent something of a danger to the public—'

'He's a lunatic on the loose,' the young policeman said, interrupting again.

The sergeant glared at the younger man.

'Mrs Bird, please ignore my young constable, will you?' he said. 'I'm afraid he's been watching far too much television.'

Christie managed a small smile.

'There is a man who lives in the woods. A man called Soldier,' she said, glancing across at Baxter. 'He's a friend of my son's. But I'm sure he's quite harmless.'

'I think we should be the judge of that, Mrs Bird,' the sergeant said seriously.

He turned to face Baxter.

'Now, my lad,' he said. 'Do you know where this Soldier lives, do you?'

Baxter didn't know what to say. He knew he had to

answer the policeman but Soldier hadn't done anything wrong.

'Come on, my boy,' the sergeant said. 'We're not going to hurt your friend. We just want to eliminate him from our enquiries.'

Baxter didn't understand.

'You must tell the policeman, Baxter,' Christie said, suddenly by his side with her arm around his shoulder.

The sergeant bent down, took his helmet off and looked Baxter directly in the eye.

'I'm going to ask you one last time, my lad,' he said. 'Do you know where this Soldier lives?'

And Baxter had no choice. He nodded.

As he led the way across the zigzag trail through the long grass and then along the narrow twisting paths with the tree roots that had always tripped him up, as he showed them how to get through the brambles and the tall ferns to where the stream ran beside Soldier's shelter, Baxter felt more and more certain that something really bad was going to happen.

At the sergeant's insistence, his mother, Megan and baby Truman had stayed behind at the caravan. Going alone with the policemen into the woods had at first made Baxter feel somehow uneasy and excited at the same time. But as they had made their way deeper into the woods, the excitement had disappeared and now there was only the sick thing in his stomach.

Behind him he could hear the sergeant breathing hard and further back he could hear the younger policeman swear as he hit his helmet on a low branch.

'Much further, is it?' the sergeant said breathlessly.

Without looking back, Baxter shook his head.

When they got close to the stream, to where the water tumbled over the fall of pebbles and gathered in a pool, where he had tried to wash the lipstick from his face, Baxter stopped.

'I can't see anything,' the sergeant said, standing beside him.

He had taken his helmet off and was mopping sweat from his forehead with a large white handkerchief.

'There, Sarge!' the younger one said.

He pointed towards the camouflaged lean-to shelter. With ferns and branches laid with studied randomness across its roof, only the opening of the shelter was visible. Baxter could see that Soldier was inside.

The younger policeman pushed his way past the sergeant and then past Baxter. He went striding along the path towards the shelter, towards where Soldier stayed crouched low and trapped inside.

'Hey, you!' The policeman pointed at Soldier and shouted.

The path became more difficult as it neared the stream and, as he scrambled along it, his heavy boots slipped on the earth that was still wet after the storm. He slid, stumbled, fell, swore again.

Soldier chose this as the moment to emerge limping from the shelter and to edge fearfully towards the flint wall where he and Baxter had kicked their heels and listened to the silence.

'Stay where you bloody are!' the young policeman yelled, climbing to one knee.

He clambered to his feet and pulled his truncheon from his belt. Alarmed, the sergeant now set off slowly across the slippery path towards the shelter.

'Soldier!' Baxter shouted in warning.

'Take it steady, Tom,' the sergeant called to the constable. 'No need to frighten him!'

But the younger man wasn't listening. Finding firmer ground beneath his feet, he ran the last few yards towards Soldier and then launched himself at him, truncheon still in hand, in a flying rugby tackle.

'NO!' Baxter and the sergeant shouted together.

As the policeman hit, Soldier went backwards in a crumpled heap of bones and rags. He went jolting backwards into the wall, and the wall that he had built so many years before went crashing to the ground under the impact.

For what seemed like a long time, neither Soldier nor the young policeman moved – and nor did Baxter or the sergeant.

Finally, the policeman started to pick himself up from the rubble, to disentangle himself from Soldier. He had a broad grin on his face.

'Got him!' he said triumphantly to the sergeant, who had now arrived panting at his side.

'You're a bloody idiot, Tom!' the sergeant said. 'You could have bloody killed him!'

'Resisting arrest, wasn't he?' the policeman said, pleased with himself. He grinned at the sergeant, then looked back down at Soldier and swung a boot hard into his ribs.

The sergeant helped Soldier to his feet and held him upright while for long gasping moments he fought for breath. Finally Soldier was recovered enough to be able to stand unsteadily on his own. He stood there looking bent and broken and swaying as if buffeted by an unseen wind; he stood there looking towards Baxter with eyes that didn't seem to focus and then, still swaying, still looking somehow like a broken string puppet, he began to fumble suddenly, urgently in the pocket of his tattered coat. As if some terrible thought had struck him, as if something precious had been lost.

The young policeman went to grab hold of him again, to stop him going through his pockets.

It wasn't fair, Baxter thought. It wasn't fair picking on Soldier. Hurting him.

'Just leave him alone!' he yelled.

Something in Baxter's voice was enough to stop the policeman.

Still swaying, still struggling for breath, his shattered knee twisted beneath him, Soldier pulled from his pocket the rag parcel that he had placed there with such care. Unwrapping it, his hands shaking, he took from its folds the small grey plastic soldier that Baxter had given to him. With great deliberation he weighed it in his hand and then, as if to check that it remained intact, he ran his bony finger along its every surface. Finally, slowly, he raised it in his open palm and held it upwards, high to the light. And it was only then, as Soldier raised his head, that Baxter could see his face was wet with tears.

'Soldier . . .' Baxter said again, more softly now.

But Soldier didn't hear him. It was as if he couldn't hear him.

For some time after the policemen had left the shelter, Baxter heard the voice of the young one echoing through the woods as he pushed and prodded Soldier along in front of him. When they had set off to find their way back along the narrow winding path through the forest, Soldier had his hands behind him in handcuffs and Baxter knew that he would find it difficult to walk and to keep his balance with his bad knee. Every time he fell, and he seemed to fall quite often, Baxter heard the young policeman kick out at him with his heavy boots and swear.

Baxter didn't go with them back along the path; he didn't want to watch Soldier falling down and being hurt. Instead he had stayed behind at the camp to look at the wall that they had sat on together and that had now fallen down and to look at Soldier's things that the young policeman had gone through and then thrown into a small untidy heap.

Although Baxter was feeling really empty and sad, he picked up an old pair of binoculars; he put them to his eyes and tried to look through them but one of the lenses was cracked from when the policeman had smashed them on the ground. He picked up a mug and then the handle to the mug that had broken off; he tried to put them together to see whether they would fit but there was a small piece missing. He looked at the blackened kettle that Soldier boiled on the fire and the dented saucepans that didn't have proper handles that he and Soldier had eaten stew out of. There were a few blankets and a few clothes but Baxter didn't want to touch these because they didn't look very clean.

When Baxter looked at the small pile of Soldier's possessions it made him think of his own things that were still there and all broken in the empty house. Somehow, in a way he couldn't make sense of, in a way he didn't understand, he thought that it must all be connected, must all be joined up. It was something like, because that thing then had happened, so this thing had happened now. And the thought of all of it, the thought of it all joining up and being jumbled up, made him feel more empty and more sick in his stomach at the same time and it made the clockwork key ticking thing inside him turn tighter.

Tick ... tick ... tick ... tick ... tick ...

With everything that had happened, everything with his father, everything with Soldier, Baxter wondered whether it would ever really stop now, whether it would ever finally go away.

When the policemen had put the handcuffs on Soldier, yanking his arms roughly behind him because at first Soldier didn't understand what they were asking him to do, Baxter didn't want to watch. He didn't want to watch but at the same time he found that he wasn't able to turn away. It was just like it was with the man with the broken teeth and the bottle. He didn't want to see, but he *had* to see. It was as if someone, something, was making him look at everything that was happening; it was as if he was being made to look at it so that he would remember it for ever.

It was his fault.

He had done this to Soldier and Soldier was his friend. They had sat together on the wall and Soldier had saved him from his father in the storm and in return he had brought the policemen to hurt him and to take him away.

He had tried to stop them. He had shouted to leave Soldier alone. But they hadn't listened.

It was his fault and he would have to remember it for always now. And every time he would have to think about it, he knew it would be the same. Every time he would feel the same hot crimson flush of shame.

# 74

# Christie

*Suddenly it felt as if they were leaving the
one place they had that was safe*

After the policemen had left, after they had pushed
Soldier, still handcuffed, into the back of the blue-and-white
panda car and had driven back along the lane,
Christie had handed the baby to Megan and waited for
Baxter at the opening to the woods. In all the weeks she had
spent in the clearing, this was the closest she had come to the
forest.

Why did she fear it so? Why did she hesitate even now?

Finally she saw the small pale figure of the boy in the distance,
coming slowly along the dark shadowy path with his
head bowed. Forcing herself forwards, screwing up her
courage, she stepped into the woods and went quickly
towards him.

'They took Soldier,' Baxter said as she rested her hand on

his shoulder and they walked side by side back to the clearing.

'I know,' she said gently.

The forest was quiet, much quieter than Christie had thought it would be; the rustle in the leaves of the great trees was welcoming, not forbidding. She had expected a sudden chill but the warmth of the sun still found its way through the dappling canopy. Still, though, it made her uneasy.

'But he hadn't done anything bad,' Baxter said, looking up at her. 'Why did they take him?'

Christie didn't answer; she suspected that she no longer had any answers to such questions. Why did they take that strange defenceless broken-down creature that Baxter called Soldier? Why did they take him when it seemed his only offence was that from somewhere he had summoned up the courage to try to help Baxter in the storm?

'He was my friend,' Baxter said.

'I know,' Christie said softly.

They walked on side by side until Christie could bear it no longer, the hurt that was inside her son. She had to try to make it right for him. At the opening to the clearing, she stopped and turned him towards her. She knelt down so that she could look into his eyes.

'It will be OK, you know,' she said, brushing at his fringe with her fingertips. 'Soldier will be OK, I promise.'

Baxter looked at her as if he wanted to believe her but didn't quite.

'He needs someone to look after him, to keep him safe,' she said. 'And the policemen will find someone. I'm sure they will. And then he will be OK.'

She pulled Baxter close to her. She too wanted to believe it but wasn't sure that she did.

'Soldier's just the same as everyone,' Christie said. 'Just like you and Megan and baby Truman . . .' She held him closer still. 'Because we all need someone to look after us, to keep us safe and make everything OK,' she said.

That much she *was* sure of. Of that she had no doubt.

'And that's *my* job,' she said. 'To watch out for you and Megan and baby Truman. My only job.'

She realised that she was explaining it to herself now as much as she was saying it to reassure him. She realised too, in a way that she never previously fully understood, that it was the children who somehow kept her safe even as she was caring for them. Her love protected them; theirs gave her purpose, made her strong.

'And it's the most important job in the world,' she said. 'Nothing is as important as that.'

That was the truth of it. The only truth now.

Once Christie had finished, the inside of the caravan was polished and clean, as clean as she could make it, much cleaner than it had been when they had arrived. She had also done everything she could, she told herself, to make it as secure as possible. The windows were fastened, the curtains drawn and all the cupboards locked. One thing bothered her about the caravan though; she would have to leave the key in the door, as she had no way of knowing where to return it. It felt so wrong, so irresponsible, to walk away and leave the key where anyone might find it; it felt like something that Truman would do. She tried to dismiss the anxiety from her mind but it kept coming back, nagging away at her.

It hadn't taken long to pack and the large leather suitcase now stood by the low step of the caravan, waiting to be loaded into Mrs Chadney's wheelbarrow. Christie felt bad about the wheelbarrow too; they would have to leave it at the top of the lane when they reached the road and hope that someone would find it and take it back to the cottage. Given that so few people passed that way, she was worried that it might sit by the roadside for a very long time or that it might be taken and never be returned. It was however the only way that she could see that she and the children could manage between them the heavy case, the carry-cot and baby Truman. She would have to push the suitcase in the barrow, Baxter would carry the cot and Megan would hold the baby.

Later, once they were settled, she would have to write to Mrs Chadney to apologise, to explain about the barrow and to thank her for all her help over the weeks. If she could, she would send some money.

Once were they settled? Christie shivered and pulled her white cardigan about her.

Megan and Baxter stood looking up at her, waiting to be told that it was time to go. They were dressed in their best clothes, their hair neatly brushed; their faces pale and sombre; their eyes big and questioning. The sight of them, brother and sister, side by side, so young, so sad, so serious, it was enough to break your heart, Christie thought. If you let it.

She *must* not let it. She had to be strong for all of them.

She smiled at them; there were no smiles in return. They sensed her anxiety, she knew that.

Christie wished there was something more that she could do to make the day easier for them. More practically, she wished too that she had paid greater attention to the roads on the journey from Brighton to the forest, that she could remember the towns and villages they had passed through on the way. Because, although she was reluctant to confront it, the awful truth was that she didn't know exactly where they were. If at that moment someone had opened up a map in front of her, she would have had little idea where to point to find them. She felt ashamed. How could she not know where she and the children were? What kind of mother was she? And not knowing where they were, of course, had other consequences; it meant that she didn't know how they were going to get back to Brighton.

She forced the thought away from her. It was better not to think about it too much; it was better to take it one step at a time. First the long walk to the road. With the children, the wheelbarrow, the carry-cot and the baby, that would take some time. Once they got there, they would have to go on until they found a village. And there they would wait for a bus. Would there be buses? Christie had enough money in her purse for their fares, she hoped. But how many buses would it take to get back to Brighton? And how would she know which buses to take if she didn't know where she was? How would she piece together the journey?

Once more she tried to push the thought away from her. One step at a time.

'OK, everyone?' she said, smiling again.

Pulling the caravan door to a close for the last time brought a stab of sadness that surprised Christie. She thought she would be glad finally to see the back of it but suddenly it felt as if they were leaving the one place they had that was safe, secure and familiar and stepping into the unknown, into the void.

And when they got there, when they got to Brighton, what then?

They would turn up on her mother's doorstep and they would not be welcome. Her mother would be hateful and cruel. She wouldn't want the children in the house and certainly wouldn't want the noise and fuss of the baby. And apart from anything else, there was no room, was there? The twins hadn't married and were still living at home. They would have to move in together and share a room to create just a small space for Christie and the children. The house would be crowded, full of resentment. The air would be like poison.

How long could they live like that? And what would they do for money?

Again she pushed the thoughts away. Somehow she would find a way to make it all work. She *had* to make it work. There was no choice.

'OK, Megan?' she said, settling the baby carefully into her arms.

'OK, Baxter?' she said, helping him to lift the carry-cot.

Both children nodded.

Christie heaved the suitcase into the wheelbarrow and they set off along the potholed lane towards the road.

'Let's sing a song,' she said.

She'd said it to keep their spirits up but once the words were out she knew it was exactly right. It was exactly what they should do, she thought. She felt her own spirits lift. Everything *would* be all right; she would make sure of it, whatever it took. And whatever the future held, they mustn't be afraid of it. They would get there together and they would arrive singing.

'What shall we sing?' she said.

Megan didn't wait for an answer and Baxter soon followed.

'*Love, love me do . . .*'


They sang intermittently as they walked along the lane; Megan would remember a song she had learned at school or Christie would start them off again. Between the songs there were other thoughts, which Christie resisted; thoughts about what Strachan had told her; about the five thousand pounds, about the home in Brighton that she had created and that was now stripped bare; thoughts about a woman called Sally, another called Doll, about a suitcase full of cut and torn clothes; thoughts about Truman's unknown mother; about Soldier striding through the storm to try to save Baxter from his father.

One by one she fought them off. There would be time enough for all of them in whatever the weeks, months and years ahead held.

Making their way back along the lane took even longer than she had imagined it would. They had to stop often so that she could take the baby so that Megan could rest for a while and Baxter could ease his aching arms.

Finally though they reached the road and found a place in the twist of roots of an oak tree to leave the wheelbarrow. Christie now had to carry the suitcase and her heart sank as she tried to lift it, as she felt its dead weight, and as she tried to walk with it. After just a few yards she had no choice, she had to put it down again.

'Wait, children!' she called as Megan and Baxter walked ahead.

She bent again, lifted the suitcase and staggered a few more paces. It was an insult too far on top of all the injury, it was too much and Christie felt tears of frustration threatening to well in her eyes. Arrive there singing? She couldn't even lift the case.

It was at that moment, as Christie was trying to decide whether to laugh or cry, that a green single-decker bus swung around the corner towards them. Instinctively, Christie stuck out a hand and miraculously the bus slowed to a halt a few yards ahead of them.

'Where to, love?' the bus driver said as the doors opened.

Taken by surprise, Christie didn't know quite how to answer him. Megan and Baxter looked up at her expectantly. The bus driver must have seen her confusion.

'If it helps, love, this bus is for Crawley.'

Crawley?

Christie took her purse from her pocket; she clicked it open and removed the slip of paper that Strachan had given her.

Crawley: it was where Truman's mother lived.

It was a ridiculous idea. Until yesterday she hadn't known this woman existed and she had no idea what she was like, whether they would be welcome there. And Truman's mother didn't know about her, didn't know about the children, didn't even know what her own son called himself now.

No, it was impossible.

And anyway, she could hardly turn up unannounced and

penniless on her doorstep with three children, one of them a baby in her arms and all their worldly goods in a single suitcase, could she?

'Sorry, love,' the bus driver said. 'We haven't got all day, you know . . .'

Could she?

# 75

# Truman

### *It had even worked a treat on his wedding day*

A powerful thing, the thumb, Truman thought. With an outstretched thumb and a carefree smile he had hitch-hiked all the way down and across country to Margate and it hadn't cost him a penny. The thirty was still in his pocket, he'd swapped jokes with lorry drivers, he'd been kept hand-somely in cigarettes and a travelling salesman with a lazy eye and a lisp had even bought him a cup of tea and a bacon sandwich in a lay-by on the Thanet Way. Not bad, eh?

Catch a bus or a train? Mug's game.

Leaning on the black iron railings, staring out to the dis-tant sea, listening to the calls of the seagulls, breathing in the warm salt air, checking out the swimsuited girls on the lux-urious sand that stretched to the harbour wall in front of him, it felt good, it felt as though Margate would do him fine. The sun was on his face and, although they were not nearly as grand, the white stuccoed buildings that lined The Parade and Market Street behind him reminded him just enough of Brighton. It felt better than good, it felt like coming home; maybe Christie and the kids might even like it here one day, once he'd smoothed things over, once she'd got over it and everything was sweet again.

All he needed now to make the day perfect was a drink.

He picked up the empty suitcase and jogged across the road, dodging through the oncoming cars with a cheerful wave.

When he reached the pavement, he looked up and like it was meant, as if it was there waiting for him all along, The Welcome stood in front of him. Truman pushed at the heavy polished door and stepped into the saloon bar. The carpet on the floor was worn thin, the leather on the chairs was cracked, the ceiling was yellowed by cigarette smoke but it wasn't bad. In the corner there was an old upright piano. No, it wasn't bad at all.

As the door closed a bell rang faintly and a barmaid came through from the adjoining snug.

'Can I help you, sweetheart?' she said.

She had something of the look of that Christine Keeler, the one that did for Jack Profumo. She was a bit bigger than her, not as skinny, and she was a bit what Truman's old mum would call tarty, a bit brassy. But she was none the worse for that.

'You most certainly can, princess,' he said, leaning across the counter, breathing in deeply.

He smiled. She smiled.

'What's it to be then?' she said, lowering her eyes.

'A pint of your finest, please, princess,' Truman said.

As she pulled at the long dark wood handle of the pump, she glanced up at Truman.

'That's quite a shiner you've got there,' she said.

Truman's hand went to his face; he winced playfully.

'You should see the other bloke,' he said.

'Oh yes ... ?' she said archly, playing along, playing the game, handing him the pint.

'Not a mark on him!' Truman said.

She laughed; it was a terrible strangled laugh, like a cat in a sack in the dead of night. But he'd get used to it.

He turned away from her and looked across to the piano.

'Anyone play that?' he said.

'Not for a long time,' she said. 'You play, do you?'

Truman walked across to the piano, lifted the lid to the keyboard, pulled out the stool. Slowly, dreamily, he played.

'*Unforgettable,*' he sang, looking back across to her, looking into her eyes, '*that's what you are ...*'

It worked every time. It had even worked a treat on his wedding day. She leaned forwards, rested her elbows on the bar and cupped her hands around her face.

'*Unforgettable ...*'

When he was done, he softly closed the lid, pushed back the stool and walked back across the bar towards her. She clapped her hands delightedly.

'That was lovely,' she said breathlessly.

He paused, reached into his pocket for a cigarette and his lighter. He drew on the cigarette and let the smoke work its magic before he sent it in a spiralling plume towards the ceiling.

'Do you know something, princess?' Truman said, coming closer, picking up the pint, lifting it to his lips.

'What's that?' she said.

'You're a bit of all right, you are,' he said.

She looked up at him, her eyes dancing, her cheeks ever so slightly flushed.

'You're not so dusty yourself . . .' she said.

Bingo.

# FOUR MONTHS LATER

# 76

# Soldier

*He had tried this name they said was his*

Through the latticed living-room window of the crooked half-timbered house at the top of the hill, Soldier watched as the two Golden Retrievers went hurtling across the lawn, as they scampered together side by side along the rolling contours of the meadow and as they ploughed a furrow through the long grass of the blue-green fields that lay beyond. Rain had been falling steadily since dawn and a sparse grey blanket of morning mist lingered at the foot of the valley. Soon the dogs would disappear into that mist and plunge helter-skelter down the worn muddy bank and into the fast-flowing, shallow waters of the river that ran there.

In the distance, the animated barking of one of them announced that they had reached their destination. They would return to the house in due course, sleek and glistening from the river, their breath steaming in the cold November air, to be met at the door of the conservatory with protestations and old bathtowels. After a brisk rub-down and their genial daily finger-wagging lecture about staying out of the river, they would slump together on the rug by the boiler and sleep the rest of the morning through.

Many years before, there used to be another dog here, Soldier had been told. His dog.

There was a series of black-and-white photographs of them together in the album that lay open on Soldier's lap as he sat in the upright chair and gazed through the rain-streaked window. Max, a huge square-headed black Labrador, with a lolling tongue and laughing eyes, had his paws on his shoulders as a young carefree Soldier sat smiling in a garden chair on the lawn. They would walk together for miles, apparently; exploring the ancient network of foot-paths, bridleways and narrow high-hedged lanes that criss-crossed the Devon countryside around the old house. They were such happy days, his mother had told him as they had turned the pages of the album together.

Such happy days.

Did he remember?

Soldier didn't remember.

No, it was much more than that; much more than simply not remembering. Not remembering implied forgetting. And that suggested some temporary lapse, a lapse that could be overcome. With Soldier it was more profound, it was per-manent, it was unshakeable. It wasn't that he didn't remember; it was that he didn't *know*. It was as if he had never known.

He didn't know the dog they called Max, he didn't know

the small proud white-haired woman who said she was his mother, or the bent balding man who walked with a stick who was his father, or this old lopsided house that stood at the top of the hill looking down across the gently sweeping valley. He didn't know anything of his life here.

He didn't even know that his name had been Joseph Cottrell.

Joseph. Joe. Joey. Joseph Cottrell.

He had tried this name they said was his. He had tried it over and over in his mind; he had tried it on for size. It felt wrong, as if it didn't fit.

He had tried so hard with all of it.

Day after day he had sat staring at the photograph album; he had examined every last detail of every one of the snapshots that had been so lovingly mounted in the thick leather-backed album's heavy black pages. Since the summer he had spent countless hours listening to this person who was his mother, and to his father talking about his life before. His life as it was, or as they said it had been. They had shown such love, such patience, such tenderness. They had shed such tears, these people. These people he didn't know.

The doctors had said that it was important to talk, that it would help, that something might suddenly unlock and that the memories might come flooding back.

Nothing had unlocked.

Or if the memories didn't come back at once, the doctors had said, then perhaps Soldier would at least find his voice again.

He hadn't.

Still they persisted.

Soldier had been a teacher, they said. Did he remember

going up to university? Classics at Oxford; just like his father before him. They had been so proud.

How about this, Joe?

*Arma virumque cano, Troiae qui primus ab oris*
*Italiam, fato profugus, Laviniaque venit*
*litora, multum ille et terris iactatus et alto*
*vi superum saevae memorem Iunonis ob iram*

Do you remember how we used to recite it? The *Aeneid*. We'd trade it line for line, the pair of us sitting together in the study. Both showing off, we were! Showing off something rotten. Remember, son?

He had taught for seven years at the local primary school after graduating. Did he remember? It had only been ten years before that he had sat as a small boy in the same classroom. And he must remember some of the children in his class? He couldn't have forgotten those terrible Robinson brothers! Such young tearaways, they were; had their own car-repair business now, who would have believed it? Did he remember the school itself? What a draughty old place it was! They would take him there to see it when he was stronger. Would he like that? Would he?

He had a sister, Rosie; surely he remembered Rosie? Lived in Australia now. They were inseparable as children, he and Rosie; they used to climb trees together. The one to the left of the field down there; yes that one, that big one. Rosie was coming to visit him soon. That would be good, wouldn't it? He was an uncle now, with a handsome nephew and the prettiest niece.

And he had been engaged to be married to Alice. Alice: the

girl who had been his childhood sweetheart? Alice: the girl who lived down the road in the next village? Look, on this page, there was a photograph of her. Remember, Joey? You should have married her years before; but you were so quiet, so reserved, so shy. It took the war to make you ask her. She thought you'd never get round to it!

She had waited for him for years after the war, they said; waited for him to come back to her, with her heart broken. But finally she had found someone else and she had moved on.

He had been twenty-eight when the war came and took him away, they said. And that had been twenty-three years ago. Twenty-three years and they'd missed him every day ... Twenty-three years and now he had come home to them again ... Wasn't that wonderful? Could he remember the day he left? Could he remember the way his father shook him by the hand? So formal! Did he remember his mother's tears, the catch in her throat and the sob in her chest? Did he remember? Did he?

There had been a young reporter from the local newspaper at the police station when the sergeant and Tom had arrived with Soldier in the back of the panda car. It had been a slow week and the reporter had been hoping for more from his daily call. Instead he had found that he had to content himself with the usual meagre diet of petty thefts and minor bumps and scrapes on the roads; at most all they were going to make was a paragraph or two in that week's edition. The sooner he got off the local rag and on to a proper paper, the better it would be, he had told the duty inspector.

'Hello, Sarge, who you got there then?' he called to the sergeant as he trotted down the station steps.

'Just some poor old sod we found in the woods up at Tabell Ghyll,' the sergeant said, helping Soldier from the back of the car.

'We had a tip-off,' Tom said proudly.

'Oh, yes?' the young reporter said, his ears pricking up.

'Turned out to be nothing,' the sergeant said, propping Soldier against the car. 'Just this mystery man here.'

'Looks like he'd been living up there for years,' Tom said. 'We thought we'd better bring in him. See what we can find out about him.'

The reporter walked over to Soldier; Soldier shrank from him, muttering almost inaudibly.

'I wouldn't get too close,' Tom said. 'The stink of him is enough to knock you off your feet. Bloody terrible in the car, it was.'

'It says "Soldier" on his coat,' the reporter said.

'That's what they call him, apparently,' the sergeant said. 'That's all we know. And there's no sense to be got out of him.'

'How do you think he got up there, up to the forest?' the reporter said. 'And how do you think he managed to live there for so long?'

'Beats me,' the sergeant said.

'He'll be like one of those Japs,' Tom said. 'You know, living in the forest, still thinking the war's going on.'

'Make one hell of a story, that would,' the reporter said, smiling, taking out his notebook. 'Can I quote you on that ...?'

\*

The national newspapers had picked the story up as soon as it appeared and the television news had followed quickly after.

'Mystery man living in the forest', a British soldier still fighting the war eighteen years after it was over; true or not, it was the stuff of tabloid dreams. WHO IS THE MYSTERY MAN? they asked. They ran a photograph of Soldier with his long matted hair, his tangled grey beard, his face grey with the grime of the years spent in the forest. His eyes stared wildly from front pages across the country. The following day they ran another; this time with his hair neatly cut and his face scrubbed and clean-shaven.

The haircut and shave had revealed a younger man; a man instantly recognisable to a mother and father living in a crooked house at the top of a Devon hill.

WAR HERO IDENTIFIED! the papers proclaimed the following day. The mystery man was fifty-one-year-old Joseph Cottrell, they said. An unnamed soldier had been shipped home, having been found wandering dazed and lost in a field in France in 1945; he had lost his identity discs and was suffering from amnesia and shrapnel wounds to his knee. Taken by ambulance to a nursing home in Sussex, records showed that he had vanished before being treated and before he could be identified. It seemed that while the staff were busy admitting another patient, he had simply stepped out through the open ambulance door and started walking.

Somehow that soldier, now known to be Joseph Cottrell, had found his way to the forest, and against all the odds had survived. They'd tried looking for him at the time but they were chaotic days after the war and he had quickly been forgotten.

When his parents came for him, there was one final photograph. *A joyful reunion* the caption read under a picture of Soldier looking uncertain and unsmiling.

The rain had eased and Soldier had watched the two Retrievers make their leisurely, weary way back up through the valley. They'd left bursting with energy and enthusiasm; they'd come back spent.

The Home Service was playing on the polished mahogany radiogram that took pride of place in the living room. The news came from America: a man who meant nothing to Soldier had been shot dead the day before in something called a motorcade in a place called Dallas. It was, the newsreader said, the end of an era; the world, he said, would never quite be the same.

Soldier could make no sense of it. His world had already changed entirely.

The photograph album lay abandoned on the floor next to his chair. In the palm of his hand now, held upwards to catch the morning light from the window, held upwards so that he could see its every line, its every contour, so that he could run a finger over its every curve, was a small grey plastic soldier with a damaged knee.

Soldier didn't hear the living-room door opening and he didn't see his father and mother exchange glances as they came bustling into the room.

'The dogs are back,' his father said briskly, turning the radio off.

Soldier's hand closed around the plastic toy. He turned to face them.

422

'They'd been in that river again,' his mother said, setting down a clinking tray of tea.

'Here, Joe, look what I've found,' his father said, coming busily to Soldier's side, leaning on his stick, depositing a new, slimmer album on Soldier's lap.

'Do you remember, son?' he said. 'Summer of 1919 it was. Just after the Great War.'

Dutifully Soldier opened the album and began to turn the pages.

'It was the year we had that holiday in the forest,' his father said. 'You were only about eight.'

Every stiff page of the album contained a series of six tiny black and white prints held in place by brittle yellowing corner mounts.

'Remember, Joe?' his father said.

Each print showed a small caravan, a small white hump-backed caravan standing alone in a wide grassy clearing in the woods.

'Look, there's you, your sister and your mother ...' his father said.

Three people were sitting, squeezed together, side by side on the low step in front of the caravan. Next to a pale serious-faced fair-haired boy was a smiling confident ponytailed girl; next to her was a young woman in a white cardigan with shoulder-length coal-black hair.

'Do you remember it, Joe? Do you?' his father said.

Closing his eyes, Soldier gripped the small grey plastic toy more tightly.

'You do remember something, Joe!' his father said, delightedly.

Soldier could no longer hear him.

Instead he could hear the echoing call of a wood pigeon, far in the woods, greeting a new day. He could hear the dull and distant beat of a crow's wing. He could feel the misty chill of a rising forest dawn. He could follow a twisting track to where the bracken thinned and fallen branches lay like bleached bones. And he could feel a gathering warmth as he crouched low and still in an earthy tangle of brambles and musky ferns.

And from there, from beneath the spreading shadows of the beech trees at the ragged edge of the wood, he could see out across a great green, rolling sway. He could see out to where a ponytailed girl had once skipped, to where a boy had hidden deep in the long grass, and to where a woman had run.

'Bring anything back, Joey?' his mother said, brushing away a tear from his face with the back of her hand.

*Sunt lacrimae rerum.*

There are tears at the heart of things.

'Does it, Joey? Does it?'

# Author's Note

Aeneas visits the temple of Juno in Carthage and marvels at its size and magnificence. He finds himself drawn to a series of murals depicting the deaths of his friends and countrymen in the Trojan War, the war in which he had lately fought. He is moved to tears and says: '*Sunt lacrimae rerum et mentem mortalia tangunt.*'

It is a line often quoted and its meaning is much argued about. It is understood here as: There are tears at the heart of things, and men's hearts are touched by what human beings have to bear.

# Songs

♪ 'Take These Chains From My Heart': Ray Charles, HMV, 1963. By Fred Rose and Hy Heath.

♪ 'How Do You Do It?': Gerry & The Pacemakers, Columbia, 1963. By Mitch Murray.

♪ 'Falling': Roy Orbison, Monument, 1963. By Roy Orbison.

♪ '(I've Got a Gal In) Kalamazoo': Glenn Miller and His Orchestra, RCA Victor, 1942. By Mack Gordon and Harry Warren.

♪ 'Night and Day': Frank Sinatra, Bluebird Records, 1942. By Cole Porter.

♪ 'Unforgettable': Nat King Cole, Capitol Records, 1951. By Irving Gordon.

♪ 'Love Me Do': The Beatles, Parlophone, 1962. By John Lennon and Paul McCartney.

♪ 'Bo Diddley': Buddy Holly, Coral Records, 1963. By Ellas McDaniel.

♪ 'The Night Has a Thousand Eyes': Bobby Vee, Liberty, 1963. By Ben Weisman, Dorothy Wayne, Marilyn Garrett.

♫ 'Welcome to My World': Jim Reeves, RCA Victor, 1962. By Ray Winkler and John Hathcock.

♫ 'Do You Want to Know a Secret?': Billy J. Kramer with The Dakotas, Parlophone, 1962. By John Lennon and Paul McCartney.

# Acknowledgements

I would like to thank Emma Beswetherick, Caroline Kirkpatrick and the outstandingly talented team at Piatkus for their enthusiastic belief in this book. For a former newspaperman, it was a joy to work with a group of people who were so consistently creative and so committed to hitting all those tight deadlines. I am also hugely indebted to Eve White, my agent, for her invaluable suggestions, her critical insight and for her knowledge of the business. A special thank-you must also go to Philippa Donovan at Smart Quill who was the first to suggest that this book might make it to publication and who pointed me towards Eve. And finally and most importantly, I want to say thank you to the one person who made this book possible. My wife, Annie, never doubted that *Love, Love Me Do* would be published. She was right. But then again, I have learned in the extraordinary adventure of our life together that she invariably is.

READ ON FOR
AN EXTRACT FROM
MARK HAYSOM'S NEW NOVEL

*SEE MY BABY JIVE*

# 1

# Crawley New Town

One behind the other, the two men led the way from the bus station with the battered leather suitcase hoisted high above their heads. They were identically dressed in long drape jackets with velvet-trimmed collars, suede shoes with thick crepe soles, drainpipe trousers and bootlace ties. One had a cigarette that bobbed dangerously from the corner of his mouth; he squinted as the smoke snaked into his eyes. In sashaying polka-dot circle skirts and sling-back heels, their bottle-blonde girlfriends followed on in single file. Behind them went the children, Megan and then Baxter. Christie brought up the rear, carrying the baby.

And they were doing the conga.

A minute before, everything had seemed beyond her, everything seemed hopeless, and Christie had felt tears coming to match those gathering in Megan's eyes. But now they were doing the conga with strangers through a strange town and Megan and Baxter were giggling and kicking out their feet in time to the breathless voices.

'Let's all do the conga,
La la la la,
La la la la ...'

It was difficult for Christie to take it in, to adjust to what was happening. They had nothing in the world and nowhere to go and yet here they were dancing through the streets with people she didn't know, people she would normally have ushered the children across the road to avoid. And they were dancing her joyously, recklessly towards an unknown future.

'La la la la,
La la la la ...'

Baxter turned to look up at her. She held the baby close with one hand and waved to him with the other. He stumbled. Almost fell. Kicked out his leg again and laughed.

# 2

# Earlier that day in the
# Ashdown Forest, Sussex

I t was madness. Even as she had dragged the suitcase on to
the bus and then fumbled for the fares for herself and the
children, Christie had kept telling herself that it was an
entirely ridiculous idea.

And, if it had been ridiculous then, it had become even
more obviously so when she sat down, shook out her purse
and found that she had just five shillings left in the world.

Madness.

There were so many reasons why she should have been
doing the safe and sensible thing, the only rational thing;
however difficult and distasteful that might be. And of the
three that mattered most (in the end the only three that
mattered at all) two were sitting in the seat in front of her
and the third was screwing up his face in complaint in her
arms.

She leaned forwards, put her head between those of
Megan and Baxter.

'OK, everyone?' she said.

They half turned towards her and nodded. Megan managed a small smile of reassurance.

They had no idea where they were going or what to expect when they got there and yet still they were trying to be brave for her. They sat close together and in silence, staring intently ahead as the bus pulled away from its stopping place in the forest. They looked so small, Christie thought; so heartbreakingly small, so pale and tired.

As the bus manoeuvred steeply around the first bend, Christie glanced back to the potholed track that led to the clearing far in the woods. The branches of a great twisted oak hung in a dense forbidding canopy over its entrance; brambles spilled menacingly from its tangled verges.

Christie shivered, closed her eyes and held the baby tightly.

They had left the clearing just a few hours before, but for a moment so much of what had taken place there seemed like a dream; it was as if it had happened long ago and to someone else, not to her and the children. It was impossible to believe that they had lived in that cramped and ugly caravan for six weeks. And for a moment, it was as if the storm that had broken yesterday at sunset was something she must have imagined.

Leaning against the window with her eyes still closed, Christie could feel the August sunlight playing on her face as the bus slowly followed the meandering twists and turns of the road through the forest. She breathed deeply, letting the warmth soak into her. She was suddenly strangely calm, drifting almost towards sleep.

The bus turned a tight corner and the sunlight disappeared behind a tall hedgerow. Christie's eyes snapped open.

The ache in her arms from hauling the suitcase reminded